THE WATERSHED

FRANCES COWIE

THE WATERSHED

Published by Blue Butterfly Press.

Re-edited version May 2025
www.francescowie.com

Second Edition.
ISBN: 978-0-473-39972-6 (paperback)
ISBN: 978-0-473-39973-3 (e-book)

A catalog record of this book is available from the National Library of New Zealand.

Cover Design: Steven Novak | www.novakillustration.com

Editor: The Error Eliminator | www.theerroreliminator.wordpress.com

250529

To Margaret Rita

THE WATERSHED

PART I

LOUISA GRACE CHURCHILL

1

BITTERSWEET

EARLY NINETEEN SEVENTIES

Louisa Churchill was barely sixteen when she experienced two of life's most inevitable moments at the hands of Roger Walker.

The first, a moment of loving passion.

The second, a moment of sorrowful loss.

Both over in an instant and both life-changing all the same.

The Churchills lived across the street and three doors down from the Walkers, in a small weatherboard house with a big backyard filled with passion fruit vines, feijoa trees, and a huge walnut tree that dropped its fruit each year with the Easter winds. Louisa had one sister, a music-mad teen named Rose, and parents who were still together. Just like every other kid in the street.

Roger, older than Louisa by several months, was someone she looked up to. More than that, he was the boy she watched with a secret gaze as he walked home from school. The boy she dreamed about when lying in her room on lazy, wet Sundays. And yet, in her mind, he'd never noticed her.

From their living room, which faced the street, Louisa could just make out the open window of Roger's upstairs bedroom. She'd never seen him looking out before, but tonight, with the sky clear and stars aglow, he leaned on the windowsill, his attention on the heavens. When

Louisa realized he'd seen her staring, she quickly closed the window and turned out the light.

She climbed the stairs to her room, closed the door, and lay on her bed, his image filling her mind. Roger wasn't handsome in a manly way but beautiful—as some adolescent boys are—with a stunning face and physique and skin tanned to golden by summers past.

Louisa had noticed a change in him over the past few weeks. He'd sometimes walk with her as she pushed her bike home from school, asking about her classes and the sports she played. Occasionally, she'd catch him staring at her across the hall in assembly, and each time she met his gaze, he'd offer her a slight, crooked grin as if they shared more than just living in the same neighborhood and attending the same school.

Louisa grabbed a magazine off the nightstand and opened it. As she started to flick through the pages, she wondered if Roger Walker would ever be her boyfriend.

Leaving the window open to clear the stale air from the room, Roger flopped on his bed, his thoughts turning to Louisa Churchill. Her big brown eyes and the way her cheeks flushed coral pink whenever they spoke. There was no one particular moment at which Roger decided to pursue Louisa. He'd contemplated it for months, knowing they should wait until she was a little older, but time was no longer on his side.

Despite his young age, Roger often reflected on the mysteries of life—its point, lessons learned, and reasons why. Now, those reflections held more significance. Summer break was only a few weeks away, but he no longer looked forward to it.

He cast his mind back to previous summers. Long, humid days when he and his friends would hike to the waterfall to swim in the frigid water cascading into the pool below and balmy evenings spent at the beach with his family.

This summer would be different.

. . .

The following day after school, Roger strolled across the street, his new LP tucked under his arm. The Churchills' back door stood wide open. Strips of multi-colored plastic filled the void, flapping in the breeze to deter grass flies. Roger knocked and stepped into the kitchen.

"Hi." Kathy Churchill's smile was warm and welcoming, as always. "How's that hip of yours?"

"Not too bad, thanks. The doctor said it was bursitis, but who knows. Is Louisa here?"

She wiped floured hands down her floral apron. "She's in her room, doing her homework. Go on up. But leave the door open."

Roger ran up the narrow staircase. The treads were almost too small for his feet, which amused him. He knocked.

Marking her page with a notepad, Louisa glanced up from her textbook. She set the book on the desk beside the bed, her gaze fixed on his. "What are you doing here?"

He stepped into the room. "Want to listen to my new LP?"

"Aren't I too young and flat-chested to be your friend?" Her lips held a slight smile but also a hint of pout. "Isn't that what you told everyone?"

Roger laughed at her effort to express indifference. She was an interesting girl, stuck up and quietly sure of herself, and he thought about her from the moment he woke in the morning until he fell asleep at night.

He placed the LP on her nightstand, sat on the bed without invitation, and studied her. Even with her body slowly moving into womanhood, she had a slight, girlish frame with long arms and legs tanned to the color of liquid honey. "Who told you that?" he asked. "Anyway, things change."

"You mean, I grew boobs, and suddenly you're interested?"

"I just thought we could hang out. I have to go away soon." He let his eyes drift to her chest. "And anyway," he said with a grin, "your boobs are still tiny."

Louisa's cheeks flushed as she studied him. "Away where?"

He pulled aside the sheer curtain on the window to glance at the street below, hesitating with a sharp inhale before he spoke. "To Wellington. I have a lump on my hip. They want to zap it."

"Will it be okay?"

"Yeah, probably." Roger turned to her and smiled.

"What's the LP?"

"*Harvest.* I've listened to it all week. Shall I put it on?"

"Play me your favorite track first."

Roger stood, removed the record from its sleeve, and set the B side on the turntable, his hand trembling as he aligned the stylus with track four.

Louisa smiled at the distinctive intro. "I love this song. Can you play it? On your guitar, I mean."

"Not quite yet."

Roger returned to the bed and sat beside Louisa, their fingers close enough to touch and breathing in rhythm. He wondered what Neil Young's words meant to her and whether she understood their meaning for him. It never ceased to amaze him how comfortable he felt around her—like everything was okay in his world.

Roger didn't admit it to anyone, but his time in the hospital dragged like a hundred gray Sundays.

His return to Clifton Falls brought with it a measure of acceptance, and he couldn't wait to see Louisa—to play music and talk about nothing much as they sat on her narrow bed in her small bedroom. Music was always the common denominator. She loved the poetic musings of John Denver, Cat Stevens, and Carole King. He, the raw truth of Neil Young, James Taylor, and an Irish band called Thin Lizzy.

It was a hot day. They sat on the veranda, sipping lemonade as they watched the sun slip behind the shaded hills. Mustering the courage to break the silence, Roger looked out onto the street and beyond, to the flat landscape of their small slice of suburbia. "What are you thinking about?"

He caught Louisa's sharp inhale.

"Mum and I had a long talk yesterday," she said.

"I suppose she's told you, has she? The whole damn street knows." In a way, Roger was relieved. It meant he didn't have to spell it out, didn't have to shelter her.

She took his hand and traced a vein back and forth with her thumb. "I'm so sorry."

"Yeah, me too." He squeezed her hand in response. "But being sorry won't buy me more time, will it?"

"Don't say that. What about the treatment?"

"It's finished." He stared into space, trying not to think about where he might be going next. "I'm all out of chances, Lou. No more hiking, chasing waterfalls, or sliding down mountains."

Louisa rubbed her thumb over his knuckles. It made him feel safe for some reason. He didn't know why.

"So if you could do one thing, just one thing, what would it be?"

"You mean what's top of my bucket list?" Roger gazed at her with sadness, wondering if honesty would be the best policy. After all, it was too late for him to be anything but honest. "Make love to you." He paused for a reaction, but she gave none. "I don't want to die a virgin."

She hesitated. "Don't say that."

"Why? It's the truth. I want to do it before I'm too sick to know how amazing it is."

"Roger, I can't. I'm only sixteen."

"But we care about each other," he whispered. "If we do this, you'll always be mine, no matter what."

"It's not that I don't want to, but I'm too young."

Roger knew he was no longer just the boy from across the street. He wanted to be her soulmate, her teacher of knowledge, her first. The one she'd always remember. "I get that, but I sense you around me, Lou, all the time."

It would be another week before they were alone again. It was another hot Sunday, and humid rain clouds rolled in from the coast on a light but steady easterly. Her parents were out for lunch with friends at a vineyard down by the river, and Rose was playing next door.

Roger and Louisa sat on her bed in her room, the dark pink candlewick bedspread soft and plush beneath their skin. With the curtains drawn against the world, light and shadow floated in and out on the breeze.

He entwined his fingers with Louisa's and rubbed his thumb over her pink nail polish and fingertips, noticing where the steel strings of her guitar had left their mark. He wasn't nervous or worried. After all, what would be the point?

He lifted her chin with a determined finger and returned her gaze without a single blink or hesitation. His hands cupped her face, caressing either side of her jawline before their lips touched. He'd never experienced such a moment, and in his heart, he knew it was the right thing to do.

Her lips were soft and needy, and Louisa melted into his touch, before pulling back. "What if we get caught?"

"We won't."

"I'm scared."

"Don't be. There's nothing to be scared of, Lou."

She chewed her bottom lip, frowning in thought.

"Undress me," he whispered, peppering kisses under her jaw. "Just jeans and Jockeys. Leave my T-shirt on."

Roger didn't want her to see the tumors on his torso, and he knew she'd respect his wishes. Louisa unbuckled his belt and inched down the zipper of his fly, then tugged his jeans to the floor, where he kicked them aside. He sat on the edge of the bed, removing his watch as she stood and unbuttoned her blouse.

His attention moved to her small breasts encased in a white cotton bra, and he reached around her back to unclip the hooks and set her free. Long dark hair, straight as strands of polished silk, fell over pink peaks to where it rested, almost touching her waist.

He said nothing more as he pulled her between his legs before cupping her face in his hands as they kissed—gently, cautiously. He didn't want to hurt her but knew he had no choice either way.

They lay, rocking back and forth through her initial pain. He increased his rhythm, coaching her with his imagination.

Roger's release was swift and strong, but he wasn't mature enough to understand if Louisa's experience matched his own.

Afterward, they clung together in spills of silent tears and stifled laughter. "That was incredible," he whispered. "I love you so much." Roger didn't care if he'd overstepped the mark. It was too late for unnecessary fears about what Louisa thought of him. "I'll remember this moment forever and beyond. I can't tell you what it means to me."

"Don't say that." Tears tracked down her cheeks. "We still have time, plenty of time."

He held her close, planting soft kisses on her hair while selfishly willing his God to take him as he lay in her arms, still inside of her. While he remembered the impression, the warmth, and before pain took its strangling hold.

"I never imagined it would be like this." He pulled back, his fingertips tracing the pulse beating under the skin of her wrist. "How beautiful you'd feel."

She tugged up the comforter from the end of the bed, surrounding them in its warmth.

"Hey," he murmured into her hair. "You cold?"

"No. I'm making a cocoon. Spinning my silk around you until you fly free."

"I love you, Lou. I'll love you till the sun stops shining."

Louisa raised herself on both elbows. "Shh. What's that?"

"What's what?"

The door flew open, flooding the room with light. "What are you two doing?" Her sister's silhouette hovered in the doorway.

"Get out of here," Louisa yelled. "Get out and shut the door."

"You're a hussy. I'm telling on you. Mum and Dad are gonna be so mad."

Louisa jumped off the bed, covered herself with a towel, and pushed her sister out of the room as she hissed through gritted teeth, "I swear, if you tell, I'll never speak to you again. There's something you don't understand. Now promise me."

"Why should I?"

"Please. This is important. Promise me!"

Rose's expression betrayed her reluctance. "Okay. I promise."

"Cross your heart?"

"Cross my heart."

"Now leave us alone."

When Louisa turned back to Roger, he propped himself up on one elbow, a huge grin plastered on his face. His grin turned to laughter.

"What's so funny?"

"Us getting caught, and you standing there half-naked, all fired up and fighting for me. Come back here."

Since the chemo, Roger's blond hair grew freely but short and curly where it was once long and straight. With his clear skin prickled with a hint of youthful growth on a well-defined jawline and upper lip, he looked much the same, but faint dark circles under his eyes hinted at the inevitable.

As the days stretched into harrowing weeks, Roger and Louisa never again had the chance to demonstrate their love in a tactile way. As much as they wanted to be with one another, it just wasn't possible.

Louisa thought about that special day often. There'd been nothing lustful about it. It was simply an outpouring of pure virginal love. A harmonizing of their childhood souls coupled with an amalgamation of their adolescent desires. And while she expected to feel guilty, she didn't.

Sometimes, when she dared to set her thoughts free, she questioned the significance of her beliefs—something that didn't come easily to her. But mostly, she felt scared and alone and numb.

After school each day, Louisa spent hours at Roger's bedside, her textbooks and notepad balanced on her knees. She'd paint scenarios of life without him on an internal canvas as she watched him sleep and read Steinbeck to him when he was awake.

However, as Roger weakened, his mother, who didn't understand the importance of their relationship, was less inclined to allow her to stay.

It was another tiresome Sunday. Mass was over, as was the Churchills' formal Sunday lunch. Her mother had invited two parish priests to join them for their midday meal, and Louisa longed to be anywhere but at the table while she fussed over the clergy.

After helping with the dishes, Louisa crossed the street to number forty-five. She knocked, and Roger's mother cracked open the door just enough to poke her head through.

"Can I sit with Roger?"

"Not today. He's having a bad day."

"I'll be quiet. No one will even know I'm there."

"We can't let you anymore, dear. He's too weak for visitors."

"Mrs. Walker, please. I need to be there for him."

"I'm sorry, Louisa. Now run along home."

Louisa trudged back across the street, a lump of emotion stuck in her throat. When she entered the kitchen, she took one look at her mother and burst into tears. "Some days, I don't know if I'll ever see him again."

Her mother reached for her with loving arms. "I know. Stay strong. He needs you."

After school the next day, Louisa stayed home. She couldn't bear the thought of being turned away from the Walkers' door when she knew Roger lay alone in his room. But she'd barely finished her homework when Mrs. Walker phoned. Roger wanted to see her. Louisa didn't hesitate.

When she entered his room, the curtains were drawn, leaving one dull bedside lamp as the only source of light.

He held out his hand. "Lou."

"It's okay. I'm here."

Louisa straightened the bedding that covered his now emaciated frame. She admired what Māori would call his *mana*—his power, influence, and strength—and marveled at his articulation. How he conveyed his feelings so openly for a boy of sixteen, as if he possessed the soul of a poet, a scholar. She'd never met anyone like him and doubted she ever would again.

"Promise you won't be sad for me," he said.

"I can't promise that." She shifted in her chair and took his hand in hers. "Are you scared?"

"Scared shitless. And completely and utterly pissed off. At least you actually asked me. Everyone else says get well soon and pretends I have the flu or something. I wish they'd say they'll miss me and that I've been a good friend… instead of all this get-well bullshit. Even my younger brothers don't know what to say."

"It doesn't mean they don't care."

"I guess." Roger tightened his grip on her hand and brushed his thumb gently over her knuckles. "I want to ask you something." He held her gaze.

"Okay."

"Do you believe in reincarnation?"

She hesitated. "Do you mean returning in another body, another life, that kind of thing?"

"Yeah. The progression of our souls."

"I've never really thought about it. It kind of scares me."

"Why? You're not afraid of being with me. You know I'm dying, but you still keep me company."

"That's different."

"Is it? Sometimes, we have to question our beliefs." His words caught in his throat, and he stopped to take a sip of water. "Don't you agree?"

"What do you mean?"

"Don't let religion destroy your inquisitive spirit, Lou. Question everything. When you receive what you truly believe is the right answer, that will be your truth. Be open to change, always. And remember… love is infinite. It's okay to love more than one person at a time."

Louisa leaned forward and kissed him on the forehead. "I'm going to miss you. You're the best friend I've ever had. I love you, Roger Walker."

"I love you too. And if I can find a way back, to have another crack at life, I will. Look out for me."

Roger left on a bright blue-sky summer's day around noon. He made it past the darkest hours before dawn, past the time when workers and students leave for their busy day ahead, and past the time when his mother took a break for a much-needed cup of tea. He left when the sun was high and warm, when living made sense. His mother had crept into the kitchen to prepare a light lunch when he slipped away—alone, as so many souls prefer to go.

That same afternoon, Louisa left school after tennis practice and rode her bike through the park, where lions stood guard at the entry gates and tall oaks towered upward of fifty feet. She stopped at the library to return an overdue book before hurrying home.

Two black cars stood in the street when Louisa turned the corner. She stopped outside the Walkers' wooden gate, straddling the frame of her bike, her left hand gripping the handlebars and the fingernails of her right digging into the flesh of her palm. She couldn't go in.

Toward early evening, as the sun set, Roger's older brother came over to break the news. And as the Churchill family sat at the kitchen table, there were no words—only tears and disbelief.

The next day, Louisa joined the Walkers to recite a rosary for the boy who held her heart, her fingers nimble over tiny beads of faith. She had never said goodbye, not properly.

Now, it was too late.

That night, she lay on her bed and listened to *Harvest*, trying to imagine him through her tears. But no matter how hard she tried, she couldn't sense his spirit around her.

The Walkers didn't allow her to see Roger after he died. They screwed his casket shut, not even giving her the chance to ask.

How would she know it was really him?

The morning of his funeral, Louisa dressed in the most colorful outfit she could find: a baby-doll number in swirls of orange, yellow, and pink paisley print that she'd sewn in home economics. She refused to wear her school uniform as a gesture of respect. Roger hadn't wanted his mourners to wear black, but the majority did anyway. Tradition trumped the wishes of the very soul whose life they'd come to celebrate.

Louisa felt the weight of the congregation's gaze as she walked down the center aisle toward the altar. Royal blue carpet marked the way, but her footsteps still left a deafening impact. She was the girl. The one who'd spent every spare minute of the past few weeks at his side. The girl who'd never before experienced loss but who accepted it nonetheless.

Signatures covered his coffin with scarcely an inch to spare, black waterproof ink scrawled across white lacquer in commemoration of a short life, not necessarily well lived. Louisa refused to sign her name, likening it to signing her life away on a document she didn't understand.

She sat between her parents and sister, three rows back in wooden pews designed for the devotion of suffering rather than comfortable contemplation.

As she stared straight ahead at the casket topped in scarlet peonies, she experienced a sudden rush of energy. Not the kind that gives you fervor, but the kind that assaults your heart.

Even though altar boys from Saint Francis of Assisi Collegiate and Father Bernard, an old family friend, flanked the altar, the coffin stood alone.

Father Bernard's words provided no comfort. If he spoke to her, Louisa didn't comprehend. If he grieved with her, she didn't feel the alliance. And if he offered her hope, she couldn't accept it.

Louisa had often imagined this day over the past few months, mentally rehearsing her words to his mother, father, and brothers. But her imagination was nothing compared to the reality. How could it possibly be? No one, apart from her family, offered any verbal comfort. It was beyond her young friends to articulate their feelings, but they wept for Roger all the same.

Outside, the sun shone brightly without a cloud to carry Roger's spirit away. Clutching a damp handkerchief, Louisa watched as mourners filled the churchyard and Roger's father, uncles, and brothers carried his coffin to the hearse. People mingled as hundreds of young men from schools in the district formed a guard of honor from the doors of the cathedral right along the street, ready to perform a *haka* for one of their own.

Liam O'Leary caught Louisa's attention. Slightly older than Roger, he was a young man of presence, Roger's rugby teammate and mentor, and leader of the *haka*. The men tensed in anticipation as Liam assumed his position in front of the cathedral's main steps. Liam glanced Louisa's way, offering a nod of recognition, and as he started to chant, other males—young and old alike—followed his call. When their cries of war and grief filled the air, throats burned, noses dripped, and eyes glistened.

For many weeks, Louisa struggled to believe Roger was gone.

2

FAMILY BONDS

Kathy Churchill's cousin, Maggie, and Louisa shared a special bond. More than a second cousin, Maggie had assumed the role of self-appointed aunt in Louisa's life. Kathy was aware that her daughter found it suffocating at times, especially when Maggie acted as her conscience—the voice of reason in her adolescent mind. But on the whole, as long as Maggie kept the booze at bay, their relationship remained close.

"How's Louisa doing?"

She poured Maggie a cup of tea and offered her a freshly baked scone from the basket on the kitchen table. "Not so well. Since she lost her young friend, she can't seem to shake the sadness."

"Yeah, well, maybe they were more than friends."

"What do you mean?"

"She's sixteen, and he was dying. I wonder if they—"

"Maggie!" Kathy was shocked. "Are you suggesting they slept together before he died?"

"Well…" she mused. "I was fifteen when I let that good-for-nothing Jack O'Brian spread my butterfly wings."

"Please don't say that. I can't even entertain the idea of them having sex. Louisa's a good girl. She wouldn't do that."

Kathy felt sure her eldest daughter was still a member of the purity club, but Maggie, whose early experiences forever forged her views on life, apparently thought otherwise.

Louisa smiled as she walked into the kitchen. She dropped her schoolbag on the floor and kissed her aunt on the cheek. "Aunt Maggie, when did you get here?"

"About an hour ago, pet. I'm staying a couple of days."

"Cool." Louisa frowned at her mother. "Why are you looking at me like that, Mum?"

"I'm not looking at you like anything, darling." Kathy wiped her hands on her apron and turned to put her cup in the sink. She'd never considered Louisa and Roger as being more than good friends, but what if Maggie was right? She felt sick even thinking about it. Louisa was barely sixteen when Roger passed away.

Quickly dismissing the thought, she returned the virginal Louisa to her rightful place. "How was school?"

"Same old, same old. Some days, I can't see the point."

"While we're still drawing breath, there's always a point, pet," Maggie said.

"Yeah, but some of the people we love are no longer drawing breath, are they? That's what I don't understand." Louisa let out a heavy sigh. "I better go do my homework."

She picked up her schoolbag and grabbed an apple from the fruit bowl before hurrying up the stairs and shutting her bedroom door against the world.

"I see what you mean." Maggie sipped her tea. "She's still grieving, no doubt about it, and rightly so."

"He was such a caring boy. I swear, if I hear 'only the good die young' one more time, I'll scream. It seems so senseless. His young life cut so short."

In Louisa's room, a small black record player sat ready and waiting. And like every other day since Roger's death, she sprawled on her bed, stared at the ceiling, and watched specks of dust float in her vision as Neil Young transported her to another world.

A soft knock broke the mood before Maggie stepped into her room and shut the door. "How are you doing, pet? You know, since the passing of your friend?"

Louisa sat up and rested her head against the headboard. "It's been tough. No one wants to talk about him. It's as if he never lived."

Maggie pushed some magazines aside to make space and perched on the edge of Louisa's bed. "People aren't always sure how to discuss death, love. They don't like reminding others of what they've lost. Give them permission by mentioning him first. That way, your friends will realize you're open to their words."

It had been only a few months, but some days, Louisa struggled to see Roger in her mind's eye. Yet his photograph only upset her more. His smiling, handsome image captured for all eternity remained hidden away in her nightstand drawer for those days when she gathered enough strength to look at it. "I don't want to forget him."

"Of course not. Has he visited you? You know, in your dreams?"

Louisa hesitated, searching her aunt's expression for guidance. "Sometimes. It scares me. Please don't tell Mum and Dad. They'll think I'm crazy."

"Your dreams are safe with me. I don't understand how we can believe in the Holy Spirit, the resurrection, and guardian angels, but when we talk of the dead, it's as if they're merely dust, carried away on the breeze."

"I loved him, and he loved me… kissed me like I could heal his soul. But in the end, I couldn't save him. I wasn't enough." A tear slid down Louisa's cheek, and she wiped it away with the back of her hand.

"But his soul isn't dead, pet. Don't you ever forget that. Keep talking to him. Tell him how you feel. He'll hear you."

"You think?"

"I know. I know only too well."

3

COMMUNICATION OF INTEREST

The night Louisa met David Reynolds started with two coincidences. First, Louisa's friend invited her to a family birthday party at the last minute. Second, her parents allowed her to stay out later than usual.

Not long after she arrived, she noticed him standing lost in thought, mesmerized by the bonfire burning in a field adjacent to the house. When he glanced over and caught Louisa staring, he stared back.

Every time she dared look his way, his expression communicated his interest. She didn't understand the draw, but there was no mistaking it. Louisa knew she looked much older than sixteen, but that didn't mean she knew how to respond to an interested male. When he moved to her side, she feigned indifference.

"Hi. What's your name?"

"Louisa. Louisa Churchill. What's it to you?"

"Everything." David said nothing more.

His friend laughed. "Shit, Reynolds, when did you learn to speak the language of love?"

David didn't take his eyes off her as he replied, "Piss off, Sam. I'm talking to Louise."

"It's Louisa, with an A." She returned his gaze without blinking once, challenging him.

"Well, Louisa," he said, emphasizing the A. "I'm David. Would you like to dance?"

"I guess."

"You guess?" David raised a brow. "You'll have to do better than guess."

He took her hand, and they joined other couples in the living room, slow dancing in the soft light as America's "I Need You" drifted from the record player. David held her close, and she relaxed into him. When he finally kissed her, Louisa responded the only way she knew how: with a mixture of apathy and enthusiasm.

Louisa ran down the stairs just as Rose answered the door. It had been over a week since she and David met, and she hadn't expected to see him again so soon. She hesitated on the bottom step. "David, what are you doing here?"

A slow smile lit up his whole face, melting her insides a little. "I wondered if I could take you out for dinner."

She fiddled with her hair, not quite believing David stood on her doorstep, asking her out. "Um… I'm not sure. I'll have to ask Mum. Come in."

He removed his baseball cap and followed Louisa into the kitchen just as her mother put a casserole into the oven.

"Mum, this is David Reynolds. We met last week at Kelly's."

She turned, wiping her hands on her apron. "Hello, David."

"Mrs. Churchill." He offered his hand, and she shook it. "It's nice to meet you."

"And you too, David. Anyway, what can we do for you?"

"I wondered if I could take Louisa out for dinner."

She threw a disapproving look Louisa's way. "For dinner? Like on a date?"

"I'll have her home by ten."

"I don't think so, David. Louisa's still in high school. We can't have her gallivanting around town with a much older boy. What would people think?"

"Mum!"

"No, I'm sorry, Louisa. I said no. But you're most welcome to join us for dinner."

David glanced at Louisa for guidance. She nodded. "I'd like that," he said. "Thank you."

"How old are you, David?" her mother asked.

"I'm nineteen."

She frowned. "I see. And do you have a job?"

He nodded. "I work on a family farm up the Rata River Valley, but I plan on doing a building apprenticeship soon."

"Good for you. A trade is a sound career choice for a young man, especially given how farming is right now."

"Yes. Things are pretty tough out there, that's for sure."

"Anyway, we'll just be upstairs," Louisa said.

"I don't think so," her mother said sternly. "Young women do not entertain men in their bedrooms."

Louisa caught David's grin and blushed.

"You can sit in the living room," she said. "With the door open."

On the night of her seventeenth birthday, the family ate dinner early, with her father, Tom, seated at the head of the table and David next to Louisa. As she blew out the candles on her birthday cake, David ran his hand up and down her thigh under the tablecloth. He let it linger close to her panty line while discussing the weather with her father, and Louisa chewed her lower lip, keeping her eyes on the knife as her mother cut the cake.

After dinner, they left in David's pickup for the local cinema, but instead, he headed out of town and down a deserted farm track leading to the coast.

"Where are we going?"

David stared straight ahead. "You'll see."

"But we're supposed to be going to the pictures."

He glanced at her and grinned. "I hope you've read the book."

"We should go back. What if Mum and Dad find out?"

He reached over and squeezed her hand, his fingers calloused from many hours spent working on the farm. "They won't." He paused. "You're not worried, are you?"

"No." She wrung her hands together in her lap, then held them still, not wanting David to notice how nervous she was. "Why? Should I be?"

"You never have to be scared of me, you know that."

"I know, it's just… isn't this private property?"

"It's a friend's place. I've been coming here for years."

"Is this where you bring all your girlfriends?"

He threw her a sideways glance, his hands circling the steering wheel as he parked his vehicle. "I don't have any other girlfriends. But I'm only saying it once, so stop fishing."

"I'm not fishing. You're horrible to me sometimes."

"I'm only teasing." David smiled and cut the engine. "You're such an easy target."

He'd stopped on a high embankment covered in fir trees overlooking the South Pacific coast. With the night sky now dark, the moon shone bright and full, casting a jagged vertical sheen over the ocean.

Louisa sulked.

"Hey, come here." David pulled her toward him, took her face in his hands and kissed her, his lips tender on hers. "Happy birthday, Lou. You look so pretty, all dusted in moonlight.

"Thanks." Louisa relaxed. David wasn't typically one for romantic words, so when he did use them, she knew he was sincere. She sometimes felt guilty that she'd replaced Roger with David, but her love for David was different from her love for Roger. Not better, just different.

He held her gaze, rubbing his thumb over her lips. "Give me another kiss, and I'll give you your present."

"You bought me a present?"

He kissed her again, this time with a hungry tongue, then reached into the glove compartment and pulled out a small package. "Just a little something."

"Can I open it now?"

"Course you can."

Louisa undid the ribbon and lifted the lid off the tiny pink box. Inside, a dainty gold locket dangled from a delicate chain. "David, it's beautiful."

"Look inside."

She opened the clasp. Embossed into the back of the locket was a four-leaf clover fashioned from sterling silver. "I don't know what to say. I love it."

"It's for good luck."

"You're gonna make me cry."

"Here, let me put it on." David draped the chain around Louisa's neck and fastened the clasp.

She touched it, the metal cool under her fingertips. "I've never had a present from a boy before."

David caressed along the line of her collarbone. "I'm not a boy, Louisa." He kissed her again, his tongue hot and demanding. "I want to show you how much of a man I am," he whispered.

"David, we shouldn't." Her voice acquired a husky note as her breathing grew labored.

"Yes, we should. We've been building up to this for weeks. You're saying no, but your body's talking an entirely different language."

"I want to… but I'm scared."

"Shh, I'd never hurt you. You understand that, right? I need you, Lou." David skimmed his hands over her breasts. "You have beautiful tits, so firm." He unbuttoned her blouse, moved his hands around to the back of her bra, and unhooked it with a tug. "I love you, want you so much."

She arched her back and stretched upward. Following her lead, David kissed from her earlobe to her collarbone. And each time he caressed her and blew his hot breath over the barely wet mark, her control slipped further away.

"David… I…"

"Help me out here, please. I can't stop thinking about you. I need to be inside you." He reached down to the lever under the seat and slid it back as far as it would go, then lifted her to straddle him.

Louisa felt his arousal, stiff and thick behind the zipper of his jeans, and when David slipped his hand under her skirt and into her panties, she responded with an enthusiasm that shocked her.

"Just say the word if you want me to stop. I don't want to hurt you."

"No… don't stop, please." She unzipped his jeans before tugging them down as he lifted off the seat.

David held her in position and kissed her softly. "Tell me if it hurts." Gently guiding her hips, he entered her with care. She held on to his shoulders as he stilled to kiss her before rocking her back and forth, their rhythm matching stroke for stroke.

Their sex was tender and loving, and all throughout, David reassured her with gentle words and steady hands. Louisa never told him she wasn't a virgin, and while he didn't mention it either, he must have realized.

Afterward, David helped her clean up with tissues from the glove compartment, all the while murmuring assurances of how good it was for him and how much he loved her. They'd spent a lot of time together, but that night was entirely different, and her shyness took hold.

"What should I say if Mum asks me about the film?"

"You haven't read the book?"

"I'm not into the classics," she murmured. "I prefer quick romances full of greed and passion."

"Well, it will suit you down to the ground then. It's all that and more. I have a copy at the farm. I'll bring it down next week."

"You're coming next week?"

"Do you want me to?"

"I guess."

David simply smiled. "*I guess* we're on the same page then."

In the following weeks, David didn't know what to expect of Louisa, but she gave herself to him with an enthusiasm that amazed him every single time. When they were together in public, Louisa bordered on aloofness. But when alone, she demonstrated her love for him without a single selfish moment. She wanted to please him as much as he did her. And please him, she did.

Now, what the hell was she saying? That she was pregnant?

"What do you mean, you're late? You can't be pregnant, can you?" David ran his hands through his hair as he contemplated what this would mean for their relationship.

"I don't know! How would I know what being pregnant feels like?"

"We've only done it a few times without a condom, for God's sake."

"There's no need to take the Lord's name in vain, David. I need support here, and you're scaring me."

David said nothing for a long moment. "Hey, come here." He held her face and kissed her softly on the forehead. "I'm sorry, Lou. We'll figure something out."

"We have to go away. Mum and Dad will flip out if I tell them I'm pregnant. They'll send me to a home in the country to work for no pay and force me to give up our baby for adoption."

David realized that if she was pregnant, marriage would be their only option. The solution was plain and simple. However, his feelings for Louisa were complicated. He loved her, but having a child would take their relationship to a whole new level. A level he wasn't yet ready for.

"We can't do that, Lou. Even if we wanted to, we don't have any money." David was always one for practicalities. "Go to the doctor and take a test. Get Rose to go with you. Once we know for sure, we'll make some decisions, okay?"

"I can't take my sister with me for a pregnancy test. She's too young. You need to come with me."

"I can't at the moment," he said, remaining firm. "And Rose is a mature kid. You need to confide in someone, and I don't want it to be one of your gossipy friends. Even if you are pregnant, it's still early days."

After Mass the following Sunday, Louisa nudged her sister as they finished the dishes. "Come upstairs. I want to ask you something."

"What?"

"Not here," she whispered. "Not with Mum and Dad around."

Rose followed Louisa upstairs to her bedroom and flopped down on the bed. "What's going on? You're acting weird. And make it quick because I have to do my cello practice. I'm learning 'Eleanor Rigby.'"

"You and that darn cello. This is more important than any cello practice." Louisa shut the bedroom door and sat on the stool in front of her dressing table, her back to the mirror.

"Fine," Rose said. "Tell me."

"I'm late."

"For what?"

"With my period... What if I'm pregnant?"

"What? Like pregnant with a baby?"

"Rose, honestly. That's what pregnant means." Louisa sighed and raised her eyebrows, wishing her sister were a few years older.

"But aren't you on the pill? I thought you couldn't get pregnant when you're on the pill."

"I was too scared. You hear so many stories about it making you fat and all that."

"Louisa, sometimes you're so clueless. You have to tell Mum and Dad."

"No. And don't you dare say a word! I have to go to the doctor and take a test, and you need to come with me."

"What? I'm not coming. David should go."

Louisa chewed the inside of her cheek as she searched for a solution that wasn't there. "But he can't get time off work during the day, and I'm too scared to go alone. Please, you have to come."

"Rose, Louisa," their mother called up the stairs. "What are you two doing? Don't forget your cello practice, young lady."

Rose opened the bedroom door and called out, "I'm coming." She stood with her hand on the door handle. "Look, wait a few days. Mum and Dad are away next week. We'll come up with a plan then. But you'll have to tell them sooner or later." She patted Louisa on the shoulder. "You might not even be pregnant. How many weeks late are you?"

"Two months and my boobs hurt."

Rose sighed. "That's a sure sign."

"What? How do you know this?"

"What can I say? I read."

4

LOVE AND LOSS

Disillusioned with school, Louisa had secured a job at a local department store through a friend of her mother's. She'd initially applied for a position on the beauty counter, but much to her disgust, they started her in haberdashery instead.

Each day, she walked to work with her lunch in its brown paper bag and stood behind the counter with boredom for company. At the end of the working day, she walked home again and ate dinner with her family, wishing every minute that her period would announce its presence.

During the last week of August, two days before their parents' trip to Tom's family farm to help with early lambing, Aunt Maggie arrived, suitcase in hand and a smile on her face. Maggie had no children of her own, and she loved Louisa and Rose dearly.

Maggie took the same back bedroom she always did. A small room of no more than eight feet by nine, it contained a dressing table and a narrow bed covered with an orange candlewick bedspread.

"Are you sure you're okay in here?" Louisa asked. "It's kind of cramped."

"It's perfect. Don't you worry about me."

While Maggie arranged her toiletries on the dressing table, Louisa studied her aunt's reflection in the small, beveled-edge mirror hanging on the wall from a tarnished chain—every line on her face and every crease of her hands a testament to her life's difficult path. Once attractive in a common way, Maggie was now too thin, her cheeks too hollow, and her hands shook. The booze had taken its toll.

Maggie had turned forty-eight last birthday, but looking at her, one would swear she'd seen more than sixty years. She often told Louisa, "We don't appreciate the beauty of our youth until it's gone, and then it's purely a retrospective indulgence." Louisa didn't fully understand what she meant but nodded anyway.

Back in the kitchen, Louisa took an apple from the fruit bowl and bit into it as she watched her mother fuss about with last-minute tasks. Kathy loathed spending time with her mother-in-law, but rather than admit it, she insisted she didn't want to leave the girls, and Louisa felt sorry for her.

"Now, you two behave yourselves. And be kind to Maggie. She doesn't need any grief," her mother said as they hugged goodbye. "We're lucky to have her."

"Mum, I'm sixteen. We don't need a sitter. I love Aunt Maggie, you know that, but if she's out drinking every night, we might as well be on our own anyway."

"Louisa, that's enough. Maggie's lived a life you wouldn't understand. She just goes a little overboard occasionally, that's all."

"But—"

"I won't hear another word," she snapped. "We're not leaving you two girls alone for a week, and that's final."

A few days later, on a longed-for Saturday, Louisa woke with a splitting headache. According to Rose, Maggie had left for the pub before she'd even eaten lunch, and Louisa welcomed her aunt's absence.

But by midafternoon, she could hardly drag herself out of bed to use the bathroom. Smudges of blood stained her panties, and cramps gripped her gut. By early evening, she could no longer bear the pain.

Calling out to Rose, Louisa staggered to the couch and lay back on the cushions, beads of sweat gathering on her forehead.

"You okay?" her sister asked as she entered the living room. "You're as white as a sheet."

"Something's wrong." Louisa winced in pain, covering the life inside her with delicate hands in an effort to protect it. "Can you phone David? His number's in my diary… on the back cover. Hurry."

"What do I say?"

"Tell him… to come straight away. I need to go to the hospital… He should bring his dad's car."

"I'll call Mum at the farm."

"No! Phone David, please. And hurry."

By the time he arrived, Louisa was doubled over, retching into a bucket. They helped her into the back seat of the car and took the shortcut road bordering the cemetery to Clifton Falls General.

Rose chatted as they drove, more due to nerves than anything else, and Louisa closed her eyes against the intrusion.

"Why's the cemetery right next to the hospital?" Rose asked as David turned into the hospital grounds.

Neither Louisa nor David replied.

"It's bad town planning. I think about it every time I pass those ghastly gates. I've decided to become an architect. When I'm older, that is."

"Shh, Rose," Louisa said with a sigh. "I can't think straight."

David and Rose waited outside Women's Surgical for over two hours. Doctors and nurses bustled in and out of the ward, but no one gave them a second look.

Finally, a lanky young man dressed in scrubs and with a stethoscope around his neck approached them.

"Are you Miss Churchill's family?" he asked curtly, pushing his thick-framed glasses up his nose.

"I'm her boy-boyfriend." David spoke with a slight stutter when he was nervous, and hospitals always made him nervous. "And this is her s-sis-sister."

"Your name?"

"David. Sorry, D-Da-David Reynolds and Rose."

"I'm Doctor Evans." The doctor ignored Rose. He barely made eye contact with David. "Where are Miss Churchill's parents?"

Rose went to speak, but David beat her to it. "They're away for the week. We haven't been able to contact them. An aunt's looking after Rose and Louisa, but she's unwell."

Rose remained silent.

"Okay, Mr. Reynolds, come with me." He pointed a finger at Rose. "You, stay here."

"How is she?" David asked as they entered a small office. "Is she all right?"

"Louisa's stable at this point. They'll have her back in the ward soon." Doctor Evans glanced at her notes. "It appears your girlfriend, if that's what she is, was pregnant. Did you know that, Mr. Reynolds?"

"No, not for sure, no."

"What do you mean, not for sure? Either you did or you didn't. Which one was it?"

"Well, she's a few weeks late, you know, with her period." David stuttered his response.

"Yes, well, your baby… I presume it was your baby, was it, Mr. Reynolds?"

A nurse entered the room and handed a file to the doctor. David sat in the chair, looked at him, and waited.

"As I was about to say, have you heard of an ectopic pregnancy?" Doctor Evans didn't wait for a reply. "That's when the embryo forms outside the uterus and has no possibility of reaching full term. It's uncommon in a child of her age. But, of course, a child of her age doesn't generally do what one must to become pregnant. Louisa suffered an ectopic pregnancy. Our only option was to remove the offending fallopian tube."

"Does that mean she's lost the baby?"

"Precisely. And, because of Louisa's age, I'll need to talk to her parents." Doctor Evans flicked to the front page of her file. "I presume they know about the pregnancy?"

"No. We hadn't told them yet."

"Indeed?"

David took a breath of courage and sat up straighter. "Well, we weren't sure she was pregnant. Until now, that is." Hundreds of thoughts lined up in David's mind, awaiting his consideration. He knew what an ectopic pregnancy was and what it could mean for Louisa. On the farm, they culled ewes that had miscarried and fed them to the dogs. Why that thought came to mind, he had no idea.

David carefully weighed up his words before speaking again. "And as Louisa is almost eighteen, I'd appreciate you keeping her parents out of this."

"I'm not sure that's possible. Miss Churchill will need to stay in the hospital for at least three days, so how will you explain that to her parents? I can see no other option."

"I'll talk to Louisa." David now spoke with confidence. "It's her decision."

Doctor Evans sat back in his chair and arrogantly regarded David. "As you wish. Come back to me tomorrow, will you?"

David left the doctor's office suffering from information overload. It wouldn't be easy keeping the pregnancy from her parents, but ultimately, it was Louisa's decision.

He edged his way into the ward, Rose following several steps behind.

"Hey." He bent down to kiss her. "How are you feeling?"

"Groggy. Can I have a glass of water? I'm so thirsty."

"I'll get it," Rose said.

"You okay?" He pressed a hand to Louisa's forehead as a mother would to her child and frowned down at her. "What are we going to tell your folks?"

"Nothing."

"But it's not that easy, Lou. You know what this town's like. It won't be long before someone puts two and two together."

"David, no. I don't want them to know."

"Okay, okay. Settle down. So what am I meant to say?"

"I'll be out of here before they get back. They're not coming home until Friday now."

"And what about the scar and Maggie?"

"They'll never see it. They went in through my belly button. Look, David, I can't deal with this right now. I've just lost my baby." Louisa's voice sounded hollow. "Promise me you won't tell. And talk to Rose and Aunt Maggie. They have to keep this a secret."

"Fine. And we've just lost *our* baby."

Louisa fiddled with the locket around her neck. "What?"

"You said, 'I've just lost my baby,' but it was my baby too."

"I'm sorry, but it's different for guys. You don't understand."

David let out a heavy sigh. He understood only too well.

It was after midnight when David and Rose returned to the Churchills' home. He waited until breakfast to break the news. Maggie listened carefully as she brewed coffee, ate dry toast, and smoked the first of her many cigarettes for the day.

And as he told of their baby's loss in his no-nonsense monologue, David knew if anyone could keep a secret, Maggie could.

Louisa loosened the waistband of her pajama pants, trying to get comfortable as she watched Maggie dry the dishes.

"How are you feeling today, pet? A bit better?" Maggie, forever the trooper, had been sober since Louisa arrived home, playing the role of aunt with compassion.

"I feel like I've been run over by a truck." Louisa smiled at the older woman. "I wanted to say thanks… you know, for your support. I couldn't have managed this without you."

"You're welcome, pet. Glad I could help. But what's all this talk about not telling your parents?"

"They wouldn't understand. Mum's so self-righteous when it comes to 'the sins of the flesh,' as she calls it."

"Sometimes there are secrets we shouldn't keep, that's all I'm saying. Do you understand, love? Give her a chance. She may surprise you."

"You know how Mum is. She thinks we should all stay virgins until we marry."

"Well, after everything you've been through over the past few days, you'll understand why, eh." Maggie accompanied her pointed message with a concerned smile.

Louisa thought for a moment. Despite her reluctance to disrespect her mother, she wanted to confide in Maggie. "I don't get her. She's so staunch."

"Yeah, well, with good reason."

"What do you mean?"

"It's not often I tell secrets of the past, pet, but you may understand her better if I tell you this one. I need you to promise never to repeat it. Not to your mum, your father, Rose, or David. Promise?"

"I promise."

Maggie sat at the table. "The day she turned thirteen, Dennis O'Brian, one of her foster brothers, tried to rape your mum. I came home to find out he'd almost succeeded."

"No!"

"Oh yes. The bastard. She had to be a strong wee girl, living in that O'Brian household."

Sadness washed over Louisa as she let Maggie's words sink in. "She never talks about her time there."

"Nothing much to say now. It's all over and done with, but she'll carry that with her to the grave and beyond."

"What happened when the O'Brians found out?"

"They never found out. I said it at the time, and I'll say it again. There was no one to tell."

"But that's not right. He should have paid for what he did."

"That's what your mother said. But when you're an orphan, pet, you're treated like no one owes you a damn thing."

It now made perfect sense to Louisa. Her mother's judgment had been clouded in the worst possible way. "It can't have been easy for you to share that with me. Can I ask you one more thing?"

"Fire away."

"Why do you drink so much?"

Maggie looked at Louisa, her eyes weary with pain and acceptance. "To forget, pet. My fella, he was killed in an accident on the docks when I was in my twenties. He was a bastard to me most of the time, with his fists as well as his words, but I still loved him. He wanted to marry me, or so he said. Came courting with flowers wrapped up in promises. But the day of the accident, we had a huge row, and I said a whole lot of ugly words I shouldn't have. So did he. I wanted him to change, to be my knight in shining armor. I didn't realize it at the time, but he didn't have it in him. He left for work in a huff, and we never said goodbye."

Maggie stood and slung the tea towel over her shoulder. She opened the oven to check the scones, removed the baking sheet, and set it on a wire cooling rack. "That night, a crane hook knocked him off the dock and into the water. He couldn't swim. They didn't find him until the next morning."

"I'm so sorry. I didn't realize."

"Yes, I know, love. But that's the thing about life. We so often judge others when we don't know their stories. Better to ask and get it all out in the open. Then, we have the choice to understand. I've liked men since, but the passion's gone now. I'll be alone now until my dying day. Men annoy the shit out of me with their little-boy wants and needs. Better to be single than clean up after some stupid fella all my life." Maggie laughed loudly.

She poured a cup of tea for Louisa and set it on the kitchen table, along with a basket of freshly baked scones, raspberry jam, and butter.

"When I was about fifteen," she continued, "younger, if I'm honest, I fell in love with one of the O'Brian brothers, Jack. He was after me for sex, nothing more. I get that now, but he disguised it well." Maggie gathered her thoughts while buttering a scone. "Full of sweet talk and small gifts when we were alone, he didn't acknowledge my existence at any other time. He ended up marrying his childhood sweetheart the day he turned twenty-one. I gave myself away too soon and kept on giving. The men, they kept on taking. So, you see, we all have our story, pet."

"Thank you for telling me yours." Louisa swallowed past the lump forming in her throat. "You're a good sort, Maggie."

"Yeah, so they say, but look where it got me."

5

INCHING INTO AUTUMN

In the months that followed, Louisa fell into a deep malaise, her mood distant and defiant. Her parents and David forever walked on eggshells as her hurtful tongue snapped back at them.

On the Thursday before Easter, Louisa arrived home from work to find her mother waiting at the kitchen table.

"Is everything all right, Mum?" she asked. "You look tired." Her words conveyed polite concern rather than anything deeper.

"Sit down. We need to talk."

Louisa met her gaze but remained standing. "About what?"

"What's gotten into you lately, Louisa?"

"What do you mean?"

"Well, for one, your room is a pigsty."

"How many times have I told you to stay out of my room?" Louisa snapped. "What were you doing in there, snooping?"

"I was looking for a magazine."

Louisa's heart sank. She knew what was coming next.

"I wanted to make that chocolate cake recipe I saw in the *Woman's Weekly*. But instead, I found this." She held up an empty pill packet. "Please tell me this isn't yours."

"Mum, butt out. I'm old enough. What's in my room is my business." Louisa grabbed a cookie from the jar on the counter, turned into the hallway, and hurried up the stairs.

Her mother followed.

"While you're living under my roof, young lady, it is my business. And there's no need to speak to me in that tone." Her voice was steady but firm. "It's the pill, isn't it?"

"Yes, Mum. You know what it is."

"But it can't be yours. Why would you be on the pill?"

"For my acne."

"But you have beautiful skin." Kathy scanned her daughter's face for confirmation. "You're sleeping with that boy, aren't you? What have I done to deserve this? Haven't I been a good mother to you girls? Why would you do such a thing, Louisa? Go on the pill without consulting me… without regard for the consequences?"

"That boy? You mean David. He has a name."

"How can you stand there and be so flippant? Sex before marriage is a sin, you know that. Our church doesn't allow its members to take the pill."

"Please, spare me the pious talk. The church is your church, not mine. Any church that preaches sex as a sin is not my church. How can the very act that is vital for the continuation of the human race be a sin?"

"But you've always been involved in the church. How can you say that and turn your back on your beliefs?"

"I don't know what I believe. I love David, and he loves me. That's all that matters right now."

"But who you love in your teens, you may not love in your twenties."

"Yes, Mother, so you keep saying."

"Then why are you engaging in such reckless behavior with a boy who may well be a five-minute wonder?"

"We've been together for months. David's not a five-minute wonder. And he's no boy, far from it."

Louisa watched as her mother busied herself, picking up bits and pieces of nothing from her bedroom floor. She always did that during arguments. Kept herself busy with trivial tasks.

"Well, this explains everything."

"What are you talking about?" Louisa asked. "What does it explain?"

"Your recent behavior. The moods, the backchat, not wanting to go to Mass. It's that pill. I've heard it can make you depressed. It all makes perfect sense."

"Don't be ridiculous. I'm not depressed. But I am tired of having to answer to you and live by your rules. What about me? Don't I deserve happiness? I want to be free from your moralistic crap."

"No one who's on the pill will live in my house, Louisa."

"Fine, I'll stop taking it and get pregnant then. Is that what you want?"

"No, of course not. I want you to save yourself until marriage."

"Too late."

"No, please don't say that." She searched Louisa's face, her expression creased with hurt and concern for a lifestyle she didn't understand.

"Why? Don't you want the truth? You always taught me to be truthful." Louisa spat out her words. Hurting her mother wasn't her intention, but that didn't stop her from lashing out, fighting for her choices without compromise. Even so, the sight of Kathy struggling to hold back her tears had an effect.

"I want you to go out with different boys and have fun. I can't stand the thought of you parked up in his car with his grubby paws all over you."

"You're unbelievable. I thought you liked David. We love each other and have a lot of fun together."

"Yes, well, that's not my idea of fun."

"No, I didn't think it would be," Louisa muttered.

"What did you say? Why do you have to hurt me? May I remind you, young lady, that I've experienced situations you wouldn't even dream about. But, with the help of my faith and your father, I got through them."

"Mum, stop. You had a difficult childhood. I get that. I feel your pain more than you realize. I have compassion for you, but I don't have to relive your life. It's the seventies, and we think differently now. Anyway, it doesn't matter. We'll never see eye to eye."

Her mother picked up a magazine from her desk and stacked it on the bookshelf. "Of course it matters. It matters to me, and it matters to your father. We don't want our daughter flouncing around town like some trollop. What will people think?"

"Some trollop? How can you say that about me? And stop tidying my room. Leave it!"

"I don't understand. I'm trying, but I can't. You need to pack your bags and go. Unless you're willing to change your ways, you're no longer welcome in this house."

With that, her mother stormed from the room and slammed the door.

As Louisa packed an overnight bag, she wondered why her mother could never let an argument go, never be wrong, and never see any point of view other than her own. Louisa pondered briefly whether the idiom "like mother, like daughter" applied. After all, reflection can teach us many things if we choose to look. But Louisa knew her mother kept her eyes firmly shut when it came to situations she struggled to understand.

A soft knock pulled her from her thoughts. "It's Dad. May I come in?"

"It's your house."

He opened the door and frowned as he glanced around the room at the clothes, magazines, and records littering the floor. "I'd like a little chat."

Louisa sighed but continued packing. "Sure, Dad, fire away."

"Your mother told me what happened."

"Of course she did. Well, she told you her side of the story."

"Look, you have to stop treating her the way you do."

"Oh really? And what about me? What about me, Dad? When is she going to butt out of my life?"

"She's worried about you, that's all."

"Well, she can stop worrying because I'm fine. But I'm sick and tired of her moralistic crap. All this 'sex is a sin' garbage. I'm over it."

Her father sat on the edge of the bed, sighed deeply, and shook his head. "Come on, Louisa. Your mother loves you very much. I don't understand why you treat her this way. It hasn't been easy for her."

"I get it. I do. She's had a hard life, but that's not my fault. That's her unhappiness, not mine."

"Keep your voice down," he whispered. "Show some compassion."

"I know she tries her best, but she's suffocating me. I want to live my own life, not relive Mum's."

"That's not fair. Your mother and I have enjoyed our life together."

"If you say so."

He sat in silence while Louisa packed makeup from her dressing table into a small bag.

"This David, do you think he's the one?" he eventually asked.

She turned to face him. "I'm barely eighteen. How would I know who's 'the one' at my age?"

"Well, if you're…" He cleared his throat.

"Making love. We're making love."

"Yes, well, that may be so, but you still have responsibilities. If you insist on carrying on with this foolishness, there's only one thing for it. You and David must get married."

"What? But he hasn't even asked me." She closed her makeup bag with an exaggerated tug on the zipper. "And I don't want to get married yet."

"Well, you seem to think you're old enough to enjoy what marriage has to offer. And you say you love him."

"I knew you wouldn't understand. This isn't the fifties. We want to be free of all that stifling rubbish you grew up with."

"Look, make more of an effort and meet us halfway, for your mother's sake. That's all I ask."

"Well, she's thrown me out, so I guess I won't have the chance to meet you halfway."

He looked at Louisa but remained silent.

"I have to go. David will be here soon. I'm staying with a friend from work tonight. After that, we'll see, okay?"

"How did it come to this, eh? It only seems like yesterday you were riding your little bike around the backyard. Now you're working at Harris', all dolled up in a short skirt and pale lipstick. Where's my baby girl gone?"

"I'm still here." Louisa smiled at her father. "But I grew up."

"Don't shut us out, Lou. We understand more than you realize. I get that your mother can be difficult, but I'll always look at her with love. I have no other option."

Louisa followed him down the stairs and into the kitchen, where he removed his dinner from the oven. She sat for a while, watching him eat, the smell of lamb chops, gravy, and mashed potatoes making her stomach grumble. She patted his hand. "You okay?"

He rested his silverware on the plate. "Why do the women I love complicate things more than necessary? Surely it doesn't have to be this hard?"

"We'll work it out."

"You do realize the damage is well and truly done for your mother? She'll forever hold the rope. Even when it rubs her raw, she won't let go."

"Yeah, I know."

"Anyway, off you go. Just give it a couple of days."

By the end of the following week, her father had persuaded Louisa to return home. Hoping that an apology to her mother would suffice, Louisa strolled in one afternoon, bearing chocolate éclairs as a sweetener. She knew her father understood, but she also knew that for her mother, conditioning from her difficult childhood ran deeper than any sense and sentiment.

6

THE CHAPEL

Louisa stopped at the chapel's entrance, adjusting her veil with a nervous smile before linking arms with her father. As they waited, he patted her hand affectionately and told her to take a deep breath.

Many months had passed since the loss of her baby, and her parents still had no idea about the pregnancy. Now, on an overcast day that threatened rain, their families and close friends had gathered in a quaint ivy-covered chapel overlooking the bay to celebrate the wedding of Louisa and David.

A wedding Louisa had insisted upon.

She wore a flowing white gown with a wisp of veil attached to a garland of white rosebuds and baby's breath. Rose, as her only bridesmaid, looked pretty in pink polyester satin, her long brown hair pinned in curls at the back of her crown and fingernails painted the color of luminous pearls.

As they walked down the aisle, Louisa glanced at David's mother, sitting tall with the rest of his guests on the right-hand side of the chapel. Her prim pillbox hat and severe suit said it all. Louisa wasn't Pam's ideal bride for her only son. She'd made that perfectly clear ever since they announced their engagement.

However, if her parents had reservations about the marriage, they hid their opinions behind bright smiles and warm handshakes. But as they recited their vows, Louisa could have sworn she heard her mother breathe a sigh of relief.

At the sit-down reception dinner in the church hall, she and David couldn't take their eyes off each other. Louisa had insisted they abstain from sex for a month before the wedding, and the tension had built ever since. Initially, he'd told Louisa he felt rushed by their brief engagement, but today, he seemed perfectly happy as he gazed at her like she was the most precious thing in his world.

7

WANTS AND NEEDS

Each day, Louisa took her lunch packed in a brown paper bag and walked to work from their rented cottage across the street from the Clifton Falls Public Library. She stood behind the counter at Harris' Department Store with boredom for company, then walked home again and ate dinner with David, wishing every month that her period would fail to announce its presence.

As the weeks passed, Louisa no longer wanted to share her evenings with David. She seldom wanted dinner. Didn't want to sit at the table and pretend. Didn't want him to fuss.

"Are you okay?" David's tone carried a worried edge as he walked into the kitchen that evening.

She looked at him sadly, her hand fiddling with her locket. "My period came today. Another wasted month of waiting and wishing."

"Come on, Lou, you know what the doctor said. A baby may never be on the cards for us." He moved to comfort her, wrapping an arm around her shoulders. "But that doesn't mean we can't believe in miracles. We have to stop worrying about it and enjoy the life we have together."

"I knew you wouldn't understand."

"Of course I understand. But—"

"No, David, you don't." Louisa stepped away. "You don't understand what it's like to worry every day that you might never conceive. You don't understand the ache inside or the intense grief whenever I get my period. All my life, I've had it drummed into me not to get pregnant, and now, when I want to, I can't."

"Look, you have time on your side. It's too soon for us, that's all."

"How can you say that? We've been trying for ages, and you know I have only one tube. One tube, David. Half the chance. Half the darn chance."

"I understand, but—"

"There are no buts." Louisa looked at him and sighed. "Get your own dinner. I'm going to bed."

She slammed the bedroom door shut behind her.

Two weeks later, David sat at the kitchen table, his thoughts bouncing back and forth. He'd worked pouring concrete foundations since dawn. It was now dusk. Once he qualified as a builder, his weekly pay packet would be boosted by a few extra dollars. But for now, money was tight, and he needed the overtime.

His thoughts turned to Louisa, lying on the bed in their room, uninterested in eating or spending time with him. When would she shake off this malaise, and how much longer could he take her indifference? David opened the fridge and took out two cold sausages left over from dinner the night before. He buttered two slices of thick white bread, smothered them with relish, and wrapped them around the sausages.

Taking his snack with him, he strolled through to the living room and turned on the television. Small things bugged him—the coolness of the spring evening and trivial work matters. He wondered if he should try harder to please Louisa, to reach out more. Perhaps he should.

As he made his way to their bedroom, he anticipated her mood. Most nights, all she needed was a few minutes alone, and she'd be okay.

He removed his shoes and sat beside her on the bed.

"Don't touch me." Louisa moved closer to the edge of the bed, placing a frigid distance between them. "I'm not in the mood."

David sighed and rubbed her back, desperate to renew their connection. Where had the Louisa he married gone? "How will we make a baby if you won't let me touch you?"

"I can't right now. I don't feel like it."

"Fine, but you said you were ovulating. If you want to get pregnant, we can't let this opportunity pass us by."

Louisa turned to glare at him. "If *I* want to get pregnant?" she yelled. "What about you? You don't give a toss, do you? I don't even know if you love me anymore!"

"I refuse to sit here and listen to this nonsense." David grabbed his shoes and put them back on. "Sort yourself out, Louisa. I love you now as much as ever. But you, you always want more. I'm not enough for you. Never will be."

"Where are you going?"

"Back to work, to check the foundations. I'm worried about the frost." He tied his shoelaces, tugging each tightly into a bow. "I'll sleep at Mum's tonight. Give you some space."

"Don't go. Please, come back to bed."

"No, Lou, not this time. This baby thing's got out of hand. The best years of our lives are passing us by, month by darn month. Sure, you're happy when you think you might be pregnant, but that sadness each time your period comes… It has to stop. All you care about is yourself. Don't you think I feel it too? I want to be a father, I really do, but we have to trust God's plan and be grateful for what we have because I'm near breaking point."

David stormed from the bedroom, yanked his jacket off the coat stand, and slammed the front door behind him. His shoes crunched as he crossed the lawn, already crisp with frost. Seated in his truck, he dreaded the cold night ahead. The last thing he wanted was to sleep alone in his old bedroom at his mother's house, but he needed to leave before he ended it for them both.

PART II

ROSE FAITH CHURCHILL

8

IMMACULATE HEART

Immaculate Heart Collegiate, a prestigious private boarding school for girls, upheld strict Roman Catholic traditions and doctrine. The boarders, mainly young women from outlying farming communities, comprised eighty percent of all pupils. But Rose Churchill was a day girl, and that's the way she liked it.

On the evening of the midyear music festival, several of the city's high schools, including Saint Francis of Assisi Collegiate, Immaculate Heart's brother school, were gathering for the recital in the assembly hall. Rose entered the school grounds dressed in her winter uniform—a black blazer, crisp white blouse, and kilt of Munro tartan. She loved how the woolen fabric swung around her mid-calf as she lugged her cello up the steps and into the school hall.

Their headmistress, a tight-lipped woman nicknamed Sister Mary Big Tits, greeted Rose at the door with a stiff nod. She was tough and sometimes not particularly fair but had her pupils' best interests at heart, and Rose respected her very much. Some of the other nuns didn't fall into this category, and she found it hard to accept their conservative ways.

The in-crowd flocked together as usual. Those who didn't make the cut, including Rose, stood on the outskirts of the throng, secretly envious of those in the inner sanctum.

"You all set?" her friend and fellow musician Emma asked as they moved backstage.

"I'm kind of nervous. The hall's packed."

"You'll be fine. Big deep breaths."

"But there are heaps of guys here."

"So? They don't bite." Emma laughed. "Well, some of the older ones might if you ask them nicely."

A soft smile played on her lips. At fifteen, like many girls her age, Rose dreamed of having a boyfriend but was too shy to express her interest. "Stop it. You're making me blush."

Nikau Hughes slid into his seat beside Billy Cook as Whā and Away walked onto the stage. "What the heck? Don't tell me we have to sit through a boring string quartet."

"It won't hurt you," Billy said with a grin as he stared at the girl with the cello. He'd noticed her before, with her long, straight hair and kissed-by-nature features.

"Have you seen what they call themselves?" Nikau scoffed. "Who'd come up with a name like that?"

"You do get it, right? Whā, the Māori word for four, pronounced with the English 'F' as in far—"

"Mate, I get it. I'm Māori, aren't I?" He scowled at Billy in mock indignation, then laughed.

Billy glanced at their housemaster, who shook his head and frowned. "Shh, be quiet. Grove's looking this way."

"Shit. Check out Cello Girl," Nikau whispered. "She's hot."

"Piss off. She's mine."

"No way. What gives you that idea?"

"Because I've had my eye on her for a while. I saw her at rugby last year and in the Valley over Easter."

"What? On the farm?"

"No, walking along the road by the river. So, I get first shot. It's fate."

"Good luck with that. She's way out of your league, mate." Nikau dug his friend in the ribs. "Anyway, you may never see her again."

"Oh, I'll see her again. I feel it in my bones."

"Shit, Cook, you and your touchy-feely hippy crap."

Mr. Grove walked up behind the two boys. "Hughes, Cook, in my office first thing tomorrow. Now, shut your mouths. Show some respect for the performers."

"But they haven't started yet, Sir," Nikau said. "Give us a break."

"Hughes, why do you always have to answer back?"

"Quiet, Sir. They're just about to start."

A hush fell over the auditorium as Sister Mary Monica stepped forward to introduce the performers. "Over the past few months, this quartet has fused pop, rock, and classical music. They've performed all over the district and at many school music festivals. May I present, Whā and Away."

The crowd clapped as the Sister left the stage, and Billy watched Rose fiddle with the locket dangling from a fine gold chain around her neck. She took a deep breath, closed her eyes briefly, and walked up to the lectern.

"Good evening. My name's Rose Churchill. Tonight, we'd like to play a medley of Beatles classics, starting with 'Lucy in the Sky with Diamonds,' also recorded recently by Elton John, moving on to 'Here Comes the Sun,' then 'Eleanor Rigby,' and my personal favorite, 'In My Life.'"

Billy could tell she was nervous from the slight tremor in her voice, but she spoke well. He leaned back in his seat, folded his arms, and for the next fifteen minutes, didn't once take his eyes off Rose.

"I'm in lust," he said to Nikau once they'd finished their set. "She's under my skin and moving to you know where."

"Is that all you think about? Getting your twig and berries out of your pants?"

"Piss off. I'm approaching my sexual peak, and Cello Girl can help me get there. I'm not getting anywhere with that tease I've been dating. Besides, she's dumped me."

"What? When did this happen?"

"Last weekend. Said I didn't respect her. It's not true. Still, if a girl's not interested, it's her loss."

"Unless they're under your skin like Cello Girl."

"Exactly."

Nikau laughed. "Dreamer."

From the stage, Rose couldn't help but notice the two boys sitting at the back of the hall. They'd chatted and laughed with one another all night, but at least they'd had the decency to stop during the recitals. People who talked through a performance annoyed her. If they didn't like it, they should leave.

The boy seated on the side aisle was familiar, and his handsome face and demeanor intrigued her. Taller than many of the other boys and with long dark hair, he looked like the surfer type—with tanned skin polished by the salt of the sea.

"Who's that guy at the back of the hall?" Rose whispered to Emma as they packed away their stands and music scores. "Last seat on the right."

"Billy Cook. He's a boarder at Saint Frank's, in the same year as us. His parents own a farm in the Rata River Valley. He's cute, don't you think?"

Very cute. "A bit."

"He has a girlfriend," Emma said. "She's a B-I-T-C-H, so you'd better watch out. But he's been staring at you all evening."

Rose blushed. "No, he hasn't."

"Oh yes, he has. And don't look now—he still can't take his eyes off you."

9

THE BUS TRIP

Every second weekend of that unusually warm spring, Rose caught the bus for the hour-long journey to her grandmother's farm in the Rata River Valley. Since the death of Rose's grandfather years earlier, Nana Annie had stubbornly managed the place herself. But even with the assistance of two farmhands, the farm soon slipped into disarray. Now, the once profitable unit barely made enough to pay the workers' salaries, let alone support her grandmother's meager lifestyle.

Rose looked forward to her weekend trips to the Valley like a child anticipating Christmas. She loved the fertile farmland surrounding the river but didn't much care for Nana Annie's house, with its musty feeling of stories past.

As she sat at the bus depot, her thoughts turned to Billy Cook. Lately, it seemed everywhere she went, Billy followed. He was a cocky addition to the Saint Francis debating team just that week and had played in the junior basketball final the week before. She'd even seen him at the movies and surfing with a group of guys at Petrie Bay one Sunday afternoon. But he was never on the bus. He didn't seem to go home on the weekends. Still, if he played cricket on Saturdays, he'd have to stay in town.

Rose opted for a middle seat, shoved her bag in the overhead compartment, and removed a novel from her string shoulder bag. Just as the bus was about to pull away, Billy Cook strolled down the aisle, staring as he passed by to take the seat behind her.

She gazed out the window. Why would he pick that particular seat when the rest of the bus was almost empty? She hadn't had time to shower before leaving home, and now, would Billy take one look at her lank hair and think she wasn't well-groomed? She removed the hair tie from around her wrist and pulled the offending locks into a high ponytail.

All the way to the Valley, Billy invaded her personal space, resting his hand on the rail at the back of her seat. When they arrived, he grabbed her bag and handed it to her before reaching for his own.

"Thank you," she murmured.

"You're welcome." His eyes danced when he smiled, like he kept a secret she'd never share. As they disembarked, he loomed over Rose, his closeness unsettling her.

"Excuse me." His voice was deep for his age, and as she turned to meet his intense stare, the heat crept up her neck and face. He offered her an envelope, his smile now slight and stare blatant. "I think you dropped this."

"Um… it's not mine."

"Yes, it is. Please, take it."

She hesitated before accepting the envelope and stuffing it into the side pocket of her bag. Her heart raced as he strolled across the street without once looking back and climbed into a waiting truck as if he owned the world. As Rose watched him drive away, Annie pulled up, her elbow resting on the open window as usual.

"Rosie." Her nana always called her that. "How are you, my girl? It's a beautiful afternoon for a trip to the Valley."

"I'm good, thanks" She opened the car door and slid into the passenger seat.

"And who's that young man?"

"Um, I'm not sure, but I've seen him at school. He's a boarder at Saint Francis." Rose lowered her head to hide the blush.

"Is he now? What a handsome fellow. Come to think of it, that's

Grant Cook's truck. Must be his son. He goes to Saint Frank's and his sister's in her last year at Girls' High," her nana said with a grin as she started the car. "Anyway, that's enough gawking. Let's get you home."

Back at the farm, they sat at the kitchen table, eating cold mutton with thick slices of Annie's scrumptious oat bread spread with freshly churned butter and, to top it off, last summer's tomato relish.

Her nana put another slice of bread on Rose's plate. "I may have found you some causal work if you want to stay with me for a few weeks the new year."

"Really? Where?"

"At the general store. They need someone to help out in the mornings occasionally."

"But what about Mum and Dad? Mum thinks I'm too young to have a summer job, even a casual one."

"I'll sort that out. I told Shelly you'd pop down and see her tomorrow."

"Sounds great. I can't wait to get out into the world and earn my own money." Even as she spoke, Rose was certain her mother wouldn't approve of her staying in the valley for more than a few days, let alone a few weeks.

"Now, don't go wishing your life away. Just be thankful for each day. That's what I say."

"There's just so much to look forward to. Anyway, let's get these dishes done, then I might go to bed and read."

Rose flopped down on the bed, emptied the contents of her overnight bag, and slipped her hand into the outside pocket, looking for the envelope. He'd addressed it with her initials and added "Cello Girl" underneath. Billy's handwriting was unusual for a boy his age, uniform and mature. But then, his height and deep voice were also unusual.

She removed a sheet of lined paper and unfolded it. *An Interview with Cello Girl*. Neatly written in black ink were five questions, and beneath each one, he'd left several lines blank for her reply.

He must be joking. Rose mumbled the questions aloud. She

refolded the paper and tucked it into the back of her novel before flicking to the title page, eager to immerse herself in her latest romance. Every now and then, she'd stop to reread Billy's note, questioning if the joke was on her.

Early the following day, Rose arrived at the general store for her interview. The small rural store was packed to the rafters with everything from bread to milk, magazines to newspapers, and all manner of fruit, vegetables, and dried goods.

"The job's for the first week of January and a few days here and there after that," Shelly, the owner, said, "but I could do with a hand this morning if you're free."

"Sure. Can I use the phone to let Nana know?"

"Of course. There's one in the office."

Shelly was a crazy lady with a heart of gold, and the two of them clicked straight away. Over the next few hours, she showed Rose the ropes: how to make milkshakes, sort the various newspaper orders, and dip ice cream cones into the liquid chocolate in a small stainless-steel urn next to the freezer.

"I'm not sure I'll ever get my head around this cash register."

"Course you will," Shelly said. "It's a piece of cake. And, Rose, you can't be shy here. A store's a stage, so put on your happy, confident face. Okay?"

"Yes, okay." Happy and confident were two words she wouldn't usually use to describe herself. But she'd try.

Around midmorning, Rose returned from the storeroom to find Billy Cook staring at her over Shelly's small frame. Their eyes locked, and she struggled to look away.

Shelly called out as he approached the counter, "Billy, what can I get you on this beautiful summer's day?"

As Billy continued to study Rose with blatant interest, the phone rang in the office.

"That'll be the phone." Shelly pushed her to the front of the counter. "Rose, you're it."

"Just the paper, thanks." Billy picked up the *Weekend Press* and handed her several small coins. "How long have you worked here?" he asked, maintaining intense eye contact.

Heat traveled up her neck to her cheeks. "It's my first day. I'm helping out for a bit in the New Year."

A slight smile caught his lips as he studied her. "Looks like summer in the Valley just became a whole lot more interesting." And then, he was gone.

"Oh, and by the way." He was back, both hands leaning on the top of the doorframe. "Did anyone leave an envelope here for me?"

Rose looked back as her boss returned from the office. "Shelly, have you seen an envelope for… Sorry, what's your name?"

He flashed a knowing smile. "Billy. Billy Cook."

"For Billy Cook?"

"No, darlin', but I'll keep an eye out."

"Thanks, Shelly," Billy said. "Guess I'll pick it up another time." He left without looking back.

Rose didn't see Billy again for two weeks. However, when she arrived at the Clifton Falls bus depot the Friday before the end of the semester, there he was. He boarded before her and sat in the back row while she took the same middle seat, relieved he wasn't behind her. But as the bus joined the Eastern Pacific Highway, he approached her.

"Do you mind if I sit here?" He indicated the seat beside hers.

Rose glanced at the empty seats surrounding them. "I guess not." She moved her bag onto her lap, clutching the straps as she stared out the window.

"You don't sound too enthusiastic about it."

"You're free to sit wherever you want," she mumbled.

"Do you have the note?"

"No."

"I want it back, completed." He looked at her and grinned.

"You're so full of yourself," she said, averting her gaze again.

"Guilty as charged." He reached over and traced an index finger around the filigree pattern of her locket. "This is pretty. What's inside?"

Every muscle in her body tightened, and he hadn't even touched her. "Nothing."

Billy leaned closer. "It's engraved with a tiny figure eight."

"Eight's my lucky number," she murmured. "I was born at 8 a.m."

"And you don't carry a photo close to your heart? What about your dog or your boyfriend?"

"I don't have a dog… or a boyfriend."

"Good."

Billy said nothing more for a while. When Rose finally relaxed, he moved closer, twirled a lock of her hair around his fingers, and whispered, "Come swimming with me tomorrow afternoon, down under the old bridge."

His invitation took her by surprise. No boy had ever paid her any attention, let alone touched her hair or asked her to go swimming. She pulled away. "I can't. My nana worries about me." She had no idea why she was telling him this.

"Come on." Billy moved closer still. "I know you want to."

"And how do you know that?" She stared straight ahead, fiddling with the hem of her sweater.

"I feel it under my skin, like a warm energy. I could pick you up."

"And what would I tell Nana?"

"That you're going swimming with a friend. It's no big deal."

"I don't think so." Rose stared out the window at the sunset, flushing the sky pink, and felt her face do the same.

She froze as Billy spread his legs wide, his thigh touching hers as if they had an intimate friendship. He leaned toward her and whispered, "Bring the note."

Rose cast him a sideways glance and caught his smile.

They traveled the rest of the way in silence, and when they reached the Valley and disembarked, he sauntered toward the same truck, still without saying a word.

Despite his invitation, Rose didn't see Billy that weekend, and his note remained in the back of her novel while she considered her responses. It would be another few days before she finally spread the page out on her bed and answered all his questions. She read over her words, second-guessed her choices, and scolded herself for being foolish.

As Christmas came and went, Rose thought of Billy and his swimming invitation often, still questioning why he even suggested they spend time together. After all, he was a popular boy with looks that could melt the hearts of a hundred girls, whereas she considered herself plain and uninteresting.

And yet, as her father drove her back to the valley on New Year's Day, Rose couldn't wait to see Billy again.

10

MOODY SKY

Rose glanced up when Emma walked into the store. Emma, whose father was principal at the local school, was a born and bred Valley girl who now boarded at Immaculate Heart. "Hi there."

"Good morning," Emma said. "Can you please make me a milkshake? It's so hot out there."

"Sure. What flavor would you like?"

"Lime. No, wait, strawberry." Emma stood at the ice cream counter and watched Rose prepare her shake. "Hey, there's a party tonight in Hansons' barn. Want us to pick you up?"

"I'll ask Nana, but I won't be able to stay long."

"Billy Cook will be there."

Rose clicked the milkshake cup into place and added pressure to turn it on. The noise of the machine meant she had a moment to consider her reply.

She grabbed a straw from the holder and speared it into the shake. "And that matters why?"

"Don't pretend. I know you like him." Emma accepted the shake and took a sip.

"How do you know that?"

"Well, if he stared at me like he stared at you that night, I'd like him too. Although he spends heaps of time with Vanessa Blinkly. I have no idea why. She's weird."

Rose frowned. "Maybe they're going steady."

"Nah. She likes Nikau, and Billy definitely likes you." Emma dropped several coins on the counter, laughing at Rose's reaction. "Be ready by seven."

Rose had seen Billy that morning, and while he welcomed her back, he hadn't mentioned the party, or anything else. Perhaps Emma was wrong.

When they arrived, the barn was packed, mainly with the mid-teen set, but half a dozen older boys sat on hay bales in the corner, drinking beer and laughing at each other's jokes. Rose hovered behind Emma, not wanting to be noticed.

"Here." Emma pulled a hip flask from her jacket pocket. "Have a swig of this. It'll help you relax."

Rose screwed up her face. "What is it?"

"Bacardi. I stole it from the old man's liquor cabinet. Goes really well with Coke." She poured Rose a Coke and added a splash of rum. Rose nursed the drink, taking a few sips before discarding it behind a hay bale.

"You okay?" Emma asked.

Rose spotted several Saint Frank's boys at the far end of the barn, but there was no sign of Billy. "Parties make me nervous, especially if guys talk to me."

"Yeah, me too. Come on. Let's dance." The two girls joined the group on the makeshift dance floor, where they stayed until the music slowed. When Rose went to grab another Coke, Emma followed her.

Emma tilted her head toward the door. "Look what the cat's dragged in."

Rose didn't turn to see. She knew it would be Billy. "Who?"

"Billy and Vanessa." Emma craned her neck to get a better look. "What are they up to? I thought she liked Nikau. Everyone says she's a tramp, but it's probably just gossip."

Rose cast a sideways glance at Billy and Vanessa, huddled together just inside the door. He leaned in as Vanessa spoke and smiled at her as he replied. His arm snaked around her shoulders, and he pulled her close, then kissed her on the cheek.

Rose turned to Emma, her fingers playing with the small locket around her neck. "Anyway, I might get going."

"Is it because of Billy? I'm sure they're just friends."

"Course not. I have a headache, that's all."

Emma walked with her to the door. "How will you get home?"

"I'll run up to the house and phone Nana. She said she'd pick me up."

"Okay. See you tomorrow."

Rose left the barn just as Nikau's mother was dropping him off, and they greeted each other in passing. She knew he was Billy's friend, but as they hadn't officially met, nothing more was said.

"Hey." Nikau slapped Billy on the back. "What's up?"

"Where have you been?" Billy asked. "I've been calling your place all day."

"Hanging out with the old man, mending fences." Nikau checked out the crowd. "What's with Cello Girl?"

Billy scanned the barn, hoping to catch a glimpse of her. "What do you mean? Where is she? Is she here?"

"She's just left. She looked kind of upset."

"Shit!"

Billy dashed outside. Rain had started to fall in intermittent droplets, but the evening was still light. He spotted Rose as she approached the cattle stop, striding along as if her life depended on it.

"Rose," he called after her. "Wait up."

She kept on walking as if she hadn't heard him.

"You're leaving already?" Billy asked as he fell into step beside her, his boots crunching on the gravel.

"I'm just going up to the house to call Nana."

"Let me drive you home. It's starting to rain." He caught hold of her elbow. "Rose, stop, please."

She stopped. Turned to look at him. The few spits of rain had turned to a light drizzle, and the smell of damp gravel filled his nostrils. "Stay there. I'll get the car, okay?"

Billy ran back to his mother's car. The rain fell heavier now, and as he pulled alongside her and reached over to open the passenger door, he watched her consider her options. "Hop in."

She hesitated before climbing into the front passenger seat.

They drove in silence until he turned off the highway into Churchill Lane.

"Are you mad because I was with Vanessa? We're just friends, honest."

"Why would you think that? It's not my business who you spend time with."

"Yeah, but—"

"You can drop me off here. I'll run the rest of the way."

"You sure?" Billy parked on the grass shoulder beside the gate that led to her grandmother's house.

"Yes, I'm sure." Rose grasped the door lever. "Thanks for the ride."

"You're welcome. And Rose…?"

She waited.

"Come swimming with me tomorrow? Just you and me."

"Why don't you go with Vanessa?"

Billy sighed. "Because I want to go with you." His hands hugged the steering wheel as he stared straight ahead. "I thought you were interested."

"A girl has a right to change her mind." She opened the door, sending her string bag tumbling onto the ground. Bits and pieces spilled out, and she bent down to pick them up.

Billy jumped out of the car and came around to crouch beside her. "Here, let me help."

"Please, just go. I don't want Nana to see you."

As she ran up the driveway without looking back, he glanced down. Floating in a puddle at his feet was a white envelope addressed with his initials, BC. He picked it up, shook off the muddy drips, and turned it over. It was sealed with a blob of red wax pressed with a treble clef symbol. And as he sat in the car, skimming over her five responses, Billy couldn't keep the smile from his face.

No doubt about it, Rose Churchill was interested.

Rose spent the next hour lazing in a hot bath with thoughts of Billy for company, wondering why she'd been so mean to him. He was tall, tanned, and muscular, with a kind, open face. Shelly thought he was nice, so he must be. But he possessed an edge. Not arrogance; something else. Pride? Sexy pride?

Her nipples tightened as she contemplated what it would be like to kiss him, and an unmistakable sensation between her legs intensified. Each time she dared to imagine, her physical response was the same.

And later, as she tossed and turned, trying to fall asleep, he continued to invade her thoughts. She wanted to touch herself, to release the overwhelming need she'd felt lately, but her moral conscience stopped her.

Sunday's overcast sky went perfectly with the day's events. First, ten o'clock Mass. Next, a heavy midday meal of roast mutton, gravy, and vegetables, followed by apple shortcake with cream, and lastly, nothing on TV. Rose moped around the house, bloated and bored.

It was late afternoon when she finally rummaged through her string bag for the letter, planning to tear it into tiny pieces.

It was gone.

She ran down the driveway, combing the grass as she went. The tire marks of his mother's Honda were still noticeable in the muddy gravel where Billy had dropped her off, but the envelope had vanished.

11

THE BLUE NOTES

Carrying a large box of bananas, Shelly entered the store through the saloon doors and looked Rose up and down. “What’s up with you this fine Monday morning? Boy trouble, is it?”

“No, of course not,” Rose said. “Bit of a headache, that’s all.”

“Oh, is that right?” Shelly placed the box on the shelf beside the fruit bins. “Well, don’t look now, but your headache’s just about to walk through the door. I’ll serve him if you like.” She wiped her hands on her apron and smiled. “Billy, what can I get you?”

“Just the newspaper, thanks. Oh, and can you please give this to Rose?” He handed Shelly a small blue envelope. They chatted freely about the weather before he left without once looking at Rose.

“That boy has you in his sights, young lady, and he’s about to pull the trigger.”

“Stop it. He has not.”

“Just saying. What’s with the envelope?” Shelly passed it to Rose. “Love letter, is it?”

“Of course not. I’ll read it later,” she said with a shy smile. “And stop teasing me.” Rose tucked the envelope into her apron pocket and busied herself with the newspaper orders. Her lunch break couldn’t come soon enough. She wanted to see what Billy had to say.

But later, as she sat in the sun and unwrapped her sandwich before opening the envelope, she was almost too scared to look. He'd folded the note neatly into quarters. Written on delicate blue paper, the type used for airmail letters, it was almost transparent. Rose loved the feel of it. She used the same paper when writing to her pen pals. Fit for words that would carry one far away to unimaginable worlds.

An Interview with Cello Girl
Question One
What's your favorite color?

That you answered this question with a palette rather than a single color suggests a multi-faceted personality. You weren't happy to settle on one color but instead picked black, white, gray, and a hint of fire, being red. If one were poetic about it, one might call it a moody sky.

Simply black and white would be concerning. We shouldn't view life in such a conservative, non-yielding fashion. However, the addition of gray adds leeway to your thinking. A middle ground.

Still, your choice of red is the most interesting of the mix. Red is the color of fire, of love and passion, but also of rage.

You have passion in your soul, which manifests in your music. Once you allow that passion to seep into other areas of your life, you'll be truly living.

BC.

She shook her head and smiled, wondering if Billy had even written the note. His sister must have written it for him, surely. Or perhaps Rose had misjudged him. If so, this boy was no fool. *A moody sky*. What an interesting observation.

On Tuesday, another perfect blue-sky day, Shelly pounced as soon as Rose arrived at work. "You have a letter."

The night before, Rose had slept with the first note under her pillow, wondering if, or when, he'd deliver another one.

"Really? Who's it from?"

"Do you even need to ask?" She handed Rose another blue envelope. "I've always been fond of young Billy, but that glint in his eye will get him into trouble one day, mark my words."

Rose bit her bottom lip and smiled sweetly at her boss. "Well, he won't be getting into trouble with me."

Shelly chuckled. "We'll see."

During her lunch break, Rose made herself comfortable in a shabby cane chair that faced the river at the back of the property. She opened the envelope and withdrew the folded note. It was the same blue paper, the same hand, the same fountain pen ink.

An Interview with Cello Girl
Question Two.
What's your favorite song right now?

I must admit, this one had me stumped. It's not a song I'm familiar with, so I phoned the radio station to request it. When they finally played it, it almost sent me to sleep.

At first, I couldn't figure out why it would be your favorite song of the moment. Harry Chapin's tale of fresh-faced love and youthful ambition gradually descending into inevitable middle-aged mediocrity. Really?

I finally clicked (it sometimes takes me a while). A contemporary song with an expressive cello piece. That's why you love it. I hope you'll play it for me one day…

Once again, his assessment was spot-on. Her spark with Billy Cook was smoldering into a flame. Yet, now that he had his questionnaire back, Rose wasn't entirely comfortable with him analyzing her answers.

"Has he been?" Rose whispered to Shelly on Wednesday as she took her apron off the hook behind the office door.

"Has who been?" Shelly whispered back with a grin.

"You know—that boy."

"He has a name, darlin'. It's Billy. You do know that, don't you? And yes, he's been. His note's on the table out the back. And we don't have to whisper. There's nobody in the store."

Rose went to take off through the saloon doors to the storeroom.

"Hold on a minute," Shelly called after her. "Read it on your break, okay? Otherwise, you'll be good for nothing all day. Now, put that apron on and get to work."

"Sorry. I forgot about work for a second."

Shelly nodded. "Thought so."

The store was busier than usual that morning, so Rose didn't take her break until almost one. She made herself comfortable on the back porch with a cup of tea and an oat-bread sandwich, then opened the envelope. The paper, font, and smell of the note were the same. Billy had a slight scent about him—there, but barely.

An Interview with Cello Girl

Question Three

Which novel has inspired you the most?

We read to enliven our souls. Fantasy keeps us from sinking into the depths of an ordinary life. Even so, your choice of novel surprised me. It's evident you have an intellectual mind—you're a straight-A student, I hear—but I still expected some trashy tale full of handsome heroes, damsels in distress, and a happy ending. Jumping to conclusions is a bad habit I try to curb, often without success.

I, too, have long admired W. Somerset Maugham. Therefore, I compliment you on your choice. I also enjoyed his tale of love and betrayal involving Kitty, Walter, and Charles. In my opinion, compassion is one of life's greatest gifts.
I wonder if Kitty would agree...

Rose held the note open, pondering his response. She'd almost convinced herself he wouldn't know the book, but once again, he'd surprised her with his analysis and prose. *Fantasy keeps us from falling into the depths of an ordinary life.* Could he have written that, or had his sister written it for him?

"So, little Miss Secretive. What's in today's letter?" Shelly asked when Rose walked back into the store.

"Nothing much. And it's a note, not a letter." She slipped the envelope into her pocket. "Just a whole lot of puzzlement."

"What do you mean, puzzlement? I'd have thought Billy was an open book. But what do I know?" Shelly pulled her apron ties tight. "Men. If you ask me, they're all after the same thing. Mark my words."

"I'm not so sure." Rose still believed in the notion of men making romance. "He might be different."

Shelly shook her head and chuckled. "Well, it looks like whatever Billy's putting in those little love notes is having the desired effect. He's circling to collect his prey."

Thursday's question, number four, was the movie one, and she wondered if he'd scoff at her choice. It wasn't the kind of movie some guys would enjoy, so his response would be interesting. Their blue-note game had added excitement to her week, and Rose smiled as she contemplated the days ahead once he'd addressed all her answers. Would they have a proper conversation?

"Good morning, Shelly. Another gorgeous day."

"That it is. And before you ask, no, he hasn't been."

"What makes you think I was going to ask?"

"The words were dancing on the tip of your tongue before you even opened the door, darlin'." Shelly stopped what she was doing and looked at Rose. "If he comes in, I want you to serve him. You could even speak to him, you know, face-to-face."

"I do speak to him," Rose murmured.

"Barely. So how about you smile and put on a brave face. Remember, this is a store—"

"And a store's a stage." Rose finished the mantra, grinning at her boss.

"Now you're onto it."

As it turned out, when Billy delivered blue note number four, Rose was out the back taking a break. She'd just finished her milkshake when Shelly dropped the envelope into her lap. "Special delivery for you. You have ten more minutes."

As per his previous notes, Billy had folded this one into quarters. When she opened it, a tiny scrap of card, smaller than a postage stamp, fluttered out and landed face down on the wooden porch. She tried to pick it up but couldn't, so she licked her fingertip and touched it to the back. When she turned it over, there he was, smiling up at her.

He'd given her a photo for her locket.

An Interview with Cello Girl

Question Four

What recently viewed movie spoke to your soul?

Ah. The humble story of Saint Francis of Assisi and the innocent, fresh-faced Clare. Fields full of fire poppies, yellow wheat shifting in the soft breeze, and constant birdsong.

So, Miss Rose, you are a hopeless romantic after all.
I bet you wished Francis and Clare ended up together, rolling around in those fields of wildflowers.
Go on—admit it.

While this movie's not to my taste, I can see why you liked it. It just goes to show that there's no right or wrong when it comes to individual inspiration.

My favorite scene is the one where he cuts her hair and lets it float on the breeze.
Most symbolic!

BC.

His cheeky comments made Rose smile as she slipped the tiny photo into the frame of her locket and clicked it shut. When she walked back into the store, she was still smiling.

"That beau of yours was in again this morning," Shelly said to her on Friday, flashing a knowing smile.

"He's not my beau. I hardly know him."

"Is that right? Well, you won't mind if there's no note today, then?"

A wave of disappointment washed over Rose as she wondered why Billy's response to the last question hadn't arrived in the usual manner. "I don't mind a bit."

"Hold on. I spoke too soon." Shelly craned her neck to watch Billy park his farm bike in front of the building. "Look who's here."

"I might go grab some more Coke from out the back."

"No, you don't, missy. Stay here and serve your young man." Shelly headed into the storeroom, leaving Rose and Billy alone.

"Hi. How are you?" He looked every inch the farm boy in his tight jeans, work boots, and black tank. He was well-built for his age, with strong shoulders and veins protruding proudly along sculptured forearms, and every time she saw him, her tummy fluttered just a little.

"Fine, thanks. And you?"

"I have the final note. But you can't see it unless you come swimming with me tomorrow."

His invitation filled her with unexpected dread. "I don't care. You had no right to open my envelope. It was private."

"Really? I wrote the questions in the first place, and you addressed it to me."

"That doesn't mean I wanted you to read my answers."

He turned serious, his expression defiant. "So, you're turning into Miss Hurtful now, are you, with that sting in your voice?"

Rose lowered her eyes to hide her discomfort as she folded his newspaper. She pushed it across the counter. "I didn't mean for it to come out that way."

"Yeah, well, the more you open that pretty little mouth of yours, the more you piss me off." Billy picked up the paper and tossed some coins onto the counter. He turned to leave but looked back. "Meet me under the main bridge at one tomorrow. Otherwise, I won't bother you again."

Rose watched him leave, immediately regretting their exchange as the sound of his motorbike faded into the distance.

"Well, well, well." Shelly reappeared from behind the saloon doors. "You sure ruffled a few feathers that time, young lady. What do you reckon? Are you gonna meet him?"

"You were listening?"

"Only heard the last part." Shelly raised both hands. "I swear."

"He's pretty mad at me. I think I might've blown it."

"You think? Look, men aren't the enemy. You just have to learn how to manipulate them. Don't be afraid of a little boy-girl communication. That's how we get what we want. Go meet him."

"I'm not sure. Mum and Dad don't like me spending time with boys."

"I hear ya, but, hey, Billy's a nice kid. You both could do with some innocent fun."

Rose chewed her lower lip. “I guess.”

“Look, you’re fifteen. I’d dated half a dozen boys by your age.” Shelly smiled. “But, come to think of it, look where it got me. Knocked up at sixteen and married to Joe three months later.”

“But you’re happy, right?”

“Yes, happy as a little pig in mud. Joe’s a great guy.”

The bell above the door chimed, and Shelly looked up. “Vanessa, darlin’. What can I get you?”

“I’d like a word with Rose, please In private, if possible.”

Those “I’m not good enough” butterflies stirred in Rose’s stomach. She knew Vanessa only by reputation. She was often the target of schoolgirl gossip, and Rose had no idea whether the rumors were true. Rose took a deep breath and released it.

“Of course. Go in the back for a minute.” Shelly opened the door to the storeroom for the girls to walk through. “I’ll hold the fort.”

Rose ushered Vanessa into the storeroom. “What can I do for you?”

“It’s about Billy.”

“What about him?”

“He said you saw us at the party. There’s nothing going on between us. We’re just friends.”

“It’s not really my business who Billy spends his time with. I hardly know the guy.”

“But that’s the whole point. It is your business. Billy likes you, and I don’t want to ruin his chances. I know some of the snooty girls at school say I’m a piece of trash, but don’t judge me until you’ve walked in my shoes.” Vanessa stepped toward the door but stopped and looked back. “Billy’s a great guy. Give him a chance.”

“Thanks.” Rose’s staunch resolve crumbled. “Vanessa?” She called after her. “I thought he had a girlfriend.”

“Not anymore. She dumped him last year.” Vanessa smiled, and her whole face softened. “He’d like one, though. I’ll see you around.”

Rose followed Vanessa back into the store and stood behind the counter, watching her leave. She was such a pretty girl, but she always seemed troubled.

"Well, it looks like you might be off to meet Billy after all," Shelly mused once Vanessa had gone.

Rose grinned at her boss. "Why do you do that?"

"What? What did I do?"

"You were eavesdropping. Don't try to deny it."

"Guilty as charged," Shelly said. "But it's exciting. Kind of like a story out of a *True Confessions* magazine."

Rose frowned. "What's a *True Confessions* magazine?"

"Never mind, darlin'. You had to be there. Back when I was a teen, those magazines helped us in our quest for knowledge, if you catch my drift." She winked. "Right. Let's put the kettle on."

Rose and her nana usually spent Friday evenings together watching TV. Sometimes, Annie would ask Rose how she felt about life's issues, and she'd respond openly. Often, their souls were linked, and they'd comfortably share stories and philosophies. But that night, Rose kept her thoughts to herself because those thoughts were consumed by Billy.

"I have to work again tomorrow if that's okay?" Rose switched on the TV.

"Of course. More money in the bank. It's always good to see a young person doing an honest day's work."

"Thanks for letting me stay with you, by the way."

"I love your visits, you know that. Being alone sucks the life out of us oldies." She smiled sadly. "Loneliness is for the young. They can dream of a better life ahead. The elderly realize a better life isn't going to show up."

"Don't say that." Rose sat on the arm of her chair and hugged her tightly.

"It's true. People talk about us oldies waiting for God. That's me, patiently waiting for God. But when you're here, I have a purpose. I feel alive again."

Her honesty surprised Rose, and she wasn't sure what to say. She hated the idea of her grandmother getting older. "What time are Mum and Dad arriving?"

"Around five, so don't be late home. Not sure what's going on with Louisa, but according to your father, she's back home at the moment."

"Oh, okay."

Puzzled, Rose waited until her nana had gone to bed before calling her sister. They'd always been close, but the loss of Louisa's baby had moved their relationship to a whole new level of understanding.

"How's my favorite sister?" Louisa asked. "It sure is quiet around here without you and that noisy cello."

"I'm good. What about you? Is everything okay between you and David?"

"I guess. But he's spending some time at his mother's again, so I'm staying with Mum and Dad tonight. We needed a break." She sighed. "But we'll figure it out. So, don't you worry, okay?"

"Okay." Rose hesitated. She did worry. David was a good man, and she wondered if Louisa had lost sight of that lately. "Anyway, I need your advice about something."

"What? I don't believe it. You, Miss Perfect, are asking *me* for advice?"

"Are Mum and Dad home?"

"No, they're at some dinner party. Why's that?"

"Well." Rose hesitated. "I've met a boy."

Louisa fell silent.

"I've kind of known him for a while. He goes to St Frank's, but we're in the same year. Anyway, he asked me to go swimming with him tomorrow afternoon." Still silence. "What do you think?"

"What's there to think? It's about time you went out and lived a little. You're fifteen. Old enough for a summer romance and an afternoon date with a boy."

"Yeah, I guess."

"But no hanky-panky. Take it from someone who knows."

"We've hardly even spoken to each other, so there won't be any hanky-panky."

"It's all well and good to say that now, but once he starts working his 'I want you' magic, saying no is never easy. Are you blushing?"

"How did you know?"

"Just a hunch. Look, it's about time you came out from behind your cello and lived a little. But remember, Mum and Dad will be there in time for dinner, so don't be late home. You know how Mum is about boys and sinfulness. The Lord will strike you down if you so much as look at a boy in lust, so keep that in mind, and close your eyes when he kisses you."

"He won't kiss me."

"Want a bet?" Louisa chuckled. "Would you like him to?"

"Yes. I'd like him to… very much."

12

THE PUMP SHED

Just after one that Saturday, Rose stood waiting for Billy in the burned-off grass, with the words "stood up" invading her thoughts. She stayed under the bridge for another fifteen minutes, enjoying the shade and frustrated by the heat.

Under her white peasant blouse, a new orange toweling bikini hugged her figure, its cups joined in the center by a wooden ring. Even though Rose loved how it made her feel, she'd never owned a bikini before and wasn't sure if she'd be comfortable wearing it in front of him, so she'd popped a T-shirt in her bag just in case.

At the sound of a farm bike approaching, Rose glanced toward the highway, willing her butterflies to still as Billy rode into view. He came to a stop in front of her, removed his sunglasses, and smiled. "Sorry I'm late. I stopped to help an old ewe tangled in a fence."

"I was just about to leave. Thought you'd stood me up."

"Well, after yesterday, I considered it… to teach you a lesson." He searched her face for a reaction as he steadied his bike. "And if you're going to be all snooty about it, you can go home right now. Life's too short for regrets and compromise."

Rose held his gaze. He was bossy. A take-charge kind of guy. "No,

I'm okay. I want to come." A flirty smile curled her lips, as if they had a mind of their own.

Billy grinned, his eyes glinting in the harsh sunlight. "Now, that wasn't so hard, was it? That little smile. Hop on."

A towel hung around his muscular shoulders, but otherwise, his torso was bare. Rose hesitated, distracted by the thought of touching his naked waist. "I'm not sure. I haven't ridden on the back of a bike before."

"Don't worry, I'll be careful. Lean with me on the corners, and hold on tight, okay?"

"Okay."

Billy flashed her a knowing grin. She hopped on and clutched the back of the seat. He reached around and pulled her hands tight around his waist. "There. That's better," he said with a chuckle.

Dust billowed in the air as they rode down the gravel road that ran parallel to the river. Rose had never been so close to a half-naked boy in her life, and excitement blended with her discomfort.

Billy turned off the road and parked in the shade of a willow tree opposite a rusted farm gate. Standing beside the bike, she brushed the dust off her jeans, unsure why she'd agreed to come.

"There's a track here that leads down to the river and the swimming hole by the old bridge." Billy reached under the seat and pulled out his T-shirt and camera.

"Why the camera?"

"I take it everywhere. In case I see something interesting that I want to shoot." Each time he spoke, he commanded her attention, and she couldn't look away. His smile drew her in, inch by inch, tug by tug. He opened the gate and waved her through. "Just as well you wore jeans. The bracken's pretty dry this time of the year, and the bank's steep, so be careful. I'll go first so I can catch you if you fall."

Rose followed him along the narrow track, and true to his word, Billy helped her down.

He dipped his head to meet her gaze as she held on to his arms. "You okay?"

"Fine."

He continued to hold her. There was no smile, and for a split second, she thought he might kiss her. “Come on. It’s not far.” The spell broke.

The river flowed swiftly in the center as it hurried beneath the bridge, but by the willows, where the water stilled and darkened, was a deep swimming hole. Along the banks, rātā trees boldly displayed their crimson brushes—the river’s namesake brazen in full bloom.

Billy plunged into the water as soon as they reached the edge. “Coming in?”

“Is it cold?”

“Not once you go under. Come on, get in.”

Rose unclasped her locket, slipped it into the change pocket of her jeans, and tugged them off. Now that they were alone, removing her blouse didn’t seem such a good idea, so she left it on. Her toes gripped the slippery stones as she moved to the river’s edge. Goosebumps assaulted her skin, and her legs tingled as the cool water flowed around them. “I might just paddle.”

“No way.” Billy floated closer and skimmed his arm across the water, splashing her from head to toe.

She squealed as the white muslin of her blouse clung to the toweling bikini top and her breasts tightened. “That was just mean.”

Billy laughed. “Hurry up. Get in.”

Rose removed her blouse and spread it on a large boulder to dry before wading into the river, arms crossed timidly over her chest. Billy swam up behind her and snaked his arms around her waist. She flinched at his touch.

“I love your bikini, but I’d love it even more if you took off the top.” He faced her now, so close she could see droplets of water dripping off his chin.

“What? No!” She moved away.

“I have my top off.”

“But you’re a boy.”

“I’m a man, not a boy.” He flashed her a grin full of cheek. “Go on. It gives you such a sense of freedom, swimming without restrictions.”

"That's like me telling you to take off your swimming trunks," she flirted, then internally scolded herself for being so forward.

Billy removed his trunks and threw them onto the bank. "Done."

"Don't come near me."

He moved closer. "Why not?"

Rose waded away from him. "Because you're naked."

"So?" he said, laughing.

"Honestly, if you come near me, Billy Cook, I'm getting out and walking home."

"But then you won't get the last blue note."

"Well, you'd better behave!"

He slipped under the water and swam toward her again but stopped a few feet away. Stared.

"Please don't look at me like that," she said. "You're making me self-conscious."

"You have nothing to be self-conscious about." Billy waded to the river's edge and grabbed his towel, his white butt a stark contrast to the rest of his tanned body. He turned toward her, rubbing the terry cotton through his hair, naked as the day he was born and without an ounce of shame.

Embarrassed, she dipped her head below the surface and swam against the current toward the old bridge.

By the time she reached the shore, his trunks were back on, and he lay face down in the sand. As she approached, Billy flipped over onto his back and propped himself up on both elbows to take in every inch of her. "Why are you ashamed of your body?"

Rose covered herself with her towel, picked up her jeans, and fished the necklace out of the pocket. "Don't most girls feel uncomfortable about boys seeing them in a bikini?"

"You'd be surprised."

She sat at his side, and as she slipped the chain around her neck, he leaned forward to help her with the clasp. The brush of his fingertips against her skin intensified her awareness of him. "You don't seem to have a problem with yours."

"Should I?"

"I guess not."

"But you didn't answer my question."

"I used to be overweight," she said, staring out over the river, "and I can't get used to the new me."

"But you were still cute when you were heavier."

Rose turned to look at him. "How do you know?"

"Because I've watched you for a while." His features softened. "You've always been beautiful to me."

Heat rushed up her neck and face. "Sorry. I'm not sure how to respond. You don't need to say that when you must have heaps of other prettier girls after you."

"I mean it. I noticed you at the St Frank's rugby final a while back." He held her gaze. "You intrigued me."

"That was ages ago. We were thirteen."

"Well, I'd just turned fourteen." Billy's grin, now soft and caring, lit up his face. "If this was the Middle Ages, we'd be married by now."

"What?" She giggled. "To each other?" Rose stretched out, letting the sun bathe her in much-needed warmth. Did he really think she was attractive, or was it just a line?

"That's an interesting thought," he replied. "Anyway, I can't change your thoughts about yourself, but I'm free to think you're beautiful. And, in my opinion, if a guy says you're beautiful, he usually means it. Now, at times, he only means it in the heat of the moment, and other times, he means it for always. It's up to you to learn the difference."

"Thank you." His compliment stuck in her head, and no matter how hard she tried to ignore it, she couldn't.

Billy leaped to his feet. "Come on. Let's go exploring."

Their swim and the heat of the summer afternoon relaxed Rose more than anything had in a long time, and as they dressed, contentment washed over her.

Billy took her hand and led her along the track toward the mouth of the river, where it merged with the coast. Dry grass and bracken edged the gravel path, and when he stopped, she almost walked into him.

"Sit over there in the grass. I want to shoot you."

"No. I hate having my photo taken."

"Go on, just a couple," he coaxed. "You have a picture of me."

"Do I?" Rose said with a smile. She sat in the long grass and, despite her initial reluctance, felt peaceful and happy as he clicked away.

He replaced the lens cap and offered his hand. "Come on. I want to show you something."

As the gravel track gave way to a clearing, Billy let go of her hand. Rose stopped and then took several steps forward. "What is it? A hay barn?"

"It's the old pump shed. If you go around the side, you'll see the original waterwheel. It used to belong to my grandparents."

"I love waterwheels. Will it ever work again?"

"Doubt it. An earthquake changed the river's course years ago. Now it's just a pile of rotting timber, rust, and crumbling stone."

"What's that amazing smell?"

"Lavender. The guys who bought the land turned it into a lavender farm. Come on. I'll show you."

Billy grabbed her hand again and guided her to the back of the building. There before her, not thirty feet away, fields and fields of blooming lavender swayed in the light breeze, releasing its rich fragrance into the summer air. Rose inhaled deeply and smiled.

"Lucky we came today," he said. "They'll start the harvest soon, and the sprigs will be gone."

"What an incredible sight. I love lavender. What do they do with it once it's harvested?"

"Press it for oil. It's medicinal."

She glanced back at the shed. "Can we look inside?"

He cocked a mischievous brow. "Thought you'd never ask."

Rose pushed the pump house door open and stared up at the wooden beams crisscrossing the double-height ceiling. "Wow. It seems a lot larger inside. Do you know when it was built?"

"In 1898. There's a placard over the door. I remember my grandparents used it to store hay at one stage."

The smell of hay, timber, and dust enveloped her as she stepped inside. “Imagine this place converted into a summer house.”

Billy spread his towel on the floor and watched as she did the same. Sunlight filtered through gaps in the timber, casting shadows across the room. The soft light accentuated the cut of his muscular frame, and Rose struggled to take her eyes off him.

“If you sit down and let me kiss you, you can imagine it’s your summer house, and I’ll give you the final blue note.” He reached for her hand, his expression full of mischief.

Her face heated again. “You’re not trying to blackmail me now, are you?”

Billy gently guided her to the floor. “Of course not. It’s purely a suggestion. Have you put a photo in your locket?”

Rose settled beside him on the towel and smiled shyly. “Maybe.”

“Good.”

She glanced around the interior again.

“You okay?” he asked.

Rose nodded.

“Sorry about yesterday. I didn’t mean to be an asshole.”

“That’s okay. I was kinda mean to you as well. It’s just…”

He entwined his fingers with hers. “You’re not nervous, are you?”

“I’ve never kissed a boy before.” She couldn’t look at him.

He chuckled. “What? Never? You’re kidding me.”

“Why are you laughing? You’re acting like a typical rugby jock.” She went to stand. “Maybe we should go.”

Billy reached out and pulled her back down. “I’m sorry. I didn’t mean to laugh.” He explored her face with his hands, his fingertips tracing her lips and cheekbones. “Will you give me one more chance? I’d love to be your first kiss. You have such gorgeous lips.”

Until that moment, Rose hadn’t understood the current that passes between two people who desire one another. She’d never comprehended why some girls at school were already sexually active. Louisa was right. It was all well and good to be virginal when at school with no male contact. But when a good-looking boy held you in his arms, telling you that you’re beautiful and wanting you with all his soul, it was a different story.

"Rosie," he whispered. "Is it okay if I kiss you?" His lips skimmed her neck, his breath hot against her skin as she closed her eyes.

"Yes."

Billy cupped her face, his thumbs at the base of her jaw and fingers holding her with gentle pressure. His lips were soft and full, but the kiss was a fleeting caress, no more than a brush. He trailed his mouth across her neck and collarbone, moving toward her earlobe.

"Do you want more?" he whispered.

"Yes."

He did it again. Just when Rose thought he would dance his tongue into her mouth, he pulled away, back to her earlobes and the hollow at the base of her throat.

"More?"

"Oh, yes." She wanted more, so much more.

Billy sat back, his expression puzzled and eyes hooded with want. "You're so beautiful."

She glanced down, her knuckles tight as she gripped the waistband of his jeans.

"Look at me."

Rose met his gaze. "Why are you doing this?" Once again, her voice was a hint of a whisper.

He flashed that flirty grin. "Doing what?"

"Teasing me."

"Payback."

"What do you mean?"

"You've teased me for weeks. I'm just playing the game."

"No, I haven't. I thought you said you wouldn't act like a rugby jock." She pulled away.

"I won't." He tugged her close again. "Promise."

This time, when he took her face in both hands, he didn't hold back. His tongue searched her need, sucking her in deeper and deeper. Their kiss flowed like warm caramel—sweet, rich, and fluid. And when his tongue explored her mouth, Rose fully understood her sister's warning.

Resistance was futile.

Her nipples hardened as Billy traced his fingertips up and down her torso, the thin muslin of her blouse no barrier to his touch.

She pulled back.

"Sorry… too much?" Billy reached up to brush wisps of hair from her face—reading her, reassuring her.

"It's okay." Rose pulled her knees to her chest and hugged herself in defense. "You've had your kiss, so now I want the note."

"You said you didn't care."

"I lied."

"One more kiss." His eyes captured hers. "You're an incredible kisser for a novice."

"No." Their flirting felt naughty but nice. No boy had shown an interest or desired her before, and she liked it. "Give me the note."

"Say please."

"Please give me the note."

Billy reached into his jeans pocket, pulled out the note, and unfolded it. He started to read:

"An Interview with Cello Girl
"Question Five
"What do you want most out of life?

"Your response to question five is the most insightful yet. Once again, you intrigued me. To, and I quote, 'know your soul's purpose' comes from a philosophy many of us don't understand. The point of my questionnaire was to find out more about you. Not the shy, self-conscious girl on the bus, not the girl who hides behind the cello at school functions, not the girl who has a summer job at the general store, but the real you. Your answer is honest and true. You trusted me enough to share what you want out of life, and for that, I thank you."

Billy offered her the note. "Here, you read the rest."

Rose held the page steady and glanced at him before running her gaze over the words in the filtered light.

"Aren't you going to read the last part?" he asked.

"I can't. I'm sorry." She returned the note to him, knowing if she spoke his words aloud, she'd cry.

Billy picked up from where he'd left off, watching her as he voiced the last few words.

"May we always be true friends, passionate lovers, and soulmates into eternity."

"That's so beautiful. Thank you," she whispered. "It makes me sad. I don't know why."

He took her hand. "Hey, don't be sad."

Rose attempted to regain her composure by making light of his words. "Are you sure you didn't get your sister to write the blue notes for you?"

He chuckled. "Who, Anna? You must be joking. She'd laugh in my face and then tell all her friends about it. They took me a while to write. I had several attempts at this last one."

She smiled softly.

Tender kisses touched her neck, her lips, and back again. His hands moved from her face, traced over her arms, then around to the small of her back. Rose wanted him to touch her breasts again, so she arched into him, knowing it was wrong, but…

"You're gorgeous. I want you so badly." Billy's kisses intensified, his tongue firm against hers. He undid the top button of her blouse. "Let me see your bikini again. Orange is my new favorite color."

Rose shook her head. "I'm sorry. I can't." His erection, solid and larger than she'd expected, pressed into her pelvis as they lay on their towels, him now half on top of her.

"Let me make love to you," Billy whispered as he caressed her earlobe with his tongue. "You want to… I know you do."

"I'm sorry. I can't," she repeated.

"Why not?" Hot breath caressed her neck and throat, leaving a trail of want.

"I'm scared."

"You don't have to be scared," he soothed. "It's just you and me... No one else needs to know."

"It's not about that."

"Well, what then?"

"It's against our beliefs, you know that. Wrong in the eyes of the church."

"But how can something so wonderful, so natural, be wrong? Do you think God sees it as wrong?"

"Please don't do this," Rose said, not looking at him. "I don't need this pressure. Mum and Dad would ground me for a year if they found out I was here."

"But they'll never know, will they?" Billy kissed her neck, sucking her skin with his talented mouth, leaving his mark. "No one will ever know. It can be our secret." His hand moved down her body to unzip her jeans. "I have protection."

"Billy, don't. I can't." She pushed him away and sat with her knees hugged to her chest. "It's not about whether I want to or not. I can't."

"Rosie, I want you to be my girlfriend. To spend time with you... To be your first and for you to be mine. I want us to be passionate lovers like I said in my note."

"We don't even know each other, and I'm underage."

Rose stood, zipped up her jeans, and reached down to grab her bag as he raised himself onto his elbows and watched. "We'd better get going. Mum and Dad will be here soon. I'm going back to town tomorrow."

"Seriously?" Billy shook his head as he got to his feet. "Can't you talk them into letting you stay? When will we see each other again?"

"There's no talking my mother into anything. She makes all the rules. But I'll be back the following week."

"Good."

They lingered in silence at the gate where they'd left the bike, its seat cool from the shade, but Billy was in no hurry to return to the main bridge. He held her hands possessively. "So, Cello Girl, how did you enjoy your first kiss, or rather, kisses?"

She smiled and then came the blush he expected. "Very much."

"Me too." He pulled her close, his arms around her waist and chin resting on her crown. "I don't want you to go home." He dipped his head and kissed her again, his lips a light touch on hers, then pulled back, one hand still cupping her cheek. "And how will we see each other once we're back at school? Saint Frank's is a hell of a place to escape from, especially during the week."

"Do you want to see me?"

"Of course." Billy brushed the hair from her face and smiled as he sensed her relax. He liked her and saw no point in pretending otherwise. "Always."

Rose stepped back. "There's a movie I want to see. We could go together if you can get a pass out."

"Okay. Which one?"

"The latest James Bond. I don't like soppy girl films. I prefer movies with a bit of grit and guts."

"Is that right? I'm keen, more than keen."

"Cool. I love Carly Simon."

"You do realize she's not in the movie, don't you?"

"Really? I thought she played the part of M as well as singing the theme song," she teased.

Billy laughed now, enjoying their banter. "M's never played by a female. It's a male part."

"Is that so? Someday, a woman will play M."

"No way."

"I don't see why not. The world's changing, and even James Bond movies have to move with the times."

"I like you, Cello Girl. I like you a lot." He tossed his keys in the air and caught them. "Come on. We'd better get back. Don't want to keep Mummy and Daddy waiting, do we?"

"There's no need to be sarcastic." Rose flung her bag over her shoulder. "Let me ride your bike."

"What? No way. Not today, anyway."

13

COMING HOME

Kathy and Tom Churchill drove over Rata River Bridge on their way to Annie's farm at exactly 4:31 p.m. As they passed the yellow road sign, Kathy sensed something approaching them from the T-intersection. But when she glanced right, she saw nothing untoward.

As they drove, Kathy stared down at the swiftly flowing river, its strong current making her uneasy, although she wasn't sure why.

When they arrived at the farm, Kathy's somber mood intensified. There'd always been an uncomfortable air between her and her mother-in-law. They maintained an awkward relationship—constantly keeping score. Ever since Tom told his mother he was marrying a Catholic, Kathy had sensed a hesitation in Annie. And from that day forward, she'd never felt good enough.

She greeted Annie with a stiff hug, over in a moment. "Where's my darling daughter?"

"Out swimming with friends. She said she'd be home by five."

"But it's almost five now."

Annie glanced at the clock on the wall above the kitchen sink. "So it is. She'll turn up soon enough. She's never late for dinner, you know that."

"I hope she's not hanging around with farm boys."

"Come on, love," Tom said. "Let's not jump to any conclusions."

"Well, you can't be too careful at her age. She's a pretty little thing. I bet there are lots of boys wanting to get their hands on her."

"Oh, for goodness' sake," Annie muttered. "I'll start dinner."

Over an hour later, there was still no sign of Rose, and Kathy couldn't settle the panic gaining traction in her gut. "Perhaps we should call Shelly. What if Rose had to work late?"

Kathy listened on the phone in the living room as Tom made the call from the kitchen. He ignored Shelly's pleasantries and got straight to the point. "We were wondering if Rose worked late today. We expected her home by five. It's now after six, and we can't think where she might be."

"No, sorry, Tom. She left here at one, and I haven't seen her since. She was going swimming with a friend—Billy Cook, as I recall."

"I see." He paused. "And this boy, does he live around here?"

Kathy's heart skipped a beat. She played with her wedding ring as she listened.

"His parents, Grant and Doreen, have a farm up by the cutting. Their number's in the book. I wouldn't worry, Tom. Billy's a lovely boy. Maybe they're visiting friends. Or she might be at his place."

"Right. Thanks anyway."

Grant Cook answered their phone on the first ring. They hadn't seen Billy since he left on his bike after lunch and were about to go looking for him.

Tom met Grant and two of his farmhands at the intersection of Rata River Road and the main highway. As the summer light faded toward dusk, the younger men walked the track while Grant and Tom drove along the road, searching for any sign of Rose and Billy.

"Hold on. Stop the car," Grant said. "There's skid marks in the gravel. And a sheep in the ditch. Looks like it's been hit."

Tom pulled onto the road verge, and the two men jumped from the car.

"Billy? Rose?" Grant yelled. "Billy? Billy?"

"Grant! Grant, down here," came the faint reply from a farmhand.

"Grant," Tom said. "Did you hear that?"

"We need help," someone shouted.

They found Billy six feet down the bank with the front wheel of the bike on top of him. He was unconscious, his femur piercing the skin of his thigh.

"I see the girl," the other farmhand yelled. "She's down here."

"Thank God!" Tom scrambled farther down the bank to the river's edge. "Is she all right?"

It took him all of two seconds to realize his youngest daughter was dead. He'd seen the dead before; their eyes communicated the horrible truth. But he didn't need to look into her eyes to know Rose's life had ended. She lay face down on the water's edge, her white blouse twisted around her neck, her exposed skin covered in pinpricks of purple bruising, and her orange bikini top ripped apart.

When they turned her over, mud and sand caked her hair, neck, and chest—the indentation of the impact now frozen on her innocent face. There was a gaping gash on the side of her head, where she'd struck a sharp rock, but blood no longer flowed from the wound.

Rose was already cold.

"Someone! Please," Tom shouted, his hands shaking. "Go to the nearest house and call the police."

He cradled Rose in his arms. How was he going to tell Kathy? What would he say? Tom held her for the longest time, rocking back and forth as the seconds stretched into minutes and the flashing lights of an ambulance and a patrol car reflected across the river.

"My beautiful, talented girl. I'm sorry I wasn't here to save you. I'm so sorry." He wanted to say everything he wished he'd said when she was still alive. Now, words deserted him, and as he pulled her closer to his chest, he noticed the silver chain around her neck, its locket resting between her shoulder blades. As he slipped it into his pocket, a voice broke into his grief.

"Mr. Churchill, I'm Constable Milton. Shall I send a patrol car to tell your wife?" The police officer was little more than a kid himself.

Tom had heard him vomiting in the bushes earlier, and he still looked green around the gills.

"No." He sighed deeply and looked to the heavens before returning his attention to the young man. "I'll do it. We'll head back to town tonight. Please, take good care of her."

"Of course. We'll get the boy away first, but there's a second unit on its way. If you want, I'll ask the driver to wait at the highway turnoff until you arrive, and you can follow it back to town," Milton said. "We'll be here for a while yet."

"Thank you. We'll be half an hour at the most."

Back at the farm, Kathy struggled to remain still due to the uneasy sense of dread in the pit of her stomach. She looked over at her mother-in-law when she entered the kitchen. "We'd better call the police."

Annie set a basket of laundry on the table and started to fold its contents. "I'm sure Tom will be home soon."

"Why did you let her do this? Why is she out with some boy, getting up to goodness knows what?"

"The girl's fifteen," Annie snapped. "You can't wrap her up in cotton wool and that religion of yours forever. It's not right."

The telephone rang, breaking their tension.

"You get it. It'll be her."

"Rose, where have you been?" Kathy blurted into the receiver, her tone a mixture of relief and anger.

"Mum, it's me," Louisa said. "What do you mean? Where's Rose?"

"We don't know. She went for a swim with some boy this afternoon. She's not home yet. I'm worried sick."

"Look, calm down. Rose told me she was spending the afternoon with a guy she's friends with. They'll be down at the swimming hole under the old bridge."

"You talked to her about this? When?"

"She phoned last night, and we chatted about it. She wasn't sure whether she should go."

"And you told her to go?" Disbelief muscled its way into Kathy's voice. "What were you thinking, Louisa? She's a kid, for goodness' sake."

"Mum, she's fifteen."

"Yes, so your grandmother keeps reminding me." Kathy's tone softened. "Anyway, I'll call you later. Your father's out looking for them. We'd better keep the line clear."

"Do you want me to drive up?"

"No. I'll let you know when she's home. Or call back in an hour. She's bound to be here soon."

Kathy ran out of the house as Tom's headlights swept the driveway. He stopped in front of her and stepped out of the car. Without saying a word, he stood with his hands pressed to his face, covering his nose and mouth.

"Did you find her? Is she all right?"

"We found her, love." Raw, thick sobs rose from his belly. "She… she's gone. I'm so sorry. She's been killed… in a farm-bike accident."

"No! Tommy, no! Don't say that. Please don't say that."

Tom reached out to comfort her, but she was having none of it. He'd never understood this side of his wife, but that's how it always was—Kathy's way.

His mother appeared, clutching a tea towel. "What's going on?"

"What's going on? What's going on!" Kathy screamed in grief and disbelief. "She's dead. You let her go with that boy. And now she's dead! What am I going to tell Louisa?"

"No. Not my Rosie." Annie fell to her knees on the parched lawn and sobbed into the dirt. "It can't be true. Why, God?"

"It is true. Why did you let her go? You let her go. Now she's dead."

"It's not Mum's fault, Kathy," Tom said. "Come on, let's get you inside. We need to go home. They're taking her down in an ambulance.

Said they'd wait for us at the turnoff. The boy's already gone to the hospital. Apparently, he's touch and go."

"He survived?" Kathy shrieked. "He survived, and Rose is dead?"

"They're not sure if he'll make it. It's too soon to tell."

"I want to see him. It's his fault," Kathy said. "I want to see him tonight."

"You know that's not possible, love. They're operating as soon as they get him back to town, and we have Rose to attend to."

The phone rang. Annie ran into the house, and Tom followed.

"It's Louisa." She handed the receiver to her son, her face lined with sorrow and stained with dusty tears.

"Dad, what's happened? Nana sounds upset."

He sighed. "Is David there?"

"No, he's still at his mother's. Dad, what's going on?"

"You'd better call him and tell him to meet you at our place, Lou. Do it now."

"Have you found Rose yet?"

"We'll talk about it when David's there."

"No, Dad. Tell me now. I have a right to know!"

Tom hesitated, bile rising in his throat as he held his wife's tormented gaze.

"Dad? Are you still there?"

"We found them, sweetheart. I'm so sorry. There… there's been an accident…" He twisted the telephone cord between his fingers and sobbed. "She's dead, Lou. She died. This afternoon."

"No!" Louisa screamed. "She can't be dead. I need her."

"I'm sorry." Tom swallowed hard. "There's no other way to say it. We'll be home in about an hour. We're following the ambulance down the highway. Go next door and stay with the Browns until we get there, okay? We'll pick you up on the way through. Okay?" he repeated.

"Okay."

He hung up the phone and turned to his mother. "Mum, call the Browns and explain. Louisa needs support until we get home, and David's gone AWOL."

Tom drew his wife and mother into a hug. He now had to carry the burden for them both. Their grief matched their resentment for one another, and he was the only one holding their fragile relationship together.

Once home, Kathy went straight to bed, the sounds of her grief muffled behind the bedroom door.

In the living room, Louisa sat on the floor, hugging her knees to her chest. Tom took his daughter's hand. "Have you tried calling David?"

"Yes. But they aren't answering. I don't know where they are. David hasn't talked to me in two days."

"We'll try again shortly."

"But I'm worried. David's God knows where… and my beautiful sister's lying in some cold, dark morgue. And he has no idea. No idea at all."

"Don't worry, Lou. We'll find him."

When she redialed the Reynold's number a while later, Tom observed the exchange with concern. "Pam, it's Louisa. I need to speak to David."

She listened.

"Please put David on the line."

Louisa waited, then opened her mouth to speak. She dropped the receiver back into the cradle.

"She hung up on me. The bitch hung up on me." Louisa ran up the stairs. Her old bedroom door slammed shut.

Tom redialed their number, and the woman didn't even wait to find out who was calling before she spoke.

"Look, Louisa, David doesn't want to talk to you right now," she said curtly. "I thought I made myself clear. He needs space. Don't you agree?"

"Pam, it's Tom Churchill here."

"Oh, Tom. I'm sorry. I thought you were Louisa."

"Yes, so I gather." He sucked in a breath. "May I speak to my son-in-law?"

"He doesn't want to be disturbed. He said he'll call Louisa in the morning."

"Is that so? Well, Rose died in an accident a few hours ago. So I'd appreciate it if you told David to get his sorry ass out the door. His wife needs him. She's at our place." He slammed down the receiver, furious at how people dragged petty grievances into situations that were none of their business.

David arrived fifteen minutes later and enfolded his mother-in-law and Tom in a firm hug. He took the stairs two at a time, tapped on the door of Louisa's old bedroom, and let himself in. He sat on the edge of the bed.

"Hey," he whispered. "I'm so sorry, Lou."

"David." She threw her arms around his neck. "It's Rose. She's gone. She's dead."

"I know. I'm so sorry." He was already crying.

"In an accident." Louisa struggled to release the words. "She died. In a farm-bike accident."

He pulled her closer. "I know. Come on, let it all out."

"How am I going to live without her?" Sobs rose from deep within her throat. "How will I cope?"

"We'll cope together."

"But you don't even want to be with me anymore."

"That's not true. I still love you," he murmured. "Love you with all my heart."

Kathy and Maggie dressed Rose for her Requiem Mass in the three-quarter-length pastel pink dress she wore to her junior school ball eight months before. They washed and brushed her hair, leaving it to fall freely around her shoulders. White ballet pumps—purchased especially for the occasion—were placed on her delicate feet, and a tiny posy of blush pink rosebuds, lily of the valley, and sprigs of lavender nestled in her hands.

As soon as Kathy returned from the funeral home, she sought out Louisa. A strange sense of detachment had conflicted with other emotions while they prepared Rose, and Kathy needed a comforting hug from her firstborn.

"I want to see her."

"No, Louisa. I'm sorry. Not a good idea."

"Why?"

"Because she doesn't look like Rose, sweetheart. I don't want you to remember her like that. I want you to remember her full of life, sitting behind her cello, doing what she loved."

"But how will I know it's her in that darn box? How will I know?"

"Come on, Lou. How about you go sort a few bits and pieces for her? The record by that Harry Chapin guy and *The Painted Veil*. She loved that book. Oh, and the little locket we gave her for her birthday. Go on. I'll make sure they go with her."

14

RECOLLECTIONS

Billy lay in his hospital bed and stared at the moody sky beyond the window. It reminded him of Rose's color palette from blue note number one. But today, there was no passion in the mix.

Initially, his recollection of the accident had been patchy, but as the hours dragged into days, the images in his head shifted into focus, and he remembered the impact clearly.

The rest came to him in flashes, but the time before the bike ride home, when he lay with Rose in the dappled light of the pump house, would remain seared into his memory forever.

Today was the day. His parents had called in earlier and talked about the funeral, but no matter how many times he told himself to get a grip, Billy still couldn't get his head around the fact that Rose was gone.

Footsteps broke his train of thought.

"Hi there."

He turned his head toward the door. "Vanessa. What are you doing here? Aren't you going to Rose's funeral?"

"Of course, but it's not for a while yet. I figured I'd come and sit with you." She held his hands. "Then I can take your energy back to Rose."

Emotion lodged in his throat. "Thanks," was all he managed to say.

"Have any of the others visited?"

"Shelly. Niko. A few of the guys from school." He looked toward the window and sighed. "But no one knows what to say, Ness. And I can't concentrate. My mind's all mushed up with a whole lot of crap."

"You and I, we don't have to say a thing."

Her warmth washed over him. Vanessa was the kind of person most people didn't appreciate. He didn't understand why. To him, she was a beautiful soul and a friend in the truest sense of the word.

"I just want to sit here," she said. "Hold your energy and let you know you have a friend."

"What am I going to do, Ness? It should have been me. Why didn't I die instead? I've fucked up."

"Don't talk like that. Who knows what's meant to be?" She handed him a tissue. "In some ways, I blame myself."

"Why would you say that?"

"Because I visited Rose at work and asked her to give you a chance."

"Shelly did too. I guess most of us have times in our lives where we feel we've messed up at someone else's expense when all we wanted to do was help. You did what you thought was best out of friendship. That's special. Remember that."

"I liked Rose. She had an elegance about her that… Well, I wish I was more like her."

"I keep seeing her smiling face in my mind. That long hair and those cute freckles across the bridge of her nose." Billy swiped his eyes with the back of one hand. "It's so unfair."

"It is."

They sat in silence for a while longer, then talked in short sentences until it was time for her to leave.

"Anyway, I'd better go." Vanessa bent and kissed Billy on the forehead. "I'll visit again once I'm back at school."

"Thanks." He choked back a sob. "And say goodbye to Rose for me. Tell her I'm sorry."

"You can tell her yourself." She took his hand again and squeezed it. "I'm sure she'll hear you."

As Vanessa left the ward, Billy pondered life—how fleeting it was for some and how long-lasting for others. Who made that decision?

"Now, son, tell me in your own words what happened. Take your time. I have all afternoon." Detective Sergeant Aaron Benet sat on the chair beside Billy's hospital bed, his large frame spilling over the edge of the blue plastic seat.

"I don't remember all of it."

"Tell me what you can. Everything you do remember."

Billy searched his memory. "I picked Rose up just after one. We swam in the water hole under the old bridge, then walked along the track to the stone pump shed."

"And you took the bike from the farm, is that correct?" Benet made notes in his small notebook with a pencil as Billy nodded. "And Rose Churchill, the deceased, she was your girlfriend, was she?"

"Not really… kind of."

"Well, which one is it, son? Was she your girlfriend or not?"

"I guess." Billy lay back on the pillow and closed his eyes, but he could still feel the weight of Benet's judgmental stare. "I'd just asked her."

"What happened next?"

"We walked along the river track. It was overgrown with dry bracken, and I remember thinking her jeans would protect her legs from being scratched. I showed her the lavender fields, and then we went inside the pump shed."

He hesitated. Frowned.

"Then what did you do?"

"We talked and, you know—"

"No, I don't, son. You tell me."

"I guess we made out for a while."

"So that's how she got that hickey on her neck, is it?"

Billy sighed, shaking his head as he recalled the feeling of Rose's warm skin against his lips. "I suppose."

"And did you have sex with this fifteen-year-old girl, Billy? You are aware that sixteen is the legal age of consent?"

"We didn't have sex."

"Are you sure about that?" Benet scribbled in his notebook, his whole hand gripping the pencil as he wrote. "You do realize that information will be in the autopsy report?"

"What autopsy?" Billy's mind flashed to his delicate Rose, lying on a cold slab in the hospital basement, waiting to reveal her secrets.

"Individuals who die in a motor vehicle accident in this country are required to have an autopsy, son, and Rose Churchill was no exception." Benet shifted in his chair. "Carry on. I realize this is hard for you, but it has to be done."

"We lay on our towels on the wooden floor—"

"And the sex?"

"I've already told you we didn't do anything… just kissed."

"Yes, so you keep saying." Benet hesitated. "But she was a pretty girl, and you're a virile-looking young fella. You wanted to, you know, do the deed, is that right?"

"Sure, but she was a virgin and didn't want to."

"And that stopped you, did it?"

"What are you trying to say? That I forced her to have sex with me? I'm a virgin too. It was the first time we'd been alone together."

"Okay, son, settle down. I have to ask these questions. It's just part of the job. We need to get a handle on what took place, that's all. Carry on. What happened next?"

Billy picked up his water cup, took a sip, and then closed his eyes briefly. "We walked back upstream to where we'd left the bike. It was almost four thirty, and Rose needed to be home by five. She wanted to ride back down the road to the hay barn. I didn't want her to, but she said her dad had been giving her lessons on her grandmother's farm bike."

"And you let her, is that what you're telling me?"

"I didn't want to." Billy broke down. "I said no at first, but then—"

"So what are you saying here, Billy? You, a farm boy your whole life. How long have you been riding bikes on the farm, three or four years?"

"About that."

"And how long have you held a driver's license? Let's see." Benet flicked through his notebook, turning back several pages.

"Three months." Billy sighed. "I passed the day after I turned fifteen."

"And you're telling me you let a girl, with no driver's license and little experience, get on the front of that bike and ride with you as her passenger down a road that's no more than a farm track?"

"Yes. I think so."

"You *think* so?" Benet studied him for a long time. "Let me tell you what *I* think, shall I?" He shifted in his chair again, searching for comfort. "You wouldn't be so stupid, would you?"

"It wasn't like that. She wanted to have a go, that's all." Billy let out another dispirited sigh. The pins holding his leg in place were uncomfortably tight and itched like mad.

"Right, let's get the facts straight." Benet huffed out a breath. "A young girl is dead, her life cut short, ending years before it should have. Her family's grieving beyond belief, and you're trying to shift the blame to save your precious hide. It's not looking good here, Billy."

"She was driving, I swear. I'm not trying to shift the blame. I'm not a liar." Benet's questions irritated Billy. He wanted out—out of bed, out of the ward, out of life.

"But you've already told me you can't remember everything."

"I remember that."

"No, son, I'm not sure you do. You're saying Rose was driving because you don't want to take the blame or lose your license. That's what I think."

"Think whatever you like. I know the truth."

Billy wriggled around in the bed, tense with pain and frustration. He watched Benet flip over a page in his notebook and wet the tip of his pencil with his tongue.

"So, how did the accident happen? Tell me what you recall."

"We were coming up to the bend by the hay barn, and as we took the corner, a sheep ran out in front of us. I yelled for Rose to brake, but she didn't have time. We hit the sheep, skidded on the gravel, then slid into a spin and ended up going over the bank.

"I landed halfway down with the bike on top of me and couldn't move. I remember the pain. Clear as day. The bone was sticking out of my thigh, and there was blood everywhere. I tied my towel around the top of my leg as best I could. I couldn't see Rose—kept calling out, but she didn't answer." Hot tears trickled down Billy's face and off his chin in a single drip. "That's all I remember, honest. I don't even know what happened to her."

"That'll come out soon enough, son." Benet sighed. "Look, I realize you're hurting. We all do stupid things when we're young, make bad decisions. But most of us scrape through, learn from our mistakes, and move on. It'll take time, but you'll mend. Rose Churchill won't mend, though, will she? She's broken forever."

Detective Sergeant Benet stood and closed his notebook. "Take my advice, Billy." He slipped it into the top pocket of his sweat-stained shirt. "Do the right thing, son, and let's not hear any more of this 'she was driving' nonsense. Think of her family. What they're going through. Don't tarnish their memory of Rose."

Kathy didn't answer the door when the bell rang. She stayed at the kitchen table, trying to make sense of the tea leaves clinging to the inside of her empty cup. Maggie read tea leaves, but to Kathy, the tiny flakes' message remained elusive.

"Aaron Benet's here, love," Tom called from the hallway. "From the police."

Benet's bulk filled the small kitchen. "How are you, Kathy?" he asked. "Please, don't get up."

"I'll make some fresh tea," Tom said as he filled the kettle.

"I'm not too bad, thanks, Aaron," Kathy replied. "Better than yesterday and the day before. Some days are worse than others." She indicated a chair. "Please, sit down."

Benet sat. "I thought I'd swing by to tell you the boy's improving. He has a broken femur and pelvis, but other than that, he'll mend."

"I suppose he will. But what about us?" Kathy stared down at her cup once again, searching for answers. "Will we ever mend?"

He shifted in his seat, glanced at Tom, and sighed. "Also, I thought I'd better tell you the latest."

"What's that?" Tom asked.

"The kid, Billy, he's making noises about Rose driving."

"No! Why would he say that?"

"I suspect he's trying to save his hide. He knows he'll get a youth conviction and lose his license. To tell you the truth, Billy doesn't strike me as a blatant liar. I'd say he's just having a little memory trouble. I wasn't going to mention it. This whole sorry business is painful enough as it is, but I thought I'd better. Then everyone knows what's what."

"I want them to lock him up and throw away the key." Kathy rubbed her fingertips across her forehead, too exhausted for visits from people she hardly knew.

Tom returned to the table with a pot of tea, cups, a plate of muffins, and sugar and milk, all sitting neatly on a tray.

"He's a minor, so that's not happening." Benet picked up a muffin, broke off half, and stuffed it into his mouth.

"Tell us what he said about Rose driving," Tom prompted in obvious disbelief.

"He said they went to the river for a swim, a bit of fun… You know these teenagers. On the way back, she said she wanted to ride down to the hay barn, and he reluctantly agreed. That's his story, anyway."

"No, that can't be," Kathy said. "She wouldn't do that."

"I gave her a few lessons recently," Tom said. "She was getting the hang of it. But riding with a pillion passenger is a whole different kettle of fish."

"Yep. And I'm sure you're right, Kathy, but I just wanted you to know. Oh, and another thing. It seems they were more than friends."

"What? What are you saying? That he was her boyfriend?" Kathy asked.

"Seems so. Well, according to the boy."

Kathy couldn't comprehend his words. "But she'd never even looked twice at a boy in her life. She was only fifteen."

"I realize this is hard for you, but you need to know the facts—no surprises later that way. They spent the afternoon down at the old pump shed by the river."

"That little prick," Tom said.

"Look. They are… were, kids. There wasn't anything going on, apart from innocent teenage stuff. You know the drill."

"But how can you be so sure? We never even knew she had a boyfriend. We thought she was working at the store that afternoon. What else was she hiding from us?" Kathy crossed to the sink and rinsed her cup under the faucet.

No one answered.

She turned to look at her husband. "You don't think that boy took advantage of her, do you? What if he took advantage of her, Tom? I couldn't bear it."

Benet cleared his throat. "According to the autopsy report, there was no evidence of sexual activity. Your daughter was a virgin. And I'm sorry to bring it up, but we're required to explore all avenues. And I grilled him pretty good on that score too."

"Thank God for small mercies," Kathy said.

"Oh, I almost forgot. Her shoulder bag's in here." Benet handed Kathy a large brown paper bag. "Hard, I know, but we have to return these items. You might want to take a look at the letters. It may help you understand that their association was no more than the beginnings of an innocent courtship. Her watch is in there too. It seems the time of the accident may have been four thirty-one. That's what time it stopped, anyway."

15

FOREVER GOODBYES

"I want to go to the cemetery."

"What, now?" Billy's father helped him into the car. "You've only been out of the hospital five minutes. Here, give me those crutches. I'll put them in the back."

"Dad, if I don't go before we leave town, I won't get another chance for ages."

"I guess you're right," his father said. "I'm not trying to stop you. It's getting late, that's all."

It was a frigid autumn day. The trees were as bare as his heart, and the dirt on her grave was damp and pungent. Billy stood there, expecting to feel her spirit around him, but the void in his soul gaped and wept silent tears. He studied the headstone, murmuring the inscription aloud:

"Rose Faith Churchill
"1962-1978
"Flowers bloom forever in the hearts
of those who remember them."

"Come on, Son, we'd better hit the road."

Billy lingered to reread the inscription, mumbling it under his breath. "Just a little longer."

"Look, you shouldn't be standing on that leg. Come on. Mum will be worried."

A car pulled into the parking space at the edge of the burial plots, and Billy glanced over with disinterest as the driver cut the engine.

"Who's that at Rose's grave?" David asked as he removed the keys from the ignition and stared out the windshield. "It looks like the boy. We can't get out, not yet."

But Louisa was already out of the car, running toward Billy. "You sick bastard. What are you doing here?" she yelled, tears streaming down her face. "You killed my only sister. Now you're visiting her grave?"

"Louisa, come back. What are you doing?" David ran after her. "Louisa, get back in the car." He grabbed her by the arm and tried to hold her still.

"Let go of me, David." She broke free. "Billy, you waste of space. All you wanted was a quick screw. You felt nothing for her. Now she's dead. And you're here 'paying your respects.' Unbelievable! Get out of here." Louisa was screaming now. "Never come back. Understand? And you," she snapped at Grant. "You brought him here. What were you thinking?"

"William, get in the car." Grant came to the aid of Billy, who stood glued to the spot, his face pale and breathing shallow. "Come on. Mind that leg."

"You make me sick," Louisa spat out. "It's a shame someone wasn't there to help Rose. I'll never forgive you as long as I live, Billy Cook. You killed my sister, and I hope your life is ruined, just like mine is."

David stepped in front of her. "Louisa, that's enough. Back to the car," he said through gritted teeth. "You're making a spectacle of yourself."

She opened her mouth to continue her attack, but David took her by the arm and pulled her away. "Stop it. Get back to the car. Now!"

He opened the car door and stood his ground until she sat in the passenger seat, her face like thunder.

"What do you think you're doing?" David asked as they watched the Cooks' car leave the cemetery.

"He shouldn't be here. It's not right. He killed her. Now he's at her graveside, playing the grieving boyfriend."

"The boy has a right to pay his respects. They were friends. He's just a kid, for shit's sake."

Louisa slumped in her seat. "I don't understand how you can be on his side."

"This isn't about sides, and you know it."

"Well, what *is* it about?"

David rested his elbows on the bottom of the steering wheel and rubbed his temples with his fingertips, wondering if he could ever make this better. "It's about compassion."

"Really? And while everyone's showing compassion to that kid who killed my sister, who shows compassion to me?" Louisa looked out of the car window toward the grave. "Take me home. I can't get out again now. He's tainted the space, her space."

That night, after a lackluster dinner he didn't taste, David sat at the table, his second cup of coffee cold and untouched. Louisa hadn't let him make love to her since Rose's accident, and he felt her withdrawing from him one lonely day at a time.

"I'm going to bed." Louisa stood at the kitchen sink and stared out the window into the darkness. She filled a glass with water and took several gulps. "It's been a shit of a day."

David watched her move around the room, tidying this and that. He hadn't noticed before, but she looked so much older. "Lou, we need to talk." He pushed out a chair with his foot and indicated for her to sit.

"Not tonight. I'm not up to it. Please don't do this." She remained standing.

"If you won't talk to me, let me in, I'm not sure our marriage can survive." He glanced down into his mug before meeting her gaze.

"What do you want me to say? I've lost my baby, I've lost my sister, and now, what are you implying? That I'm losing you as well?"

"That's not what I said—"

"You just said you weren't sure our marriage can survive."

"I want us to go back to how we were, to love each other again. I want you back. The old Lou."

"There's no going back for me, don't you understand? My sister's dead, and all I want is a baby. But I can't conceive, can I?" Louisa stayed remarkably calm, too calm. "So, what's left in my life?"

"You have me. I'm here now. I'm ready to make a baby, to love you, to help you through." He stood and reached for her. "I'm willing to work on our marriage, but I need you to meet me halfway. Even part of the way."

Louisa sobbed, her hands covering her eyes. "What will I do? My world's falling apart." She stepped closer and rested her head on his shoulder, her tears dampening his shirt. "I miss her so much. Some days, I can hardly breathe."

David held her tighter than he had in months. "I know. Come on, let's get you to bed. But I'm sleeping with you. I need you, Lou," he pleaded. "We need each other. No more of this spare room business."

Several months later, Louisa announced she was pregnant.

16

THE SESSIONS

Kathy stared through the thin blinds filtering light across the psychiatrist's office, barely registering the children playing in the park next door or the cars driving back and forth along the road. She hardly even heard Doctor Duncan Wiseman's questions, but she replied anyway.

"The iceberg roses bloomed like never before last summer," she said. "Out of all the roses in the garden, Rose liked icebergs the least. Said they were too showy, with little scent and no substance once out of their environment, meaning they didn't last long in a vase. She jokingly likened them to some of the in-crowd at school—pretty girls with shallow personalities and no staying power. I remember wondering how young people gain such insight. She was wise beyond her years in many ways, my Rose. I was so proud of her."

"So, how have you been since the accident?"

"I can't believe it's been all those months already," Kathy answered. "Tom always said the sun shines down on us, but not now. Not since January past. I have good days, not-so-good days, and darn horrible days. I keep reminding myself that Rose made an unwise choice that day. That's all. It was an accident. But still, the questions keep coming. What if she'd made a wise choice? Would she still be here?"

Kathy fiddled with the blinds, varying the light's direction from up to down. "Was it her time? What if she hadn't got on that farm bike with that Billy boy? What if they'd never met? What if she'd stayed at home for the summer? Would she have found her way to the Rata River Valley anyway? Or would she have been struck down by a car while crossing our street on the same Saturday afternoon?"

She avoided the doctor's gaze as she sat in the chair opposite his desk. "The 'what-ifs' keep swimming in my head, and no matter how hard I try to drown them, they keep bouncing back to the surface."

"What you're experiencing is the natural progression of grief, Kathleen. It's a path all parents tread when they lose a child."

Kathy continued as if she hadn't heard him, "I used to love being in my garden. Trimming and shaping plants is like cutting the troubles from your life, reshaping it to how you want it. Neat and tidy."

"I agree, gardening can be most therapeutic."

"Not now. The garden's too full of what would have been. A reminder of how far I've fallen into this pit of grief." Kathy perched on the edge of the chair, rolling the hem of her handkerchief between her fingers and thumb. "What if I could cut this grief from my soul, prune my inner tree, so new growth appears in the spring?"

"Something to discuss next week, perhaps. Time's up for today, I'm afraid. Although we could carry on for a few more minutes if you wish."

During her hour-long appointment, Kathy had talked of nothing but Rose. However, she knew the doctor had a schedule to keep, no matter how caring he seemed. "No, thank you, Duncan. I appreciate your time."

"Don't be too hard on yourself. Take time to grieve and have a good cry. The shower's one of the best places to let go. The water can help cleanse the sorrow—metaphorically, of course."

She stood and picked up her bag from the floor.

"Wait, Kathleen, one more thing." Duncan spoke gently as he rose from his chair. "Have you thought about talking to the boy?"

"What?" She stared at him in stunned disbelief. "Of course not. I have nothing good to say to him."

"I'm not suggesting you ignore your grief, but meeting with him may help in the act of forgiveness."

"So, what are you suggesting? That I forgive him?" Kathy raised her voice ever so slightly. "That's ludicrous."

"Finding it in yourself to forgive may help you move on."

"Let's get one thing clear, Duncan. There's no moving on from here. They say time heals all wounds, but a mother's broken heart never heals from the loss of her child."

The following week, Kathy stood at the reception desk of the law firm Shand Shand and Harrow, Tom almost an afterthought at her side.

"Kathleen and Tom Churchill," she said to the receptionist. "We have an appointment with Henry Shand."

While Henry Shand and the Churchills weren't friends in the social sense, they belonged to the same parish, and his daughters attended Immaculate Heart. In happier times, they'd shared pleasantries on the sidelines of sports tournaments, but this visit wasn't about pleasantries.

"Kathleen, Tom, please come down." They followed Henry along a narrow corridor, passing small offices filled with busy workers. In his office, files, law books, and papers piled high, held together with dust and anticipation. "How are you both?"

"As well as can be expected under the circumstances," Tom said.

"Yes, well, once again, my condolences. Please, take a seat." He waited for them to settle into their chairs before handing Tom an official-looking document. "You're aware of the coroner's findings?"

"We are," Tom said as he passed the report to Kathy.

"I'm not sure I can add anything further to make the process easier for you or your family."

"We want to know what can be done about the boy," Kathy said. "That's why we're here. In our opinion, a six-month loss of license and a five-hundred-dollar fine is an unacceptable outcome."

Henry sat forward in his chair and pressed his fingertips together. "What did you have in mind? A private prosecution?"

"Can we do that?" Tom asked.

Henry hesitated. "I'm not sure you want to go down that route. The police have already prosecuted Billy for driving an unregistered vehicle on the road. Given his age and the fact it was a tragic accident, I feel justice has been served to the best of the court's ability."

Tom cleared his throat. "I'm sorry you feel that way. We don't accept the outcome and never will."

"I understand, but as your lawyer, it's my job to advise you." Henry paused as if anticipating a reaction, but the Churchills remained silent. "My advice is to let sleeping dogs lie. Billy's fifteen, a teenage boy. Granted, he made a massive error of judgment that day, one he'll carry with him for the rest of his life. Do you honestly believe that dragging him through the courts again will make a difference to how you feel about him or, indeed, how he feels about himself?"

"It doesn't seem fair. Our Rose is gone while that boy, as you call him, gets off scot-free," Tom said.

"I agree, I agree," Henry mumbled. "But even so, Billy's world's been turned upside down. He hasn't managed to return to school, which is a shame for such a bright boy, and his rugby career is all but over. No doubt, he'll be finding out who his real friends are right now. He is… *was* a well-liked kid with a bright future. But now, well, he's living a life sentence of his own."

"Sorry," Kathy said, "but I can't feel sympathy for him. I just can't."

Henry rubbed his chin while studying them. "Look, take a few more days to think it over. There are certain avenues we can pursue, but the longer you drag this out, the harder it will be for the both of you."

"You're right," Tom said. "But I can't see another way forward."

"Just give it time," Henry replied.

Kathy rose to her feet, tears welling in her eyes. "May I use the bathroom?"

"Of course." Henry stood and opened the door. "Down the hall, second on the right."

As Kathy pushed through the restroom door, she caught sight of the pale, drawn face staring back at her from the mirror above the basin. She looked older, so much older, and her many sleepless nights had smudged their presence with a smoky finger beneath her bloodshot eyes. She splashed cold water on her face, wondering how she'd ever be brave enough to get through.

Less than a week after meeting with their lawyer, Kathy returned to Doctor Wiseman's office. She sat in the same chair, staring straight ahead.

"How's progress since your last visit?"

"What progress? To be honest I'm struggling. It never seems to end."

He scanned his notes. "What never seems to end?"

"The grief. Is there ever any progression after the loss of a child? Right now, I can't see a way forward, let alone the light at the end of the proverbial tunnel."

The doctor hesitated before speaking. "I've been thinking about what you said last time. About roses."

"What do you mean?"

"Perhaps we could run through an exercise, with your consent, of course."

Kathy didn't want to run through an exercise. She was exhausted, buried in a hole of sorrow and murky sadness, and her appointments with Duncan never seemed to help. "An exercise?"

"Let's align your thoughts and feelings with the analogy of a rose."

She stared at him in disbelief, her stomach tied in knots.

"I'm sorry. I realize your daughter's name was Rose, but please, stay with me on this one." Duncan fidgeted with his pen. "Imagine your grief as a rose."

Kathy sighed. "Sorry, I don't follow."

"We prune roses in the winter, so they develop strong growth in the months ahead. But, if we prune them too early, the new growth dies back with late frosts. So timing is the key. We can align the pruning process with human grief. It's okay to sit and stagnate for a while. This is nature's way… Hibernation, if you will. But at some stage, grief must be tackled and pruned from your heart. Do it too soon, and you have to start over. Leave it too late, and the grief grows unruly, with no formal structure, making it harder to control. But the most difficult part of the pruning process is the dead wood, is it not? It's brittle and requires extra effort to remove. But if you leave it on the bush, it holds the plant back."

"So, you're saying I'm in my dormant stage, and soon it will be time to prune?"

"That's one way of looking at it, don't you agree?"

Kathy shook her head, wondering yet again whether therapy was a complete waste of time. "No, not really."

"Well, an unwillingness to forgive is the dead wood in your soul, is it not? It sits, becomes brittle, and ultimately strangles any new growth. In the end, it can destroy you."

Duncan examined her face for a response. When she gave none, he continued, "Do you remember what you said at our last session?"

She frowned. "Not really, to be honest."

"What if you could prune your inner tree to let the new growth appear? You can, but you'll have to talk to the boy first. Remove the dead wood before cutting back to an outward-facing bud to encourage that new growth you crave. Remember, the hardest part is eliminating the dead wood."

"So the dead wood symbolizes an unwillingness to forgive?" Kathy repeated his analogy, struggling to accept the lesson.

"Precisely."

She left Duncan's office furious. How could he even entertain the idea of forgiveness? But over the next few weeks, her thoughts and feelings held court in her mind. The arguments flew back and forth in heated debate, but the verdict was always the same. An unwillingness to forgive equated to a life sentence of torment.

Kathy looked up from peeling potatoes as Tom entered the kitchen. "I want to see the boy."

"What boy? Billy Cook?" Tom was forever cautious. "Do you think it's wise after all this time?"

"I've been thinking about it for weeks," Kathy said as she rinsed a potato and placed it in the colander. "It's a chance to break the ice, to talk to him and give him the cello."

"What? You can't do that. That cello belonged to Rose."

"I can't bear to look at it. He can look at it. It might remind him of what he's done. I want to move on, Tom. Not to erase the memory of Rose… not to forget, but to honor the life she led."

"You're right. Rose wouldn't want to see you so sad all the time." He grabbed a beer from the fridge and flicked off the bottle top. "She'd want you to be doing something worthwhile with your life." He poured it into a glass and took a sip.

Kathy studied her husband, questioning what made him tick. *Men, they just don't get it.*

"I am doing something worthwhile. I'm a wife and a mother, and I want to enjoy my grandchild without constantly thinking about that boy. You've always told me to be thankful for my lot. You said the sun was shining down on us. But the sun hasn't come out in a long time. Bad things happen to good people, Tommy. That's just the way it is. No matter how positive you are, my life will never be the same. It will never be better."

She ran from the room in tears and slammed the bedroom door behind her, the potatoes still in the colander on the kitchen counter.

On the last day of September, Kathy and Tom drove out to the Rata River Valley. They stopped at the accident site and laid freshly cut spring flowers under a small white cross standing solemnly on the roadside. Kathy wondered who was responsible for the cross. No one had consulted them about it, but perhaps the boy had taken it upon himself to mark the spot.

She decided to let it go. After all, they should have erected a memorial themselves, but while they'd considered it, it hadn't happened.

September was unusually cold in the Valley that year. The sun peeked out, but as if not wanting to intrude on the somber occasion, it ducked back behind the clouds. Daffodils, snowdrops, and jonquils stood proudly under massive oak trees, softening the driveway to the Cooks' home. Work boots lined with thick woolen socks stood on the front porch next to terracotta pots full of cheerful polyanthus in winter colors of yellow, red, and blue.

In the back of their station wagon, the cello rested in its black coffin. As they waited at the screen door, Kathy wondered if Billy would ever lift the lid… ever touch its strings.

Grant appeared in worn blue jeans, work socks, and a thick woolen jumper. The two men shook hands. *This isn't a social call,* Kathy thought. *Why are they shaking hands?* But when men shake hands, it's like starting anew. They don't even have to discuss the issue. They simply shook hands and carried on.

"Kathleen, Tom, please come in. William's in the sunroom." They followed him through the dark kitchen, across the living room, and into a small conservatory. When Billy rose from his chair to greet them, Kathy noticed an air of vulnerability about him. She'd expected him to be much bigger. He was tall but thin—gaunt—and pale, his hair long and unruly. She'd often imagined him as a grown man during those times when blame was fierce. But, in reality, he was still a boy.

They took a seat. The air was thick and uncomfortable, and Kathy struggled to breathe.

"I'll open a window," Grant said. "Let in some fresh air. Doreen sends her apologies. She had to take her mother to the hospital for an appointment this afternoon."

"No problem," Tom said. "It's William we're here to see."

They sat in awkward silence until Billy spoke.

"Thanks for coming," he said shyly. "I wanted to explain and tell you I'm so sorry for your loss. I liked Rose very much, a lot. She was special." He exhaled loudly. "I'm having trouble adjusting. I won't be going back to school." He frowned. "I don't know who I am anymore. I'm so, so sorry."

Kathy noticed he didn't mention who was driving, and although she wanted to, she didn't ask. That fact hung in the air, along with so many other lost opportunities and redundant words.

"We've brought you her cello," she said. "And these." Billy's face crumpled as she handed him the blue notes. "They're in your hand and private. I wanted to return them to their rightful owner."

Looking at Billy now, Kathy finally saw him for what he was. A scared, broken kid whose life, like her own, would never be the same. But it didn't help prune the grief. The dead wood still splintered her heart, holding on for dear life and sucking her dry.

PART III

JESSA ROSE REYNOLDS

17

JESSA ROSE

Jessa Rose Reynolds arrived at 8:00 a.m. on the last day of March, which just happened to be the warmest day of the year. She fought for twenty-two hours to enter this world, struggling for liberation until her mother managed one final push and set her free.

Tom cuddled his granddaughter with pride. He longed to say how much she looked like Rose as a baby but held his tongue apart from saying, "She's a precious gift."

"She's also a noisy little miss. Keeps screaming for food," David said.

"The sooner you settle her into a four-hourly feeding routine, the better," Kathy offered. "It has to be done right from the start."

"Mum, you don't put breastfed babies on a four-hourly feeding schedule these days. They can get dehydrated. You feed on demand." Louisa smiled as she looked up from her hospital bed to the tiny bundle in Tom's arms. "We've waited such a long time. I want to cherish every moment."

"Well, you're making a rod for your own back," Kathy said. "All this demand-feeding rubbish. It's not right if you ask me."

"We want to do it our way, Kathy," David said firmly. "As first-time parents, we're sure to make mistakes, but we have to go with what they teach us."

Tom gave David a knowing wink and passed the baby to Kathy as Louisa moved the conversation away from feeding schedules. "She looks like an old soul, don't you think, Mum? So alert."

"All babies look like that. Like they're summing you up from day one, but she won't be seeing properly yet," Kathy replied.

"Have you thought of a name yet?" Tom asked.

"We have," Louisa said. "Jessa. Jessa Rose, if that's okay."

"Of course." Kathy cooed at her granddaughter. "She'll never know her aunt, but she'll carry her name. What a lovely thought."

18

CERTAIN STIMULI

MANY YEARS LATER

The Friday of Labour Weekend brought new challenges to the Reynolds household. That afternoon, two hours after she collected Jessa from school, an unexpected diagnosis rocked Louisa's world.

Louisa followed the young duty doctor down the hospital corridor. He ushered her into a side office, a small space devoid of warmth or windows.

"Please, take a seat," he said as he stepped behind the desk.

She sat in the offered chair, clutching her purse in her lap. "How is she?"

"Jessa's fine. What your daughter is experiencing isn't asthma. She had a panic attack."

"Panic attack? But that can't be right." Louisa considered the doctor, fresh out of med school by the look of him. "Jessa has nothing to panic about."

"That's not necessarily the case. She also said she's been having nightmares."

"Don't all children have nightmares occasionally?"

"With all due respect, Mrs. Reynolds, Jessa's no longer a child. The fact she's such a dedicated student in her last year of high school may mean she's under self-imposed pressure. Or, indeed, family pressure may be taking its toll. In some instances, nightmares, or even repressed memories, can be triggered by certain stimuli."

Louisa frowned. The consulting room's clinical smell and the closeness of the air were difficult to ignore, and she needed a drink of water. "But there is no family pressure."

"That may be so, but high-achieving girls of her age can sometimes experience some form of mental instability. That's why we're seeing so many young women with eating disorders these days."

"Well, what can we do about it?"

"Apparently, she's been having these attacks for some time." He checked his notes. "Let's see… Since she was fifteen."

"I'm sorry," Louisa murmured. "I had no idea. She's kept this from us until now."

"Why do you think that is? Are there troubles at home or concerns about her sexuality? Is she sexually active?"

"What? No! Well, I hope not. She doesn't even have a boyfriend. She has friends who are boys. But not in that way, as far as I'm aware."

"It's not unusual for a girl of her age to have a love interest, but she's not on the pill, so—"

"Why would Jessa be on the pill? She's still at school. What are you implying?"

"I'm not implying anything. I'm merely trying to ascertain the facts." He paused. "Is she an overachiever?"

"She's focused on what she wants, if you call that overachieving."

The doctor glanced at Jessa's notes again. "And what about friends? Does she have a social circle?"

"Of course. She has a great group of friends. They're close, have been since preschool days."

"Do you think she's confided in her friends about the attacks?"

"I don't know. I wasn't even aware she had panic attacks until now." Louisa didn't bother hiding her cynicism. "We thought it was asthma."

"Okay, well, she seems fine now." He scribbled a note on the sheet of paper in front of him. "I'll book a follow-up outpatient appointment with a psychologist for next week."

"Do you think that's necessary?" Louisa frowned. "Jessa's not mentally ill."

"That's not the point. Something's going on, and talking to a professional may help."

"But surely she can talk to us?"

"That's not standard treatment in these cases. One's parents cannot be all things to all people."

Louisa hesitated. "Should I go with her to the appointment?"

"Feel free to wait in the waiting room, but Jessa should spend time alone with the psychologist. That way, she can be honest about her feelings with the safety net of confidentiality. If you're there, she may feel vulnerable, which could strain your relationship. Jessa will confide in you when she's ready."

"I'm sorry, but I don't understand what you mean."

He leaned back in his chair. "Well, exposing our weaknesses to our nearest and dearest is not always beneficial. When we do, judgment can become an issue."

"I see. But I still believe friends and family are the best people to confide in."

"Why's that? They're not professionals, are they?" he said curtly. "If you had an infection, would you ask your friends or family to treat you?"

"I guess not." Louisa realized she was being dismissed. "Thank you for your time, Doctor… Sorry, I don't recall your name."

"James, Jack James."

Still struggling with her thoughts, Louisa joined Jessa in the waiting room.

She looked up from the magazine in her lap. "So, what did Hot Doc say?"

Louisa rummaged in her bag for her car keys. "Behave. You could barely breathe earlier, and now you're eyeing up the doctor? Honestly."

"But, Mum, you have to admit. He is cute, don't you think?"

"I suppose. If you like that type." Maybe Jack James had a point. Perhaps Jessa did have a secret boyfriend. "Too old for you, young lady."

"You think?"

"Enough of that talk. Let's go home. We'll discuss his suggestions later."

Misty rain hugged the coastline to the north of the parking lot. It was cold for spring, but patches of calm blue sky had formed in the southwest. Tomorrow would be a better day. "Here, let me help you with your schoolbag."

"Mum, please don't fuss. You know how I hate it when you guys fuss over me."

"Sorry, darling. I just worry about you, you know that."

They climbed into the car, and Louisa started the engine. Neither of them spoke as they left the hospital grounds, and as they headed for home, Louisa stayed strangely silent.

Jessa loved Labour Day weekend. By the time the late October holiday rolled around, the days were longer and radiated longed-for warmth while budding fruit had replaced the pink and white blossoms of spring. She usually spent holiday weekends at her grandparents' farm in the Rata River Valley. But this weekend, all plans were shelved.

Tom and Kathy, who'd inherited the run-down farm after Annie died, had built a new house on a knoll overlooking the main road. From the bay window in Jessa's bedroom, the farm stretched out as far as the eye could see. It was a special place.

Jessa gazed out the car window at a white-capped Carter Bay as her mum drove past the port and turned into their perfect street. She pulled into their perfect driveway and parked in front of their perfect house.

"I might go to my room. I don't feel like dinner."

"You should eat, darling," Louisa said as she opened the front door. "Also, we need to talk."

"Do we?" Jessa dropped her backpack on the floor. "I'm tired."

"Why don't you have a hot bath? We'll chat later."

"Okay."

As she poured some bubble bath under the stream of water, Jessa thought about her day. The panic attacks had intensified recently, but she didn't understand why. It would be easy to blame stress, but she sensed there was more to it. She stayed in the tub until the water cooled. Why she always did that, she didn't know, as it spoiled the experience.

"How was your bath?" her mother asked as she strolled into the kitchen later, already dressed for bed in checked flannel pajamas and her hair tied up in a ponytail.

"Nice."

"And how are you feeling?"

"Fine."

"Do you want to talk?"

"Not really."

"Well, we need to talk about it at some stage, darling."

"Do we?"

"You can't go on like this. We'll have to ring Immaculate Heart. They need to know what to expect if you have another asthma attack at school."

She sat at the table and looked at her mother. "But the doctor said I don't have asthma."

"I'm aware of what he said, darling, but how else can we explain what's happening?"

"We don't have to explain it. Why must we label everything? Put it in a neat and tidy box?"

"But we're worried about you."

Jessa sighed. "I know, Mum, but I want to move forward. I don't want to own this. It's not who I am." She softened her voice and continued, "I don't want to look back. Life's too short."

"You used to be such a bubbly girl with not a care in the world. But that doctor, he said you're having nightmares. Why didn't you tell us?"

"This is why. You overreact."

With his empty plate pushed to one side, her father watched their conversation volley back and forth. "We're only trying to help, Jess."

"She doesn't want to discuss it, David." Her mum rose from the table, collected his plate, and sat it in the sink. "She thinks I'm overreacting."

"So what did the doctor say?" he asked.

"He wants Jessa to see a psychologist."

He turned to Jessa. "I agree with the doctor. You should talk to a professional."

"What are you saying?" Leaning back against the counter, her mother folded her arms over her chest. "That Jessa needs to see a shrink? I can't believe you think our daughter needs therapy."

"It's up to Jessa," he said firmly. "She's old enough to make that decision."

"I'm sorry, but I don't agree. She's a child."

"Would you two stop it?" Jessa said, shaking her head. "I'm right here, and I'm not going to see anyone. And now, I'm going to bed. It's been a long day."

Kathy waited several days after Louisa's worried phone call, allowing her some time to process Jessa's diagnosis. As she drove from the Valley to meet her daughter for lunch, she hoped she was in a better frame of mind and more accepting of Jessa's needs.

They met at a café on the waterfront, ordered over small talk, and sipped glasses of rosé.

Louisa removed the paper napkin from around her knife and fork and dug into a chicken salad with couscous, grilled halloumi, and greens. "I told you that Dr. James wants Jessa to see a psychologist, didn't I?"

Kathy glanced up from her bowl of steaming pumpkin soup. "Yes, and it's an excellent idea."

"Mum, how can you say that?" Louisa rested her silverware on the plate and fixed her gaze on Kathy, her brows knitted. "I don't want the stigma of going to a psychologist hanging over my daughter's head."

"Sometimes you lock the door to that mind of yours and throw away the key."

"What's that supposed to mean?"

"Look, there's no stigma attached to counseling these days." Kathy searched her daughter's face for acceptance but found none.

"That may be so, but do you know anyone who goes to a psychologist? Because I don't."

An enthusiastic server collected their empty plates and offered the dessert menu. They surveyed the choices. "The lemon cake sounds good," Kathy said.

"Yes. I'll have the same."

Kathy waited for the server to leave, then exhaled slowly. "I saw a psychologist for a while. After Rose died."

Louisa's eyes widened. "What? You never told me that."

"Your father was the only one who knew."

"If you're so in favor of it, why didn't you tell anyone?"

"Because that was years ago. Times have changed. If you're lucky enough to find someone you click with, they can help you transform your life. Clear the mud."

"I'm not convinced. Do you think it helped?"

"It did. I needed to put my thoughts into perspective, you know, after the accident. Therapy helped me do that, helped me surround the memory of Rose with love rather than grief and anger."

Louisa waited while the server delivered two slices of lemon cake drizzled with yogurt and sprinkled with toasted coconut threads.

She scooped up a forkful of cake and popped it into her mouth. Louisa and Kathy rarely discussed Rose. They both found it too painful. "Do you ever feel her around you?"

"For the first couple of months, I did, then nothing. It felt like she'd moved on. It sounds crazy, I know, but—"

"I felt the same," Louisa said. "I dreamed about her at first but haven't since."

"Jessa's helped fill the void. She's a special kid. A wise girl. And so astute."

"Yes, and I love her to bits. But I keep thinking about Rose." Louisa sipped her coffee. "I can't help myself. I guess that's why I'm overprotective. Jessa's too precious, and she looks so much like Rose. If we'd been blessed with more children, I might feel differently, but I struggle with letting her go."

Kathy nodded. "Your father taught me early on in our marriage that we don't have to repeat the patterns of our past. I was convinced I'd end up making dubious decisions like my parents did, but he sees life differently, your dad. He taught me to use my early life as an example, not to emulate but to break the mold. Let Jessa have this chance. She'll learn from it, whichever way the tide turns."

"You're right. I know you are."

Kathy chuckled. "Louisa Reynolds, that's the first time you've ever said those words to me."

"What words?"

"'You're right.'"

Louisa laughed. "That's what happens when you're a mum. You see your own mother differently."

"Yes, maybe you do. Anyway, I'd better get going. I don't want to get caught in the afternoon traffic." Kathy rummaged through her purse for her wallet. "I'll pay."

19

CONVERSIONS

"I'm not sure Jessa should come to the Valley this weekend," Louisa said into the phone a few weeks later.

"Mum," Jessa muttered. "I'll be fine with Kathy G. I'm not a baby."

Kathy disliked being called Grandmother, Nana, or any of the other titles one would usually bestow on the female parent of one's parents, so Jessa had called her Kathy G. at a young age, and that name had stuck.

"Hold on, Mum." Louisa put her hand over the mouthpiece. "Jessa, please don't interrupt." She returned to her phone conversation. "I'll see what David says and call you tomorrow."

David strolled into the kitchen, draped his jacket over the back of a chair, and pecked his wife on the cheek. "See what David says about what?"

"Jessa wants to go to the farm on the bus this weekend."

"Well, that's fine, isn't it?" David helped himself to a can of beer from the fridge and pulled the tab. He took a sip. "She's been on the bus before."

"Finally, someone's talking sense," Jessa said. "I've no idea what Mum thinks I'll get up to."

"I worry about you, that's all."

"But Lea's coming with me. She's going home for the weekend."

"Lea?"

"Mum, you've met Lea. She's a boarder at Girls' High, remember? Her parents have a farm in the Valley."

"Of course. The redhead."

"Any problems, just call," David said. "I can always shoot up and get you. It's only an hour's drive."

Jessa shared a smile with her father. "Thanks, Dad. I'll be okay. Kathy G. will take care of me."

Lea Ellison was a gorgeous free spirit with a quick smile, throaty laugh, and a stubborn tomboy streak. Jessa attributed these qualities to her hair. Flaming red, it fell in ringlets well below her shoulders. Lea insisted it was auburn, but the boys in the Valley had always called her Ginger Lea.

A beautiful girl, both inside and out, Lea possessed a carefree disposition and sun-shy porcelain skin salted with tiny freckles across the bridge of her nose. The first time Lea introduced herself to Jessa, she made a point of explaining her name by saying, "Hi, I'm Lea, as in tea. Lea with an A."

Her parents, Anna and Rob, farmed a small herd of dairy cows on the northern side of Rata River, but even though Jessa had visited her home more than once, she'd never met them.

With the two girls chatting all the way from Clifton Falls, the bus ride passed in a flash. They didn't attend the same school, so they had lots to catch up on, and as usual, Lea couldn't stop talking.

"See that house down there." Lea pointed to a stone dwelling as the bus crossed the Rata River bridge. "It belongs to my uncle. He's an architect and has converted it into a weekend retreat. I'm cleaning it over the holidays."

"For money?"

"Yep. Mum owns a cleaning business."

"What was it before? It looks like an old pump shed."

"It was. And a hay barn back in the day."

Jessa craned her neck as the building came into view more clearly. She'd noticed it before, and it had always intrigued her.

"He's owned it for years," Lea continued. "It was overgrown with blackberry and weeds before he started working on it. You can still see the old water wheel around the back. He calls it the Watershed."

"I love buildings with names."

"Come with me tomorrow, and I'll show you inside. It's amazing."

"If your mum needs extra help, I'm good at housework, and I'd love a few hours work over the summer."

"I'll ask her, okay? If she's here instead of Dad, I'll introduce you. But be warned, she's a bit of a hippy feminist." Lea laughed and cocked a brow. "But no mother's perfect."

As the bus pulled into the depot, Jessa immediately spotted Anna. With her curly hair and broad smile, there was no mistaking the resemblance.

Anna stepped forward and kissed her daughter on the cheek several times. "Hi there, sweetheart."

"Stop it." Lea playfully batted her mother away. "I've only been gone two weeks."

"Yeah, but I've missed you."

"Mum, this is Jessa. The friend I told you about. She's keen on some work over the summer."

"Hello, Mrs. Ellison." Jessa extended her hand.

Anna shook it. "Jessa. Pleased to meet you finally. Lea's told me so much about you. So you're after some casual work?"

"I'd love some. I'll be staying with my grandparents after Christmas for a while."

"Well, it's your lucky day. One of my staff's taking time off in the new year. Let's start with a trial, shall we? I'm not sure if there'll be anything later in January, but we'll play it by ear."

"Sounds great." Jessa glanced over as Kathy G. pulled into the depot parking lot in her brand-new station wagon.

"Oh, and, Jessa, next time you shake hands, do it like you mean it."

She smiled with warmth. “There’s no need to be shy. A firm handshake says a certain something about a girl. And, please, call me Anna.”

Lea raised her eyebrows at Jessa and mouthed, *“Told you,”* before following her mother to the car.

Jessa inhaled a deep breath of crisp valley air and relaxed. It was good to be back.

Having persuaded her mum to let her stay in the Valley over the summer break, Jessa started her trial at Ellison Cleaning the week between Christmas and New Year. The Watershed, with its sun-filled rooms and windows overlooking the river, was by far her favorite house on their list. It always appeared spotless, but they still went through the motions. Mr. Cook liked things just so, and who were they to question him?

Now, with Jessa’s trial over and Lea in bed with a head cold that particular day, Anna sent her to the Watershed alone. She let herself in through the large entry door, a rustic piece covered in flaking powder-blue paint and sporting a dull brass knocker.

A distinctive smell greeted her inside—fresh and clean, with a hint of brewed coffee about it. Jessa dropped her sweatshirt on a chair in the living area and opened the French doors onto the deck. As she pulled the sheer blinds, sunlight flooded the interior with warmth.

Jessa had never met Lea’s uncle, although she imagined what he’d be like. Anna was such a warm soul—open and full of fun, just like Lea—and she assumed he’d follow the family trait. The jolly teddy bear type, probably with a chubby belly to match.

According to Lea, her uncle William was single and in his thirties, and he was obviously a neat freak, judging by how he kept his home.

She studied his extensive record collection stacked beside an expensive-looking stereo system. Their sleeves were in pristine condition, making her wonder if he ever played them. She wanted to play one or two herself, to release their mute existence while she worked, but thought better of it.

Task by task, Jessa checked off her list. She cleaned the bathrooms, ran the vacuum cleaner over the floors, and mopped the flagstones, leaving the beds until last.

In the main room, a small stereo sat on a dresser beside the walk-in closet. She switched it to the local FM station, stripped the bed, and collected the towels, which she stuffed into a laundry bag along with the sheets.

She began to remake the bed, singing as she worked.

"Who the hell are you?"

Jessa spun around in fright. A tall man stood before her, briefcase in hand, staring as the music from the stereo pounded in her head. She turned it off, then stood perfectly still.

With a face like thunder and his jaw tight, he waited for an explanation.

"Um… I'm a friend of Lea's. I work for Ellison Cleaning, but—"

He didn't let her finish. Instead, he picked up the phone from his bedside table and pointed an index finger at her. "Stay right there."

She did as she was told, the pit of her stomach in knots as he pinned her with his gaze, his visual hold firm and unbreakable. His eyes were a deep crystal blue, the most intense blue she'd ever seen, with white rays evident in the iris—but cold—and a faint scar ran into his hairline from above his left eyebrow.

"Anna, I've just arrived to find a stranger, not only in my home but also in my bedroom with the stereo on." He paused. "Yes, okay. Well, in future, I'd appreciate being informed." He listened. "Right. Okay." He paused again. "Of course I'm happy with Lea, but I won't have strangers here making themselves at home."

He spoke with perfect diction, even with his voice elevated. Jessa flinched as he slammed the phone back into its cradle, not waiting for a reply. His steely gaze never wavered.

"What's your name?" He appeared tired and preoccupied, his ashen face accentuating the light growth of stubble—neatly clipped along the cheek line and under his chin.

"Jessa. Jessa Reynolds."

"Well, Miss Reynolds, you may leave now, thank you."

"Shall I finish the bed and—"

"That won't be necessary. Go."

Jessa picked up the laundry bag and took two steps toward the door before turning back to face him. "I'm sorry for putting the stereo on."

His eyes narrowed as he considered her, but he said nothing more.

She dashed for the front door, tugged it open, and slipped out into the humid air. She spun back to speak, but the door shut firmly in her face.

Jessa knocked.

"Yes?" he snapped as he reopened it.

"Sorry. Your car's blocking my way."

He grabbed his keys from the hall table and, mumbling something under his breath, bounded down the steps in front of her.

After moving his vehicle to the parking space at the back of the barn, he stormed back inside without uttering a word.

The large door slammed shut for the second time.

Jessa drove about three hundred meters toward the highway turnoff before pulling over. She glanced across the road to a small white cross, struggling to focus as her eyes filled with tears. But one thing was crystal clear; she never wanted to see that horrible man, with his superior tone and aggressive demeanor, again.

With the many holiday homeowners flocking to the countryside for the summer, Ellison Cleaning was busy and short-staffed. Jessa wanted to confide in Lea about her encounter with Mr. Cook, but it took her two days to find the courage to bring it up.

"I met your uncle the other day," she said as she watched Lea ready herself for work.

"Really? He's meant to be away. Was he grumpy?"

"Very."

"He's always like that with strangers," Lea said.

Jessa grabbed Lea's brush to tame her unruly curls, then pulled the auburn locks into a high ponytail. “We didn’t get off to a good start. And I left my new sweatshirt there.”

“Don’t worry. Knowing him, it’ll be washed, ironed, and sitting in a plastic bag on the hall table. He likes things just so.” Lea checked her hair in the mirror and smiled. “Thanks. Looks great.”

The girls joined Anna in the family room, and Lea flopped down on the sofa, her bucket of cleaning cloths on the floor beside her. “I’m starving. Can we have morning tea before we start?”

Anna placed a jug of iced tea and a freshly baked orange cake on the breakfast bar. “Actually, I wanted to talk to you both about being discreet. I’m sorry about what happened the other day at my brother’s, Jessa. But remember, we must be professional and not take advantage of our clients’ homes, no matter who they are. This includes stereos, books, and TVs. And confidentiality is a must, understand?”

Both girls nodded their agreement.

“I realize it was my fault,” Jessa said, “but he scared me half to death.”

“Don’t worry. William’s abrupt but harmless.” Anna flashed her signature warm smile. “I’ve been meaning to ask if we’ve met before. You seem familiar.”

“I don’t think so.”

“But your grandparents have a farm in the Valley?”

“Yes.” Jessa helped herself to a slice of cake and broke it into thirds. “They’ve lived here since my great-grandmother passed away.”

“Really? Is their surname Reynolds too?” Anna asked.

“No, Kathy and Tom Churchill.”

Jessa noticed Anna’s sharp inhale.

She nodded. “What’s your mother’s name again?”

“Louisa.”

“Of course. Louisa and David,” Anna said slowly.

Jessa popped a piece of cake into her mouth. “Do you know them?”

“Only by name. You know what farming communities are like. Everyone knows everyone else.”

“Mum, can Jessa stay for dinner?”

“Not tonight, sweetheart. Scary Uncle William’s coming over.”

Anna smiled, but this time, it lacked the usual warmth. "Maybe next week."

"I'd like that, thanks. This cake's delicious. Can I have another slice?"

As William drove to Anna's for dinner that evening, he couldn't get Jessa Reynolds out of his mind. Had his sister failed to join the dots? He arrived right on time but didn't get the chance to discuss the young housekeeper with her before they ate.

"So, Uncle William, what's happening in your neck of the woods?" Lea asked as they finished their main course.

William took another slice of naan bread from the basket on the table and mopped up the last remnants of his curry. "Not much. We're crazy busy at the office. What about you? Hope you're not breaking too many hearts?"

"Not yet. Me and my friends have a rule not to make out with the local guys. They all talk about you if you do. I'm waiting until I get to Dunedin. I hear those southern boys are hot." Lea raised an eyebrow at her uncle and giggled.

William chuckled. He enjoyed his niece's company. Her love of life and sunny disposition helped him relax.

Rob frowned at his daughter. "Don't you think you're a little too young to be thinking about hot guys?"

"Give it a rest, Dad. I'm eighteen. Bet you were making out with Mum years before that."

"Your mother wouldn't let me touch her until we were married."

"Whatever," Lea said with a grin.

William observed their back-and-forth banter with amusement. He often wondered if he'd ever get the chance to be a dad. "So, where's your young friend tonight?" he asked. "Jessa, is it?"

"She stays with her grandparents, Tom and Kathy Churchill."

William chewed his bread and swallowed slowly. "They live on the other side of the cutting, is that right?" He shot his sister a look.

"That's them," Lea said.

Anna stood and gathered up the plates. "Right, who wants dessert?"

After dinner, as William prepared to leave, he turned to Anna. "Come out to the car with me. I have that book you wanted."

"I'll get it another time."

"No, come and get it now, or I'll forget." He grabbed his jacket from the coat stand in the hallway. "Thanks for the meal and company, Rob."

"Anytime," Rob replied. "Let's do it again soon."

"And you, young lady," he addressed Lea, "behave yourself."

She giggled. "Always."

William and Anna walked to his car in silence. He opened the door and turned to her. "What on earth were you thinking?" he whispered.

"I had no idea who she was until today, I swear."

"What? She's your daughter's friend, and you didn't think to ask her name? Don't you keep records of your staff?"

"Of course I do, but she's just a casual. And, honestly, I didn't connect her to Louisa until she told me who her grandparents were."

"But she's the spitting image of Rose."

"That may be so. But to be fair, William, I never met Rose Churchill. I've only ever seen her in photographs. And I don't know much about Louisa or the child's grandparents, apart from what Mum's told me. Sorry. I've just been so busy, and I messed up. I'm so sorry."

"For shit's sake, Anna, I thought I'd seen a ghost."

"I didn't realize you'd be there yesterday. Jessa's a great worker, and I'm struggling to find staff at the moment, but I'll try to move her to other jobs when you're around."

"Good. Because what would happen if Kathy and Tom, or worse, Louisa, found out she was in my home?" William thought for a moment. "I wonder if she knows who I am."

"Look, they won't find out. I've explained the importance of confidentiality, and she understands. If she knew about the Rose connection, she'd have mentioned it, don't you think? Maybe no one's ever told her the story."

"Yeah, that's true."

"And if you do happen to see her again, remember, she's a teenage girl. You scared her half to death the other day."

He frowned. "Shit, really? I guess I did. Point taken."

20

CONSERVATIVE AND UNYIELDING

The following day, eager to retrieve her new sweatshirt from the scary Mr. Cook, Jessa parked on the roadside and walked through the garden to the Watershed's front door. She rapped the brass knocker and waited several minutes before peeking through the garage window. He wasn't home, so she let herself in with her key.

Each time she stepped through the large blue door, inspiration hit her. The Watershed was exactly how she imagined a French country cottage would be. A generous open-plan space ran the full length of the building, with large windows and doors overlooking the river. A relaxed living area occupied one end, while a galley kitchen with a long breakfast bar stood at the other. The kitchen moved through to a mudroom slash bathroom, barn-like garage, and woodshed.

It was beautifully appointed, as Kathy G. would say, with off-white rendered walls, hardwood flooring, and flagstones softened by woven woolen rugs. In the living area, slouchy, oversized cream sofas kept a large river-stone fireplace company, while whitewashed and lightly sanded furniture added to the casual feel.

The style was mainly contemporary, but a few antiques sat comfortably in the space. Color infused the living area courtesy of the country landscape beyond the floor-to-ceiling windows, where nature provided an ever-changing palette. Additionally, several large unframed canvases in hues of white, black, gray, and red enlivened the interior walls, and in the main bathroom, exposed beams and a high-backed French-style tub added a distinctive air.

Mr. Cook kept it immaculate, and although he used the house only occasionally, it still felt like a home. Comfortable and familiar, the way certain homes do.

Two bedrooms flanked the central hallway, which also led to the living area. The main bedroom offered a walk-in closet and ensuite, along with a king-size bed. This was his domain, where masculine energy quivered in the air.

The second bedroom was neither masculine nor feminine, making it suitable for anyone who wished to enjoy the pleasure of resting in its space. Jessa had never ventured up the stairs. The door at the top was kept bolted shut.

Outside, the original water wheel, now rusted and broken, stood cradled between two pillars of stacked river stones. Hard landscaping surrounded the north face of the building, incorporating a step-down deck bordered by lavender and French vanilla roses and a stone path providing access to the river below.

Jessa searched the ground-floor area, but no matter where she looked, inside or out, her sweatshirt was nowhere to be found.

By the time her next workday arrived, Jessa had relaxed a little. She was still worried about running into Mr. Cook again, but cleaning the Watershed was part of her job, so she needed to toughen up. She arrived at the Ellisons' to find Lea making her bed.

"Morning. What's on the list today?"

"Just the usual." Lea plumped up her pillows. "No Watershed, though."

"I still feel guilty about that. I messed up, big time."

"No, you didn't. My uncle's a grump, so don't worry. He needs a girlfriend, or a woman friend, or whatever old people call it." Lea giggled. "But you'll have to clean it while we're away at my aunt's wedding. Why she's getting married in January, I don't know. Dad's in the middle of making silage, and Mum has to get Mrs. Winter to run the business."

"I enjoy going there. It's your uncle that I'm not sure about. He's kind of creepy if you ask me."

"He's okay. Had some stuff happen in his early life that Mum says affected him, and he's a total nerd. But he's still my fav uncle."

"What kind of stuff?"

"Not sure. Girlfriend stuff, I think. Mum's not one for gossip, especially about family. Hey, I have photos of him when he was younger." Lea reached under her bed and pulled out a photo album, which she passed to Jessa. "See if you can find him."

Jessa flicked through the pages. "There." She pointed at the younger William. "Look at his hair. It's so long in this picture." Jessa studied the photograph more closely. His face was strangely familiar. She turned the page. "Holy cow! What about this one with his shirt off? All six-pack abs, surfer tan, and pretty-boy hot. And I do love a leather bracelet on a guy."

"Noooo! Stop it. He's my uncle. That's totally weird."

"I know it's weird for you, but you get what I mean, don't you? He's mysterious and brooding, like Heathcliff. If you look at him objectively, he's still an attractive man—for an older guy. He's young-looking, even now."

"Okay. This conversation is over." Lea giggled as she threw a cushion, which hit Jessa head-on. "Get a grip."

Jessa spent the following morning cleaning two houses back-to-back. She had one final job after lunch, returning the Watershed's sheets and pillowslips, which he preferred sun-dried rather than in a clothes dryer. Jessa smiled to herself as she thought about how fastidious he was. She wondered if he ever relaxed, ever left his house in a mess, ever ate ice cream for dinner.

When she pulled into the wide driveway, the garage door was

closed, and the place looked deserted. Jessa knew he wouldn't be there, but that didn't stop her gut from clenching as she grabbed the laundry bag from her back seat.

It was another sticky day. She couldn't wait to return to the farm for a shower and a glass of iced tea. Jessa opened the gate at the side of the house and followed the shaded path to the back door. In another few weeks, the lavender bordering the deck would be past its best and ready for trimming. But in the meantime, industrious bees were having a field day. She inhaled the calming fragrance and unlocked the back door with her key.

"Don't you usually knock before letting yourself in?"

Jessa froze, the memory of their first meeting flashing through her mind. William sat at the large dining table, plans and sketches spread out before him. He scarcely bothered to glance up.

"Sorry… Mrs. Winter asked me to drop off your linens. I assumed you'd be away at the wedding, or I would have left them at the door." The butterflies in her stomach morphed into moths as her determination to remain calm deserted her.

She tightened her grip on the laundry bag as he looked her over. "That's Rob's side of the family." He smiled ever so slightly. "I'm here for a few days, and to be fair, I'm a day early. Please, come in and do what you have to do." His cold eyes danced into life. "I'm William, by the way." He stood and offered his hand.

She reached forward and gripped it firmly. The laundry bag dropped to the floor. "Jessa."

His amused smile caught her off guard. "Of course. Jessa Reynolds, isn't it? You have quite the handshake for a young woman."

Her cheeks burned, the heat moving to her neck and chest as his gaze lingered. "I'll put these away if that's okay."

It bugged her that he reminded her of someone, a boy from school perhaps, but she couldn't put her finger on who. He had a lot going for him in the looks department. Dark hair peppered at the sides with molten gray, those crystal-blue eyes, a muscular physique, and immaculate grooming. He was a handsome man, but all the same, he had a solemn persona—conservative and unyielding.

"Oh, and about the other day. I may have overreacted. I realize you were only doing your job." He looked at her steadily. "I'd had a stressful week, but that's no excuse."

"I'm sorry about the stereo. It's inappropriate for a cleaner to make themselves at home. I understand that."

William returned to his chair. "Even so, I don't tend to make a habit of scaring people half to death." He rested his chin on his left hand and ran his index finger over the central depression between his nose and upper lip as he stared.

Jessa realized Anna must have told him what she'd said.

"Don't you get tired of cleaning other people's homes?" he asked. "Ever think of setting your sights higher?"

He might be hot, but he's a smug bastard. Just when she was starting to warm to him, the wind changed, and he turned back into his arrogant self. "No, I'm happy being a cleaner for now. It's a worthwhile job, and it keeps me fit."

"Of course. I wasn't implying there's anything wrong with it. It's just… Never mind."

She picked up the laundry bag and tugged the cord tight. "Is it okay if I put these away in the hall closet?"

"Sure."

Jessa hurried down the hallway, stacked the linens, and made a beeline for the back door. "All done. Sorry for disturbing you."

"No problem."

21

UNEASY WORK

The Crawford residence, a grand old lady over by the old sawmill, occupied all of the following morning, so Jessa looked forward to cleaning the Watershed with its tidy interior.

The day dawned unusually cold for midsummer, with light rain drifting across the ranges, misting the hills and cleansing the air. As Jessa drove down Rata River Road, she spotted William's Range Rover in the driveway. For some reason, the thought of seeing him again unnerved her. She didn't understand why. He'd been pleasant enough, almost charming, the previous day.

As she approached the house, steam billowed from his en suite window on the far left of the entry door, and she could hear the shower running. She knocked anyway and waited for a response. Nothing.

After a slight hesitation, Jessa let herself in. As usual, everything was neat as a pin. It reminded her of a story from her childhood about a house with a place for everything and everything in its place. She ran her fingertips over the coffee table, expecting dust. Not a speck. She imagined him cleaning the house before she arrived, then giggled at the absurdity.

William appeared from the bedroom, a small white towel sitting low on his lightly tanned hips. "Shit! You gave me a fright."

Her sight came to rest on his muscular upper body—the well-defined shoulders, perfectly cut upper arms, and powerful V-line abs.

He tightened his towel, following her gaze with an unreadable expression. "Jessa, isn't it?"

"Yes." It surprised her that he remembered her name.

He filled a glass with water from the fridge, seemingly perfectly comfortable with having his half-naked body on display.

"I'm sorry, but the door was unlocked. I hope I'm not intruding. We have a busy week with Anna and Lea away, and Mrs. Winter told me to finish here. She thought you'd be out at golf. I can come back later."

"No need." He looked her up and down. "Anna said you'd be here this week. Anyway, I want to talk to you about something. But let me get dressed first."

Jessa set a soft smile free as she watched him walk down the hallway. He might be a grumpy old shit and arrogant too, but he was seriously hot, in a "don't touch" kind of way.

And that white towel!

Minutes later, he returned to the kitchen dressed for golf in a white polo shirt and navy chinos. "Here." He offered her the missing sweatshirt, neatly folded in a clear plastic bag. "You left this here the other day."

She hesitated, unsure why he'd have it in his bedroom, and suppressed a smile as she recalled Lea's words. "Thank you. I thought I'd lost it."

"I was wondering if making some extra money on the side might interest you."

She frowned. "Um… doing what?"

He tilted his head to one side and smiled. "Don't look so worried. Can you type? I have a document that needs word processing and thought maybe you'd be interested in working a few extra hours."

The charming William unnerved her, and she hesitated again while considering her response. "I did a typing course at school to help with my computer skills. What kind of document is it?"

"Just specs for a project I'm working on. Nothing too technical.

I've made quite a few edits. Would you like to take a look? I'm sure your typing skills would leave mine for dead. I'll go grab it."

"Sure." As he entered his office, Jessa asked herself why that word had left her lips.

He returned with his briefcase and removed a black folder, which he offered to her. "Here, see what you think. I don't want you to say yes if you're not up to the task. Unfortunately, my work computer crashed, and I lost the original file."

Jessa flicked through the document. In the margins of each page were neatly written notations in what she called architect font—uniform, black ink, stylish.

"Looks okay. When do you want me to start?"

"I'm off to golf now the rain's stopped. You can stay on after you've finished cleaning if you want."

"Um, I'll come back after lunch if that's all right. My grandparents are expecting me."

"Sure. You know where the computer and printer are. Are you familiar with *Windows 95*?"

"Yes, we have it at home."

He studied her before continuing, "Good. I don't need it until late next week, so take your time, and don't forget to save as you go. Do you live with your grandparents?"

"No, I live in Clifton Falls but I often stay with them for holidays."

He nodded. "Can you read my writing?"

Jessa glanced at the document and his neat handwriting. Why he'd even mention it was beyond her. "Yes, it's perfectly legible." She didn't have the nerve to ask about the pay rate.

He picked up his car keys from beside the phone. "What's a fair hourly rate?"

Jessa had no idea what to say. "I'm not sure."

"Well, what does Anna pay you?"

"Six fifty an hour."

"Right, how about seven fifty?"

"That's way too much. Six fifty's fine."

"Okay, but remember, everyone's time is valuable, and if you don't think your time is worth reasonable recompense, no one else will."

He was almost out the door when he turned back. "We'll see how you get on, shall we? Oh, and, Jessa…" He waited for her to meet his gaze.

"Yes, Mr. Cook."

"I've left a key for you on the hall table. That way, you won't have to check in with Anna. It's best if we keep this between ourselves, and that includes Lea and your family, okay? And please"—his eyes danced with that smile again—"call me William."

When Jessa returned after lunch, the Watershed was church-like still. Warm sunlight streamed through the north-facing French doors and windows as she sat at the desk and booted up the computer. By late afternoon, she'd processed a quarter of the document. She read each page aloud, correcting mistakes and typos as she went, then left the finished work on the desk for his attention.

The next day, the papers sat next to the keyboard with a few alterations and a note saying: "*Well done, please continue, W.*"

His bed was neatly made, the nightstand clear of clutter, and his briefcase and leather weekender were nowhere in sight. An unexpected disappointment washed over her. He'd gone back to his city life.

The Watershed's pull intensified each time Jessa walked through the large blue door. To her, the house possessed a soul-like strength, held stories of journeys past and the promise of an optimistic future.

By late Friday afternoon, she'd completed all but three pages of the document, so she decided to stay a little longer and get the job done.

Once she'd finally finished, Jessa straightened in the chair, squeezed her shoulder blades together, and rolled her neck from side to side before standing to stretch.

She opened the French doors and ran her hands over the tips of lavender as she strolled down the path to the river. Water soothed her, and Jessa loved to swim, but her mother had made her promise she'd never swim alone. So instead, she paddled in the shallows, inhaling the soothing scent of lavender through cupped hands, and stood in a daze as diamond-like orbs of afternoon sunlight danced on the cool water's surface. Usually, the river made a frantic run to the sea, but with the heat of the summer evaporating its strength, it now flowed leisurely toward the coast.

William strolled onto the deck, his focus on Jessa wading along the river's edge below. He felt a surge of fascination as he watched her. Her long brown hair reached the small of her back and hung in silky strands over her chest, while messy bangs sat in wisps across her forehead. The loose-fitting black polo printed with Anna's company logo didn't do her figure justice, but today, the muslin blouse and cutoff denim shorts, fraying white cotton over her long legs, certainly did.

His thoughts turned to Rose as he contemplated alternative outcomes. Would they have been childhood sweethearts who married and had a child like Anna and Rob, or would their relationship have petered out over the years?

He recalled Jessa standing straight and still the day he yelled at her for being in his bedroom. He hadn't meant to scare her, but she'd given him such a fright that he'd overreacted. That look of alarm on her face and those eyes—wide and bewitching in a deep shade of gray, not a blue-gray, almost charcoal. He knew he was staring, the familiarity of her face unnerving, but he couldn't tear his gaze away. She had that air of vulnerability about her that young women have when they're beautiful but unsure of themselves, and in the days that followed, he couldn't stop thinking about her.

And although his inappropriate interest in the young housekeeper didn't sit well with his morality, William couldn't help but wonder whether she ever thought of him, or if she had a boyfriend waiting for her in Clifton Falls.

Following the path through lavender and roses, William smiled.

"How's the water?"

Jessa spun around, one hand on her chest. William stood on the river's edge, not two feet away. "Don't you know not to sneak up on people? You gave me such a fright." Her nipples pebbled inside her bra. She told herself it was out of fear rather than something else she didn't want to consider.

He laughed. "Guess now we're even."

Jessa had never witnessed him laugh before. It brought his face to life.

"Sorry," he continued. "I didn't mean to scare you."

"I didn't know you were coming up today," she said coyly. "I've just finished the document. It's on your desk."

"I didn't know I was coming myself. But I needed a break from the office." He kept staring. "Are you going in?"

Jessa focused on the sandy bottom beneath her feet, which gave way to the smooth river stones beyond. She wanted nothing more than to take a dip in the crystal-clear water. "Not today. Mum made me promise a long time ago that I'd never swim alone. She's a worrier."

"That's a good rule. But you're not alone." His smile faded. "I'm here."

She strolled out of the water, keeping her eyes cast downward.

"Are you a strong swimmer?" he asked.

His attempt at conversation amused her. "Not too bad." She glanced his way. "I swam for the school team last year but don't see the point of long-distance training. Life's too short to spend hours in an indoor pool. There's a water hole under the old bridge that I love. I remember going there when I was younger. Mum said we never did, but I went there with Kathy G. and Poppa. The memory's clear as day."

He stilled for a moment. "I know it well. I swam there with my friends as a teenager."

She stepped forward. "Anyway, I'd better go before Kathy G. gets worried."

"Does she know you're working for me?"

"No. You told me not to say, remember?" Jessa stared at him for a few seconds, then glanced away. He gestured for her to go first and followed her up the track. She could feel his gaze and sense him in her personal space but didn't stop walking until they reached the house.

"I'm here all next week," he said. "If you call in on Monday, we'll go over what you've done and sort out payment. Say, one thirty on Monday afternoon. Does that suit?"

"Yes, that's fine. I should be finished cleaning by then."

He opened the side gate for her. "Okay, good."

"I'll see you then."

22

THE WEEKEND

When Jessa returned from the Watershed, she was surprised to find her mother's car in the driveway. Over the past year, they'd struggled to get along. She often accused Jessa of being headstrong, while Jessa found her too overprotective. Why her parents had agreed to her spending the summer at the farm was a mystery, but she figured they probably needed a break from her just as much as she needed a break from home.

Her mother smiled at Jessa as she walked into the kitchen.

"What are you doing here?" Jessa kissed her on the cheek.

"Your father's away on a fishing trip, so I decided to come up for the night. You're home late."

Jessa looked away. "Yeah, I had a last-minute job."

"How's your week been? What have you been doing?" She didn't wait for Jessa to answer her rapid-fire questions before moving on. "Where's the redhead?"

"Good, working, and away, in that order." Jessa sat at the table with her mother while Kathy dished up their meal. "Where's Poppa?"

"He's down at the pub," Kathy said. "I'll pop his in the oven."

Jessa had barely taken a bite before her mother brought up university.

"I'm worried about you going to Victoria this year."

She set her silverware on her plate. "Mum, you know I want to study architecture. I don't want to clean other people's houses all my life."

"Take a gap year, that's all I'm suggesting. I can get you a job in the factory office, and that way, you can stay at home for another year, find your feet, and save some money."

Jessa concentrated on her meal.

"What do you think?" Her mother pushed her food around her plate while she waited for a reply.

"We've already discussed this a thousand times. I want to go at the same time as all my friends. There's no point in taking a gap year. Architecture's five years as it is."

"Look, sweetie, we're only trying to protect you. You're not yet nineteen, way too young to move away from home."

"Mum, I'm nineteen in March." Jessa kept eating. She was tired of having the same old conversation.

"Yes, but… You know what I mean."

"What age were you when you left home, Kathy G.?"

"She has a point," Kathy said. "I was sixteen when I was forced to leave, if you could call that foster place a home."

Louisa shot her mother a dirty look. "Times were different back then. All I'm saying is we want you to make the right decision."

"The right decision for who?" Jessa asked. "You and Dad? Because Dad thinks I'm ready to leave the nest."

"When did he say that?"

"Recently. The other day, in fact."

"See, this is the whole point. No one ever backs me up. What about me? When is it my turn to get what I want?"

"You can't keep me home forever. I'll be fine."

"Let the girl be. Just because you didn't have the gumption to move away doesn't mean Jessa's the same."

"Gumption? What kind of word is that? That's so typical. You always take her side."

"Unbelievable. This isn't about taking sides." Jessa rose from the table, rinsed her plate, and stacked it in the dishwasher. "Conversation over. I'm going to my room."

Half an hour later, she breezed into the living room wearing jeans, a cute lacy top, and a hint of makeup.

"Where are you going?" her mum asked.

"To the Smiths' party. I told you about it the other day." Jessa winked at her to keep the mood light. "Coming?"

"Don't be ridiculous. Be home by eleven."

She kissed her on the cheek. "Twelve."

"Remember, no drinking and driving… and don't offer to drive anyone else home."

As she passed the small white cross on Rata River Road, Jessa recited a silent prayer. She'd started this ritual not long after first noticing the cross, and now, it was second nature. The lights were on at William's and an unfamiliar car parked in his driveway. She wondered if he now had a girlfriend but quickly dismissed the thought. It was none of her business.

The Smiths' barn was about ten minutes farther down the gravel road. When Jessa arrived, there were cars parked all along the grass shoulder, and the barn was already packed. Used paper plates littered the makeshift tables, and Jessa was pleased she'd eaten at home.

"Jessa! Welcome, babe. What ya drinking?" The voice belonged to Scott Smith. Jessa had dated him for a few weeks just after turning fifteen. He was a sloppy kisser and couldn't keep his hands to himself, but they still moved in the same social circles. "How kind of you to grace us with your presence."

"Figured I'd show my face. Catch up with a few friends." She handed him a six-pack. "I'll have a beer."

"That's the spirit. Where'd you get this?"

"Borrowed it from my poppa's stash, but I'm driving, so I'll just have one, two at the most."

"I'm glad you're here," he whispered, his breath hot on her neck. "Maybe we could have a little fun before you leave for Vic."

She laughed. Surely he wasn't serious. "In your dreams."

"Come on, babe," he mumbled. "You know I've been in love with you since we were fifteen."

"Is that right?"

"Hey, Jessa. What's up?" Scott's brother, Nick, broke the tension by offering her a joint.

"No, thanks. You know I'm drug-free forever—well, until I'm old and on painkillers."

Jessa mingled, making sure to keep her distance from Scott. The last thing she wanted was him trying to shove his tongue down her throat. That wasn't her idea of fun.

After a couple of hours, two beers, and several dances with various guys who all had the same idea as Scott, she'd had enough. With Scott monitoring her every move, it was time to leave.

Mini M turned over three or four times before finally starting.

"Come on, come on," Jessa muttered as she pulled onto Rata River Road. Her Mini was her freedom, but it was well past its use-by date. Her grandfather had warned her about buying such an old car, but a lack of cash also meant a lack of choice. Five hundred meters or so from the Watershed, it missed a beat, then another. She pulled over to the side of the road, and that's where her Mini died.

After weighing up her options, Jessa locked the car and set off down the road toward the Watershed as the humid rain clouds, which had been brooding all afternoon, finally broke. She cursed her choice of footwear and lack of a jacket. By the time she reached William's, she was soaked to the skin, and her feet were covered in mud.

The car parked in his driveway earlier was nowhere in sight. Jessa hesitated before knocking, not wanting to wake him, but knocked anyway.

William switched on the outside light. He couldn't help but smile as he answered the door. "Well, well, well. Who do we have here?"

Jessa stood before him—wet clothes clinging to her body and her nipples tight against her top. "My car broke down by the felled willows. Can I use your phone to call Poppa?"

"Of course. Come in."

"No. I'm all muddy." Her teeth chattered, and he now noticed she'd been crying.

"You're freezing. Go around the back. I'll open the door. You can use the shower in the mudroom."

"No, please. I'll be fine."

He studied her face. Slightly heart-shaped with a nose that turned up a touch at the tip, pretty didn't begin to cover it. She was so much more. The word *sensual* slipped into his mind, but he quickly dismissed it. Her eyes were full of expression, even when she was serious, and her lips appeared darker and fuller in the soft light from the hallway. She'd never looked more alive.

He cocked his head toward the side gate. "Go on."

William watched through the living room windows as Jessa hurried along the path, passing the lavender and roses, now dripping with droplets of summer rain. He unlocked the door and stood to the side. The vulnerability of a young woman in need made him feel surprisingly alive—something he hadn't experienced in a long while, and he closed his eyes against the inappropriate thought.

While Jessa showered, William's unruly thoughts turned to Rose. Her teenage body concealed beneath a white muslin blouse and jeans of dusty denim. The orange bikini encasing her pert breasts. Her mid-brown hair, thick and silky, almost reaching the small of her back. Her arms around him as she rode pillion on his bike and the taste of her innocence on his lips.

Just as quickly, his mind returned to the young woman in his mudroom.

He shook his head. Sighed.

Jessa stretched her arms upward, soothing water from the rain showerhead tumbling down her back as blood flowed from a cut on the bottom of her foot. She turned off the shower, toweled herself dry, and grabbed the robe hanging from a hook on the back of the door. Its plush softness enveloping her, she searched in the small cabinet for a Band-Aid. Unable to find one, she wrapped her foot in toilet tissue.

"Do you have a Band-Aid?" she asked as she hobbled into the kitchen. "I've cut my foot, and it won't stop bleeding."

William pulled out a stool from the breakfast bar and motioned for her to sit. "Here, let me take a look."

She froze. "No, it's okay, honestly. I just need a Band-Aid."

"Sit," he commanded. "Let me see."

She sat. William held her ankle in one hand and inspected the cut with the other, smoothing his fingers over the sole of her foot. Her skin bumped at his touch, and Jessa struggled to ignore the rush.

"Looks okay, but it needs some iodine." He rested her foot on the stool beside hers. "Wait there."

William returned from his bathroom with Band-Aids, cotton balls, and a bottle of antiseptic. "Right. Hold still." He raised an amused brow as he dabbed the cut.

"Ouch. That stings." Jessa had always hated her feet. Her toes were long and misshapen, and now, William was touching them.

"There, that should do it."

He returned the antiseptic to the bathroom. "What were you doing out on your own at night in that crazy car of yours?" he asked as he strolled back into the room and sat beside her.

With the beer still in her system, she felt a little lightheaded. "I went to a party, mainly to get away from my mother. She arrived for the night and immediately started on at me about uni. I didn't expect Mini M to let me down halfway home."

"Mini M? Is that what you call that heap on four wheels?"

"Excuse me. We can't all drive a swanky Range Rover." Jessa waited for him to continue the conversation. When he didn't, she realized she may have outstayed her welcome. "Anyway, I better phone Poppa."

"I'll drive you home." His mood turned serious. "Your grandfather wouldn't appreciate picking you up from here."

"Why's that?"

He stared at her for a moment. "It's all water under the bridge."

She wanted to press for more detail, but he didn't seem the type who'd provide it. "I couldn't ask you to take me home."

"Fine, stay here, then. I have a spare room."

"You're not serious."

William grinned at her response, and a flush of heat crept up her neck. "Of course not. And you're not asking. I'm offering. What time's your curfew? How about a hot drink first?"

"Thanks, I'm freezing. I probably shouldn't have been driving. I've had two beers. But that was ages ago. And I ate before the party, so…" Jessa often talked too much when nervous, and now, words tumbled from her like an uneasy tide in a summer storm. "Also, I said I'd be home by twelve."

William fought to conceal his amusement as Jessa prattled on. "Well, the evening's but a young pup," he said when she eventually stopped to take a breath. He walked into the kitchen and flicked on the kettle.

"Is hot chocolate okay? I don't drink coffee at this time of night. Keeps me awake."

"Me too. Hot chocolate's great, thanks."

"What's this talk about university?" he said as he searched the pantry for leftover chocolates from Christmas. "Didn't you say you were happy being a cleaner?"

"I am. But after your comment the other day, I've been giving it some thought." Her voice held a teasing tone, almost like there was a wink to go with it. "Perhaps it's a good idea."

"Really? Good for you." Her change of heart impressed him. "Do you get decent grades?"

"I guess so. I scored an A-minus on a calc paper last semester."

"Well done."

"Do you need to be smart to get a degree?"

"What were your other grades like?"

"Not bad. Mostly A's. All A's, in fact." She glanced at him through her lashes as he carried a tray from the kitchen and placed it on the coffee table. Two mugs of hot chocolate, a plate of peanut cookies, a small bowl of pink and white marshmallows, and another brimming with Belgian chocolates all sat neatly on the tray.

William stared, a slight smile curving his lips. "You're having me on, aren't you?"

"It's too easy," she said with a cheeky grin. "Sorry, but I couldn't resist. You were jumping to all kinds of smug conclusions."

"Ouch. That stung." *One nil to her.* "You, Jessa Reynolds, are a heartless little brat."

"Can be." Jessa picked up a cup, dropped three marshmallows into the chocolate liquid, and took a cookie off the plate. She looked up and flashed a knowing smile. "I've already been accepted into Victoria, but Mum wants me to take a gap year. She thinks I'm too young."

"What's your degree?" He watched as she broke off a piece of cookie and popped it into her mouth. It surprised him how animated their exchange was, and he found himself genuinely interested.

"Architecture."

That Jessa wanted to work in his profession amused him. "Why architecture?"

She finished her cookie. "Why did you choose it?"

"That's not an answer."

"Well, I love homes, commercial buildings, symmetry, and intelligent use of space and proportion. I enjoy analyzing shape and form."

He was impressed and intrigued. "So that word processing job hasn't put you off?"

"No, not at all." She took a sip from her mug before setting it down on the coffee table. "Can I have another cookie?"

"Go for it. It's nice to see a young woman enjoying her food."

"What do you mean?" She took a bite.

"Aren't most teenage girls on diets these days?" William mentally kicked himself. He knew not to discuss such topics with young women. He needed to pull himself together. "Not that you need to be, of course."

"Not me. Life's too short for regrets, compromise, and diets." She looked at him and reached for her mug, her expression full of mischief.

Days gone by flashed through his mind, but he steadied himself back to the present. "Is that the world according to Jessa Reynolds, or did you steal it from a hippy love song?"

"It's all me. I can think for myself."

"I bet you can." He wondered briefly if, or what, she was thinking about him.

"So, what are your thoughts on what I've done here?" He motioned to the room. "With the conversion?"

Jessa glanced around the interior. "It's amazing. Why did you call it the Watershed? It's hardly a shed."

He sipped his drink, studying her over the rim of his mug. "Can you suggest a better name?"

"No. The name's perfect, but I was just curious how it came about." She took a chocolate and sucked it slowly, moving the creamy treat around her mouth. "Was the renovation a turning point in your life?"

William struggled to think straight as he watched her. "I didn't think so at the time, but possibly."

She smiled but said nothing.

"When I was younger," he continued, "I'd come here whenever I needed solitude… when I was despondent, I guess. Now, it feels like home."

"The Watershed. A place to shed tears of despondency. Very fitting."

Her poetic assessment amused him. His gaze held hers, and a hint of sadness flickered in her expression. "So, where's your boyfriend on this stormy summer's night?" he asked, changing the subject.

"No boyfriend." She stared at him, eyes wide and pupils dark. "I'm not attracted to guys my age."

William immediately regretted his question. Her dating status was none of his business. And yet, each time she glanced his way, her raw sexual energy pulled him closer with a sharp tug. A tug so intense it bordered on discomfort.

Clearing his throat, he stood and picked up his keys from beside the phone. "Come on, let's get you home. I'll lend you some flip-flops so that Band-Aid stays put."

"Thanks, but what's Mum going to say when I arrive home in a bathrobe?" She giggled.

"I see your point." He went into the guest room and returned with a sweatshirt, an old T-shirt, and a pair of yoga pants. "A friend left these when she stayed last. They're probably too big, but it's all I have, sorry."

"Thank you."

William kept his Range Rover immaculate just like every other aspect of his life. Jessa wondered if sex with him would be the same. Immaculate and tidy, or messy and passionate. Not wearing a bra or panties made her feel more connected to her sensual side—heightened her senses like moody music and literature could—but her attraction to him was misplaced. The guy was twice her age. She needed to snap out of it.

As they drove along Rata River Road, Jessa lost herself in the music playing on the stereo.

"I love this song," she said.

He seemed surprised. "I wouldn't have expected Harry Chapin to be to your taste."

"Why not? I enjoy all types of music. There's a moving cello bridge coming up." Jessa leaned back in the seat and closed her eyes. "Mum has this album. She played it all the time when I was little."

"You like the cello?"

"I do. I want to take lessons when I move to Wellington. Kathy G. has a cello, or at least, she did." She frowned. "I can't remember what happened to it. I love songs from your era. The Beatles, Elton John, Neil Young."

"Songs from my era. What do you mean by that?" His laughter was relaxed. "I like music from your era too."

"Sorry, I didn't mean to imply you're old." Embarrassed by her candidness, Jessa realized she was still talking way too much.

"I'm old compared to you."

"I guess. How old are you?"

William cast her a sideways glance. "Isn't it rude to ask a person their age?"

"Women, maybe, but I thought guys were cool with it."

"I'm thirty-five. Anyway, wait until you start learning the cello. It will be all about old music, string quartets, and Brahms." As he turned into Churchill Lane, his expression betrayed his amusement.

"What's so funny?"

"You." He clicked the gearshift into park. "You're an unusual girl for eighteen."

"Am I?" She rested her hand on the door lever. "Anyway, thanks so much for the lift."

"Are you okay to walk from here?"

"Sure. Mum's probably waiting up for me, so…" She turned to get out of the car.

"Jessa?"

She looked back at him.

"See you Monday afternoon. Good night."

The next day, Poppa, forever a reliable presence in Jessa's life, donned his mechanic's hat and drove with her to pick up Mini M. He tinkered under the hood, attached jumper leads to his old Ford truck, then followed her home, ensuring she arrived without incident.

During the first half of the following week, with only occasional work from Anna now, and Lea spending time with some guy she'd met before Christmas, Jessa fell into William's comfortable routine. She retyped more of his contracts while he played golf and tennis, ran the river track, and sat at the dining table, drawing people's dreams on thin sheets of drafting paper.

He arrived home early most afternoons. They sat and talked while drinking iced tea and eating sliced pear and cheese with fresh walnut-

and-fig bread from the artisan bakery in the village. Their afternoon meetings had become rather too familiar, but neither of them cared.

On Thursday, as they soaked up the sun on the deck, William broached the subject of Jessa's mother. "Why don't you get on with your mum?"

"She smothers me. But that doesn't mean I don't love her." She paused. "Mum has an unusual personality. She's fearful, mostly about me. I wish she'd chill out and enjoy her life instead of surrounding herself with negative energy."

"What do you mean?"

"She's kind of… how you were when we first met. Angry at the world."

He smiled at her. "Is that right?"

"I don't mean that in a judgmental way. It's more of a casual observation." Jessa reached for more bread, her hair trailing over her bust in silky strands. "But, hey, I haven't walked in your shoes," she said softly. "I don't know of your past troubles."

"What makes you think I have past troubles?"

"Isn't everybody fighting some internal battle?"

"I guess." William paused in thought. She was right. Everyone had their own cross to bear—he was reminded of that fact every time he drove down the road. "And what about you? What are you battling internally?"

Jessa gazed out to the river and beyond. She didn't speak for several seconds. "Nothing much."

"You don't sound too convinced."

"We all have diamonds to cut from our coal. Metaphorically speaking."

He regarded her with a mixture of amusement and admiration. "You're an intriguing girl."

"Am I?" She shrugged. "Come swimming with me?"

"What? Now?"

"Why not? It's so hot. I need to cool off. At least come and sit with me so I'm safe. Mum would be upset if she knew I was swimming alone."

"She'd even be more upset if she knew you were swimming with me, believe me."

"Why's that?"

He hesitated. "Some would see our friendship as inappropriate."

"I guess. But it's not, is it?"

"Do you have a swimsuit?"

"No, but I have a T-shirt in my car. I can swim in that."

His hesitance vanished, tucked away for later. "Okay, why not?"

Despite the humid weather, the river was refreshingly cool until they got used to it. William couldn't stop staring at Jessa as she floated around in the small water hole beneath the willows. Who was this girl —full of empathy and insight and wise beyond her years? He tried in vain to avert his gaze from her wet T-shirt and the nipples peaking under her soft cotton-knit bra. He thought of his teenage years with sadness, swimming with Rose underneath the old bridge farther downstream. But Jessa's question drew him back to the present.

"How did you get that scar on your leg?"

"I fractured it when I was fifteen. The bone came through the skin. I broke my pelvis at the same time."

"Ouch. That must have hurt."

He struggled to suppress the flashback. "It did. More than you could ever imagine."

"Anyway, I'm getting cold." Jessa waded toward the bank, her arms across her chest. Soaked panties clung to her bottom, and goose bumps tightened her skin. She turned, bunched the T-shirt, wrung out the excess water, and tied it in a knot above her navel.

As she reached for her towel and covered herself, he mentally questioned the appropriateness of them swimming together. Arousal stirred in his groin, and if he didn't know better, he'd swear she was in total control. He reminded himself that Jessa was only eighteen, with teenage-girl hips and teenage-girl breasts—and he, a man of thirty-five, who felt entirely out of his depth and was about to drown.

"Is it okay if I have a shower?" she asked.

"Go for it. You know where the towels are."

He stayed in the water, shuffling his thoughts as he watched her stroll up the track. Once out, he lay face down on his towel, the sun's warmth soaking into his back and his erection uncomfortable beneath him. He turned his mind to the mundane, doing his best to ignore his blatant desire. Making love to an eighteen-year-old, who also happened to be his housekeeper and his niece's best friend, could never be an option. William chose to ignore the fact that Jessa and Rose were related by blood. That detail would stay buried along with the dead.

She called out from the deck, "I'm off home now. I'll see you tomorrow. Thanks for the shower."

"You're welcome." William lingered at the river's edge for a while longer. When he finally entered the mudroom, her tiny red panties greeted him as he opened the shower door. He chuckled and shook his head, suspecting she'd left them there on purpose. The hot water soothed his need as he moved his hand in an urgent rhythm, bringing himself to a much-needed solo climax.

That night, William unlocked the door at the top of the stairs. Boxes of books, unpacked office files, and plans were stacked on the floor, along with sketches of homes he'd designed and photo albums from his teenage years. On an antique desk, an eight-by-ten picture frame held a photo he'd taken of Rose the day she'd died.

Holding the frame in both hands, he marveled at the similarities between Rose and her niece. The shape of the nose was different, but the full lips in muted red and the eyes—dark as the water hole in which they'd swum—were intensely familiar.

The water might be murky, but even so, William couldn't wait to see Jessa again.

23

THE PANIC

It's not always easy to find solitude as a teenager, and while Jessa loved her mother dearly, her negative energy doused Jessa's spirits like wet sand on a flame. So when Poppa mentioned he was off on an overnight fishing trip, and her grandmother and mother had tickets to a concert in Clifton Falls, Jessa looked forward to spending some time alone.

After a stroll along the river and an afternoon swim with Lea, she made herself comfortable in the sunroom with a cup of peppermint tea and a novel. Someone had once told her that reading exposes us to lives well-led, and for Jessa, that summed it up perfectly. As long as she had a good book, she was never bored. But there'd been a shift in her mood over the past couple of weeks, and that shift had to do with William. Every time his eyes threw a lazy glance her way, she felt a tug. And each time, that tug was a little stronger.

Jessa read for a while, then watered the pots of petunias on the veranda before strolling to the cornfield to pick two cobs for dinner. As she ate, her thoughts returned to William. The company he kept, what food he liked, and his disposition. She wondered how he felt about her. Was he interested? Did he sense that same tug?

She was just about to turn on the TV when the phone rang, jolting her back to reality.

"Hey, it's Rachel. I'm going to Mass with Mum. Do you want to come?"

Jessa considered her friend's invitation. Perhaps a little Catholicism wouldn't hurt. "Okay. Will you pick me up?"

"Be there soon."

Rachel was an angelic girl who Jessa knew from school. She wore a purity ring and encouraged Jessa to do the same. But Jessa had no interest in wearing a purity ring. It would be like telling everyone you were on a diet without wanting to lose weight. Jessa wanted to have sex. In fact, she wanted to have sex with William—tangled together in crisp white sheets on his comfortable bed in his masculine bedroom to the left of the large front door. The thought of it prickled her skin. Even the sound of his voice sent shivers straight to her core.

Mass was uneventful until it came to Holy Communion. The wafer stuck to the roof of her mouth, and despite taking a decent sip of red wine from the chalice, it wouldn't budge. As she watched Rachel kneel at the altar to receive the symbolic *body of Christ*, a familiar lightheadedness surfaced. Jessa took three deep breaths. She held each one for a few seconds, exhaled slowly, and then returned to the pew to wait for the final blessing.

"May the Lord be with you."

"And also with you."

Rachel's mother, who belonged to the generation that treated clergy with absolute reverence, prattled on about "Father this" and "Father that" all the way home. Jessa, who preferred to judge people on their merits rather than their vocation, remained silent until they arrived at Churchill Lane.

"You can just drop me off at the end of the driveway, thanks. I need some fresh air."

"Are you okay?" Rachel asked. "You looked pale at Mass."

For the first time since their friendship began, Jessa found Rachel's concern suffocating. "Just tired. Nothing an early night won't fix."

"Right, well, I'll call you tomorrow."

"Okay. Goodnight, and thanks for the ride and invitation."

As Jessa walked up the gravel driveway toward the dark and empty house, her mood flattened and her heart raced. By the time she reached the veranda, she was struggling to catch her breath.

Unable to remain still, she paced the living room, vague recollections of sunlight peeking through cracks in slotted timber and dust motes dancing in shafts of light, flickering through her mind.

She slipped on a pair of running shoes and tied the laces with unsteady hands, then stuffed her backpack with the clothes she'd borrowed from William.

Small pillows of gravel dust puffed around her feet as she ran down the driveway and onto the main highway, heading toward Rata River Road.

William opened his front door and frowned at the sight before him. "Hey, are you all right?"

"I don't feel too well. Can I come in?"

"Of course." He stepped back. "What's the matter?"

"I feel faint." Jessa stayed outside. "And… nauseous."

He touched her hands. They were cold and clammy. "Come inside. How did you get here?" He led her into the bathroom, dampened a washcloth, and handed it to her.

"I ran. I run when I"—she held a hand to her chest, trying to calm her breath—"need to clear my head."

"You ran? All that way?" William lowered the toilet seat lid. "Sit. Put your head between your knees."

She sat and pressed the washcloth to her forehead.

"Better?" he asked after a few minutes. "Can you stand?"

Jessa nodded.

He ushered her into the living room, then picked up a paper bag from the kitchen counter and offered it to her. "Let out a sigh, then breathe into this. In for four quick beats, hold for seven, out for eight. Keep breathing into the bag and try to ride with it. Don't fight it." He took her left hand and wrapped his fingers around her pinkie for some time before doing the same to the corresponding finger of her right hand. It was something Vanessa had done for him when he needed calming. Something he'd always remembered.

Jessa sat back on the sofa. "What was in this bag? It's making me hungry."

"Sorry, bread I bought at the market." William regarded her with concern. He narrowed his eyes. "Are you okay? Feeling better?"

"A bit." She picked at her nails. "I'm sorry. I didn't mean to bother you," she said, blinking back tears.

"Hey, it's no bother." William handed her a tissue from the box on a side table, then poured her a nip of brandy. "Here, sip this, then you'd better call your grandparents. Let them know you're safe."

"They're not home. Poppa's away fishing, and Kathy G.'s at a concert in town with Mum and Aunt Maggie."

He filled a glass with water from the fridge. "Here."

"Thanks." She drained the glass and held it out for a refill.

He studied her for a moment. "Jessa, have you taken something?"

"What do you mean?" Her brows knitted together. "Like drugs?"

"It's just… you appear to be reacting to something. You're hungry and thirsty."

"Well, I haven't. And you're not helping by accusing me," she snapped. "I don't do drugs. I hardly even drink alcohol."

"Okay, calm down. I'm not accusing you. I'm just trying to understand. Has this happened before?" William rubbed his palm over her back and felt her relax.

"I had an accident a couple of years ago and bumped my head. The doctors at the time diagnosed me with panic attacks."

William understood how frightening they could be. He'd suffered from them after the accident. "How do you feel about that?"

"You sound like my shrink. That's what she always asks." Jessa fiddled with the buttons of her blouse, an uneasy silence separating them. "I'm starting to feel a bit better."

"How about I make you a hot drink before I drive you home?"

"I don't want to go back to the house."

"What about staying with Lea?"

"She's at the movies with her new boyfriend."

Jessa looked at him through thick lashes framing her dark eyes. He caught her drift. "You can't stay here."

"Please. I don't want anyone else to see me like this. Don't make me leave. I'm scared."

"Shit." William shook his head, the words "big mistake" screaming at him on repeat. "Look—"

"Please?" she repeated. "No one will know.

He hesitated, telling himself just this once wouldn't hurt. "I'll get you that drink."

They talked for a while. Small talk. But as they sat opposite each other at the dining table, sipping hot chocolate, he realized they could easily cross the line with just one step.

"Come on, let's get you to bed. It's getting late." Jessa followed him into the guest room, where he took a woolen blanket from the closet and draped it over the ivory feather quilt. "It's a bit chilly in here, but you should be warm enough."

"Thanks."

He checked her expression. "Why does your family leave you alone, considering the panic attacks?"

"They don't normally, but I promised I'd be okay. Mum worries, but the farmhand and his wife live next door. They usually keep an eye on me."

"Now you tell me. Your family wouldn't be happy if they found out you were here. You do realize that, don't you?"

She nodded and pressed the side of one index finger to her lips. "Our secret."

"And by the way"—William gestured to a small plastic bag on the dresser—"you left those in my shower. Goodnight."

"Goodnight, Billy."

He frowned at her. "Why did you call me Billy?"

"Isn't it short for William?"

"No one calls me Billy." He hesitated. "And I prefer it that way."

He left the bedroom and shut the door behind him.

24

MOONLIGHT FANTASY

If ever there was a raw nerve to hit, Jessa struck it by calling William Billy. His sudden cool detachment reminded her of their first meeting, and that same fear formed a tight knot in her gut. Then she recalled what Lea and Anna said about him and knew she'd be safe.

The knot relaxed.

Jessa cracked her door open, undressed, slipped into William's T-shirt from her backpack, and snuggled into bed. The sheets were fresh and crisp, and the bed neatly made, just how she'd left it after his last guest stayed. She pictured William alone in his large bed across the hall and smiled. She wondered whether he slept naked, on his front or on his back.

Did he lie awake thinking of her?

After many frustrating minutes of tossing and turning, Jessa slipped out of bed and tiptoed across the hall, her heart racing in her chest. "William," she whispered. "Wake up."

"Jessa, what's wrong?" William flicked on his bedside lamp, blinking as his eyes adjusted to the muted light. "Are you okay?"

She stood beside his bed, shivering from the cold. "I'm freezing. Can I sleep in here?"

"What? Jessa, it's late. I'll get you another blanket, but you can't sleep with me. You know that."

William grabbed a quilt from a padded blanket box at the end of his bed, then ushered her back to the guest room. He sat on the edge of her bed, naked from the waist up, and brushed a lock of hair from her face as if she were a small child. "Now stay put."

"I don't want to be alone."

"You're not alone. I'm just across the hall."

An hour later, she was back.

William switched on his bedside lamp for the second time that night and sighed. "What now?"

"I'm still cold and kind of anxious."

"Jessa, go back to bed."

"I want you to keep me warm. Please."

"Shit. I shouldn't be doing this." But he opened his bed to her anyway. William turned his back to conceal his erection, struggling with his conscience. He'd overstepped that line, and the fictional life he'd imagined in which Jessa played the leading role was fast becoming a reality.

Jessa lay with her back to him, and he sensed her gradually relax into sleep. But a short while later, she turned and slid an arm around his naked waist. Her firm breasts pressed against his skin, sending fire to his groin, and his abs contracted as she cuddled into him.

He longed to turn over. To hold her, kiss her, and take her in love. Instead, he lay there, listening to the rhythm of her breathing along with his internal admonishment. His sleep, when it eventually came, was unsettled as he tossed in a sea of aching wants and needs.

William woke late, struggling to reconcile the morning light with his tiredness. He expected to find her making breakfast in the kitchen, but the blinds were still down and the doors locked. Jessa was gone. He felt stuck, unable to move forward or back, and as he faced the insight daylight brings, he realized Jessa Reynolds could never again share his bed. "Welcome to purgatory," he muttered.

All Sunday long, William let his imagination get the better of him as he pictured holding her in his arms. He realized it was inappropriate, but he had to stay another day just to see her.

He approached Monday morning with trepidation. Jessa arrived early, breezing through to the living room, seemingly without a care in the world.

"Hi." Her tone was friendly and fresh, her shiny locks tied in a high ponytail with wispy strands flying free. "Why are you still here? Don't you have work today?"

He felt as if he would burst.

"I'm working from home this morning." William swallowed hard, his throat dry and uncomfortable. "I'll leave after lunch. How are you after the weekend?"

"Great. Another gorgeous blue-sky day." Jessa flashed her carefree smile, flanked by tiny dimples. "Can I make a start, or would you rather I came back this afternoon?"

William studied her.

"Why are you staring at me like that?" she asked.

He rubbed the back of his neck, but the tightness remained. "About Saturday night."

Her smile faded, replaced by a slight frown.

"It can never happen again, understand?" he said with certainty.

Her frown deepened. "What do you mean? Nothing happened." She busied herself with her bucket of cleaning supplies, ignoring his gaze. "I thought you were my friend, and I needed you, that's all."

"But it's not all, is it? If we're honest, it's not all—"

"I'm sorry, but I can't deal with this right now." She grabbed her keys from the hall table. "I'll come back after lunch."

"Jessa, wait."

"No, William. Please don't do this. Don't spoil what we have."

For the rest of the week, Jessa drove past the Watershed every day, anticipating William's return, but there was no sign of him.

She knew he desired her and was convinced her imagination played no part in it. Boys had desired her in the past. Scott, drunken boys at parties, and guys from school. But this was intensely different. William was a man, she guessed of some experience, and she found his self-assuredness exhilarating.

On Thursday morning, just as Jessa was about to leave for work, the phone rang.

"Jessa, can you get that?" Kathy called from the kitchen. "My hands are covered in scone dough."

"Hello. Jessa speaking."

"What day are you coming home?" Her mother didn't wait for a reply. "I'm having lunch with Maggie on Saturday. You should join us. She'd love to see you before you leave for university. Let me speak to Mum."

"Kathy G., Mum's on the phone," Jessa called before resuming their conversation. "Mum, listen for a minute. I'm not coming home until Monday. I have a party tomorrow night, and I'm staying at Lea's. Also, I have to work tomorrow."

"Jessa, you have so much to do next week."

"Just packing. All I need is a toothbrush, chocolate, and plenty of cash."

"It's no joking matter, young lady."

"Mum, chill out. Monday. End of story." Jessa handed the phone to her grandmother. "Please talk some sense into her," she whispered. "I'm off to work."

By Friday evening, Jessa was nervous but determined. She'd imagined being with William all week. After drawing a picture in her mind, she'd added the dialogue and lived the moment. There was no party. Most of her friends had already left the Valley, and while the little white lies didn't sit well with her moral compass, Jessa felt stifled for choice.

As she drove past the small wooden cross, she noticed several bundles of lavender surrounding it. She stopped to take a look. The sprigs leaned against the memorial like a small haystack. It made her smile, knowing that someone still cared about the person who'd died there.

The Watershed stood honest and proud, a solid old form lovingly restored to life. Jessa parked around the back of the garage, out of sight of the road. She noticed the lavender along the deck had been neatly clipped, awaiting next spring. Inside, apart from a note on the hall table, everything looked the same.

J

I'll be back on the weekend. If you see this note, please be here. We need to talk.

W

Jessa left her backpack in the guest bedroom and strolled into the bathroom. She loved this room, with its vintage-style faucet, chunky church candles, and jars of rock salt. On impulse, she ran a bath and, as the tub filled, added an assortment of salts and oils.

She soaked for a while, trying to rid her mind of all distractions. But later, as she stood naked before the large distressed timber frame mirror, she questioned what William thought of her body. Did he find her pretty and sensual, or was she too skinny and young for his liking?

Back in the kitchen, Jessa helped herself to crackers with peanut butter and made a green tea, then sat on a sofa and flicked through back issues of *Architectural Trends*. Being alone in the Watershed was a luxury she'd often dreamed about, but now, all she wanted was for William to come home.

Jessa undressed to her lacy orange bra and panties. His scent wafted from the pillows, and as she slipped into his bed, the cool sheets made her skin bump. Through the windows, the night sky, peppered with country stars, put on a dazzling display.

She woke with a start. The readout on the alarm clock showed a disquieting 1:07 a.m. Why wasn't he home yet? She put on his robe, wandered around the house, and peered out the front door. Still no William.

Jessa found a paper bag in the kitchen, held it to her mouth, and breathed deeply while counting—four, seven, eight. Her pulse slowed with each breath as fragments of recollection flickered through her mind like a subliminal television advertisement. She returned to bed, but the butterfly circus performing raucously in the pit of her stomach made sleep impossible.

She leaped out of bed and flew to the door at the sound of a key in the lock.

"Where were you? I've been so worried." Struggling to catch her breath, her neck muscles tensed as she spoke.

"Hey, calm down. Stop and breathe, okay?" William dropped his overnight bag and held her hands together as if in prayer. "It's okay. Big, deep breaths. Remember the numbers. Inhale and hold. Go with it."

He guided her to a sofa. It was now after two, and the house was dark save for a lone lamp on a side table.

"Where were you?"

"At a party." William crouched beside her. "What on earth are you doing here?"

"You left me a note. Said to be here."

"Shit, Jess. I didn't mean for you to stay the night. What have you told your grandparents?"

"They think I'm at Lea's."

"Lea's? For shit's sake, Jessa, you shouldn't be here. You know that. We've discussed this."

"But I thought you wanted me to stay."

"I told you last weekend. You can't be here. It's not fair on either of us."

"What do you mean, it's not fair? Why isn't it fair?"

"Do I have to spell it out?"

"I want to stay," she whispered. "We're friends."

"If you spend one more night in my bed, we'll pass the point of no return." His jaw tightened. "You have to go. We'll talk tomorrow."

"No." She stood her ground.

"Jessa, get dressed," he ordered. "I'll drive you home."

Her eyes burned with imminent tears. "Please don't make me go."

"For shit's sake." William stood, ran his hands through his hair, and sighed. He picked up the box of tissues from the phone alcove and handed them to her. "Hey, come on. Don't cry."

"What's wrong with me? Why don't you want me?"

"It's not about what I want." William shook his head. "How can you be sure of what you want at your age?"

"You don't get it, do you? Just because of our age gap, you want to disregard what we have."

"Our age difference is only a small part of it."

"So what's the rest?"

"Your family, friends… Anna and Lea. You're leaving for Wellington soon. What we have is special. But it can't be anything more than friendship."

"Why? No one else needs to know, and anyway, what does it matter what others think?"

"It matters. Believe me, it matters a lot. People can't find out about us. Your family would be furious if they knew you were here… knew we were friends."

"We don't need to tell anyone. Life's about taking opportunities when they're presented. If we don't act at the time, we lose the chance. When I'm unsure about my choices, I ask for guidance… for a lesson."

"Is that right?" He sucked in his top lip, suppressing a smile as this intriguing young woman tried to seduce him. "So what are you saying? I'm purely a lesson to you?" Sitting beside her, William set his smile free. Despite their circumstances he loved her innocence.

"No, of course not."

"Well, that's a relief." He chuckled.

"It's not funny." Jessa wasn't laughing. "We don't have to be together for always and forever, but I want you to teach me." Tears slid down her cheeks as she struggled to speak. "I'm eighteen, and I've never had sex, never been desired by a real man—"

"I find that hard to believe."

Jessa hesitated. "I've hardly even kissed a boy. Just because I'm young, it doesn't mean I don't have needs. I don't want to give my virginity to some sweaty, drunken boy who slobbers all over me in the back seat of his parents' car with no preparation or foreplay. I want to choose my own time and place." She pulled another tissue from the box. "Why are you looking at me like that?"

"Come here." William held her gently. "Sorry, but you're too adorable, too irresistible." He sighed. "This isn't right." He pressed his lips to her crown. "We shouldn't be here together. You know that."

Her eyes were wide with invitation. "Why not? It's what I want. It feels right, and life's too short not to act on such moments."

William brushed the back of his hand along her jawline, worshiping her youth and innocence, their desire suspended in the surrounding air. His lips barely touched her forehead as his hold firmed. Warm with lust, he tenderly kissed her neck and throat.

"I want you. Never think that I don't," he whispered. "I've waited for you for a lifetime, but we have to take it slowly." He lifted her chin slightly, his passion for her invading any sense of consequence. Their eyes met. "Understand?"

She nodded.

Their kiss was all he'd imagined and more. A loud and clear kiss with undertones of tenderness and respect but laced with dominant intent.

"I want you to take me to bed."

"No, Jess. It's too soon."

"Please. I want you and no one else."

William studied her for some time, his thoughts loud and conflicted. He longed to take that next step but realized how rocky the ground would be once he did. He finally stood and offered his hand. She rose to accept. He led her into his bedroom and shut the door.

Still wearing his robe, Jessa sat on the bed without saying a word. They'd reached the point of no return, and at that moment, his desire overrode his blaring conscience.

They stared at one another as he undressed in the filtered light from the outside security lamp. He reached into the nightstand drawer for a condom and put it on the pillow, then kissed her gently, his hands cupping her face. "We don't have to do this. If you want me to stop, say so."

"I don't want you to stop."

Jessa untied the robe, exposing her orange lacy panties and a matching bra, and William shook his head with an uncertain thought. She was just a girl in an innocent set of girls' lingerie. But as she reached for him, all doubt was pushed aside.

Her lips and tongue responded to his, her vulnerability and inexperience enhancing the intensity. He took his time, soothing her with tender words and assurances she was in complete control. That they could stop at any time.

William almost convinced himself he was meeting her needs with loving affection. But as he pushed through her physical resistance, he was mesmerized by her expression and lost all comprehension of himself.

Her stunning heart-shaped face conveyed a blend of discomfort and desire as she finally gave herself to him, and he accepted her with reckless abandon.

William woke to the sound of tires crunching on the gravel driveway. His bedside alarm clock glowed an empty 6:20 a.m.

He was alone.

Once again, Jessa had left without saying goodbye.

Their lovemaking was everything he'd dreamed of, but when he noticed the red droplets of her innocence speckled on his white cotton sheets, remorse took hold. He stripped his bed and put the sheets in the washing machine with the cycle set to *soak*.

As the shower rained soothing hot water down on him, he wished she were still there so they could talk. He longed to wash away his guilt and justify his actions, but dread sat on his skin like an itchy rash he couldn't scratch. He pressed his forehead against the tiled shower wall.

What the hell had he done?

Instead of playing golf as planned, William sat in his office, searching for inspiration as he fidgeted with pencils and blueprints. He made coffee, ate half a slice of toast, and sat some more, thoughts of Jessa disrupting his concentration. Her full lips and petite breasts, her scent, her taste.

William reminded himself, more than once, that Jessa was Rose's niece and Louisa and David's only child. How would they react if they found out he'd spent half the night making love to their daughter? Being her first, taking her without thought or concern for her future. As his untouched coffee sat cooling, his guilt grew warmer.

He'd made a massive error of judgment.

Without pausing to consider the consequences, William picked up the phone and dialed the Churchills. Tom answered, which he hadn't expected, but he doubted the older man would have recognized his voice. When Jessa came on the line, her response to his question, "What time are you coming over?" was abrupt and to the point.

As soon as William opened the front door, he could tell something was up.

"What do you think you're doing, calling me at home?" Jessa stormed down the hallway and into the living room as he followed. She set her bag on the floor. "I had to lie to Poppa when he asked who you were. I hate being deceitful, and that's all I seem to be these days."

No-nonsense Jessa had just introduced herself in no uncertain terms.

"Sorry. We need to talk." William rubbed the back of his neck, where his conscience had dumped a shitload of guilt.

"Do you know Poppa? He said you sounded familiar."

"Not really." He hesitated. "Why did you leave without saying goodbye?"

"You looked so peaceful. I didn't want to wake you." Jessa reached for him, but he resisted.

"Shit," he said, still rubbing his neck. "This is a mess. We shouldn't be here together." He opened the door onto the deck to let the morning air freshen the space. Summer would soon move into autumn, typically his favorite time of year. But not this year. He loved how Americans called it fall. Fall was right—he was falling, falling from grace.

"But last night, you said—"

"I'm aware of what I said," he interrupted, "but I shouldn't have made love to you. You're too young."

"How can you say that after what happened between us?"

"I'm sorry. I went too far."

"You said you wanted me."

"I did… I do. But that doesn't alter the fact that you're young and impressionable. You're off on a big adventure soon, and now, I've put my selfish needs before what's best for you. It can't happen again, do you understand?"

"No, I don't." Jessa searched his expression for an explanation, her eyes darting back and forth between his. "I don't understand any of it. There's someone else, isn't there? That's why you're doing this. You have a girlfriend."

"How can you say that?" This time, he took her hands and rubbed his thumbs over her knuckles. "There's been no one in my life for over two years. But I can't be your boyfriend. I'm thirty-five."

"So what are you saying? You make love to me… more than once, hold me, kiss me, and now what? It's all over now because I'm a silly schoolgirl?"

"No. Yes. Shit, I don't know. It's just… I feel guilty about what happened. I'm twice your age. You were still a virgin. I took that from you."

"You didn't seem too concerned at the time. You knew what you were doing. Me, I'm a teenager, remember? But you, you're a grown man. You hold all the power here."

"Come on," he protested. "How can you say that? You've been working away at me for days."

"What do you mean by that?"

"You know exactly what I mean. The wet T-shirt, lace panties in my shower, barging your way into my bed in the middle of the night. Shit, Jess, what the hell do you expect? I am a man, after all. It's like you're two different people. One minute, you're lost and vulnerable, and the next, you're reckless and seductive."

"I'm sorry." Jessa cast her eyes downward. "I thought it was what you wanted."

"And what about what you want? Do you honestly think I can give you what you want? You're still in school, for shit's sake." William's words caught in his throat. He didn't want to hurt her, but his remorse allowed no other option.

"I'd better go." She picked up her shoulder bag.

"Look… don't go. We need to talk. Sort this out."

"But it doesn't really matter anymore, does it."

William shook his head and sighed as he followed her down the hallway. "Of course it matters."

"And I'm no longer in school. I'm about to be a university student, and we like to push the boundaries and sometimes, live our lives with blatant disregard for any consequences. But I'm not about to beg you to desire me, William. You either do or you don't."

"Of course I do. But that doesn't mean I'm right for you."

"Fine. I knew the moment we met I should stay away. You were horrible, made me cry, and now you're putting on a repeat performance." Jessa yanked the front door open.

William came up behind her and pushed it shut again. She stood still, her body leaning into the timber as he pressed into her back, his arms caging her in.

"Jess, I'm so sorry. I didn't mean to make you cry," he whispered into her neck. "I never want to hurt you. Please don't go. I want you, but I can't do this unless you're absolutely sure." He briefly questioned whether the term "absolutely sure" meant anything to her, but once again, his desire overrode his concerns.

"It's up to you. I know what I want, but for a man your age, you seem so unsure of yourself," she challenged. "But then, maybe I didn't do it right. I realize I'm inexperienced, but I'm willing to learn."

William unbuttoned her top and slid his hand over her breasts. Her nipples contracted as his fingertips circled the small buds, and his erection pushed into her buttocks, his intention clear. Holding her chin with his free hand, he caressed her earlobes and throat with searching lips and tongue.

"You were wonderful. More than wonderful. I told you that last night." He lifted her from behind, carried her front forward into his room, and placed her face down on the bed.

William didn't speak; instead, he let his lips, tongue, and hands communicate his mood. He observed her through his passion—hands outstretched on either side of the pillow as he gently entered her, then clenched into balls of intensity, gripping fistfuls of Egyptian cotton until her knuckles turned white with fire.

"Tell me. Tell me how you feel."

"I can't. I'm too—"

"Tell me," he ordered. "Just one word."

"Uncontrolled," she cried.

25

SHADED SUN

When William woke the next day, Jessa still lay beside him. They slept late, made gentle love, and dozed in each other's arms until midmorning. Later, they swam naked in the swimming hole under the willows, then lay in the cloud-shaded sun before rain drizzled onto the dry summer earth.

Over lunch, their conversation flowed comfortably, as if they'd known each other for years. Perched on a stool at the breakfast bar, Jessa swung her legs free as she bit into toast topped with sliced tomato. "Was it supposed to hurt?" she asked shyly. "You know, the first time."

He regarded her tenderly while waiting for his toast to pop. "Everyone's different. I've only been with one virgin before." He leaned over and kissed her. "I'm sorry I hurt you, but was it okay after the first time?"

Jessa took another bite of toast and sipped her juice. "It was… okay."

William laughed freely. "What? Just okay? It certainly wasn't just okay to me."

"More than okay, if you must know." The silent seconds stretched into minutes as she ate. "So, when you lost your virginity, was the girl a virgin too?"

"She was."

"Who was she?"

"You can't ask me that," he teased. "Why all the questions?"

"I'm just curious."

William thought for a moment. He'd never discussed his sex life with anyone before. "A friend from my high school days, Vanessa. We were at a party, and both drank too much. I was seventeen and going through a bit of a rough patch, so we went to the beach to talk. I think she felt sorry for me."

"Ah, a sympathy screw. Was it special?"

"A what? You young people have such interesting terminology. And to answer your question, no. It was just sex. Messy, awkward sex. I don't remember much about it, to tell you the truth, but I do recall things being uncomfortable between us afterward. We didn't see each other for ages after that night."

"Are you still friends?"

"Yeah. But she lives overseas now."

"So how many women have you made love to since?"

"Do you mean how many women have I had sex with?"

"Is there a difference?"

"Absolutely." William buttered his toast, sliced tomato and avocado on top, and ground black pepper over it. "Having sex and making love are entirely different. Sensual intimacy is so much more than just sex. In my opinion, sex is purely a physical act. It's about need rather than a desire to couple with someone you love and adore. And to answer your very personal question"—he paused in thought—"half a dozen, I guess."

"What about at university? You must have had hundreds of girls falling at your feet. You're a good-looking guy."

William chuckled. "Thanks. I was twenty-five when I decided to go to Victoria, and being a mature student, I didn't mix with the younger girls."

"Why didn't you go when you left high school?"

"I left school at fifteen and worked on the farm for ten years."

"But you're a smart guy. Why did you drop out at fifteen?"

He considered his reply. Was this his opportunity to tell her about Rose? What would it mean for them? Would he have to let her go? Within a split second, he decided to keep the past buried. "Circumstance. All water under the bridge and swept out to sea now."

Jessa looked puzzled. "Okay, if you've 'had sex' with half a dozen women"—she punctuated the quotation with her fingers, "how many have you made love to?"

Her innocence intrigued him. He caught her gaze and smiled. "Just the one."

After lunch, they relaxed in the living room. William wanted to be still, to immerse himself in the project spread out before him on the dining table, but Jessa chatted away about nothing in particular. At times, their age difference became more apparent. This was such a time.

"Is it okay if I pick some roses from along the deck to take back to town?" Jessa asked.

William glanced up from his work. "Sure."

"They're so elegant when in bud. Their color reminds me of French vanilla ice cream."

"They're called *Renate*. I love the cream with the lavender."

"Me too." Jessa picked up her novel and opened it to the bookmarked page, then closed it again. "Kathy G. has a garden full of roses. She loves being outside with her secateurs."

"Do you always talk so much?"

"No, not always." She shielded her expression with the paperback and didn't speak for a moment. "Only when I'm tipsy or nervous."

He leaned back in his chair, regarding her with amusement. "Are you nervous now?"

"Kind of."

William narrowed his eyes. "Why?"

"It's been an interesting weekend. Overwhelming."

He sat forward, elbows on the table and hands under his chin. “Do you feel overwhelmed by me?”

“Sometimes.”

“And uncomfortable?”

“Occasionally… and tense.” Jessa returned her attention to her novel.

“Look at me.” He waited. “Tense?”

She met his gaze. “Kind of.”

William suspected she hadn’t yet learned how to read him and that his self-confidence could come across as controlling and arrogant. He chuckled. “Interesting.”

“What do you mean, interesting?”

“You’ll see.”

Heavy rain pelted the iron roof, cooling the afternoon air and washing the summer dust from the building as he headed down the hall and into the bathroom. The sound of the tub filling drowned out the rain’s din, relaxing his mood.

“Jessa,” he called. “Come here.”

After discarding his clothes on the floor, William settled in the tub and rested his arms along the rim. When she peeked around the bathroom door, he smiled, his legs spread wide as a blanket of foam surrounded him. “Stand at the end of the tub and undress.”

She stepped closer. “But then you’ll see me naked.”

His smile was gentle and reassuring as he moved to sit on his haunches. “There’s nothing more erotic, more intense, than two people sensing the essence of each other through sight and touch.”

He reached out, took her hand, and guided her to the end of the tub. “May I?”

Jessa nodded. William unfastened the buttons of her top with wet hands, slipped it off her shoulders, and let it fall to the floor. Next, he unzipped her fly and slid her jeans over her hips, and as she wriggled out of them, the sight of her white cotton boy-leg panties amped up his desire. “Turn around.” William unclasped her bra and also let it fall.

He watched her, every touch and movement reflected in the full-length mirror opposite, the glass obscured by steam around the frame but clear in its heated center. His eyes kept returning to her reflection as he pulled her panties over her knees and trailed kisses up her back and across her shoulders. Both hands moved down over her bottom, and he squeezed gently before lifting her into the tub. Her back rested against his chest, and the firm cheeks of her butt nestled into him.

His legs entwined with hers as he reached for the lavender soap. He washed her slowly—her arms, then her throat and breasts, over her flat tummy, and down between her thighs.

"I adore you," he whispered against her glistening skin as his hungry lips brushed her delicate earlobe.

"Please don't say that."

"It's true, so true. You're absolutely adorable." Jessa's back arched in request, but he wanted her to wait, to anticipate. He turned her toward him and kissed her without restraint, his full erection pressing against the softness of her lower torso.

"Please," she said. "I need you."

But William still didn't make his move. Rather, he savored the moment, caressing her neck, ears, and lips while sponging her naked form.

"Tell me what you want," he whispered, pressing gentle kisses to her crown as the rain trickled down the steam-covered windows and dull light—gray and moody—engulfed the room.

"I want to… do it again. Make love."

"Do you, now? Well, I'm all yours. Do whatever you want."

She closed her eyes as he sucked each nipple into his mouth, taking his time with increased pressure until she cried out.

"I don't know what to do."

"Course you do. You're in safe hands." William grabbed a condom from the stool next to the tub and held it out to her. "Here." He chuckled at her stunned expression.

"Um—"

He lifted himself above the water line. "Let me help."

Jessa straddled him, her hands grasping his shoulders for balance. They kissed, rough and hungry for each other, his tongue holding her hostage until he stopped to change position.

With her back now pressed to his front, they locked eyes in the mirror as he pinched her nipples and caressed her nape with his lips and tongue. Each new sigh held a touch of song until she reached the brink of complete arousal.

"Hold on to the edge of the tub," he murmured as he sat on his heels and pulled her down onto him, his hands encircling her waist. Her discomfort reflected back from the mirror as she gasped. "You're in control, Jess. Take your time," he soothed. "It's more intense this way. Gently does it."

Jessa lifted slightly, holding William's reflected gaze. Each time her eyes closed, he commanded her to open them. Ordered her to watch. Her rhythm increased hesitantly, her hands gripping the edge of the tub and his firmly on her waist until they moved as one.

"Tell me," he murmured.

"One word is never enough."

"Tell me."

"Adored!" she cried.

26

FREE SPIRIT

Jessa and William stood on the front porch, breathing in one another's essence. They'd talked freely the night before, but now, their conversation stopped and started with awkward pauses.

William slipped his arms around her waist and looked down at her. "You'd better go. You don't want your grandparents to worry. Are you okay?"

"Yes. Why?"

"I don't know..." William hesitated. He found the mornings difficult, confronting even, and the fear of her family finding out niggled away at his mind. "So many things about us make no sense."

"Let's not talk about it now."

"Okay, bossy pants. Come over tomorrow afternoon. I'll cook dinner."

"You cook?"

"Sure. When you live alone, you either learn to cook or you starve."

"Don't you get lonely, living all by yourself?"

"Occasionally." He stroked her hair and kissed the tiny summer freckles covering the tip of her nose. "I'll be lonely when you leave, but I'll be back in town next week. You can come to my apartment and stay over if you can manage it."

"That could be difficult."

"We'll sort something out. And once you're settled in Wellington, I'll visit the odd weekend. We can stay in a hotel."

Jessa dropped her sunglasses into place. "Can I see you later?"

"I thought you were spending the evening with your grandparents?"

"They go to bed around ten. I could come after that."

"You can't do that. They'll hear your car."

She thought for a moment. "Drive to the back of the hay barn on the side road. I'll run over and meet you around ten thirty."

A slow smile curled his lips. "You, Jessa Rose, are trouble. I feel it in my bones."

She returned the smile. "Is that so?"

William pulled his Range Rover into the side road, cut the headlights, and parked at the back of the barn as instructed. He leaned forward and looked out the windscreen. He loved the night sky, especially in the country, where the absence of city light pollution allowed for an unobstructed view of the constellations. Tonight, as usual, the stars put on a dramatic display.

He rested back on the headrest and closed his eyes. He'd almost dozed off when Jessa opened the front passenger door.

"Sorry I'm late," she said, puffing. "They only went to bed ten minutes ago."

"All this cloak-and-dagger business. I'm not sure I have the energy for it."

"Well, you are thirty-five," she teased.

He leaned over and kissed her, little pecks of hello, her lips soft against his. "But I feel like a teenager when I'm with you. You make me do things I wouldn't normally do."

"Oh really?" She skimmed his neck with searching lips. "Like what?"

"Like making out in my car." He climbed into the back seat, taking her with him. "I get hard just thinking about you."

"But we're not making out." Her tongue moved to his earlobe as she straddled him. "We're just talking, aren't we?"

"Is that right?"

Their kisses increased in intensity, matching their desire until William pulled back with a smile. "I almost forgot." He reached underneath the driver's seat and pulled out a box wrapped in red paper. "I bought you a present."

"What for? It's not my birthday."

"Open it."

Jessa tore off the wrapping paper and glanced inside. "You bought me shoes?" She lifted the lid and stared at them in disbelief.

He switched on the interior light. "Do you like the color?"

"It's gorgeous. I've never seen a red like it."

William laughed. "Your expression. You look like all your Christmases have come at once." He patted his lap. "Here, put your feet up."

He removed her tennis shoes and slipped the stilettos onto her feet. "You like?"

She lifted one foot for a better look. "I love. Thank you so much. It may be a challenge learning to walk in them. I've never worn heels before."

"They're not necessarily for walking in."

"Then what are they for?" Jessa frowned, meeting his gaze.

He grinned at her. "For wearing when you're naked."

She giggled and shook her head. His hand cupped her breast, kneading tenderly as he ran kisses along her already aroused skin.

They stayed in the car for over an hour. As always, Jessa started out confident but became coy and modest as they continued. William liked that, and as the force of her orgasm took hold, he murmured into her neck, "Tell me."

"What?" she panted.

"One word."

"Just one?"

"Yes. Just one."

"Reckless."

"Take me for a swim. It's such a beautiful night."

"But it's almost midnight."

"That's the best time."

Jessa's enthusiasm for life filled him with an intoxicating mix of hope and fear. While he wanted to be with her, his conscience had plenty to say about that, and he knew how her family would react if they ever found out.

He also knew being with the niece of Rose Churchill would soon become a moral issue he couldn't ignore.

They drove in silence to a water hole by the main bridge, William pushing all negative thoughts aside as he buried his head deeper in the sandy mud.

Despite the humid and still night air, the water held a sharp bite. Even so, it felt liberating, swimming naked under the country stars in the river that had caused him such pleasure and pain.

"I love the freedom of swimming without restrictions." William swam to Jessa's side and slipped his arms around her waist.

"Yes, so you keep saying."

He stared at her and frowned. "When?"

"Um, I'm not sure. Somebody said it."

He turned her back on and cupped her breasts while kissing her nape, the earthy taste of river water sharp on his tongue. "Your tits are hard."

She giggled. "It's the only time they stand at attention. When they're cold."

"It's not the only time, believe me."

When Jessa sneaked back into the house, the clock on the kitchen mantel glowed 1:34 a.m.

"Where have you been?"

"Poppa." Her hand flew to her chest. "You scared me."

Her grandfather sat at the table, a cup of tea in front of him and the bright moonlight accentuating the lines on his face.

She turned on the light over the kitchen sink, relieved she'd had the foresight to hide her new shoes in the barn. "I thought you were in bed."

"So I gather. Why's your hair wet?"

Her face heated. "I couldn't sleep, and it's such a beautiful night with the full moon, so I went for a quick dip in the creek." She poured a glass of water and leaned a hip against the counter while holding the glass tightly in both hands.

"I noticed a Range Rover drive out of the side road by the hay barn."

"When?"

"Just now." His gaze didn't shift. "Look, you're eighteen, so what you do is your business, but I know who you've been spending time with over these past few weeks, and it's not right."

"What are you talking about?"

"Who phoned you the other day?"

Jessa hesitated. "A client. I clean his house. And I did some word processing for him."

"Where? At the Watershed on Rata River Road? The Cook place?"

"Have you been spying on me?" She sat at the table, her expression defiant.

"There's no need for that tone. I wasn't born yesterday, and this William Cook, he's twice your age."

"It's just a summer fling. I'm leaving next week. Don't tell Mum or Kathy G., please."

"A summer fling? One where you lie about where you've been and who you're with? Did he tell you to lie to your family?"

"What? No! We decided to keep it quiet since he's Lea's uncle."

Her grandfather was a man of few words, but when something

needed to be said, he stood his ground until he was heard. "Let me get this straight. Lea, your friend, is William Cook's niece? Anna's daughter? Anna Cook and her grandparents are Grant and Doreen?"

"Do you know them? Anna's my boss. She's Anna Ellison now."

"Oh, I know them all right."

"What do you mean by that?"

"Do you have feelings for him?"

Jessa stared down at the table, her chin resting on intertwined fingers.

"I asked if you have feelings for him," he repeated.

"Yes, I do. But as you said, it's my business. I'm sorry, Poppa, but I don't have to answer to you or anybody else. I'm old enough."

"Is that right? So while we're paying for your education, you're throwing it back in our faces by carrying on with this man!"

"It's not like that. We enjoy spending time together, but I won't let him interfere with me going to university."

"I suppose you're on that contraceptive pill, are you?"

"You can't ask me that. It's none of your business." Jessa stood and pushed her chair into the table. "I'm going to bed. Thanks for your concern, but I know what I'm doing, and I'm not hurting anyone."

Kathy stirred as Tom slipped back into bed. "Is she home?"

"She's home."

"What's she been doing out at this time of night?"

"By the look of her, necking up a storm with some boy in the back of his car."

Kathy propped herself up on her elbows. "No! What makes you say that?"

"It's written all over her face. She has that glow and is just a little too sure of herself."

"Now that you mention it, she was like that when she came home this afternoon too. And after dinner, she couldn't sit still."

"Anyway, we'll discuss it in the morning. I need to get some sleep."

As he slipped his arm around his wife's waist and settled into her familiar shape, Tom wondered why he'd referred to William as a boy.

William Cook might be many things, but a boy, he was not.

27

REALIZATION

"Tom! Can I help you?" William failed to keep the surprise from his voice as he stood at his front door. An abrupt grip tightened around his gut. He hadn't seen Tom Churchill for many years, but there was no mistaking the man. Apart from gray hair around the temples, a heavier build, and the weathered skin of a farmer, he still looked the same as he did all those years before. William seldom felt uncomfortable in another man's presence, but Tom Churchill wasn't just any other man.

"Can we have a word?" The older man looked William up and down.

"Sure. What about?"

"You know what about. May I come in? I won't take up too much of your time."

"Come around the back." William led the way to the deck, and Tom followed. Even with pillows of cloud shading the sun, the late afternoon was still warm. He could smell the sweet roses and hear the industrious bees going about their work but realized his day was about to turn sour. "Can I get you a drink?"

"Just water. This isn't a social call."

William pulled out two chairs from the table, then headed into the kitchen and returned with two glasses of iced water with lemon slices. He offered one to Tom.

The older man accepted it and took a sip. He set his glass down in front of him as William took the other chair. "I want you to stop seeing my granddaughter."

William held Tom's gaze, waiting for him to continue.

"I gather she's been working for you, and heaven only knows what else is going on."

"Jessa works for my sister. She's my housekeeper."

"But that's not all, is it? What about this word processing job? You've been paying her to spend time with you under the pretense of work."

"That's ridiculous."

"Is it? If it's not the case, please fill me in on why Jessa's been spending time here."

"I admit, I asked her to type up some notes for me. I figured she could use the money for university. But it wasn't an attempt to get her to spend time with me. Whatever gave you that idea?"

"Come on, Cook. You were together last night, parked down the side road by the hay barn."

William said nothing as Tom scanned the river.

"And I gather she's stayed the night here at least once." Tom sighed and shook his head slowly. "This is wrong on so many levels, quite aside from the fact that she's only eighteen and you're… well, I'm guessing mid-thirties. What are you thinking, man?"

William stared into his glass, searching for the correct response, but Tom didn't give him a chance to reply before continuing, "She tells me she has feelings for you."

"Shit."

"Don't insult me by thinking I don't know what's going on. Have you slept with her?"

William's response was physical rather than verbal as he rubbed his fingertips over the light stubble along his jawline. He wondered what Jessa had told her grandfather.

"How many times?" Tom asked. "Just the once? Or more?"

"Look, I'm sorry, Tom, but this is none of your business. Jessa's old enough to make up her own mind. I didn't seduce her. Our relationship is consensual."

"I know Jessa, and I realize that may well be the case. But it doesn't alter the fact that this… this fling, or whatever you want to call it, is wrong and misguided. Nothing you say will ever make it right."

"I understand where you're coming from, but we care for each other. It's not a fling. I'm falling in love with her, and I think, no, I'm sure she feels the same."

Tom's expression hardened. "You're not in love with her, man—you're in love with a ghost. And as for Jessa… Well, she says it's just a summer fling, nothing more."

Another measured silence as William processed Tom's words. "I can see how it looks from the outside," he said eventually, "but don't take this chance away from me. I've already lost someone I cared about, and so have you. Why can't I have this chance with Jessa?"

"Because she's not Rose, no matter how much you wish otherwise. Apart from that, it will destroy her relationship with her family. Louisa will disown her if she finds out she's carrying on with you. Do you fully grasp the consequences of your actions? You're twice her age, man."

William had nothing more to say. It was pointless trying to convince Tom. Hopefully time would take care of old wounds.

"There's something else." Tom's expression betrayed his sadness. "Has she told you about these turns she's been having?"

"You mean the panic attacks?" He nodded. "She turned up here in a state the weekend you were away fishing."

"What about the accident? The bump on the head?"

"She mentioned it in passing."

William noticed his hesitation. The two of them were now united in concern for the girl they both loved.

"There was no accident," Tom finally said.

"What? But she said—"

"I know what she says about it, but it's all in her imagination. She believes in incidences with no basis in fact." He stopped to sip his drink. "Says she has flashbacks, remembers things that make no sense."

"You mean she's lying? The accident never happened?"

"Maybe in her mind, but not in reality. We took her to a psychologist, but they're not sure what's going on. It seems Jessa firmly believes in experiences she's never had."

"Are you implying she's mentally ill?" William's world tumbled around him as he began to see what this meant for him and Jessa.

"We're not sure. She's not a well girl. That's why her mother doesn't want her to go to the university this year. It's not about Louisa being overprotective. But Jessa… She's not ready."

"But she seems so onto it. If I didn't know her age, I'd swear she was in her twenties."

"She's a special girl, all right. Most of the time, she's fine, but right now, things aren't adding up for her. So"—Tom let out a heavy sigh—"you'll understand my concern. She doesn't know the details about what happened to her aunt, and it's my guess you haven't told her."

"No. No, I haven't said a word."

"Well, that's for the best. If she finds out about Rose and joins the dots, it might just tip her over the edge." Tom paused. "Unfortunately, the Jessa you know is not the Jessa we deal with on a daily basis."

Struggling to find the right words, William took another sip of water.

"Look, I'm asking you, man-to-man," Tom continued. "Let her go before it's too late. I never blamed you for what happened that day. It was an accident, but that ghost must be left to lie. I can see why you're infatuated with Jessa. She's a lovely wee soul. Loving, kind, pretty in her own way, and she doesn't have a nasty bone in her body. But she's also out to get what she wants with little regard for the consequences. We've already lost a daughter. We don't want to lose our only granddaughter too."

The old man looked tired as he stood and pushed in his chair. "I hope I've made you see sense. She leaves for Wellington on Friday. We tried to talk her out of it, but she's a stubborn little miss. It's the right time for you to cut all ties. She'll forget all about you once she settles in."

"What about me? How will I forget?"

"Well, my guess is you haven't in the past, and you won't in the future. But this is how it has to be. Her mother would never welcome you. This way, Jessa doesn't have to choose. Better all around, don't you think?"

William followed Tom to his truck. Tom's hand was already on the door lever when he turned back. "Take an old man's advice. Find a girl your own age, have a couple of kids, and mend the sorrow. Find someone to love who'll love you in return."

William stood still as Tom climbed into the cab.

"Kathy drove her back into town this morning, so you won't be seeing her tonight. And if you really care about her, I beg you to leave her be."

Tom wound up his window and was gone before William could reply.

William returned to the deck and stared out over the river as dusk smudged across an overcast sky in shades of gray and rose pink. Where had the afternoon gone?

He headed inside, opened the fridge, and studied its contents—apricot yogurt, a loaf of whole-wheat bread, and two slices of bacon—before shutting the door again.

He turned on the stereo and pulled the curtains, then poured himself a nip of brandy and sat at the dining table, staring into a half-empty glass.

Leave her be? For fuck's sake!

28

BUTTERFLIES STIRRING

March 2nd

Dear William,

I'm so sorry I didn't see you before leaving for Wellington on Friday, but Dad was watching me like a hawk. I phoned you a few times, but you never seemed to be home.

It's hard being here. The lectures are huge. Nothing like high school—not sure what I expected. I keep thinking of you walking the halls all those years ago, and now I'm following in your footsteps.

I miss you and the time we spent together over the past few weeks, and I can't wait to see you again.

Yours,

J xxxxx
P.S. Please write.

March 10th

Dear William,

I'd hoped you would have written by now, but I guess you're busy. I wait each day for the mail, but nothing.

Still, the days are flying by, and I'll soon be home for midsemester break. Please say we can spend time together.

My classes are going well, but I'm homesick. Not for Mum and Dad and my old bedroom, but for you, William, and the Watershed.

Please write as soon as you get this.

Take care,

J xxxx

March 15th

Dear William,

Where are you? I miss you so much, and not hearing from you is starting to take its toll. I had another panic attack the other day, but I did the breathing thing, and it passed quickly.

I've finally started playing the cello and am amazed, as is my tutor, by how quickly I'm picking it up.

The weather here isn't like home. It's windy and cold already, and it's only the middle of March.

J xxx

March 20th

Dear William

What's going on? Should I call you at work? We need to talk. Miss you so much and the times we spent together at the Watershed. I feel sad being here without you but realize I have a job to do. Once I have my degree, we can be together.

All going well here—learning heaps. Please write or even visit. It's barely a five-hour drive if you don't have to take the bus. It would be wonderful to hold you again, to be in your bed at the Watershed.

J xx

April 1st

Dear William,

Happy April Fool's Day. I can't tell you how excited I was to receive the flowers yesterday. Thank you. Now I know you remember me. French vanilla rosebuds like the ones at the Watershed—just perfect. I secretly hoped you'd turn up, but a dozen roses are the next best thing.

What does the number on the card mean? Is it that many days since we last made love? I guess it is. Sweet.

I phoned you at work last week, but you were in a meeting. I left a message for you to call me back and sat in the hallway by the pay phone for three hours. After that, I couldn't stand it any longer and went to bed, unable to face the world that day...

William's lack of communication had overshadowed the excitement of coming home, and as Jessa caught a glimpse of her mother through the small window of the bus as it pulled into the depot, a resigned sadness settled over her. She'd questioned his motives constantly on the bus ride north to Clifton Falls, and when her mum stepped forward with open arms and a warm smile, Jessa struggled to hold back the tears.

They drove along the port road, not their usual route, and as they passed William's compact apartment building on the left, Jessa turned her head, straining to see any sign of him—a room alight with life or an open window. But his place was dark, and the windows closed.

Her stomach flipped with a touch of nerves as she wondered if he'd met someone else. Perhaps a sophisticated businesswoman, someone who suited him better. After all, he'd promised to meet her in Wellington, promised to book a hotel. But there had been no meeting and no hotel. She only knew his address because she'd looked him up in the telephone directory.

Home was the same as always—an ordered mess. Her mother had never mastered the art of housekeeping, and Jessa liked a tidy ship.

In her bedroom, she dumped her bag on the bed, then lay on the floor and gazed at the ceiling, smiling as she studied the tiny glow-in-the-dark stars she'd haphazardly arranged as a child.

"Dinner's ready," her mum called from the kitchen a while later.

Jessa entered the room and surveyed the food on the table. Her mother was a meat-and-potatoes kind of cook, and beef stew with mash was the last thing Jessa felt like. "I'm not hungry right now. I might have something later."

"But we waited so we could all eat together. Please join us."

"Mum! Don't fuss."

"There's no need to raise your voice at your mother," her dad scolded. "You don't have to eat, but at least sit with us. We want to hear your news."

"Sorry. I'm exhausted. Bus trips suck."

The longer she sat at the table talking about her university life, the more Jessa relaxed. Even if the food didn't appeal, it felt good to be home. To her surprise, her parents looked older than she remembered when she left in February.

"Do I have any mail?"

Her mother glanced over her glasses at David. "Where did you put Jessa's mail?"

"In the top drawer of the dresser," he replied.

"Thanks. I might go and sort through it and then have an early night."

"Okay, love," her mother said. "Sleep well. And make yourself a sandwich later. We can't have you fading away."

"No chance of that. Goodnight."

Back in her room, Jessa turned over the small bundle of letters and removed the rubber band. She flicked through the three or four that could wait, and there it was—Hudson Farrell Architects. Her hands trembling, she tore open the brown envelope, unfolded the white paper, and scanned the text.

Dear Miss. Reynolds,

On behalf of Hudson Farrell Architects, I wish to congratulate you on selecting architecture as your degree of choice. As part of our internship program, we regularly contact architectural students who previously resided in our area.

If you believe you would benefit from spending time in our office as a volunteer, please don't hesitate to contact us at any stage. I wish you every success as you work toward completing your degree…

The letter was signed Dan Hudson. Jessa let it fall. It seemed William had made his choice. She flopped back on the bed, the other letters scattering on the floor.

"Darling, what are you doing?" Her mother's voice broke into her doze. "You've fallen asleep on top of the bed. Come on, let's get you under the covers." She pulled back the bedding and helped Jessa out of her clothes before tucking her in as if she were a child.

"Sorry… I'm so exhausted."

"Sleep well, and don't hurry getting up in the morning."

When her mum switched off the light, Jessa buried her head in the pillow, her tears flowing freely. She'd received William's message loud and clear. Acceptance, however, remained elusive.

The next morning, as the hurt continued to flow in a steady stream, Jessa padded into the kitchen for breakfast, still in her pajamas. She studied her mum with concern. "Is everything all right? You look shattered."

"It's Aunt Maggie. She's had a heart attack."

"No. I'm so sorry." Jessa sat at her side and took her hand. "I know how close you two are. Will she be okay?"

Her mother gazed sadly into the mug in front of her. "They're not sure. Her neighbor found her this morning."

"She'll pull through."

"I hope so. Maggie's such a source of calming wisdom in my life, and I need that sometimes." She sipped her coffee. "Her life followed a tough path. She thought men loved her when they didn't and kept looking for her first-best man, as your grandmother calls them, but never found him. She's a black sheep, and black sheep have a hard row to hoe."

29

YELLOW RIBBONS

The office of Hudson Farrell Architects occupied a two-story art deco building not far from the city's retail sector. Jessa spent the first two days of the midsemester break traveling to and from the hospital with her mother and Kathy G. However, on the third day, with Aunt Maggie now out of the coronary care unit, she walked into the central business district, determined to see William.

The receptionist smiled warmly as Jessa approached her desk. "Good morning. How may I help?"

Jessa glanced around the office, expecting to see William stroll down the stairs at any minute. "I'm here to see Mr. Cook."

The receptionist frowned. "I'm sorry, Mr. Cook no longer works here. Can someone else help you?"

What? She wanted to step away. To run through the door and never come back, but she stood her ground and inhaled before letting her words coast on an outward breath. "Oh, okay. No. I wanted to see Mr. Cook."

"He moved to Australia, just recently." She studied Jessa. "How do you know William?"

"Oh… um, I did some work for him last summer. I'm studying architecture at Victoria. I didn't realize he was moving."

"You and everyone else. Incredible opportunity for him, though, and he's always loved Sydney."

"Thanks anyway." Jessa turned and trudged slowly toward the door, struggling to process the receptionist's casual words. *Just recently. Incredible opportunity. Sydney.*

"Excuse me," the woman called after her. "You don't happen to be Jessa, do you?"

Her clenched gut eased a little. "Yes, I'm Jessa."

"William left a package for you. I remember now. He said you might call in." She took a red paper bag from a desk drawer and handed it to Jessa.

"Thank you."

"Oh, and, Jessa, William asked me to take down your details."

"Excuse me?"

"For our summer program. Send us your résumé if you're interested. But keep it brief. We don't need to know where you attended kindergarten." She chuckled while offering the company's business card. "We have two internships going at the end of the year. I'll put in a good word for you."

"Thanks." Jessa slipped the card into her jacket pocket, her hand tightening around the package.

"I'm Sharon, by the way. If I can help, call me."

"That's very kind of you."

"So you're in your first year, I take it? I graduated two years ago. Love the work. But I have to cover the front desk over lunch breaks—all part of being the new kid on the block. How are you enjoying the course so far?"

"Good. Harder than I expected, but I'll get there."

"Well, all the best. It can be a little daunting at times, but it's worth it."

"I hope so. Enjoy your day."

Jessa hurried across the street to the park. Everywhere she looked, loved-up couples lazed in the afternoon sun, happy children played on swings, and coppery leaves covered the grass. Late autumn could be bitterly cold, but today felt like summer.

She sat on a bench, opened the bag, and pulled out a parcel wrapped in rough brown paper and tied with a yellow ribbon. Addressed in William's unmistakable hand—black ink, architect font, neat as a pin—the inscription simply read: *Jessa R.*

Inside were two books, *No Ordinary Moments* and *Way of the Peaceful Warrior*. The first was brand new, while the latter had seen better days. Pieces of yellowed tape held its tattered cover together. She opened it to the title page, where an inscription flowed in blue fountain pen.

Dear William
In loving memory of Rose Faith Churchill.
May this book bring insight and
help you navigate your way.
Love, Vanessa x

Jessa ran her fingertips over the faded words.

Rose Faith Churchill? *Her aunt?*

Vanessa, William's friend?

She fanned through the pages, searching for a letter, a note, any clue as to why he'd unexpectedly cut contact and moved to Australia. Nothing.

Too tired to walk, Jessa caught the bus home. With the parcel clutched tightly against her chest, she sat upright in the seat and stared out the grimy window. She half expected to see William jogging along the waterfront or stuck in traffic at the intersection near his apartment. But there wasn't an SUV or a jogger in sight.

After dinner, Jessa retired to her room and started to read. She finally drifted off just after midnight, the words of Dan Millman floating around in her head.

Over the following weeks, those books became her solace from pain. She read and reread them, opening pages at random whenever she needed to clarify her thoughts. The words spoke to her, moved her, and she wondered if they'd also moved William all those years ago.

"What do you mean, how do I feel about it?" Jessa looked across the desk at her student health psychologist. It seemed like their last session had been only yesterday instead of three weeks ago. "How do you expect me to feel?"

"I'm asking if you understood what you were getting yourself into."

"Of course I did. Please don't judge me as a child."

"There's no need to be so defensive," Doctor Chapel said. "I'm not the enemy here. However, you shared with me that you lost your virginity to your friend's uncle, a man twice your age. And now, he's left you without a word. It's my job to help you make sense of your behavior. This is not about judgment but, rather, a way forward so you can rationalize why you indulged in reckless sexual conduct with this man."

Janis Chapel sat behind her desk in her dimly lit office, and for the next few minutes, not a sound passed her pursed lips. Jessa mirrored the doctor's stance, determined to keep Doctor Chapel out of her headspace.

"Look, Mrs. Chapel, I mean no disrespect," she said eventually. "However, I think we should call it quits before I waste any more of your time. I'm not unwell, just under a bit of pressure. It's quite common at my age."

Jessa's heart beat double time. She understood why she'd been withdrawn and discontent—of course she did—but was waiting for time to heal all things, if such a concept was a reality. Somehow, Jessa didn't think so. She realized speaking to her psychologist in such a tone was inappropriate, but despite experiencing a pang of guilt over her insolence, she reminded herself that following your own truth often comes with a dose of self-doubt.

"Please leave any diagnosis to me. Don't think you have all the answers. And it's Doctor Chapel."

Jessa wondered if *Doctor* Chapel, with her cold and calculating stare, had ever personally experienced such restlessness. She struggled to make sense of it herself, and her resentment grew with each hour spent in that bleak office.

She studied the doctor's pristine white blouse buttoned to the neck, her long, thin fingers, severe haircut, and mid-length brown polyester skirt peeking out from under the desk. The doctor remained silent, her professional indifference on full display as she tapped her pen against the desk.

Eventually, she spoke. "How do you feel about what's happening to you? Does your conscience condone your behavior?"

"I had a safe and consensual relationship with a man. I'm of age. Where's the problem?"

"That's not all I'm referring to. It's this other business as well. The panic attacks, the recollection of details that have no basis in fact, the depression."

"What I'm going through is entirely different from what you describe. I admit, I'm occasionally depressed, but I still function. I've hit a rough patch. That's all."

"Yes, so you've explained. But that doesn't alter the fact that your parents are worried about you. Your erratic eating and sleeping patterns, your malaise, and these 'flashbacks,' as you call them."

The two of them sat in silence once more.

That's her thing, Jessa thought, her procedure for breaking you down. Silence.

Every now and then, Doctor Chapel would mutter, "How does that make you feel?" Or, for added interest, "How do you feel about that, Jessa?" But otherwise, stone-cold silence.

"I'll prescribe you an antidepressant. It may help to knock off the edges."

"Fine, whatever you say." Jessa didn't care. She'd only agreed to therapy to appease her parents, and the game must be played according to their rules. She understood the importance of stress management. Life had to be attended to if one wanted any semblance of normality. The answers were obvious, but learning to implement them was the hard part.

The days passed, and the antidepressants remained in her nightstand drawer, untouched.

PART IV

CLIFTON FALLS

30

ROSEBUDS WITH TEARDROPS

University life settled into a predictable routine, and for the next five years, the cycle was the same. Lectures, semester breaks, exams, and twelve weeks over summer working at various odd jobs. Lather, rinse, repeat.

Jessa never sent her résumé to Hudson Farrell or phoned Sharon for assistance, and although a strict daily routine kept her panic attacks and flashbacks to a minimum, she passed through life devoid of emotion yet swamped by it all the same.

At times, Jessa's mind struggled to be honest with her soul, struggled to connect, and a crushing sadness settled over her world. She contained her feelings while studying, but returning to Clifton Falls for the summer unsettled her.

Each year, on her birthday, March thirty-first, one dozen French vanilla rosebuds, *Rosa Renate*, found their way to her door. No matter where she was, they appeared. The first year, she was excited. It meant contact, and the number was a sweet touch.

She was dumbfounded the second year. The number on the card was a painful reminder of many days of wretched abandonment.

The third year, the roses and the number on the card annoyed her—a distressing reminder of their estrangement.

The fourth year, the number made her furious. All those meaningless days. Why?

But by the fifth year, relief flooded over her like a promise. According to the card, over fifteen hundred days had passed since they last made love, and she knew he still cared.

With a Bachelor of Architecture under her belt, Jessa returned to Clifton Falls the week after graduation. She rented a tiny cottage one block from the beach and spent the next few days making it into a home. Lea, now a fifth-year medical student, had been posted to Clifton Falls General for a twelve-week placement, and the friends often ate together when Lea had a well-deserved evening off.

The Friday before Jessa started her new job, Lea arrived right on time for their seven-thirty night-in dinner. Jessa had never met anyone so punctual, except maybe William. Lea set a frozen cheesecake and a bottle of rosé on the kitchen counter. "Meet my contribution to the occasion."

"Yum. I'm always pleased to meet a cheesecake. Take a seat. I'm just about ready."

Lea sat at the table and watched Jessa move around the kitchen. "So, did you get that job you applied for?" she asked.

"Yes. I start next week at Hudson Farrell Architects."

"You're shitting me! That's where Uncle William used to work."

Jessa inhaled sharply. "Really?"

"Yep."

"How is he, anyway?"

"Fine. We spoke to him the other day. He loves Sydney and was dating a sophisticated city girl last year. She's in marketing, but I'm not sure if they're still together."

Jessa opened the fridge, buried her head inside, and took another deep breath. At first, she'd been unsure about accepting the position at Hudson Farrell, but it was the only firm that had offered her a job. Not that it mattered now. William was long gone, and he might never return to Clifton Falls.

"What are you looking for?" Lea asked.

"The wine."

"It's already on the table. Hurry up and sit down. I'm starving."

While they ate, each talked of their day as Ryan Adams' *Gold* album played in the background.

"This is so good. I'm glad you've learned to cook." Lea put a forkful of chicken and baked pear into her mouth, then reached for the bottle in the middle of the table. "More wine?"

"Um, excuse me. Are you trying to get me drunk?" Jessa chuckled. "You know I hate being out of control."

Lea refilled their glasses. "Of course not. But honestly, it's time you got out there and met a nice guy. Let your sexy shine and live a little."

"What? In that order?" Jessa smiled as the alcohol kicked in.

"I don't get it. You're a total hottie. Guys look at you all the time. They smolder after you." Lea giggled. "Are you asexual or what?"

"Smolder after me? Really? Anyway, who says I haven't had sex?"

"What?" Lea stared at her in disbelief. "I thought you were still a virgin."

"Well I'm not. But let's skip the details. You know I can't shut up when I'm tipsy."

"Who was he? Have I met him… or them?"

"There's only been the one."

"Was it a guy from uni? A drunken one-night stand?"

"Um… no. No one from uni. I've never had a one-night stand. Have you?"

Lea giggled again, her expression telling the tale without a word spoken. "Don't change the subject. This isn't about me."

"And I don't want it to be about me, so…"

Lea gave Jessa a knowing look. "I know who it was. I even know when you met."

Jessa hesitated. "No, you don't. You have no idea." She gripped the edge of the table with both hands and quickly stood to clear their plates. "Right. Time for dessert."

Once back at the table, Jessa swirled the cold creaminess around her mouth as she tried to enjoy the sweet but pungent tang of the cheesecake and the cool assault of ice cream. She wondered how long it would take Lea to resume her interrogation.

"It was Uncle William, wasn't it? The summer you worked for Mum."

Jessa set her spoon on her plate and lowered her gaze. She went to stand but thought better of it. Instead, she sat on the edge of her chair, running her hands up and down her jeans as she cleared her throat. "I feel like I've betrayed you, and I'm so sorry."

"I admit I don't get it. He's old, grumpy, and my uncle, so I don't see the attraction. But I'm not one to judge, you know that." Silence stretched between them as they finished their dessert. "And I've made plenty of mistakes in my short life as far as men are concerned. 'Men-stakes,' I call them." Lea released a throaty laugh. "But I don't want details. That would be gross."

"I couldn't resist him. I can't explain it."

"That's okay. I understand. Been there with guys, most of them jerks, but I still want to do it again, and soon."

Jessa didn't want to elaborate, but at the same time, she needed Lea to understand. "I loved him. Perhaps I still do. But if he wanted to be with me, he'd have found me."

Lea sighed. "Yeah, I guess."

"Does your mum know?"

"I'm not sure. But looking back now, maybe she did. She was always reluctant to send you to the Watershed unless he wasn't there. It was all a bit weird."

Jessa nodded. "I called into his office during midsemester break that first year, but he'd already left for Australia."

"And he hasn't contacted you since?"

"Not once, except for flowers each year on my birthday. Well, I assume they're from him. The card's never signed."

"Crazy. So, what happened when you went to his office?"

"Nothing, but he'd left me a package. A couple of books." Jessa reached into the bookshelf behind her and pulled out the novels. "Here. I still read them occasionally."

Lea turned *Way of the Peaceful Warrior* over in her hands. "I've heard of this one. It's a classic from the eighties. But he could have at least bought you a new copy." She skimmed the back blurb. "Maybe I should read it—it might help me sort out my life."

"Look inside."

Lea glanced at the title page. "Who's Rose Faith Churchill?"

"I think she might have been my aunt. Mum's sister. She died in an accident years ago."

"No way! You had an aunt who died in an accident? When?"

"Before I was born. No one talks about her much. But they must have at some stage because I have vivid memories of her."

"And this aunt, her name was Rose Faith Churchill? Are you sure?"

"Yes, I'm her namesake, Jessa Rose, and Churchill is Mum's maiden name. Kathy G. has baby photos of her hidden in a chocolate tin in her old glory box."

"I forgot your mum was a Churchill. I wonder if Uncle William and Rose knew each other."

"They must have. But then, why did he never mention her?" Jessa picked up *No Ordinary Moments* and flicked through its pages. "I know who Vanessa is."

"Who?"

"A friend from his school days who helped him through a rough patch. He told me about her once."

"Hence the book."

"Yes. Hence the book."

The girls talked late into the night, but Jessa never mentioned the times she and William had spent together, their forms wrapped in lust and tenderness. Nor did she tell Lea about the day counts on the birthday cards or that her uncle was the most incredible lover, with a stamina that would match that of a much younger man. She didn't explain how she'd felt so desired by him that she'd melt at his touch.

Some memories didn't need to be shared. It only cheapened them.

31

WANTS AND WISHES

The first month of the year held bittersweet memories for William. The accident, where his life changed forever and he lost Rose, happened in January. Then, many years later, William and Jessa met at the Watershed on a warm January afternoon.

And in that same month, he returned to Clifton Falls for a happier occasion: the marriage of Nikau Hughes to Donna Richardson. Five years was a long time to be away from the place of your birth, and although he expected to see change, Clifton Falls looked and felt exactly the same. Like home.

Now, on another hot and dry day, he stood beneath a wisteria-covered pergola, watching the other guests greet the bride and groom. He waited at the back of the group, happy to be the last one to extend his best wishes.

"Hi." He offered Nikau his hand. "I never thought I'd see you walking down the aisle in a suit and tie. Congratulations."

"William, mate." Nikau slapped him on the back. "Glad you could make it."

"Wouldn't have missed it for the world. I have personal business here, so it's great timing on your part."

"Nothing too problematic, I hope?"

"No, not really. Both my residential tenants gave notice last month. More a nuisance than anything else."

"Let's get you a beer. I'm dying to hear all about Sydney."

William studied the old building before him as they stood chatting in the sun. Once a convent, it had recently been reinvented as a wedding and conference venue. "What a fantastic place. They've done an excellent job with the conversion."

"We were lucky to get it at such short notice," Nikau said. "The gardens are so peaceful. Let's hope that's a good omen for the marriage, eh, mate?"

"I'll drink to that." The two of them clinked their glasses in a toast.

"And to dodging the priesthood bullet," Nikau murmured, raising his beer again.

William chuckled. He'd always struggled with the idea of Nikau becoming a priest. "That too. Although judging by how you couldn't keep your hands off Donna throughout the ceremony, you wouldn't have lasted a week."

"Don't I know it!"

In one corner of the lawn, a string quartet warmed up for its relaxed afternoon set. Three girls and a guy, all dressed in classic black, faced the guests.

"Holy shit," Nikau said, staring at the quartet. "Look at that girl with the cello. She's the spitting image of Rose Churchill."

William turned his head, and for a moment, time stood still. Behind the cello—eyes closed, lost in breath and rhythm, and even more exquisite than he remembered—sat Jessa Reynolds. He rolled his beer glass in his hands, took a swig, and glanced back. His memory of her was nothing compared to the reality.

"Sorry, mate, but she really looks like Rose," Nikau said.

"The lovely and talented Jessa Reynolds. She's Rose's niece."

"Louisa's daughter?"

"The very same."

"Far out. You know her?"

"Not well."

"Shit." Nikau let out a soft whistle. "She's…"

"Yes, *shit* is right."

"I don't know what to say."

William grinned at Nikau's reaction. "You've always had an amazing way with words. It's not like you to be speechless."

The music was a relaxed mix of pop and modern classics, but William was on edge as he struggled to shift his gaze from Jessa. Her face was similar but, at the same time, intriguingly different. Poised. He watched in awe as her delicate fingers—manicured with French tips—danced on strings tuned in perfect fifths, bringing them to life. The cello was her instrument; no denying it.

As the sun dipped behind the western hills, an angelic glow encircled her. At that moment, in William's mind, Jessa and Rose could have been one and the same.

Seeking breathing space, he moved through to the dining room, found his place card, and hung his jacket over the back of the chair. He entered the bathroom and splashed his face with cold water while shuffling his thoughts. He longed to talk to her, but not here. Not now.

Back at the table, he watched Jessa through the French doors as she packed away her cello and interacted with the other musicians. She turned and looked in his direction, a slight frown on her brow. With the sun casting a reflective glow over the west side of the building, William doubted she could see him. Even so, she appeared to be searching for someone. He wondered if it was him.

A familiar voice broke his train of thought. "William! Looks like I'm sitting next to you."

"Dan." The two men greeted each other with back slaps and a handshake. "Long time no see. How's life?"

"Not bad. Not bad at all. So, you're back are you?" Dan removed his jacket and loosened his tie. "What are your plans? There's always an opening at Hudson Farrell if you're keen."

"You don't waste any time, do you?" William chuckled as he pulled out their chairs. "We haven't even had the speeches yet."

"Sorry, but seize the day and all that. I have a brochure in the car showcasing our latest projects. Remind me to give it to you before we leave."

"Okay." Dan's warm smile helped William relax. "Sydney's been good to me, so I haven't given much thought to coming back for good." He glanced out to the garden. The string quartet had left. "Until today, that is."

The next day, William removed the Hudson Farrell brochure from his jacket pocket and sprawled on the sofa to read it. On the back page, he read the heading: *Jessa Reynolds Joins Hudson Farrell.* The photo didn't do her justice, not from what he'd seen at the wedding. William relaxed and closed his eyes, lost in recollections of the alluring girl from his past. Her breasts, fitting in the cup of his hand, the delicious warmth of being inside of her—her laugh, smell, taste, and those melodic whispered sighs she made when aroused and tumbling through orgasmic bliss.

He picked up the phone, hesitated, then dialed Dan's number.

32

MOODY MONDAY

"Welcome back," Sharon greeted Jessa as soon as she walked through the door. "How was your long weekend?"

Jessa removed her jacket and hung it over her chair. "Great. Everything a weekend away should be. And the wedding was fabulous. You should have seen the food!"

"Did you meet any hotties?"

She smiled. "Maybe. But you know me. I'm saving myself for the perfect man. My grandmother calls them 'first-best' men. According to her, they're few and far between."

"I'd have to agree with your grandmother. They're a dying breed." Sharon dropped her voice to a whisper. "We need to talk. In private."

"What about?" Jessa whispered back. "And why are we whispering?"

"Come into the boardroom."

Jessa followed Sharon and shut the door.

"I'm not sure how to tell you this, but we have a new senior on board."

"What? Is it someone we know?" Jessa's interest was piqued as she wondered who it could be. There'd been any mention of this before her three-day break.

"William Cook."

Jessa sank into a chair. She'd never discussed William with Sharon, but she obviously realized something had gone on; otherwise, they wouldn't be having this conversation. Hudson Farrell was a close-knit team, and once her initial uncertainty passed, Jessa knew she'd made the right decision by accepting a position at William's old firm. Now, that decision slapped her in the face with a heavy hand.

"You can't be serious." She craned her neck to peer through the glass partition into the main office. "Is he here today?"

"No, he officially starts on Wednesday. Look, sweetie, you don't need to tell me what went on between you two. It's none of my business, but..."

"What am I going to do? I never expected to see him again."

"It's okay. We'll figure it out."

Jessa wiped her clammy palms down her skirt, her breathing labored. "Can you get me a glass of water, please?" She sat back in the chair, focusing on breathing deeply into her diaphragm.

Four, seven, eight.

"Here." Sharon's voice broke Jessa's rhythm as she handed her the water. "Look, don't let any man mess with your head. William may be back on the scene, but that doesn't mean you guys can't have a professional relationship."

Jessa stared at her, unconvinced.

"Unless, of course," Sharon continued, "something happened, you know, that's unforgivable."

"No, nothing like that." Jessa trusted Sharon to keep her secret safe, and under the circumstances, she felt the need to confide. "When I was eighteen, I worked for a cleaning firm. William was a client. We became friends, and—"

"Wait one holy minute! You're not saying you were lovers?" Sharon always cut to the chase.

Jessa nodded. "He was my first."

"What the heck! He took your virginity?"

"I gave it to him willingly, to be fair." Jessa picked at her cuticles as her first night with William came to mind. "Shit. This can't be happening."

"But you were eighteen, and he would have been, what, thirty?"

"Thirty-five." Their age gap still amazed Jessa. It hadn't seemed an issue at the time, but the more she thought about it, the more she questioned her choices. "I know what you're thinking, but I really cared for him. In the end, he cut all contact. If he'd acted differently, I might be more relaxed about it, but to say I'm uneasy is an understatement. And as my boss—that's crazy."

"I'm sorry, but I don't understand."

"What do you mean?"

"The expression dirty old man springs to mind."

"It wasn't like that. I did quite a bit of the seducing. Remember, life's too short for regrets, compromise, or—"

"Diets. Yes, I remember," Sharon said, grinning from ear to ear. "You little minx! Well, what's he like in the sack? Go on, spill!"

Jessa laughed and shook her head. "Now you've officially crossed the line of sexual etiquette. The subject's closed. Right, I'd better get to work. I'll worry about William later."

"At least you haven't lost your sense of humor. Let's do lunch."

"Yes, let's."

Sharon and Jessa sat in a small café overlooking the harbor, bowls of seafood risotto and glasses of lime and soda on the table between them. Jessa picked up her fork and put it down again. "Can I ask you a question?"

"Of course." Sharon sipped her drink. "Fire away."

"Why have you never mentioned William before?"

"It's none of my business." She shrugged. "But looking back, it did worry me a bit."

"Why?"

"Because you seemed such a sweet, young thing. Gentle and angelic."

"Not virginal, though," Jessa said with a grin.

"I thought about that as well, as I recall, but quickly dismissed it as ridiculous."

"Yeah, I was too young to be sleeping with the thirty-five-year-old uncle of my best friend."

"What! He's your friend's uncle? Which friend?"

"Lea."

"Lea is William's niece?" Sharon shook her head. "This whole business gets worse every time you open your mouth. So, what was in that bag he left for you?"

"Just a couple of books. He'd wrapped them in brown paper to signify a tree and tied them with a yellow ribbon. He wanted me to use those books to find my way home, so to speak."

Sharon picked up her glass and leaned back in her chair. "No way. That's not the William Cook I know." She took a sip. "But have your romantic fantasy if you must."

Jessa paused, contemplating their bond. "It's funny. Ever since meeting him, I've felt as if we're bound by a silk thread, so strong it can never be broken. Even now, I sense the tug."

"I have a pair of sharp scissors in my top drawer that will take care of that."

"It sounds crazy, but we had such a strong connection. Maybe we still do."

Sharon frowned. "Please don't say that, sweetie. He clearly isn't interested. He hurt you once. Isn't that enough?"

"It's difficult to explain. It's like one of those Wasgij puzzles where you have to figure out what you're looking at from the inside out. I've found a few missing pieces but still have a long way to go, and I've no idea what I'm supposed to be looking for."

Sharon reached across the table for her hand. "Don't go there again. I can see it ending in tears."

"Tears merely cleanse one's soul. We should embrace them."

Sharon burst out laughing. "Okay, way too deep for me. You're scary when you unleash your crazy side."

Jessa laughed as well. “Maybe, but I’m finding life exciting again and”—she grappled for the right word—“fascinating.”

“Well, I’m sorry, but honestly, I can’t find anything exciting or fascinating about William Cook. He must be hung like a horse because, otherwise, why would you bother?”

“Stop it. You’re making me blush.”

“I knew it! He *is* hung like a horse. So, bottom line, what are you going to do about it if you still care for him?”

“I’m not sure. Deep down inside, I know we can’t go back. He made his choice a long time ago. I’ll have to wait and see.”

“Well just be careful, that’s all I’m saying.”

The sun lingered on the horizon as Jessa walked from the bus stop along the waterfront, past the surf lifesaving club, and into her peaceful tree-lined street. Her thoughts revolved around William as she opened the gate and unlocked her front door. She loved her cottage, and walking through the door was often the highlight of her day. But today, a sense of dread hijacked her world. In recent times, she’d felt free of him and his hold. But now… not so much.

That evening, the listlessness returned. She wanted to eat but wasn’t sure what. She wanted to watch a movie but couldn’t decide which one. She wanted to wrap herself in Egyptian cotton and sleep away her disquiet, but that wasn’t about to happen.

Jessa had returned to therapy over a year ago after finally finding a doctor who understood her needs. Doctor Cameron had said to call at any time, but lately, apart from her scheduled monthly appointment, she hadn’t felt the need for wise words of encouragement from her new psychologist.

Until today.

She rummaged in her purse for Andrea’s business card, then dialed her number and booked an early appointment for the following morning. When she eventually crawled into bed, images of William spun in her mind as she drifted off to sleep.

The following day, Jessa slept through her alarm, and by the time she reached the office suite, she questioned why she'd made the appointment in haste. After all, William was just a man from her past, and most people had to deal with past lovers at some point.

"Jessa, how are you?" Andrea offered her hand and a welcoming smile. "Come in, come in. Sit, please."

With its floor-to-ceiling windows overlooking the bay and beyond, Jessa loved Andrea's office. Situated on the second floor, it was completely private. A space for shutting out the world while compartmentalizing your life.

"I'm fine. Well, I was until yesterday."

"Go on."

"William… Do you recall I told you about him?"

"I do." Andrea glanced at her notes, then looked up, a compassionate smile warming her features. "The older lover from your late teens who left you heartbroken."

Jessa nodded. "Well, he's back in town."

"And you're worried you'll run into him?"

"Yes, and with good reason. He's rejoined Hudson Farrell as part of their management team."

"I see." Andrea sat back in her chair, thought lines tracking across her forehead. "Do you see his presence as a potential setback trigger?"

"That's why I'm here. I need coping strategies." Jessa realized she needed much more than coping strategies, but she had to start somewhere.

"A way of defusing the situation at the first meeting? Does he know you also work for Hudson Farrell?"

Jessa had asked herself that same question repeatedly. "I'm not sure. Probably not."

"So, potentially, it could also be uncomfortable for him."

"I guess."

"Any thoughts on how to manipulate the situation to your advantage?"

"You make it sound like a business deal."

"Well, that's one way of looking at it, don't you agree?"

"So you're suggesting I view it from a business standpoint?"

"Why not? How would you execute it?"

Jessa considered it for a moment. "Ignore the fact that we were once lovers. Treat him as a colleague and nothing more. After all, that's what he is now."

"Can you pull it off?"

"If I focus and hold my head high."

"You're right. There's no point in intensifying the situation by playing the poor-me, jilted-lover card. Containment is power. If he has any sense of decency, he'll feel uncomfortable too."

"How do you do that?"

Andrea gave her a knowing smile. "Do what?"

"Plant ideas in my head."

"I merely offer possibilities. It's up to you to decide what's workable. Are you nervous?"

"Extremely. But I'm older and, hopefully, wiser now."

"When will you see him?"

"We have a staff meeting tomorrow morning. I'm not looking forward to it. What if I still have feelings for him?"

"You must know whether you have feelings for him, surely. You still have a strong connection with this man."

"Why do you say that?" *What a stupid question.* She knew exactly why.

"Because his name often pops up in our sessions." Andrea hesitated, perhaps searching for a way to express herself more clearly. "You two have unresolved issues, don't you agree? Has it ever occurred to you that you and William may have a spiritual link?"

Jessa frowned. "Meaning?"

"Well, it appears there's a tension that time doesn't slacken. That silk thread you talk about."

"But was it simply a teenage crush? I may see him tomorrow and wonder what on earth I was thinking. That would be the best-case scenario. After all, what's the point in allowing your feelings for a man to develop further if he doesn't reciprocate?"

"And if you have the opposite reaction?"

"I'm not sure. He scares me a little, to be honest."

"Why's that?"

"Because we were lovers. I was young. William was my first and only. He's a gifted architect, accomplished and well thought of." Jessa paused while considering her explanation. "I'm allowing myself to feel inadequate, and I don't like it. I don't want to be manipulated."

"At least you understand feeling that way is a choice. You may want to work on that tonight. Did he seem controlling at the time?"

"No, but looking back, maybe he was a little."

"Was there any hint of sexual grooming on his part from what you recall? Any of that manipulation you mentioned?"

"No, not at all. He was loving and caring, both sexually and otherwise. So tender toward me. I don't know what it's like with other men" —Jessa warmed with a blush—"but sex with him was, um… well…"

"I get the picture. It's not every day we find a sexual partner who satisfies our needs completely, especially on our first encounter. Which is why casual sex can be ill-fated." Andrea smiled. "In my humble opinion, of course."

Jessa picked up the glass of water in front of her and took a sip. "He tried to hold himself back at first."

"So why didn't he continue to do so? He was the mature adult in the relationship."

"To be fair, I wouldn't let go. I held on for dear life. My sexual desire took over. We had two weeks of concentrated buildup, foreplay for want of a better word, and another week of intense sexual communication. That was the extent of our relationship. For him, it may have been purely sex, and now, he might find the whole thing embarrassing."

"Well, that could be your answer. He's a man, after all, and they tend to think with their appendage at the best of times. I don't say that as a sexist generalization. It's just how it is for many men. And, when you think about it rationally, the continuation of the human species does depend on it."

They shared a smile. Jessa had tried to think rationally about

William many times but never seemed able to master the process. "That's one way of looking at it."

"Is it possible he came to his senses once you left for university, realizing your relationship was problematic because of your age?"

"More than possible."

Andrea nodded. "Okay. I get that acceptance is a hard lesson to learn, but hold on to that thought. He'll soon let you know otherwise, and we'll cross that bridge if and when we come to it."

"I still don't understand what you mean about the spiritual thing."

"Well, I believe we go through our life and, arguably, more than one life with a group of beings who assist us in the lessons of knowledge, love, and healing. Is William a soulmate of yours, I wonder."

33

PURELY BUSINESS

It was 8 a.m., and although Jessa had intended to arrive at work before William, he was already in his office, talking on the phone, when she walked past the open door. His voice held the same tone, but what did she expect after five years? She'd once loved the sound of it, the way he whispered words of lust into her neck and throat. But now, its cadence filled her with unease.

She thought back to the slice of toast discarded on the kitchen island—one nibble taken from a crusty corner—and the half cup of coffee she'd poured down the sink and wished she'd forced herself to finish breakfast.

Once seated at her desk, she stretched her jaw wide to relax it, then kept the panic at bay with her four-seven-eight breathing routine. While reflecting on Andrea Cameron's comments about their relationship being problematic, Jessa mentally boxed up her feelings, taped the box shut, and labeled it PROBLEMATIC. She was young. He'd enjoyed her innocence, and for a time, he'd thought with his dick instead of his head.

A typical male reaction.

Once she'd left for Wellington, he'd come to his senses and let her go. He'd moved on, and so should she. She had no claim on him, no soulmate connection, if such a thing even existed.

William stayed in his office until their morning meeting in the boardroom. Jessa sat beside Sharon, coffee in hand, and fiddled with the pen and pad in front of her on the table as William, dressed in understated black pants and a white linen shirt unbuttoned at the neck, took the chair opposite.

When he finally met her gaze, he held it for a second. But apart from a contraction of the muscles around his strong jawline and the distinct bob of his Adam's apple, William gave no indication of their lost union. She went to offer a smile but froze at his complete indifference. Clearly, it was his way of telling her she meant nothing to him.

At the head of the table, Dan Hudson glanced over his notes before calling the meeting to order. He cleared his throat. "As you're all aware, William has agreed to return to our office after five years in Sydney." He grinned at William. "I'd like to officially welcome you into the fold. It's great to have you back."

"Thank you." William returned his smile. "It's great to be back."

"I'm pretty sure you've met everyone here, apart from our newest staff member, Jessa Reynolds."

She wanted the earth to swallow her whole and burn her to dust.

"We've already met." William's smile vanished as he held her gaze. "It's nice to see you again, Jessa."

"You too, William," she murmured. Was it her imagination, or was everybody staring at her?

Dan hesitated as he glanced between the two of them. "Oh, okay. I didn't realize you two knew each other. Right, let's get down to business."

As the meeting progressed, she felt increasingly uncomfortable in her tightening skin—as if she didn't belong to who she was—and underdressed. Her black skinny jeans, white shirt, and preppy yellow sweater stood out from the others in their black-on-black business attire, and standing out was the last thing she wanted with William Cook seated across the table.

Back at their desks, Sharon muttered under her breath, "Wow, that was uncomfortable."

"What do you mean?"

"You know exactly what I mean. The way he kept staring. Didn't you notice how his jaw clenched when he greeted you?"

"Of course I did, but I need to focus. I have a busy day."

Over the next few hours, William popped in and out of his office several times. He didn't speak as he passed Jessa's desk to wherever he was going, communicating his stance without uttering a single syllable. She'd thought their time together meant something to him. Obviously not.

Facially, he looked much the same, but his physique was more defined—heavier—like he'd spent time in the gym. She didn't have to ask herself what she once saw in him, not when it stared back at her each time she met his gaze.

Finally, as she was about to finish for the day, he addressed her. "Jessa, can I see you in my office in five?" He didn't wait for a reply.

When she knocked on his door five minutes later, William glanced up from his computer as if he didn't remember asking to see her.

"Did you want me for something?" Jessa kept her voice steady.

He leaned back in his chair and stared. She expected him to mention their affair, perhaps invite her out to dinner, or suggest going somewhere so they could talk.

"How have you been?" he asked casually.

She had no idea how best to respond. Should she tell him that he'd almost destroyed her when he left? That he'd screwed up? Scream at him for his indifference?

Instead, she simply said, "Very well. Thank you."

William nodded slowly, his eyes narrowing as he studied her. Just as slowly, he returned his focus to the screen in front of him. "I'm struggling to get my head around this new computer system. I can't find the file for the Brown job."

What?

Discomfort prickled her skin as an unfamiliar rage engulfed her. She inhaled sharply before replying. "We save all files under the street address. In case we're working with more than one client with the same surname." Jessa heard herself speak but scarcely recognized her own voice.

"Right. That's as I remember, but where are the council permits saved?" William stood and indicated for her to sit.

She swallowed hard, smoothed her hands down her jeans, then sat in his leather chair, still warm from his tight butt. As he leaned forward, invading her personal space, a fruity cologne filled her nostrils, and the mint on his breath made her realize her mouth had a slightly stale taste. Jessa closed her eyes for a moment. She longed to take a sip from the water bottle on his desk. His water bottle.

"Here, in the client's dropdown menu." Jessa clicked on a file and moved the mouse around the screen. "And there's a direct link to the council's website under each client for access to historical eDocs."

"Makes sense. Thanks. I'll take it from here."

After waiting all day for William to acknowledge her in some small way, was that it? Well, as far as Jessa was concerned, he could take *it* and shove *it* where the sun doesn't shine.

As she walked home from the bus stop around six, Jessa mentally replayed her exchange with William repeatedly, questioning why she'd chosen to work for Hudson Farrell in the first place. What was she thinking?

She let herself into the cottage, dumped her purse on the hall table, kicked off her shoes, and opened the fridge. The generous portion of lasagna, green salad, and slice of apple shortcake dusted with powdered sugar on the middle shelf made her smile. Some days, she thanked the universe for having an interfering mother with a key to her home.

Jessa yanked off her sweater and unbuttoned her blouse before even reaching the bathroom, her clothes now too tight and restrictive. Her jeans were next. She tugged down the zipper and peeled them off, taking her sensible cotton panties along for the ride.

In the shower, she buffed her skin red with a loofa, trying to ignore the heat pooling between her legs. She turned the lever to cold, leaned forward, and rested her head against the shower wall. The frigid water hit the small of her back with a sting, ran down her butt, and funneled over her thighs.

Memories of their time at the Watershed flooded her thoughts. His touch, the way he communicated his desire, and the feeling of fullness after they made love for the first time. But sitting across from him in the boardroom that morning, there'd been no suggestion of their previous intimacy. To be blatantly ignored hurt more than she'd ever imagined it would and made her question her past assessment of him.

The box marked PROBLEMATIC must remain sealed.

That Saturday, William drove out to Edgewood, a rural subdivision on a hill overlooking Carter Bay, where he owned a two-acre lot. The site had a flat building platform with unobstructed views of the coast. He'd often dreamed of building a new home but sometimes questioned whether he'd ever have the energy to do so.

Sitting in his SUV, gazing out over the Pacific, William wrestled with his thoughts. It was a perfect day for surfing, with a clear blue sky and full waves, but he wasn't in the mood for visiting his partner in surfing crime, Seb. With it being the weekend, Seb's kids would be home, and those kids were dynamite.

William tapped an index finger on the steering wheel as mindless local radio station music played on the stereo. A few minutes later, he walked toward the bank, crouched in the grass, and looked out over the bay. An image of Jessa as she stood in his office, looking nervous and cute in her preppy work clothes, invaded his mind. She'd asked him if he wanted her for something. What should he have said? That he did indeed want her for *something*, and he'd wanted her for *something* from the first day they met?

Now, he wanted her for everything.

At the same time, William needed to blame Jessa. He didn't understand why; he just did. He blamed her for being unavailable, for her youth and innocence, for his decision to move to Sydney, and for his desire to return.

What the hell had he done?

That thought stayed with him as he drove along the Eastern Pacific Highway. Ten minutes later, three boisterous children assailed him at Seb's front door.

"Would you kids go outside and let William talk to Daddy?" Jenny, Seb's wife, said as she herded the children toward the backyard while Seb offered him a beer.

William took a swig. "Thanks. I needed that."

"How was your week?" Seb asked.

"Bit like pushing shit uphill with a Matchbox toy."

Seb chuckled. "You need to get laid, mate."

"You think?"

"Absolutely. Jenny wants to hook you up with one of her friends."

"Thanks, but I'm not in the market for a fuck buddy right now."

"I hear you, but who knows, it may turn into a committed long-term relationship." Seb burst out laughing at the stunned look on William's face. "You have to get that girl out of your system one day. What's her name again?"

William watched Jenny and the kids playing in the sandbox outside and smiled. He'd always wanted kids of his own. "Who?"

"The Watershed chick. That teenager."

William cursed under his breath as he pulled his wetsuit out of his bag. "Do you remember everything I tell you when I'm hammered?"

Seb continued to grin from ear to ear. "Pretty much."

"For your information, she's no longer a teenager."

"Even so…"

William downed the rest of his beer. "Come on. Let's hit the waves before you piss me off even more."

They surfed all afternoon, and later, when Jenny insisted he stay for steaks on the grill, William agreed. Returning to an empty apartment with Jessa and Rose floating around his room like ghosts on the breeze was the last thing he needed.

34

CRITICAL STARE

Back at work the following Monday, Jessa flopped down in the chair opposite Sharon's desk and kicked off her shoes. William had taken the day off, and most of the other staff had already left, so the office was unusually quiet.

"What's up with you?" Sharon asked as she shut down her computer. "Tough day?"

"You could say that. William wants my help on a project for the architecture awards."

"Seriously? Did he ask you?"

"No, Dan did. I don't think I can handle it. I'm unsure of myself enough as it is without him scrutinizing my work with that critical stare."

"Course you can handle it." Sharon picked up her jacket and shrugged it on. "Look, you have to work together, so either resign or stick to your plan. It's a professional relationship, nothing more. Otherwise, tell Dan you can't work with William and explain why."

"I can't do that."

"Well, you've made your choice, so make the best of it. Come on, let's go for a drink on the way home. We deserve one."

The next day, William called Jessa into his office. He seemed distracted and aloof. It appeared what they once had was now a distant memory, significant to her and her alone. He outlined the brief, keeping his focus on the neatly written notes in front of him. Budgets, materials, the constraints of the building site; he covered everything.

His hands—tanned and perfectly manicured—distracted her, and as she listened to his instructions, she questioned why he'd requested her and not one of the other junior architects. Once he'd finished, William excused himself to meet with a client, and she followed him out of his office, unsure what to do next.

When Jessa left the building that afternoon, suppressed emotion lodged in her throat. She'd been teary and on edge lately. Insignificant issues bothered her. She understood the key to a successful life was maintaining a daily routine, but putting it into practice was easier said than done.

The rest of the week at the office was harder than Jessa had ever imagined as they worked together more. She wondered if William found it just as difficult but told herself the difference was he held the balance of power. She was merely a bit player in his game.

He was tough and demanding.

Darn tough and demanding.

On Friday morning, William stalked by her desk without making eye contact. "Reynolds, can I see you in my office?" he snapped.

"Oh no, what have you done, *Reynolds*?" Sharon whispered with a grin. "Sounds like you're in trouble."

Jessa forced a smile as her gut clenched. "Of course I'm not in trouble. We're all adults."

"Tell that to Mr. Grumpy Pants in there. Rather you than me, sweetie. He's an arrogant prick. But if you ask me, that's what he gets off on."

Jessa knew Sharon was making light of it but still felt uneasy. "What do you mean?"

"Young girls, studying with the master and falling at his feet."

"Stop it. He'll hear you."

"Don't care, won't care. Why would I care? It's true."

A few minutes later, Jessa hovered in William's office doorway, reluctant to go farther. "You wanted to see me?"

"Come in and close the door." His tone was curt: nothing unusual there. She glanced at the drafts of the Miller project spread out on his desk and covered in red pen.

"Please, sit." His gaze found hers. "What do you call these?" He gestured toward the plans.

"Sorry? I don't understand."

"Precisely. You haven't understood a single thing about this job, have you? Please explain your reason for presenting this substandard work."

Jessa had seen William's harsh side the first day they met and wondered if he could take it further. Now she knew. There was no equality here, not like their Watershed days. Office William was very much her superior, and he had no problem putting her in her place.

Her bravado crumpled. "I thought I had a good understanding of what was required."

"Is that so? Well, let me make myself perfectly clear. This work, for want of a better word, is inadequate in every way." His eyes never left her face as he conveyed his disappointment with a stern expression. "You've overloaded it with irrelevant content. I realize you're a new grad, for which I'll make allowances, but even so, I can't find a single redeeming feature in what you've presented here."

Jessa opened her mouth to speak.

"Please"—William raised a hand—"let me finish. Do you know what makes a successful architect, Reynolds?" He didn't wait for an answer. "There are three points all architects should consider when working on a project. I call them the three B's—brief, budget, and beauty." He leaned back in his chair without taking his eyes off her.

"First, a design must align with your client's brief. It's a crucial step in realizing their vision and, indeed, your relationship with them.

Additionally, all clients have budgets to varying degrees, and disregarding this aspect of the design process borders on disrespect."

William shifted as if to get comfortable before his next assault. "You owe it to them to work within their brief and budget, not to present pretentious crap you believe they deserve. Your designs should be fit for purpose. Understand?"

Jessa nodded without speaking. His words stung, but she fought to hold herself together.

"And finally," he continued, "effective design must flirt with beauty. Granted, beauty is in the eye of the beholder, but if you don't see the beauty in your work—its grace—you can't expect anyone else to."

"I thought my design did that."

"Really?" he snapped. "I don't see it myself." William paused, then resumed his offensive. "The Millers were clear about their requirements. Designing to particular size constraints, especially when they're small, can be challenging for any of us. But it's a skill we must master if we're to meet the needs of our clients. Not all families can live in a million-dollar mansion."

"But—"

"I gave you this project so you could show me what you're capable of." He sighed. "I was skeptical from the beginning, and you didn't disappoint. You've wasted hours of the firm's time. There's no way we can charge out for this."

"I'm sorry." Her apology was sincere, but William ignored it anyway.

"I'm not saying you won't be a successful architect one day, but it will definitely require an attitude adjustment."

Jessa couldn't answer. Tears pricked behind her eyelids, and she cursed the PMS that had plagued her lately. At any other time of the month, she would have handled this better, but not today. If William didn't soften his approach, she'd lose it, and the last thing she wanted was for him to see her cry.

"So, take these concepts," he said, his tone softening, "and rework the floor plan. If you're not proud of your effort, I don't want to see it.

Have them back on my desk first thing in the morning." He pushed the plans toward her.

Jessa's heart sank along with her ambition. "But it's almost four, and tomorrow's Saturday."

He smiled slightly and raised his eyebrows. "Welcome to the real world."

As Jessa stormed from his office, her face burning with discomfort, she was determined to do better, not because of him but in spite of him. *Grumpy bastard.*

"Are you okay?" Sharon looked up from her screen. "What did he say?"

"Nothing much. I just need a minute."

Jessa sought refuge in the restroom and splashed her face with cold water. Her eyes stung with unshed tears and irritation, but determined to remain in control, she breathed deeply, dried her hands, and returned to her desk.

"It's five thirty," Sharon said later as she slipped into her coat. "Come for a drink? Friday night and all that."

"I might put in a few extra hours."

Sharon looked concerned. "I take it he wasn't impressed?"

Jessa held up the floor plan.

"You can't be serious! He red-penned you?"

"Yep. Anyway, have a great weekend. Looks like I'll be working."

"Okay, sweetie. But don't work too hard. Our ancestors went to war to keep us free. Remember that."

"I'll try."

Jessa stayed late into the night, reworking her ideas until her shoulders ached and her headache intensified. She finally knocked on his office door just after eleven.

William looked up from his computer screen and leaned back in his chair. "You're still here, Reynolds?"

"I have the reworked floor-plan concepts."

"And so soon."

She'd not witnessed this sarcastic side of him before, and she didn't like it.

"Shall we go over them now?"

"Don't you ever sleep?" Jessa asked.

He looked at her squarely. "Not much."

"I have to go, but I'll be here at eight on Monday morning."

"Monday's a holiday, remember?"

Smug bastard. Why had she ever had feelings for him? "Of course."

He glanced at the plan. "I'm working on Monday anyhow. Could you drop off the concepts for the kitchen and bathroom? I'll need them Tuesday morning."

"I'm not sure, but I'll try."

"Here." He offered her his card. "Any problems, call me. Oh, and, Reynolds." He waited for her to meet his gaze. "Learn to walk before you run. If you insist on taking the 'Pretentious Boulevard' route, so be it. But it won't be from this office. Goodnight."

Jessa struggled to contain her indignation. "Goodnight. Oh, and, Mr. Cook." He looked up again. "I do have a Christian name. It's Jessa, remember?"

She closed his office door with a heavy hand. He had the balls to use the term "Pretentious Boulevard" when he lived on that street every single day.

She saved her tears for the drive home. The guy had officially crossed the line. A line he probably didn't even realize existed.

Trying to ignore the turmoil in his gut, William reviewed her plans for the next hour. They were good, very good. She'd made efficient use of the footprint, seemingly merging the space between public and private areas. The ground floor had the usual living areas and two bedrooms. A shared bath alcove, cantilevered into the bush surrounding the back of the property, adjoined the ensuite bathrooms. A large barn-like sliding door in the mudroom concealed utilities and additional storage, and a long island counter doubled as a dining space in the kitchen.

Outside, a modest deck flanked the front facade onto which all living areas and ground-floor bedrooms opened. A pergola sheltered part of the deck, while canvas awnings protected the external bedroom doors. The mezzanine floor housed a large bunk room at one end and a multipurpose room at the other, connected by a small bathroom built into a dormer space. She'd even planned an area off the mudroom for bikes, surfboards, and wetsuits, as well as fishing gear and the like.

Jessa had nailed it. Well, as much as she could, considering the restrictions of the brief and the land contours. But most of all, her plan was a stunning use of space. The house nestled amongst the native bush like it belonged.

William stretched upward and smiled. Sure, he'd been tough on her, but at least now she'd presented a design with architectural depth, and he was proud on her behalf.

However, he also berated himself. Had he been too harsh? He knew Jessa could perform well if he encouraged her. She had the makings of one hell of an architect, and if he had anything to do with it, that's what she would be. He reminded himself he was her boss, and therefore, he'd acted professionally.

But as she'd sat in his office, her dark eyes misting with tears, he couldn't get the younger Jessa out of his mind. Her breasts and hips were fuller now, and he imagined moving her toward him, his hands encircling her waist. He recalled the color of her nipples, her light, musky scent, her hair, silken in his fingers, and that contentment as he lay inside her.

But going back wasn't an option. To even consider a reconciliation was foolish. It would hurt too many people. But that didn't stop him wanting her. If he believed in a God, and he wasn't sure he did, was this punishment for past mistakes? Karma keeping score?

If he mentored her to reach her full professional potential, it would be his way of paying his dues. He wondered how she felt about him now. Did she regret what happened five years ago? Was it a schoolgirl crush, a "summer fling," as her grandfather had called it?

William's muddled thoughts turned to the intimacy they'd shared. Her intense desire, her innocence and inexperience. What had possessed him to pursue her? A woman half his age.

The weekend was cold for late summer, with heavy rain drifting in from the coast. Jessa stayed home and worked on the kitchen and bathroom plans, not wanting to see or be seen. When she ventured into the office on Monday afternoon, thankfully, he was nowhere in sight. William's attack might have thrown her off balance, but for once, the panic remained at bay.

The following Thursday evening, on the way home from her weekly yoga class, Jessa called into Hudson Farrell to collect a book. The building was still and soundless as she climbed the stairs to her office. Light spilled from his opened door, so she stopped out of courtesy.

"Don't mind me. I just dropped in to collect something."

"Actually, I'm glad you're here." William rocked back in his chair, pencil in hand. "I have a query about the Millers' site plan. Do you have a minute?"

Goose bumps prickled her skin. Being alone with him made her more than a little uneasy. "I have something on soon."

He flashed her a do-as-I-say look. "It won't take a second."

Jessa hesitated, formulating her response. "I'm sorry," she said eventually, "but I'm not comfortable being here after hours when there's no one else around. Can't it wait until tomorrow?"

His eyes narrowed as he studied her. "But I'm here, so you're not alone, are you?"

Jessa's eyes met his, and she sucked in her top lip, holding her emotions in check. "That's what I mean."

The frostiness in his expression shifted down a notch. "What? You're uncomfortable being here with me? You mean you don't trust me?" William shook his head. "You can't be serious."

"I'm sorry, but I'm not prepared to subject myself to a repeat of what happened last week. I have to go."

Jessa ran down the stairs and out of the building before he could respond. When she reached her car, she realized the book was still sitting on her desk.

That night, her phone rang just as she was about to go to sleep, startling her. She lay her magazine face down on the bed, wondering who'd be calling this late. She answered the call. "Hello?"

"It's William."

Jessa cursed inwardly. His voice still sent shivers down her spine. "Is everything all right? It's after ten thirty."

"It's just…" He spoke softly, his breath echoing into the receiver. "I wanted to apologize for how I handled the Miller situation."

Jessa couldn't speak, didn't trust herself to sound indifferent.

"I may have crossed the line," he continued. "I didn't mean to upset you, and I don't want you to feel uncomfortable in our working relationship."

She lay in bed, fingers tight on the receiver. "Thanks for your call, but there's no need to apologize. Perhaps you were right—an attitude adjustment was in order, so let's just leave it at that, shall we?"

She hung up before he could reply. Eliminating William Cook from her headspace was proving difficult, and a prolonged conversation was not an option.

On Sunday, the last day of March, Easter Sunday of all days, the usual one dozen French vanilla rosebuds appeared at Jessa's front door. Written on the card in neat black ink was the usual number. After everything that had happened recently, Jessa couldn't believe the insensitivity of the man. What was going on in that irrational mind of his?

Two days later, he called her at the office.

"It's William." He didn't wait for her to reply. "I won't be in today. Something's come up. Would you mind dropping off the Miller kitchen specs to me later in the day? Or if you're not comfortable doing it, ask one of the other staff."

Jessa detected a hint of sarcasm in his tone. "No, I'll do it."

"I should be home by four thirty. I'll leave a key under the mat in case I'm a few minutes late. Let yourself in."

William gave her the address, but Jessa already knew where he lived. She'd driven past many times. "Do you want me to wait?" She willed him to say no.

"Could you? That way, we can have a quick look at them together."

35

ATTENTION TO PLANS

From the street, William's apartment building looked ordinary—almost bleak—the product of an era where cost dictated everything, taking priority over form and style. Jessa took the stairs to the middle floor, where 6B greeted her with an unusually bright orange door.

The moment she stepped through the doorway, she knew she shouldn't be there. What was he thinking, asking her to his home?

The apartment's interior was perfectly proportioned, with antiques, modern sofas, and objets d'art all resting effortlessly in their place. Floor-to-ceiling windows overlooked the Pacific Ocean, and the horizontal partition between sea and sky combined with the contemporary art—each piece a journey into the artist's secret world of insight and pain—injected richness into an otherwise stark white-on-white interior.

A large surround-sound system dominated the living room. Hundreds of vinyl records and CDs lined shelves on the back wall, along with volumes and volumes of books, mainly hardcover architectural tomes, but a wide range of paperbacks as well.

The apartment had two bedrooms. The main contained a neatly made king-size bed decorated with cushions in vibrant shades of green, orange, and black. On the nightstand sat a collection of books, both fiction and non-fiction, next to a mix of cufflinks and coins, a pen, and an alarm clock. In the other bedroom, twin beds stood perfectly to attention, suited in starched white covers and topped with opulent dark red embossed velvet cushions and throws.

Double doors off the living room led to an internal study, which housed the usual office paraphernalia—an antique desk, drafting table, and books of all types—and a large oriental rug in bold tones of terracotta and navy blue overlaying the charcoal-stained hardwood floor.

In a dark corner, a cello stood on a low pedestal, glowing golden in the muted light spilling from the adjoining room. It reminded her of Kathy G.'s cello. Jessa shivered. She had no idea why William owned a cello when she assumed he didn't play. She longed to bring it to life but thought better of it, aware that she had no business snooping around in his apartment and intruding on such a private space.

It dawned on her that he lived here alone, and the loneliness of his existence matched the feeling of the interior—like a late summer's day when autumn slowly sneaks its head around the corner to take a peek. Winter's coming, but not just yet.

In the kitchen, Jessa filled a glass with water from the filter in the fridge door, then stepped through French doors onto a balcony, where lush evergreen plants stood tall in terracotta pots and stylish outdoor furniture invited human contact but appeared untouched.

It was a hazy day. She could barely make out the coastline of the cape to the northeast. As the air cooled, Jessa returned to the living room, sat on a sofa, and opened a coffee-table book featuring stunning European homes.

Her thoughts turned to the Watershed and the night William made love to her for the first time. How he gently coaxed her to climax, slowly increasing his rhythm until their release. She wondered how she'd be if they ever made love again. Would she be bold and forthright or timid and shy? She flicked through the book's pages, her mind still elsewhere. What had happened to his feelings for her? It had all seemed so perfect at the time.

The sound of the front door opening interrupted her thoughts. William strolled into the living room and flung his leather jacket on a chair. He smiled. "Sorry I'm late. Thanks for waiting."

She stood, her face warming as she checked him out. Wearing blue jeans and a white V-neck T-shirt with a tan belt and boots, he looked as handsome as ever.

"Let's sit at the dining table so we can spread out, shall we?"

"Okay."

He looked drained, like he'd been up half the night. Perhaps he'd been with another woman, making love for hours on end. The type of love they once made.

Watershed love.

"Can I get you a drink?" He opened the fridge and looked inside.

"No, I'm good. I helped myself to a water. Hope that's okay."

"Of course." William played the perfect gentleman card well, a side of him Jessa would rather not see. The cold and indifferent William helped her disregard her feelings. This version of the man, not so much.

"Now"—he pulled the tab on a can of beer and took a sip—"what have you decided for materials?"

"I've kept it simple in line with their budget. I thought I'd follow the beach feel by using light woodgrain cabinets in marine ply and off-white granite countertops."

"Good, let's take a look." As he studied the specs, deep in concentration, she noticed his jaw tighten and those hands, always the hands. The same hands that massaged her nipples between his thumb and forefinger, bringing her to mind-blowing climax, and cradled her face when he kissed her.

While they spoke in general terms about the use of materials and hardware brands, she watched William intently for any sign of interest. Occasionally, she caught a flicker of the William she'd once loved in his expression, but it was gone again in an instant. Otherwise, he remained charming but distant. "Okay, these seem fine. Should be all I need."

Jessa started when his cell phone rang. He pulled it out of his pocket. "Sorry, I should take this." Flipping open the cover, he stood and then moved to the window, his sight on Carter Bay below.

"Hi." Pause. "Yep, okay." Another pause. "I'll be there around six." His voice was almost a whisper but also tender and kind.

She stood as well, experiencing a pang of regret as she wondered if it was his girlfriend on the receiving end of that affectionate tone. He held up a hand, indicating she should wait.

"Okay, let's go to the Mexican. See you soon, bye." He flicked his phone shut. "Sorry about that. Right. I think we've covered everything." Their meeting was over. "I'll see you next week. Here, let me see you out."

Jessa followed him down the hallway. William held the door open, and as she stepped out onto the landing, he didn't say another word. The door shut behind her.

She stood for a moment in the muted light, wishing she'd had the courage to confront him… to ask the big why. But as she took the stairs down to the foyer, Jessa knew the opportunity would come soon enough and that sometimes, biding time was so very underrated.

William's office was empty when Jessa arrived at work the next day. His desk was neat and tidy as usual, nothing out of place. After checking to ensure no one was looking, she pulled a plastic bag from her purse and emptied its contents into his wastepaper basket. One dozen expensive French vanilla rosebud heads sadly sacrificed to make her point. Perhaps next birthday, he'd think twice before sending her more flowers.

He arrived not five minutes later and shut his door. She could hear him on the phone, his voice muffled through the frosted glass partition. He stayed in there for at least an hour, and she'd almost forgotten about the rosebuds when his voice boomed through the office.

"Reynolds?"

Her gut clenched as he approached. Jessa hated him calling her Reynolds, but then he probably hated her calling him Mr. Cook. It crossed her mind that she should call him Billy—just to annoy him. "Yes, Mr. Cook?"

"I'm off to Scenic Hill to check out the site for the Thompson project. I'll be away for the day."

"Okay, I'll let the others know."

He flashed a wry smile and leaned toward her. "You're coming with me," he said, lowering his voice.

Surely he wasn't serious? "But I have a full day here."

"That can wait. I need an assistant. It's a two-hour drive, so we'd best make tracks. Oh, and ask someone to empty my wastepaper basket, will you?"

"But—"

William turned and walked away before Jessa could protest. The thought of spending hours in his car, just the two of them, filled her with dread. She grabbed her running shoes from her locker, then followed him down the stairs and out the door.

Bastard.

It was a fresh April day, the sky clear blue and trees turning golden, awaiting their fall. Jessa always experienced a touch of melancholy in autumn as the warm days slipped away, and as William unlocked his late-model Lexus SUV, that feeling intensified.

She felt like his prisoner.

Kidnapped.

Neither of them spoke as they headed north past the airport.

"What kind of music do you like?" he finally asked without taking his eyes off the road.

"Anything. I'm not bothered."

He pushed a control on the dash, filling the confined space with harsh, head-banging sound. "Is this okay?"

Jessa stared straight ahead. "Fine," she lied. But within minutes, Randy Crawford's version of "Rainy Night in Georgia"—one of her favorite songs—floated from the speakers. She didn't want to appear uncomfortable in his company, to give him the satisfaction, so she sat back, took a deep breath of courage, and hummed along softly.

"You like this song?"

"It's one of my favorites. I love this version."

"You're familiar with it?" He sounded surprised.

"Randy Crawford. Such an incredible voice."

"I agree."

Jessa soon relaxed, losing herself in the music. The Corrs, Phil Collins, Lighthouse Family, Gloria Estefan—it was as if he'd hand-picked the tracks especially for her.

William followed the coastal road all the way. As the day warmed, the waves put on a show, building from a gentle swell to an impressive display of strength. And despite this part of the Pacific being known for its undertows and rough surf, Jessa longed to stand barefoot on the shore, to feel the sand give way beneath her feet.

Around midday, they drove into a small provincial town and parked outside a run-down bakery. "Let's get lunch. We can eat once we reach the site."

The thought of eating at the site unsettled her. At least if they ate at the bakery, they'd have company. But he was the boss.

"Are you okay? You're a little pale." His concern sounded sincere but was unwarranted. She didn't want him worrying about her.

"I'm feeling a bit carsick, but food always helps."

"And ginger beer, I find."

Out of the car, William rested a hand on the small of her back as he ushered her inside. Why did he do that? Act like he had the right to touch her?

The variety of food on offer surprised her. Cakes, pastries, freshly baked bread rolls, and bagels filled the display cabinet. Alongside this, a gourmet twist on the humble beef pie, made with thick layers of flaky pastry, sat in the warmer. Delicious.

Jessa opted for a soft bread knot filled with rare roast beef, horse-radish, onion marmalade, and baby cos. William chose the same. She grabbed a bottle of water and went to pay.

"I'll get this." William stepped up beside her, his wallet open.

"Please, it's fine."

"I've dragged you out of the office for the day, so the least I can do is shout you a sandwich on the company credit card."

"Thank you," she murmured.

He motioned to the cabinet behind the counter as the server bagged their rolls. "And two ginger beers, please."

The building site was ten minutes farther north. As William drove through a galvanized farm gate and up the hill to a flat building platform overlooking the Pacific coast in a one-eighty-degree sweep, her imagination clicked into gear.

"Pretty special, isn't it?"

Jessa noticed him relax. "Amazing."

"Our clients bought this land about ten years ago, but the council wouldn't give consent to build," he said as he opened the back of his SUV and pulled out two folding chairs.

"Why?"

"The farm already has a substantial home, and they don't want the coastal road littered with too many dwellings. That's the official line, anyway. But they've relaxed the rules recently. Our challenge is to design something in harmony with the landscape. Once we have a concept, the powers that be will reconsider the consent."

William offered her a chair. "Let's eat first. I'm starving."

Once she sat, he sank into his seat and offered her a ginger beer before unwrapping his lunch. Even though she couldn't make out the direction of his gaze through the mirrored reflection of his aviators, she knew he was watching her. He ate slowly: she remembered that about him. He'd made love slowly too.

They ate in silence. The food was delicious, as was the cool soda, and she hadn't realized how hungry she was. But she was often hungry. Jessa wasn't sure whether it was physical hunger or the enjoyment she gained from eating. She suspected the latter. But while some of her friends joked that they enjoyed a slice of New York cheesecake better than sex, she wouldn't go that far.

Jessa's preference to a New York cheesecake sat before her, dressed in a black high-necked sweater, his shoulders broad under its woolen rib. He stood and removed the outer layer to reveal a mid-gray Henley shirt open at the neck.

She glanced away, then back. His charcoal jeans fitted perfectly around the butt and tensed boldly at the base of his fly. Jessa's physical need overtook sensibility as she recalled the essence of him. Did he ever dream of making love to her, as she dreamed of making love to him?

"I saw your résumé the other day," William said casually. "You struggled a bit the first two years at Victoria."

What? She didn't know if his words were a question or a statement. "How do you know that?"

"Your transcripts are in your file."

"Yeah, well, I had stuff going on. Anyway, why were you even looking?"

"I was helping Dan with the salary review."

She shot him a coy smile. "Ah, so it's you I have to thank for my minuscule pay rise?"

"I tried my best, believe me. You're worth more, in my opinion, but ultimately, it's not my call."

"Thanks anyway. But working life isn't only about the money."

William removed his glasses to reveal a soft smile in his eyes. "I agree. But you've shown a marked improvement over the past month."

She turned away. Sipped her drink. "Thank you. That means a lot."

They sat finishing their lunch, an uneasy silence hanging between them.

"Right, let's get to work." William's voice broke into her thoughts. "I'll grab some pegs."

Jessa struggled to look at him—not because she didn't want to, but because she did. She longed to hold him, let her simmering desire boil over, and make love in the early April sunshine. She wanted him to admit he'd made a massive mistake, one he planned to rectify.

But he didn't say a word.

"I might change out of these heels."

"You think?" He flashed a smile but said nothing more.

For the next couple of hours, they took levels, plotted the sun's movement, and discussed floor-plan options. William's tidy sketches came to life as he explained his choices. Occasionally, when he leaned in close, she could feel his energy and smell his William scent. It unsettled her. Otherwise, he was ever the aloof businessman. Sanctimonious didn't quite fit, but she struggled to find a more suitable word.

"Do you want to drive back?" William offered his car keys.

"What? You mean drive your car?"

His smile tipped her up, making her recall earlier times when he'd smiled at her like they belonged together. "Yes, drive my car. I don't mind."

"No, I couldn't do that." She grabbed her water bottle and took a swig. Drive his car? He had to be joking.

"Well, tell me if I need to pull over at any time." His smile slowly faded. "Jess?" He waited until he had her attention. "Are you doing okay?"

He hadn't called her Jess since their last day at the Watershed, and what had once been an intimate diminutive now felt like a punch to the guts. She swallowed past the lump in her throat. "I'll just run down and open the gate."

William strolled over the building platform once more, stopping at each corner peg for no reason other than to put space between him and Jessa.

He returned the chairs to the car, ran one last gaze over the site, and then drove down the hill to the gate, admonishing himself for almost crossing the line Tom had drawn more than five years before.

She hid behind her sunglasses, but even though he couldn't see into her soul, he realized calling her Jess had made an impression. He had no idea what she thought of him. He didn't know her as an adult. On reflection, he hadn't really known her as a teenager either. Their time together had been a prism inside a bubble. Real life held no significance in their Watershed world.

They traveled south with the afternoon traffic, his emotions all over the place as she sat beside him, her focus on the countryside beyond the passenger window.

"I have to make a quick detour if you don't mind," he said as he turned onto the highway. "To pick up my surfboard."

"Sure."

"My friend Seb and I planned to go surfing this afternoon." He glanced sideways. "But since you insisted on coming along, I postponed."

Smug bastard. "I'm happy to take a walk along the beach if you cover for me at work."

"I don't need to cover for you. Remember, I'm your boss." As they made eye contact, he recalled her heat under his touch all those years ago and smiled.

She turned away. "Of course."

Just before the Rata River Valley signpost on the right, William turned left and drove down a gravel road flanked by a native broadleaf hedge. He pulled to a stop just as Seb opened the front door.

"Wow. What an amazing house! Would it be okay if I used their bathroom?"

"Of course." William opened his door. "Come on, I'll introduce you."

Out of the car, Seb slapped William on the back, then made a beeline for Jessa's hand as William introduced them.

"Nice to meet you, Jessa. So, you work for this dude?" Seb looked her up and down, a wide grin on his face. "Rather you than me."

He turned to William. "So, are we catching a few waves?"

"Not today. I just came to pick up my board."

"Come on, man, half an hour. Look at that water."

William glanced at Jessa.

"I honestly don't mind," she said. "A walk would do me good."

"Okay. Why not?"

While they changed, Jessa used the bathroom and then sat on the deck, gazing out at the ocean. She stood when the men reappeared. As they approached, William attempted to pull up his wetsuit zipper, but it jammed halfway up his back.

"Here, let me." She reached over to tug it free.

"Thanks." He let his sight linger a little too long before grabbing his board.

"Help yourself to apples off the tree," Seb called back to Jessa before they disappeared down the track to the beach.

As soon as they were out of earshot, Seb turned to William. "What the fuck are you up to?"

"What do you mean?"

"With the Divine Miss J."

"We drove to Scenic Hill this morning for a site visit. Purely work related."

"Is that so?"

William studied the waves and said nothing.

"That's not what it looks like to me," Seb continued.

"We're working. I told you."

"Yeah, like when she zipped up your wetsuit. Since when did you need help with your zipper, you pussy?" He slapped William on the back and laughed. "The only work you're doing right now is trying to get into her panties. Am I right, or am I right?"

William laughed back at him. "Piss off."

"I love getting under your serious skin," Seb teased. "You're still into her."

"What makes you say that?"

"Come on, mate. It's me. No bullshit between friends, right?"

William sighed. "Right."

"Not that I blame you. I'd so go there if I were single."

"Really? Some friend you are."

"I'm joking." Seb glanced back to Jessa, now walking along the beach. "I knew she was young, but when you meet her in person, it puts it into perspective. Young and attractive."

William nodded.

"So how old was she when you met?" Seb asked.

"Eighteen."

"That's crazy. Look, I know it's none of my business, but you need to sort your shit out before some other guy claims her. I bet she'd have you back in a heartbeat."

"What makes you say that?"

"The way she looks at you. Like there's a hundred things she wants to say, but she's afraid to voice them."

"I can't go back."

"Why not? Because of the age thing?"

"That and… It's complicated."

"Aren't all relationships with the opposite sex?" Seb shook his head. "You're one stubborn bastard when you want to be."

"Yeah, but that's the problem. I don't want to be, and it's doing my head in."

"How the hell do you work with her?"

"Let's just say cold showers are highly overrated."

They paddled out, William losing himself in his memories of their lovingly innocent coupling at the Watershed. How would their love-making differ now she was older and, he assumed, more sexually experienced? The thought of it drove him to distraction.

Some days lately, he could think of little else.

While chewing on her apple, Jessa watched the men dive under the water and surface with a shout at the first shock of cold. As William paddled through the breakers, she wondered why he'd never talked to her about their past. Was he trying to protect her or just a darn coward? She'd thought he'd at least mention the rosebuds, but that hadn't come up either.

The coastal clouds had gained strength and now covered much of the afternoon sky. Back from her walk, Jessa spread Seb's rug over the soft sand and watched as he ran up the beach toward her.

"How was it out there?" she asked.

Seb picked up his towel. "Freakin' freezing, but great. William wants another few minutes. Do you surf?" He radiated an unmistakable sensual energy beneath his smile, and Jessa glanced away.

"I've tried a couple of times. I loved it, but I seriously need lessons."

Seb sat with his wetsuit undone to the waist. Seawater dripped from his long hair down his neck and chest, and he smiled as he watched William paddle in. "I can give you a lesson if you want."

"Um, thanks, but I'm a total novice."

"My beautiful wife, Jenny, and I surf together most weekends. We give friends lessons occasionally."

If he hadn't mentioned being married, Jessa would have sworn Seb was hitting on her. "Okay, thanks. I'd love a lesson."

"Get William to bring you up next time he comes."

"Um, or not. William's my boss. He wouldn't want me tagging along."

"Right, if you say so."

Jessa sensed Seb's gaze on her as she watched William carry his surfboard across the wet sand.

"Okay, call me anytime you're up for it. I promise I won't throw you to the sharks."

"Thanks. Maybe in the summer." Jessa wondered if he knew about their past relationship. Was William the type to confide in his friends? "How long have you known him?"

"Since university. He's been a good friend to me over the years." Seb looked at her again. "He's a great guy. A little tormented, but I guess you know all about that."

Finally, an unmistakable reference to the "Jessa and William" saga.

"Hey, what are you two talking about?" William peeled his wetsuit down his chest, looking happy and content. Jessa struggled with the sight of his now half-naked form, a form she no longer had permission to touch.

She shielded her eyes from the sun and stared up at him. "Just stuff."

William chuckled as he scooped up his towel. "Don't believe a word he says. He's full of shit."

"If you say so, old man," Seb teased. "I was just telling Jessa how you need friends like me."

"Why's that? So you can convince me to skip work to go surfing?"

"Yeah. I challenge you to live in the moment."

A smile remained on William's face. "I'll get changed, and then we'd better head back to reality. Pick me an apple, will you, Jess?"

She held her breath as a wave of possessive sadness swept over her for Watershed William and the half-naked William now standing before her. *Jess.* "Sure."

Their drive south mirrored the one north. William's choice of music—mellowing as the day faded into dusk—expressed her innermost thoughts through notes and verse. If he didn't like a song, he'd flick his thumb over the control in instant dismissal.

As they approached the airport, Jessa instigated a conversation.

"What does Seb do, apart from surfing?"

"He's an environmental scientist. Works in consultancy. They have three kids, so that keeps him busy too."

"Their home's amazing. Did you design it?"

"I did. We bought land at the same time, but mine's on Edgewood Place, overlooking the bay."

"I love that area. Are you building there?"

"One day. The lot's two acres, but I have a few dreams to chase first." William glanced at her but didn't smile. "I'll show you sometime. I'd welcome your ideas."

When they reached the CBD, it was almost six. Jessa pondered his "chasing dreams" comment, realizing how much of our lives we spend doing just that. As the familiar intro of "Here We Are" flowed from the car stereo, she leaned back on the headrest.

"Do you know this song?" William kept his attention on the road.

She paused, feeling the heat between them. "Not the Spanish version."

"It's Portuguese."

Jessa briefly closed her eyes, letting the English words flow over the unfamiliar in her head. *Smug bastard. Why's he doing this?*

"I'm meeting friends for dinner down at the waterfront if you want to join us." William didn't take his gaze off the road as he offered the invitation. His tone was casual, but she questioned the intent.

"I have to get home, but thanks anyway."

Days drifted into weeks, and apart from the odd smile, William seldom offered any warmth in Jessa's direction. She sensed his stare occasionally but nothing more, and it dawned on her that she didn't really know him.

Who was he?

What did he feel?

What made him tick, his heart sing?

Winter seemed bleaker than usual that year. It was the wettest July on record, and Jessa felt like her life was trickling away with the rain. On a particularly miserable day, William was waiting for her when she returned from lunch.

"Jessa, are you free to look at a job?"

"I need to finish some working drawings. I'd hoped to get a clear run at them this afternoon."

"They can wait. Meet me downstairs in five."

Jessa sighed as she glanced over at Sharon and shook her head.

"What's with that man?" Sharon asked. "He treats you like you're his private PA."

"Yep. But he's the boss."

"Puh-leeze. This has nothing to do with the fact he's your boss. He's an egotistical bastard, and in my opinion, the ego doesn't match the package."

Despite her best efforts not to, Jessa giggled. Sharon always managed to add a spark to her day. "Oh, it does! Believe me, his ego and package match perfectly."

Jessa could still hear Sharon's laughter as she left the office, William right behind her. Some days, she wondered how she'd survive at Hudson Farrell without her.

"What's Sharon laughing about?"

Jessa smiled coyly. "Just a private joke."

William looked at her and frowned. He obviously suspected they were discussing him.

As Jessa clicked her seatbelt into place, William shot her a sideways glance, and memories of their intimate time together resurfaced, making her shiver.

He reached for the temperature control. "Are you warm enough?"

She smiled. "I'm fine, thank you."

Jessa followed William onto the building site, looking cute in her hard hat and Doctor Martens and, as usual, catching the attention of the men on the job, young and old alike.

"Who's the eye candy in the frock 'n' Docs?" one of the apprentices asked when she headed up the stairs to check out the view.

Tommo, the site foreman, shook his head.

"You mean Jessa?" William asked.

"Yeah, the girl. She's gorgeous."

"She's a junior architect from our office," William offered.

"So, is she single?"

"I have no idea. Why's that?"

"I might ask her out." Reece kept his focus on Jessa as she surveyed the build. "She looks like my type."

The two older men grinned at each other.

"Don't you think you're punching above your weight with that one?" Tommo asked.

"No way. Maybe she could teach me a thing or two, talk cougar to me." He turned to William. "Shit, sorry, mate. She's not your girlfriend, is she?"

"We work together, nothing more."

"Yeah, guess she's way too young for you, mate. Can you hook me up with her number?"

"Just ask her," William said. "She doesn't bite."

"What I wouldn't give to—"

“Reece, that’s enough,” Tommo said. “Back to work.”

As they drove back to the office, William made casual conversation before broaching the subject of Reece.

“What were you and Reece talking about?”

“How good he is with his hands.” She shifted in her seat. “Actually, he asked me on a date, but I told him it would be unprofessional.”

William glanced her way. “So the fact he’s only eighteen had nothing to do with your refusal?”

“Eighteen? Really? He looks a lot older. He so well-built.” She looked out the passenger window. “Anyway, age is merely a mathematical equation once we reach adulthood.”

“Maybe, but he’s not an adult at eighteen, is he? Even if he thinks he is. Eighteen is such an impressionable age.”

“You’re right about that,” she murmured.

36

REDUNDANT WORDS

Jessa glanced up from her work as Dan Hudson sank onto the chair in front of her desk. She enjoyed having him as a boss. His face sported a perpetual smile, today being no exception.

"Are you okay?" she asked. "You look worn out."

"It's been a busy week. I need a holiday."

"You should take some time off, then."

"You sound just like the wife. Anyway"—he held up a large envelope—"drop these drawings off to William on the way home, would you? Leave half an hour early. That way, you won't have to claim overtime."

Jessa smiled at him. "I'd never claim overtime for that. What do you take me for?"

"I know you wouldn't. You're a good kid."

She left early as instructed and drove to William's apartment, Carole King confiding in her through the car stereo. As the music restored her balance, Jessa contemplated William's initial assessment of her work. How had he put it? She needed an "attitude adjustment." He gave his opinion freely, but she didn't care for his approach and often felt inadequate around him.

His bright orange door still seemed out of character. She'd never imagined William in terms of orange. To her, he was more of a "light gray with a smudge of charcoal and just a flush of red" kind of guy. The colors of a moody sky, like his paintings at the Watershed.

Four, seven, eight. Knock.

William opened the door, his expression curious but mood convivial. "Jessa, to what do I owe the pleasure?"

Pleasure?

"Dan asked me to drop this off." She offered the envelope. "He said he'll call you later."

"Come in, please. I want to talk to you about something."

As he held the door wide in a welcoming gesture, Jessa hesitated. Some days, she struggled to break free of the tug. Today was such a day.

She reluctantly followed William into the living room, intensely aware of his scent and presence. He looked casually stylish in soft blue jeans teamed with a plaid shirt in muted shades of navy and red with off-white as the accent. His face, prickled with a neat stubble, was reminiscent of his manner—precise with an edge of scratch.

She inhaled deeply, held it, and exhaled with purpose while removing her jacket. He stared as she glanced around the room.

"Have you heard the news?" he asked.

"What news?"

William smiled softly. "We've received a triple-A nomination for the Miller project."

"Are you serious?"

"I am. Well done."

"That's… I don't know what to say."

He walked over to the fridge. "Can I get you a drink?"

"Just a water, thanks."

"Come on. This nomination is a big deal, and you did an excellent job. Have a glass of wine with me?" He studied her. "Or if you're too uncomfortable being here," he added with a hint of irony, "that's fine."

Determined not to let him get to her, Jessa accepted his offer. "I'll have a Riesling if you have some."

"I'm pretty sure I do. So, you like your wine fruity and a little on the sweet side?"

"I like anything sweet and fruity." As soon as she said it, her cheeks heated. The last thing she wanted was for him to think she was flirting.

William poured two glasses of wine and arranged cheese, grapes, sun-dried tomatoes, and pâté on a platter, along with a selection of crackers. It took her back five years to their Watershed days. "Let's sit outside."

The evening sun sat solidly on the horizon, but it was suddenly cool on the balcony.

"Are you warm enough?" he asked as she sat in the offered chair.

His concern reminded her of times past. He could be caring, almost gallant, but he was also an arrogant bastard when the mood took him. "Yes, I'm fine."

"Here's to you, Jessa Rose"—he raised his glass—"and a job well done."

She sipped, hoping the alcohol would help steady her nerves. It didn't. "Thank you." She wondered why he'd use her middle name and how he'd even remembered it. He'd called her Jessa Rose at the Watershed too.

"Look, I realize we got off to a bit of a shaky start, but it's all worked out fine in the end. There's another job coming up that might suit you. It's a farm cottage, but a decent-sized one."

"Sounds good."

He offered her the platter. "Here, please."

Jessa gulped another mouthful of wine and slid forward in her chair. "Thanks for the drink, but I'd better go." She set her unfinished Riesling on the small side table.

A muscle in William's jaw contracted for a split second. "Of course. Thanks for dropping off that file."

"No problem."

He followed her inside. "Jess, wait…"

She turned to face him. "Look, William, I don't think it's appropriate for us to spend time together socially under the circumstances."

Not once in the past four months had he mentioned their Watershed summer, and because he hadn't, she wasn't comfortable bringing up the past either.

"Really? And what circumstances are those?"

She'd had enough. He was pissing her off and if she stayed any longer, she'd really lose her cool. "It doesn't matter."

The apartment was deathly quiet as she crossed the room and opened the door. William cleared his throat and held out her jacket when she glanced back at him. "Don't forget this."

She snatched the jacket and stormed down the hall, leaving him standing at his orange door, alone.

By the time she reached her car, her face was flushed with what—anger, desire, or both?

"Screw you, William Cook," Jessa muttered as she drove along Seaview Road. She parked near the surf lifesaving club, her favorite stretch of City Beach, and watched the waves ebb and flow as her thoughts did the same. Couples holding hands strolled along the boardwalk while parents sat at picnic tables, eating fish and chips out of paper as their children darted back and forth between the water and the playground.

By the time she reached her cottage, the sky was somber, and the air had chilled dramatically. Inside, she dumped her purse and keys on the hall table, kicked off her shoes, and flopped down on the sofa.

Home.

Jessa loved being at home, that sense of walking into peaceful solitude at the end of a busy day. But tonight, nothing seemed to fit.

She jumped when her phone rang, secretly hoping it was William calling to apologize.

"Hi, sweetie." Sharon's voice beamed down the line. "Are you joining us or what?"

Shit! "Maybe not tonight. It's been a long day."

"But my friend Jimmy wants to meet you. Come on, we're going to NahBar."

Jessa sighed at the thought of making small talk in a rowdy bar, but she'd canceled the week before as well. "Okay, I'll meet you when… around seven?"

"Perfect."

When Jessa walked through the door half an hour later, the bar overflowed with the usual Friday night suit set, and for a second, she wondered why she'd agreed to come.

"Jessa, Jessa," Sharon called out as she waved from a table near the window.

As she approached their group, one of the guys stood to greet her. "Hi. You must be Jessa. I'm Jimmy Charlton."

"Hi, Jimmy. Nice to meet you." She offered her hand, but he kissed her on the cheek instead.

"Can I get you a drink?" he asked.

"Thanks. I'll have a house Riesling."

"One house Riesling coming up." He made his way to the bar, glancing back once or twice.

"Well, what do you think?" Sharon whispered loudly. "Any spark?"

Jessa laughed. "I've barely said two words to him. It's too early for fireworks."

"I thought you believed in love at first sight."

"That's lust at first sight, and I'm not feeling it. But he's a good-looking guy, and a bit of eye candy is always a bonus."

At first, she wasn't interested in the Jimmy Charlton package. He was just another boy in a suit who Sharon was trying to hook her up with. But as the night progressed, Jessa gradually warmed to his quirky personality and easy-going style. Also, apart from Reece, the randy apprentice, Jessa hadn't met anyone lately who seemed interested. And Jimmy Charlton was definitely interested.

She left the table to use the restroom, and when she returned, ready to call it a night, Jimmy had the same idea.

"Let's get out of here," he said. "I need some fresh air."

He ushered her out onto the street. "Okay, where to? Back to your place for sex and hot chocolate?" he asked with a grin.

She threw him a bemused frown.

"Sorry. That was a bad joke. I've had one too many beers."

"Come on," Jessa said. "I'll drive you home."

They sat in her car at the beach for a while, watching people stroll along the boardwalk as they talked. Just as she was about to suggest they make tracks, Jimmy draped an arm around her shoulders. "Is it okay if I kiss you?"

She nodded.

He didn't waste another second before exploring her mouth with an overly enthusiastic tongue.

Jessa felt nothing.

Yet, on the drive home from his apartment, she wondered if she could settle for someone like Jimmy. After all, what more did she want in a man? He was charming, sweet, and he looked good—both physically and on paper. And although the spark had failed to ignite initially, perhaps, if she fanned it a little, it just might.

37

AWARDS

The annual regional architecture achievement awards were held each year on the first Saturday of July, and this year, the Miller project had received two nominations. If it won either category, it would progress to the nationals later in the year.

The entire Hudson Farrell team was expected to attend, and as she ate lunch with Sharon at an inner-city café the weekend before, the thought of it had Jessa's stomach tied in knots.

"What are you wearing to the awards dinner?" Sharon sipped her coffee.

"I'm not sure. Honestly, I don't even want to go. I hate being the center of attention."

"Sorry to burst your bubble, missy, but you won't be the center of attention. If you win, William will accept the award on behalf of the firm."

Jessa waited while the server cleared their plates. "But I did most of the work."

"I agree. But he's the name, and you're just the pretty face. It's all about spin."

Jessa grinned. "So does that mean I don't have to attend?"

"Absolutely not." Sharon picked up her purse from the floor and freshened her lipstick. "Come on, let's go shopping."

Jessa drained her cup and hurried after her. "What do people wear to these events?"

Sharon dragged her into a small boutique full of expensive outfits. "Black tie and gorgeous gowns. So I hope your credit card's ready and willing."

"No to the credit card. I'm broke." Jessa loved to shop but was saving for a home, so she never had spare cash and made do with a wardrobe of mix-and-match basics for work. The rest of the time, she lived in jeans and tops or sweaters. "I guess I could use my 911 credit card."

"What on earth is a 911 credit card?"

"It's for emergencies. Mum and I share it, and she pays the bills."

"Lucky you." Sharon held up a little black lace dress with a thin leather belt tied off center in a small bow. "What about this? It's gorgeous."

"Yes, but it's knee length."

"As long as it's elegant, it doesn't matter." She glanced at the tag. "And it's on sale."

Jessa tilted her head to the side. "I don't generally wear all black."

"Add some colored heels, and you're good to go." Sharon held up another dress. "I've been meaning to ask," she said, frowning at the price tag. "How's it going with Jimmy?"

"Okay. He's pretty intense. But he's sweet."

"So… are you spending much time together?"

"Maybe."

"Maybe? What do you mean by that?"

"Actually, we've been out a few times." Jessa flicked through another rack of gowns; however, nothing took her fancy. "But we're taking it slowly, so don't go jumping to any conclusions."

"Would I do that? Are you going to try that dress on or not?"

"Yes, I think I will."

As Jessa stood opposite the fitting room mirror, that "special dress" feeling washed over her. That feeling every woman gets when she slips on a dress and knows it's made just for her.

Sharon nodded her approval. "That's the one. Love it."

"What about the neckline? It's so wide. Do I need to add some bling?"

"Just earrings. What do you think? Less is more. Let's look at shoes. Red would be fabulous."

Jessa remembered the blood-red heels hidden away on the top shelf of her closet. "I have shoes. In fact, I have the perfect pair."

Jessa spent all Saturday afternoon getting ready. The awards dinner was a special occasion, so she wanted to look her best. The fact she'd be socializing with William had nothing to do with it. She had the firm's image to uphold, or so she kept telling herself.

William arrived late, commanding her attention in a perfectly tailored, thin-lapelled charcoal tuxedo. She'd never seen him formally dressed, and William Cook looked better in a tux than any other man she knew. He passed two empty chairs, approaching Jessa.

As he sat, his leg brushed against hers. The hairs on her nape lifted, and she clenched her thighs together. William looked at her and smiled. "Jessa."

She shyly smiled back. "William." She could smell his cologne. Different from what he wore to work—understated, yet elegant.

Besides a few pleasantries about the food, William ignored her throughout the meal. He mainly talked to Dan, sitting to his right, while she focused on his silver cufflinks, fascinated by the black onyx centers embossed with a dark red treble clef.

When the Miller project won the Energy Star Award for excellence in energy efficiency, William got up to give his acceptance speech.

"Designing sustainable dwellings that are both aesthetically pleasing and energy efficient has been a longtime passion of mine." He paused, skimming through his notes, before setting them down. "I'd love to take credit for this design, but in this instance, the recognition belongs to the talented and, may I add, recently graduated Jessa Reynolds." He stared straight at her, smiling like the proud parent of a child about to receive an award at a school prize-giving ceremony. "I'd like to invite Jessa to accept this award on behalf of Hudson Farrell."

The audience clapped and cheered as she stood. Heat flushing her face, she passed tables filled with her peers and negotiated the stage stairs in her blood-red stilettos. William pecked her on the cheek and guided her toward the microphone with a hand on her elbow.

"Thank you." Jessa's voice took on a vibrato of its own. "I'd like to thank my colleagues at Hudson Farrell, especially William Cook, for assisting me with this design. This award belongs not only to our team but also to everyone involved in bringing the project to life and, most importantly, our clients, Mr. and Mrs. Miller, who entrusted us with their dream of a sustainable beach house. I also wish to thank the contractors, sub-trades, and hardware specialists who were with us every step of the way. Thank you."

As everyone clapped again, Jessa couldn't wait to leave the stage.

"What a nice touch," William said as he guided her down the stairs with one hand on her elbow. "Remembering to thank the clients and tradespeople."

"Why did you do that?" she hissed once they were out of view of the stage. "Don't you ever do that to me again!"

"What? What did I do?" His hand remained firmly in place.

Jessa pulled away. "Put me on the spot like that."

"It's your design, so you deserve the recognition," he said sternly. "And besides, I wanted to give you the chance to show off that exquisite dress and those killer heels."

She threw her hands in the air. "Just don't… don't even talk to me right now."

They returned to their table in silence, and as he pulled out Jessa's chair, he smiled at her. She sat, her cheeks burning like a beacon beneath her carefully applied makeup as William accepted congratulations from the team.

"You said I wouldn't have to go up," she whispered to Sharon once the speeches were over.

"Seems William had other ideas. You should have seen him staring as you walked to the stage," she whispered back. "That guy is seriously fascinated with you."

"Don't worry, I felt it."

"Your outfit looks fantastic. Where did you get those stilettos? I've never seen a color like it."

Jessa relaxed slightly. "They were a gift. From a guy."

Sharon flashed her a huge grin. "No way. You can't be serious."

Jessa winked. "It's only the second time I've worn them. The first time, they never touched the ground."

A knowing look flitted across Sharon's face. "Well, now it's all becoming clear. He has interesting taste. I'm beginning to see him in a whole new light."

"Stop it. Now pass me that wine."

Jessa watched as William, looking impossibly handsome and very much the consummate professional, worked the room. Having never witnessed him in a social situation before, his party persona surprised her. She'd always considered him an introverted loner, but he had many contacts at this gathering and appeared genuinely charming and attentive.

As she mingled, she received just as many compliments about the color of her shoes as she did her design award.

Did she wish she hadn't worn them? Of course.

Did they make her feel special? Of course.

The light drizzle from earlier turned into persistent rain as Jessa waited outside the cloakroom. When she noticed William approach, she looked away.

"How are you getting home?" His hot breath tickled her neck, and the slight smell of alcohol now mingled with his cologne.

"I'm waiting for a taxi." His closeness unnerved her. She desperately needed some fresh air and distance from her boss, but when she moved out to the portico and stood in the taxi line, William followed.

"I'll take you home, otherwise you'll be waiting for ages. I've only had a couple of drinks." He didn't wait for her reply. "Stay here while I get my car."

Jessa cursed under her breath. She wanted to go home to bed, but getting a ride with William wasn't her intention. It was still pouring when he pulled up in his Lexus.

He leaned over and opened the passenger door. "Hop in. Quick. Before you get soaked."

She climbed in, leaving her safety net behind. "I'm at number seventeen—"

"Yes, I know where you live. I drive past your place most days on my way to the gym." He flicked on the stereo.

Jessa frowned as the first few notes of a song filled the car. "What's this song?"

"It's the Judy Collins version of a Beatles classic."

"'In My Life'?"

"You know it?"

Jessa regretted engaging him in conversation. It had been insensitive of her to wear the shoes, and now, here they were, making small talk about music as if those shoes had never touched her feet before and he'd never touched her soul.

"I'm not sure. I guess, but I haven't heard this version. It's so hauntingly beautiful."

"It is."

Jessa leaned back on the headrest, closed her eyes, and lost herself in the song as if William didn't exist. It made him smile.

He pulled into her driveway as the last note played. A late-model Subaru sat next to her Honda in the carport, but there were no lights on inside the house. He left the engine running and the headlights on. The windscreen wipers swished back and forth as he went to open his door.

"It's pouring. Please don't get out." She held her clutch purse close to her chest. "Thanks for the ride."

He sat back in his seat and looked at her. "My pleasure. I'll see you in a week."

She turned to face him. "Are you going somewhere?"

"To Melbourne for work. I fly out tomorrow afternoon."

"Well, enjoy your trip. Goodnight."

William watched her run to the front porch, the heels of her blood-red "fuck-me" shoes barely making contact with the path. He sat for a while, waiting for her to unlock the door and turn on the lights. She didn't once look back.

Raw sexual energy sparked uncomfortably around him, just as it had when she'd walked onto the stage. He wondered why she'd worn those shoes. To prove a point? That she'd moved on and was perfectly happy without him? Or did she want him just as much as he wanted her?

Driving home along the port road, William pondered the likelihood of a renewed relationship with Jessa. A secret affair was no longer his style. He wanted a wife and kids and a solid, sustainable home on his lot on Edgewood Place, overlooking the bay with lime trees and lavender bordering the driveway.

He wanted Jessa.

As he pulled into his apartment parking space, his cell phone rang. He answered the call but didn't even have a chance to say hello before a panicked voice whispered, "William…"

"Jess, are you okay?"

"I… I'm…"

"Jess, breathe slowly." He backed out onto the street. "I'll be there in a few minutes. Stay on the line until I get there."

"William!"

"Find a paper bag. Breathe in and out slowly. I'm almost there."

"Okay," she whispered.

He found her sitting on the hallway floor, breathing into a paper bag, her face smudged with mascara and tears, and the black dress and red shoes puddled in a heap beside her.

"Hey," he soothed. "It's okay, Jess. It's okay." William knelt and held her hands, trying not to focus on her silky teddy and pull-up stockings.

"I'm sorry. I shouldn't have called but didn't know what else to do." Jessa sobbed, unable to catch her breath. "I'm scared and didn't want to wake Mum and Dad."

William took hold of her pinkies, letting his energy infuse her. "It's okay. I'm glad you called."

Her scent intoxicated him as they sat together on the cold hardwood floor, lost in silence. He wished she were his, like before. If she ever was.

"Come on." He helped her to her feet and led her by the hand to the adjoining bedroom. "Let's get you into bed."

She pulled a T-shirt out from under the pillow, and he smiled. It was one of his. She'd kept it all these years.

Jessa shivered and held out a wheat bag. "Can you heat this? The kitchen's at the end of the hallway."

"Sure."

While the microwave spun heat into the wheat bag, William lit the wood stove in the living room and pulled the drapes. The back part of the cottage, thick with freezing air when he arrived, soon warmed up.

When he returned to her room, she'd climbed into bed and lay with the comforter pulled up to her chin. He handed her the wheat bag. "Here, this should help."

She hugged it close, and as she snuggled down in the bed, William moved into the hallway to pick up her discarded clothes. He draped the dress over a chair and stood the shoes to attention underneath, then grabbed a warm washcloth, cleanser, and night cream from the bathroom.

He sat on the edge of the bed beside her. She kept her eyes closed as he cleansed her face, patted it dry, and smoothed moisturizer onto her flawless skin.

"Thank you," she whispered, her eyes still shut.

He understood why she didn't want to meet his gaze. The pain was too intense. "Do you want me to call anyone?"

"Um..."

"The Subaru parked outside—do you have a housemate?"

"It's my boyfriend's." She spoke so quietly that he could barely hear her, but the word "boyfriend" echoed in his head. "He's away for the weekend."

William had never considered that she might have a boyfriend. He didn't know why. After all, she was young and beautiful. Why wouldn't she have a love interest? He experienced an immediate rush of jealousy. He didn't want to think about his Jess having sex with someone else. Not five years ago, not now.

"Okay." He looked down at her with concern. "Well, shall I stay for a while?"

"No, I should be fine." Tears returned in droplets, running down her cheeks, her voice no more than a murmur. "I'm so sorry."

"Hey, you have nothing to be sorry for." He tugged off his tie and undid the top two buttons of his shirt, then lay beside her on the bed, one arm under her pillow, the other loosely around her waist above the covers.

"You don't have to do this."

"Shh. Go to sleep. Everything will seem better in the morning."

Jessa smelled like his dreams, like he'd remembered every day for the past five years. And as William stroked her hair, brushing it back from her face with gentle fingers, she didn't resist. She needed someone, and he was there. The wrong place at the wrong time. "Do you know what set it off?"

"The song, I think."

"What? 'In My Life'?"

"I felt it. I don't know where I know it from, but the notes… they ran through me and down into my fingers, like energy trying to escape."

"Hey, I'm sorry, Jess."

As Tom's words came back to him, William realized nothing had changed for Jessa. Her mind still played tricks on her soul.

They lay there in silence, his hands stroking her hair until she relaxed into sleep. The coolness of the room intensified his discomfort, but he couldn't get underneath the covers. It was neither the time nor the place.

William woke chilled to the bone—suit crumpled, mouth dry, and bladder full. Jessa slept peacefully beside him, her angelic face showing no trace of last night's turmoil in dawn's soft light. In a few hours, he had a Sunday morning client meeting over brunch and, later that day, a plane to catch. Stiff and sore, he needed a hot shower, or a cold one, or perhaps both. He snuck out the door, leaving her to sleep and wake alone.

Back home, the shower's hot water came as a welcome relief. Wayward thoughts turned inside out, but William pushed them aside, labeling them as ridiculous. He knew he should stay away, but he couldn't keep up the pretense for much longer.

Jessa awoke sometime after dawn. Shivering, she tiptoed down the hallway to the back of the house, searching for William.

He'd gone.

The cottage was uncomfortably cold, and she felt empty and alone in a world full of people who loved her. So she crawled back into bed and shut out the day, crying softly as she focused on her breathing and stilled her internal chatter—her head trash.

She slept until late in the morning, then lay there listening to the rain pattering on the iron roof while trying to remember the lyrics of "In My Life." She'd only just managed to drag herself out of bed and have a quick shower when the phone rang.

"Hi," William said. "I'm just about to board, but I wanted to make sure you're okay."

Jessa didn't know what to say, so she played the game. "I'm fine, thanks. Sorry about last night. I had one too many wines."

"I didn't realize you were drinking." He paused. "There's my final call. I'll see you next week."

"Bye… and, William…?"

"Yes?"

"Thank you. I appreciate what you did for me."

"No problem, Jess. Take care."

When Jessa arrived at the office on Monday, some of the weekend's events were still a blur. She remembered William taking her home, the haunting voice of Judy Collins, and the panic attack, but much of what happened around those three facts, she'd blanked from her memory.

However, one thought dominated. Why would William give up his night to stay with her?

"What happened to you on Saturday night?" Sharon asked as she turned on her computer. "Did Jimmy pick you up? He can't stand being away from you for one minute, can he?"

"No, he's away at a wedding. William gave me a ride." Jessa tried to sound nonchalant, but Sharon wasn't buying it.

"What? Sweetie, no."

"It was just a ride. Nothing happened between us."

"You say nothing happened, but I can tell by your tone that something went down. I know it's none of my business, but I worry about you. He's a control freak and an arrogant bastard of a man."

"Not always."

"Really? Oh, that's right, he's well hung."

"Would you stop it? Our relationship was more than sex, so you can wipe that grin off your face."

"If you say so." Sharon stared into space. "But then, who knows why we fall in love and how that excited state between two people connects? Or why it sometimes connects for but an instant and other times, it lasts a lifetime. If we didn't have that all-important chemistry, where would we be, eh? A world full of lone pairs. Couples with no chemical reaction."

Jessa burst out laughing. "What? Where did that come from?"

"Some random course I took at uni. I wanted to do philosophy back in the day but failed my first year, so I had to change tack."

"I never knew that."

"Yep. So, I can be deep and meaningful when it suits me, sweetie. I just don't do it very often. Anyway, it's a good job he's over in Melbourne. Gives you time to think about the situation."

"There is no *situation*, so nothing to think about." However, the moment the words left her mouth, Jessa knew that wasn't true. She couldn't stop thinking about William. "Why's he gone to Melbourne anyway?"

"A sustainable housing trust conference, according to Dan. William doesn't discuss his outside interests much, but from what I've heard, he's quite the philanthropist."

38

IDLE GOSSIP

The day was cold and overcast when William arrived home late Friday afternoon. While away, he'd thought about Jessa constantly. Worried about her, imagined her. His internal chatter wouldn't shut up about her on his morning run around The Tan in the Melbourne Botanical Gardens, and every time he showered, he imagined her with him, naked and glistening with body wash, ready and willing.

When he called into the office on Saturday morning, a small package sat on his desk. Inside was his bow tie, a box of Belgian chocolates, and a card with a simple "thank you" written in her neat hand. He opened the chocolates, popped one into his mouth, and smiled at the memory of them sharing similar ones at the Watershed.

That afternoon, he did something he'd never usually do. He lay on the sofa in the sun and napped. Sometime later, a knock on his front door jolted him awake.

William jumped to his feet and opened the door to find Dan Hudson standing outside in the hall. "Dan. Come on in. Can I offer you a beer?"

His boss followed him into the living room. "I'd love one. How was the conference?"

"Great. There are some worthwhile projects getting off the ground.

You should come next year. Anyway, is this a social call or work related?"

"We have a situation, but I didn't want to discuss it at work."

"Okay." William frowned as he offered Dan a chair. "What kind of situation?"

Dan sat. "Jessa Reynolds."

William handed his boss a beer, studying him through narrowed eyes. This could go one of two ways. "Jessa? Is she okay?"

"She's fine, but I'm concerned about your relationship with her."

"What do you mean?"

"There's gossip floating around the office about the two of you."

William placed a hand on the back of his neck, where tension was suddenly building. "What sort of gossip?"

"Yes, well, that's why I'm here. To give you the chance to explain. You went home with her after the triple-A's, and your car was spotted in her driveway at three in the morning."

"I gave her a lift. She felt unwell, so I stayed with her for a couple of hours. Nothing happened."

"Look, William, it's blatantly obvious you have feelings for her."

"What? What makes you say that?"

"It's the way you are with her. How you look at her."

"I'm totally professional around her. The last thing I want is to make her feel uncomfortable."

Dan nodded. "That may be so, but remember, she's a kid and a sweet one at that."

"There's nothing *kid* about her. She's an accomplished young woman—you saw her on Saturday night—and sure, I find her attractive. What guy wouldn't?"

"I agree. But I don't want her career ruined by an inappropriate workplace affair with a much older man who happens to be her boss." He studied William. "Or is it too late for that?"

William sat with his head in his hands, rubbing his hairline with his fingertips, his jaw rigid and ticking. His only option was to tell Dan the truth. "Jessa and I had a brief fling five years ago. She's my niece's friend. She went to Wellington. I moved to Sydney. End of story. I've been nothing but professional with her since we started working together, and that's the truth."

"I see." Dan raised his eyebrows and let out a long sigh. "But she would have been, what, eighteen?"

"Yep. Not my finest hour."

He shook his head. "I wish you'd told me about this before accepting the position."

"Why? Would my private past make any difference to my professional future?"

"Did you realize she was part of the team when you accepted the job?"

"I did."

"And you didn't see a problem?"

"Should I have?"

"Possibly not, but we would've moved people around if we'd known, so you didn't have to work closely with her."

"But we work well together. You know that."

"You do, but even so, you're hard on her. According to the girls in the office, you've had her in tears more than once. It's time to take a step back."

Shit. "What?"

"Look, don't insult me by thinking I don't know what's going on within my own firm. We go back a long way. I admire your work and always have, but the last thing we want is a sexual harassment case on our hands."

William shook his head. *For fuck's sake.* "That will never happen."

"How can you be so sure?"

"Because I've done nothing inappropriate. And Jessa has a strong sense of integrity. She'd never vindictively hurt anyone. It's just not in her nature."

"Good. Just so we're clear. I'm asking you to keep it that way. Otherwise..."

Several weeks after the awards night, Jessa lounged in the sunroom of her cottage, the *Saturday Morning Herald* spread out on the floor and her journal balanced on denim-clad knees while she wrote a list. The day had dawned with a heavy frost, but by noon, the winter sun shone in a cloudless sky, filling the room with warmth. As her pen scribbled back and forth across the page, two words stood out.

Clean break.

There'd been a shift in William's mood ever since his trip to Melbourne. His tough and demanding attitude prevailed, but he seemed more preoccupied with his work than ever and seldom interacted with her unless it was absolutely necessary.

If she and Jimmy were to have a chance, she'd have to move on and leave William in the past, where he belonged.

As she scanned the newspaper's situations vacant section, an advertisement caught her eye.

Port Team Architecture had an opening.

39

REGRETS AND COMPROMISE

"I'm off now, William. Shall I lock the main door? Everyone's left."

"Please come in for a minute." His voice was like steel, making Jessa hesitate in the doorway. Their working relationship was now nonexistent. She hated to admit it, but some days, she missed his presence. He never sought her input or invited her to join him on site visits. Seldom even glanced her way. William was totally professional.

Now, she could tell by his tone that he meant business, and as she stepped into his office, she experienced that familiar clench in her gut.

He rocked back in his chair, his eyes drilling into her. "Come in and take a seat," he repeated. "Or are you still uncomfortable being alone with me? Would you like me to arrange a support person?"

Jessa perched on the edge of the chair opposite his desk. "That won't be necessary. We've moved beyond that point." She didn't bother to conceal the hurt in her voice.

"At least you've come to your senses about something." Every word he spoke carried a sarcastic undertone.

"Did you want to discuss work, or is this another insult-Jessa-fest?" She looked him up and down. He never quite managed to pull off casual Fridays. Clad in fitted charcoal jeans, a light gray shirt, and a black merino V-neck sweater, he looked stylishly elegant. As usual, a neatly clipped shadow graced his jaw and upper lip, and despite his hostility, Jessa struggled with her desire for him.

William's expression remained dispassionate, his arrogance on full display. "Grant Foster from Port Team Architecture called me this afternoon for a verbal reference."

Her heart raced to a double-time beat.

"He said you were keen to 'move over,' as he put it." William shook his head, holding her gaze captive. "You can't be serious. What the hell do you think you're playing at?"

"I can't believe he'd do that. So much for the confidential interview process."

"Grant's an old friend, so he wanted to give me a heads-up, totally off the record, about what one of my team was up to."

Jessa sat up straight, shoulders back, chin high. "Even so, I would have expected him to be more professional."

"You're seriously considering it, then?"

"I wouldn't have applied for the position if I wasn't serious."

"Why? Why now when you're starting to give us your best work? Unbelievable."

While being on the receiving end of William's anger was nothing new, it upset her all the same. She didn't deserve this treatment. "It's the right time for me."

"What? To move to Port Team Architecture? Good luck with that."

She wondered what he meant by "good luck."

"What have I done to warrant this?" he asked.

"This isn't about you. I can't believe how self-centered and arrogant you are."

William's eyes narrowed as if he'd never considered himself to be either of those things. "What's that supposed to mean?"

"Why does everything always have to revolve around you? This is about me. Me, Jessa Reynolds. I want to live my life with no regrets or compromise."

"You forgot the diet part. That's your mantra, isn't it? Life's too short for regrets, compromise, and diets."

"So you finally remember me, do you? The Jessa you once had feelings for?"

William huffed out a sigh, then stood and paced the floor. "Of course I remember you. How can you even think I'd forget?"

"Well, that's the first reference you've made to our old life since you returned from Sydney. That trip to Scenic Hill, you never said a word. Even after the awards dinner, when you lay on my bed, watching over me, protecting me, you said nothing."

"What do you expect? We're both professionals, and I plan to act accordingly."

She shook her head. "You're so rigid—it's suffocating."

"I'm rigid? That's rich coming from you. When you ignored me those first few weeks, said nothing about us, I thought you were the same—rigid, as you so aptly call it." He ran a hand through his hair and rubbed the back of his neck, as if the touch would ease his annoyance. "I'm your boss now. I assumed you wouldn't want me to remember."

"Why? What reason could you possibly have to *assume* that?"

William stood at the window, his hands clenched into fists as he gazed out over the park below. "Because your family despises me."

"What?"

He turned, his dark stare drilling into her. "I just told you *what*. End of story."

"Why do they despise you?" Jessa waited, but William merely sighed. "Why did you go away? Why didn't you want me?"

He lowered his tone. "Oh, I wanted you, Jess. You think I didn't want you? I wanted you so badly I couldn't sleep for weeks after you left. And remember? There hasn't been a single day where I haven't remembered you. I remember your taste, the warmth of your naked body, your scent, your suggestion—"

"Enough," she snapped. "Don't say anything more. I don't deserve this."

"But you asked me why." He forced his words through gritted teeth. "I still remember your perfect breasts, the sensation of being inside you about to burst, lying in the bathtub with you in my lap. I remember you, Jessa. All of you. And those chatty letters you sent me. I had to move to Sydney to put some distance between us."

"Stop it! Do you have any idea how insensitive you're being?"

"You wore your 'fuck-me' shoes to the award's dinner, and you accuse *me* of being insensitive?" William closed his eyes and pinched the bridge of his nose. "Unbelievable."

His words burned. Jessa inhaled for a count of four but struggled to hold for seven and exhaled with a sharp puff. "I'm sorry. I didn't mean to upset you—with the shoes, I mean."

"Is that right?" he mocked. "When I saw you in those shoes, I wanted to pick you up, throw you over my shoulder, and take you home to bed."

"You still wanted to make love to me?" Her words were barely audible. "After all this time?"

"No, Jess, I wanted to fuck you. I wanted to fuck you out of the ballpark. You're a big girl. I'm sure by now you understand what fucking's all about."

"William, stop it!" she yelled, leaping to her feet. "You can't talk to me like that."

"Do you honestly believe I haven't wanted you all these years? Thought about you, dreamed of you, imagined you in my arms?" William sank onto the sofa and cradled his head in his hands. "I should have stayed away, but ever since seeing you again at the wedding, I couldn't stop thinking about you. You invaded me, consumed me."

"What wedding?"

"You played the cello at my friend's wedding."

"When?" She cast her mind back. "At Donna Richardson's wedding?"

"You didn't see me, but I certainly saw you. The way you'd matured into a woman. I found you captivating. I still do."

Jessa remembered. The silk thread—she'd sensed him, felt the tug. "So why ignore me? Why don't you confide in me like you used to?"

"You might think you want to know the reason, but believe me, you don't."

"How can you say that? I loved you."

"You were eighteen, Jess. Eighteen. I wasn't right for you, not then, not now." He stared at her in desperation, his words filled with resignation and regret. "I'm too old for you, too sad, too broken. And I promised your grandfather I'd let you go."

"My grandfather? What's Poppa got to do with any of this?"

"Ask your family. They know the full story or, at least, think they do. They should be the ones to tell you, not me."

As dense sobs caught in her throat, she struggled to swallow. "But I don't understand."

William reached for her. "Come here."

"Don't." She stepped back. "Don't you dare touch me!"

"Come on, Jess, don't cry. I'm sorry. The last thing I want to do is upset you. But never think I didn't want you. I wanted you with all my heart."

"But… at the pump house. You told me I was beautiful." She struggled to set her words free. "Don't you remember? You wanted to make love to me. But I couldn't."

"What?" William appeared confused. "Jess, we did make love. We made love several times at the Watershed, remember?" He offered her a box of tissues and frowned. "Here, sit down."

She sat in the same chair, staring at nothing in particular through a mist of tears as she continued to measure her breathing.

Eventually, she spoke. "You want to know why I'm leaving Hudson Farrell? It's because of you. Some days, I hate you for what you did to me. I don't want to feel that way, but I do, and I need to break your hold over me. How could you treat me like I meant nothing to you after what we had? If you'd been honest and told me you no longer had feelings for me, that I wasn't enough, I could have moved on.

"But for you to just disappear from my life… How could you be so cruel? I've spent five years getting over that, only to have you turn up again and act like nothing happened between us. Is that who you are, William? A fucking egotistical, arrogant bastard of a man? Because if it is, I've totally misjudged you."

"Jess… please, don't. I realized I messed up by not contacting you, but I figured it was for the best and hoped you'd understand." He stood and reached for her again.

Her hands flew up. "Stay away from me."

William sighed. "I'll get you a glass of water."

As William left the room, Jessa stood and moved to the window. She stared at the blue sky streaked with gray, heard the water running in the staff room, and his footfalls as he reentered the office. But she didn't turn around.

"Here." When she refused the glass, William set it on the small table beside her.

"I have to go." Her words fell on a ragged breath.

"Please don't leave. We need time to talk."

They both remained silent for a few moments. Jessa didn't know what to do—whether to stay or go, speak or keep quiet.

"Jess, come home with me, please."

The sound of the automatic entry doors opening downstairs made them both start.

"Jessa?" Jimmy called from the foyer. "Jessa, are you up there?"

"Shit, who's that?" William murmured.

She sighed. "It's Jimmy… my boyfriend."

Jessa stepped out onto the landing, stifling her tears with willpower and small squares of flimsy white tissue. "I'll be down in a minute."

Jimmy bounded up the stairs two at a time. "I thought we were meeting for dinner, and your phone must be off." He stopped, his concerned gaze darting between Jessa and William, who stood beside her. "What's going on?"

"Jessa's upset about resigning. You should take her home." William pushed past Jimmy. "I'll get her coat."

Jimmy wrapped an arm around her shoulders. "Hey, are you okay, honey? Come on. Let's get you home." He grabbed her coat and purse off William and ushered her down the stairs.

Once outside, she glanced up at William's office window. His impassive face stared back at her for several seconds before he frowned and turned away.

. . .

Jessa didn't speak for much of the drive home. She picked at her nails and rubbed her thumbs over icy fingers. She didn't want to explain. Her energy for explanations was spent.

Jimmy reached over and covered her hand with his. "Should I call your folks and ask them to come over?"

"I don't want to see them right now. It's all Mum's fault. Poppa would have gone along with whatever she wanted."

"What do you mean, and why are you leaving Hudson Farrell? You never mentioned it."

"It's not important. Doesn't matter now."

Jimmy drove the rest of the way in silence, misunderstanding sitting between them like a wall. He parked in her driveway and cut the engine, but neither of them moved to leave the car.

"Are you having an affair?" He stared straight ahead, every muscle in his face clenched. "Are you screwing your boss… that William bloody Cook?"

"No, of course not."

"Something's gone on between you. I want to know what."

She didn't answer.

"Have you ever slept with William Cook?"

"I'm going inside. I can't discuss this right now." She opened the car door and ran up the path. He followed.

"Jessa?"

"What!" She turned to face him. "Look, Jimmy, I'm exhausted. I'm sorry about dinner, but I've had a tough week. I need some space."

Jimmy stood his ground. "I'll ask you again." She'd never seen him angry but could tell he'd reached boiling point. "Have you ever had sex with William Cook? Tell me."

"Yes. Are you happy now? We had a… a… thing the summer before I left for university. But it's over. All over and done with long ago." She wanted to shout but didn't have the energy.

"But you were, what, eighteen? He must be at least twelve years older."

"More than twelve years. And I might have only been eighteen, but I really did love him. I was devastated when he ended it abruptly."

"No." Jimmy shook his head. "What are you saying?"

"I'm sorry." She set her purse on the hall table and dropped her keys beside it, tears tracking down her cheeks. "You wanted the truth. Well, that's the truth."

Jimmy followed her into the living room. "And what, you chose to work for Hudson Farrell so you could be near him?" he shouted. "So you could be with him?"

"It wasn't like that. He was living in Sydney when I started working there, and I never expected him to come back."

"Right." His voice softened, but his jaw remained tight. "So you're telling me that the entire time we've dated, you've been in love with your boss?"

"It's not like that. There'll always be a place for him in my heart. But I don't love him."

"Really?"

Silence settled over them for a moment. "I'm sorry."

He huffed. "You're not sorry. You're kidding yourself. I knew something was up, but I couldn't put my finger on it. Now it all makes perfect sense. You won't let me touch you, make love to you. I'm not enough for you. You can't love me, and it's because of that asshole you work for."

"How can you say that?" she protested. "I'm just not ready yet. You can't rush things that need time to grow."

Jimmy paced the floor, his fingers raking through his hair. He stopped and looked at her, and she realized how much she'd hurt him.

"It's true. You just can't bring yourself to admit it. Whatever we had growing has wilted. And I can't do this anymore." He paused. "You need to lay your ghosts to rest, and I need someone who'll love me and only me, not someone who's still in love with an old man from their past."

"Jimmy, please."

He stormed from the room and slammed the front door on his way out.

"Hello?"

"I need to see you."

"Please don't call me at home, William. It's almost midnight."

"Jess… can I come over?"

"No, you can't. You've hurt me. You just don't get it, do you?"

"I'm hurting too." He paused, his sigh audible down the phone line. "Hurt people hurt people. You know that."

"Jimmy finished with me because of you."

"I'm sorry. Breakups are never easy, but he wasn't right for you."

"Seriously? How dare you say that! Who I choose to see is none of your business."

"Jess. Please."

"No."

Jessa woke in a panic. She fumbled for the phone on her nightstand and checked her alarm clock, thinking she must have slept in. But it was barely 5:30. She slumped back on the pillow, urging her eyes to open as she mumbled hello into the receiver.

"Jessa?" her mother whispered. "Are you there?"

"Mum, is everything all right?"

"It's Aunt Maggie. She went in the night."

Jessa, still half asleep, struggled to comprehend her words. "What? Where did she go?"

"She passed away. Maggie's gone."

Jessa sat up and rested her head against the headboard, suddenly wide awake. "I'm so sorry."

"She never fully recovered from the heart attack, did she?" Her mother sighed. "I'm surprised she lasted this long. At least she's in a better place now."

"I'll get dressed and head over."

As she ended the call, Jessa realized she should drag herself into the shower, but instead, she slid back down in the bed and buried herself beneath the covers, questioning what life was all about—the loves, the struggles, the heartbreak.

The second Jessa set foot in the office on Monday, William was on her case. On Tuesday, he was no better. He demanded that she modify a set of working drawings, and she left his office in tears.

On Wednesday morning, just as she was about to leave home for Maggie's service, her phone rang.

"Are you coming in today or what?" William asked in a superior tone.

"No, I'll be away for the day."

"And you didn't think to inform me?"

"I asked Dan to tell you."

"He's off sick. When will you be back?"

Screw you. "Friday. After I've buried my great-aunt. She passed away last week."

William sighed loudly. "Right. My condolences. I had no idea. In future, I'd appreciate being informed. I realize you see me as heartless, but that's not the case."

"Fine. But I assumed you knew."

After the funeral, Jessa drove to the small white cross on Rata River Road. She'd stopped there only once before, but today, she felt an overpowering need to touch it. Standing with the cross at her feet, Jessa said a silent prayer for Maggie as she contemplated how easily life could change in an instant.

She sat in the long grass, now lush and vivid green from the winter rains, and asked her guardian angel for guidance. Although she wasn't a devout Catholic, her faith gave her strength when she needed it most. She'd meant to ask Kathy G. who'd died there, but it always slipped her mind. Whoever it was, the cross served as an aching reminder of someone's loss, and that saddened her.

Back at the house, she found her grandfather sitting at the kitchen table, still in his suit and a cup of tea in hand as usual, ready for a yarn served with a slice of banana cake.

"It was a beautiful service," he said.

"Yes. I'm glad she wanted to be buried in the Valley. Where are the others?"

"Still at the church hall, cleaning up. How have you been?" He looked concerned.

"Not bad." Jessa sat opposite him and sighed. "But there's always room for improvement. Actually, I'm glad we're alone. I'd like a word."

"Okay. What word would you like?" he asked with a grin.

"London." Jessa smiled warmly at him. She'd always enjoyed Tom's dry sense of humor. "I'm toying with the idea of going to the UK in a couple of months."

"What's brought this on? What about your new job?"

"I know, but I feel like I need to get away."

"Boy trouble, is it?"

"More like man trouble."

He made eye contact, perhaps expecting an explanation, but she gave none. "Let me guess. William Cook?"

Jessa nodded. Her grandfather understood more than she realized. "We talked a while back. He told me you asked him to stay away once I left for uni."

He glanced down at his cup. "I did. Felt it was for the best at the time. Still do." He took a sip. "Are you seeing him again?"

"He's my boss. You know that, don't you?"

"Yeah, I'd heard. I figured this might happen. Wondered if he'd keep away. He's a cocky bloke—I'll say that for him."

"It's not like that."

"Isn't it? I can see the appeal. The guy's successful and has a certain charisma. He tells you that you're beautiful. Chips away at you. Next thing you know, you're under his spell, and his ego won't let you go. After all, what man wouldn't want a pretty young woman on his arm?"

"That's not how it is. Since returning from Sydney, he's not really made any attempt to see me other than professionally. But for me, it's an impossible situation."

"Why? Because you're in love with him?"

"I don't know, Poppa. I'm all mixed up. He has a brooding intensity that I can't resist." She paused to gather her thoughts. "And you're right, William is controlling, even arrogant at times. But when we were together those few weeks before I left for university, he was the most caring, thoughtful man I've ever met. I felt cherished." She sighed. "Not that it matters now."

"I see."

"He made me feel so… desired and protected."

"I bet he did."

Jessa let his comment slide. "We had a real connection, like déjà vu. I can't quite explain it. Do you know what it's like to meet someone and, almost instantly, realize you have a special bond?"

"Of course I do." His expression softened. "That's how I felt about your grandmother when I met her for the first time at a train station. We lost touch for a while, but then I found her again at a town hall dance. Happy times."

Her imagination turned to a younger Tom and Kathy dancing up a storm to the tunes of Glenn Miller. She'd always wanted to dance with William but would never do so now. "Anyway, maybe he didn't have feelings for me other than, you know, sexual."

"Look, I never approved of him, for several reasons. But for what it's worth, the day I talked to him, he told me he loved you. I'm sure he meant it in his own way."

"So why did he cut me off, Poppa? If he loved me, why didn't he fight for us? And now, he says he's not right for me, so it's too late. At least if I go away, it'll give me the chance to move on."

"And is that what you want?"

Jessa hesitated. "Not really, but I have no other option."

"So you're telling me that after five years, you still want to be with him?"

"I'm not sure. We had a chance back then—I know we did, but you and William decided otherwise."

"We thought it was for the best."

"I get that, and I don't blame you. But now, he doesn't want me anymore, and I can't make him change his mind."

"He's too old for you, Jessa. And there's something else…"

"What?"

He sighed. "It doesn't matter now. You're right. Go to London. Have some fun. Your career will still be waiting for you when you get back."

40

THE CHOICE

Each day after Jimmy and Jessa's breakup, the sun lingered a little longer in the western sky as spring winds swept the promise of new life into the orchards and market gardens of the surrounding district. William spent several weeks planning his next move, with doubt as his constant companion. His first task was to contact David Reynolds.

The two of them sat facing each other over a small table fashioned from an old wine barrel. Apart from a brief phone conversation earlier, William and David had never spoken before, and it had taken much persuading before David reluctantly agreed to meet at the pub on the waterfront.

"So, what's this all about?" David looked up from his beer.

William launched into his rehearsed speech: "I'm aware that your family has no time for me, and I understand why, so I'll get straight to the point. I plan on seeing Jessa again, and I'd like your blessing."

"What the…? You can't be serious. That's never going to happen." David sipped his beer, his focus on the yachts in the harbor competing in the Thursday evening racing series.

"While I realize that Louisa and her parents may never welcome me, I'm asking you because I think you'll understand. Also, I want to tell her about Rose."

"I assumed this was all over and done with years ago. And as for Jessa, I have no idea what's going on in that head of hers. She's changed jobs, split up with her boyfriend, and, according to Tom, is talking about going to London. Now you're telling me what? That you're back on track, after five years? When did this happen?"

"It hasn't happened yet. Jessa's avoiding me at the moment, but we can overcome that with time. Jimmy broke it off with her because he knows she still has feelings for me."

"Did she tell you that?"

"More or less."

David sighed as he looked around the pub, down at his beer, anywhere but at William. "I see."

"She's the only woman I've ever loved," William continued. "We'll be together again, make no mistake, but I wanted to tell you how I feel."

"What about Rose? It's just mixed-up nonsense, isn't it?" David finally met his gaze. "Jessa's not Rose. You're getting your lines blurred here and messing with my daughter's heart in the process."

"Rose and I had an innocent teenage crush. We hardly knew each other."

"Well, according to Louisa, she seemed pretty keen on you at the time. Rose spoke to her about you the night before the accident."

This surprised William. Rose had seemed reluctant, but perhaps it was all for show.

"And I was keen on her, more than keen. But we were barely fifteen. We had one afternoon alone together, that's all." William sipped his beer, the bitter taste hitting the back of his tongue. "I've spent the best years of my life blaming myself for what happened, and for what? Am I sad about it? Of course. Not only did the accident take her life, but it also destroyed mine for a long time. I was so incredibly angry, to the point where I had no gratitude for anything. That is until Jessa came along. She allowed me to feel again. All I want now is a chance to be with her."

"You know what Louisa will do. She'll cut all ties."

"We can't be sure of that. If I don't go for this now, will we both end up in unfulfilled relationships? I don't want to take that chance. I don't have the luxury of time."

"Then what's all this about her avoiding you? If that's the case, you have a hard row to hoe. Once Jessa makes up her mind, there's no shifting her."

"She's avoiding me because I wouldn't let her back into my life. I made that decision out of respect for your family and what happened in the past, and I'm fully aware of the impact this may have on Jessa's relationship with her mother and grandparents. It's not my intention to destroy what they have, but I don't want Jessa to be a missed opportunity because I didn't fight for her."

"So you're telling me, after all that's happened over the last five years, Jessa may still be in love with you?"

"I hope so. I realize that the age gap's a concern, but who's to say any of us will survive the dynamics of a long-term relationship? Rose taught me that life is fleeting, and we all need to believe what we truly want is possible. Otherwise, what's the point?"

William waited for him to speak.

"Well, my wife might just divorce me if she ever finds out about this, but you have my reluctant blessing. I want to see my girl happy. She sure hasn't been happy for a long time. As for telling her about Rose, you're right. It's time she knew the truth, but I'll discuss it with Tom and see what he thinks."

William cast his mind back to his last conversation with Tom. "I'm not sure he'll agree, but…"

"Even so, I'd rather I told her. If she still wants you after that, go for it."

"Thanks, David. I can't tell you how much this means to me."

While waiting for Jessa outside her cottage the following Tuesday, David breathed deeply, inhaling the aroma of freshly cut grass into his lungs. William's words, "*We all need to believe what we truly want is possible,*" hung in the air. Everyone wanted the same out of life, David mused, to fulfill their dreams. But sometimes, circumstances got in the way. The more he weighed up William's arguments, the more they made sense. William loved Jessa, and David suspected Jessa loved him back.

Now, all he had to do was convince his wife.

Jessa opened the car door and slipped inside. "Hi there. Have you ordered the burgers?"

"I have, but they'll be thirty minutes."

"Really? I'm starving."

"Actually, there's something I want to talk to you about anyway, so the timing's perfect."

She fastened her seat belt. "Okay."

The evening was mild for early spring, but the wind from the coast turned cool once dusk fell. David and Jessa sat in his car at the playground by the beach. He'd planned to walk along the boardwalk but then thought better of it. He didn't want her breaking down in public, or even in front of him for that matter. But being a parent means you have to cope with your child's tears, whatever their age. He smiled as he contemplated how parenting never stops when the bond is strong.

David wasn't one for unnecessary talk, but he'd rehearsed the story of William and Rose all afternoon, and when it came time to speak, his words flowed effortlessly.

"Dad, what are you saying? That William and Rose were boyfriend and girlfriend?"

"Well, kind of. But there's more. William was in the same accident that killed Rose."

Jessa searched his face for an alternative outcome. "No! You can't be serious. Why didn't he ever tell me?"

"They were thrown off his farm bike, and Rose died at the scene. William was in traction for weeks."

"And he was driving?" A teardrop slid down her cheek as her breathing quickened. "That's why he said my family despises him."

"Your grandmother and mother have never forgiven him. Although Kathy's let go of some of the anger. She even went to see him once and gave him Rose's cello, but she still holds him culpable."

"Her cello? Are you saying it's Rose's cello that William has in his apartment?"

"I have no idea. Possibly." He sighed. "Unlike Kathy, your mother keeps the anger alive. She can't forget and will never forgive. That's why she doesn't talk about Rose. The grief still runs deep, and you know what they say: 'Words not spoken are wept.'"

He shifted in his seat, searching for comfort. "Now you understand why William couldn't be with you. He's protecting you from your mother's wrath and honoring Tom and Kathy's wishes."

Jessa's brows knitted together in a question. "So that's why Poppa warned him off?"

"Your mother doesn't know about you and William. We never told her. It would've broken her heart. You were unstable at the time, so Tom spoke to William and told him to back off."

"But I loved him. He meant everything to me."

"I realize that now, but you were sleeping with a man twice your age. To us, it wasn't right, so we did what we thought was best. You looked, look so much like Rose, and we figured William was playing some kind of sick joke."

"What are you saying? That he confused me with Rose and thought she'd come back to him? That it wasn't me he wanted but Rose?"

"I'm not sure, love. How would I know what he thought or thinks? He's not a bad bloke underneath, I suppose. You're over twenty-one now, and it's time for you to make up your own mind."

"I'm not sure what to do. His intensity makes me nervous, and now that I know the truth about Rose…" Jessa cradled her head in her hands. "How do I even process that?"

"This London thing. Why don't you go? Put some distance between yourself and everyone." David patted her hand in a rare display of physical affection. "I get that your mother can be overprotective."

"How do you know about London?"

"Tom might have mentioned it over a glass of Johnny Walker," he said with a grin.

She smiled back. "Of course he did."

"Go, be with your friends, live your life. Get some closure, or at least some clarity. If William's still keen, he'll find you."

"When did you become so wise? Or have you always been that way, and I just haven't noticed?" Jessa leaned over and hugged her father. "I know I don't often say it, but I love you, Dad."

"Come on," he said with a self-conscious chuckle. "Enough of that sort of talk. Let's go get those burgers."

41

MISSED CONVERSATIONS

Time has a way of standing still when you're at a crossroads, not knowing which way to turn. Jessa understood her thread with William had broken, but an overwhelming sorrow engulfed her whenever she recalled their Watershed days. He'd been in love with the manifestation of Rose, not her at all.

Once she'd decided to leave Port Team Architecture, the cogs of time inched forward again. Her new boss tried to talk her out of resigning, but while Jessa felt guilty about letting them down, she was determined to take up the challenge. Telling her mother about London was the next step.

It had been three weeks since she'd learned about Rose, and Jessa hadn't yet mustered the courage to speak to her mum about the trip.

That Saturday, Jessa waited until midafternoon before leaving for her usual jog along the boardwalk. After reaching the port area in record time, she stopped to stretch out the tightness in her hamstrings while gazing out over the bay. The ocean was as smooth as a millpond, with just a ripple of whitewater tiptoeing into the shore.

Her phone's ringtone interrupted her contemplation. "Jessa Reynolds speaking."

"Jess, it's William. Sorry, have I caught you in the middle of something? You sound puffed." His tone was light, almost cheerful. She pictured his smile, and a lingering sadness crept over her.

"No, it's fine," she said bluntly. "What can I do for you?"

"Can we meet for a drink?" He sounded charming, like the old William. "I want to clear the air."

Jessa had thought about contacting him many times over the past few weeks, but today, doubt cast a shadow. "There's no need. You've already said more than enough."

"Thirty minutes is all I ask."

"Okay, I'll think about it and be in touch." She hung up on him.

He rang back. She considered ignoring him but couldn't. Wasn't it what she wanted, after all, to see him one last time?

"Jess, hear me out, please. I want to do this now. How about later today?"

She sat on a nearby bench and pondered his request. "I'm not sure. Where do you want to meet?"

"My place?"

"The lion's den? I'd rather not if you don't mind."

He laughed at her joke. "It's just… I'd prefer to meet in private."

She hesitated. "Okay, I guess you could come to the cottage."

"Great. Shall we say in two hours, around six?" He sounded almost excited.

"Six is good." Jessa ended the call and dragged herself along the boardwalk, William's impending visit now a distraction that spoiled the rest of her run.

At the entrance to her street, apprehension intruded on her carefully constructed world. Physically, she'd never felt stronger, but thoughts of William constantly sparked old desires. It annoyed her, but the fact remained: he still held a tight tension on the silk thread. The thread she'd convinced herself was already broken.

Once home, Jessa ran a bath, adding essential oils of lavender and clary sage, and slipped into its warmth. When she finally reached for her towel, the water had cooled, but she felt relaxed and calm.

She applied light makeup before dressing in soft blue torn-at-the-knee jeans and an oversized cream cable-knit sweater. Jessa wanted to look good for him. She knew she shouldn't, but she did.

By the time she'd poured herself a glass of wine and grabbed a handful of almonds to snack on, the sun was descending in the western sky in a blaze of fiery passion. Dusk was on its way, along with despondency.

William knocked on her front door at 6:02 p.m., his impeccable timing the product of an organized mind or, one might say, pedantic bloody-mindedness. The thought made her smile as she opened the door.

"Come on in." She stood aside and let him pass. Dressed in dark blue jeans and a fawn-and-white striped Henley shirt, he looked as handsome as ever. Even after all this time, her heart still fluttered at the sight of him. He leaned in to kiss her on the cheek, but she pulled away.

"This is a pleasant space. It looks different in this light." William analyzed every detail of her living room, then set the large white envelope he carried on the coffee table. "It's very you."

"Thanks. Too casual for your taste, though." Her tone held an edge of confrontation.

"That doesn't mean I can't appreciate what you've done here." He was equally positioned for defense.

"Please, take a seat. Would you like a glass of wine or a beer?"

"I might stick to juice if you have any."

Jessa opened the fridge and pulled out a carton of juice. "Is grapefruit okay?"

"Perfect. I thought you liked your drinks sweet?"

"People change." Jessa spoke coolly, trying to stay in control. She poured him a juice and set it on the coffee table, along with a small platter of cheese, crackers, and pickles, then took the chair to his left. "So, what is it you wanted to see me about?"

"Rose."

Jessa inhaled deeply and released a heavy sigh. "There's no need. Dad's already filled me in on the story."

"Yeah. He mentioned he planned to discuss it with you, but there are always two sides."

"You talked to Dad? When?"

"We met for a drink recently. I wanted his permission to discuss Rose with you."

"You're a grown man. Why do you need permission?"

"Because I'd promised Tom previously that I wouldn't mention her. He knew your mother would never agree to us spending time together, and he indicated you were having a few health issues at the time."

"Poppa said he'd talked to you. But that doesn't alter the fact that you had plenty of chances to tell me about Rose."

"When do you mean?"

"At the Watershed, the time we spent together before I left for Wellington. Before you made Poppa a promise."

"I thought about it many times, believe me, but in the end, I couldn't. Don't you understand? I assumed you'd leave me if you found out, and I couldn't risk losing you."

"But you soon made the choice to leave me, didn't you? You cut me off without a thought for my feelings."

"Your feelings were all I thought about, and you know it," he said bluntly. "I wasn't right for you back then."

"Yes, so you said last time we met." Jessa didn't try to conceal her hurt. "I get it. You don't have to keep going over old ground."

"Look, I don't want to fight. I want to put all this behind us so we can be friends."

"We can never be friends, William. You gave up the right to be my friend when you left for Sydney without a word. I don't understand how you can think otherwise."

"Okay. Well, respected colleagues then."

"Except it's obvious you don't respect me."

"Is that honestly what you think? That I don't respect you? I can assure you that's not the case."

"If you say so."

William held her gaze for a moment, then sat forward on the sofa, leaving his juice untouched, and picked up the white envelope. "Anyway, I brought you these." He handed it to her.

She carefully removed the contents. Inside were eight photographs. The first four were of her, taken during that Watershed summer. She looked happy, smiling into the lens, her face kissed by the sun with tiny freckles peppering her nose. Jessa smiled softly at the recollection.

The next four were of a girl sitting in long grass down by a river, her face similar to Jessa's but younger and fairer.

"Rose?" She studied him as he nodded his response. "Where did you get these?"

"I took them the day of the accident. I never expected to see my camera again, but a cop dropped it off weeks later, along with the negatives. I sent your mother copies, but she returned the envelope unopened."

"So Mum and Dad have never seen these?" Jessa shuffled through the images as she spoke. "What about Kathy and Poppa?"

"I don't know. The police may have shown them."

She traced Rose's features with her fingertips. "She looked like me at the same age, apart from lighter hair."

"She does, or did," he said softly. "Maybe now you'll understand why I reacted as I did at our first meeting."

Jessa swallowed hard as she moved to the next print.

"I admire your ability to be in the moment, Jess. I've noticed you do it when you're working."

His frankness embarrassed her, and she shifted uncomfortably in her chair.

"I'd like to do another shoot with you," he said. "Down at the river."

Jessa looked at him sadly. "That won't be possible. But I'd like copies of these if you don't mind."

"Sure, they're yours."

"Thank you. I want my children, if I ever have any, to know about Rose." She examined his face, feeling his pain. "It must have been hard for you after what happened. With the accident, I mean."

William closed his eyes. He took a deep breath and shook his head. "I lost my life as I knew it. But I lived…"

Silence stretched before them. With a lump rising in her throat, Jessa rose from the sofa and crossed to the window overlooking the bay to the north. On the far side of the bridge, children sailed on P-Class yachts, casting white dots across the estuary.

"I wondered if I could have her cello," she said eventually.

"Of course. If you want it, it's yours."

"Thank you." She turned to look at him. "What was she like?"

William's face softened. "Gentle, shy, unsure of herself. But smart, with a quick wit. And pretty. Very pretty. Still, she could be prickly when pushed. That sting you sometimes get in your voice reminds me of her."

"Did you love her?"

"We didn't have a chance to get that far. We spent one afternoon alone together. A few hours. The rest of the time, I admired her from afar with all the lust my youthful self could muster. As the years passed, I loved the memory of her and put her on some self-indulgent pedestal. To try to ease the guilt, I guess."

Emotion caught in her throat. "Do I remind you of her?"

"In some ways. As you can see from the photos, you look similar, and your voice sounds almost the same." William stood and took two steps toward her. "Jess, I'm sorry. I—"

"There's no need to explain." Jessa stared straight ahead for a moment, then turned to face him. "I'm sad, incredibly sad. Can you imagine how I felt when you left without a word? Then, all that stuff at the office. In the end, I couldn't bear being near you."

"I figured if I let you go, you'd find someone younger. Someone your parents approved of."

"Yeah, well, I've had plenty of attention from men, lots of attention. I'm not saying I don't enjoy it, but I… can't get close to anyone."

He offered his hand. "Jess…"

"I thought you wanted me, but I was too young for you. You said so yourself. And now it's all water under the bridge and swept out to sea, as you say."

William went to touch her face, but she shrugged him away.

"I want you to go," she said. "Maybe we'll meet again someday, and you can tell me more about Rose. But I can't do this right now. I need to stay focused. I can't let what I once felt for you blur my world."

After a trip to the Turkish café downtown, William drove to the beach on the west side of the port. With the moon rising, he absently watched the surf crash and foam over the sand, eating his chicken kebab and pondering Jessa's question. "*Did you love her?*" His mind flashed back to the pump house: Rose lying on her towel, her blouse half undone and lips full and arousing. He smiled at the recollection.

Until Nikau's wedding, William's career had taken priority over everything else. Any past attempts at relationships were purely sexual liaisons, void of intimacy and fueled by an aching physical need with little or no emotional connection.

All that remained was regret.

It was after ten when William knocked softly on Jessa's front door for the second time that night. He was just about to leave when her approaching footsteps greeted him. The door opened a fraction, restrained by the security chain.

She frowned. "William, what are you doing here? I'm about to go to bed."

"I need to ask you something. May I come in?"

Jessa unlatched the chain and stepped out onto the veranda. Unruly strands of hair tumbled free from a high ponytail as she pulled her blue toweling robe around her.

She closed the door behind her. "Not tonight." She sighed, as if she couldn't wait to go back inside. "Lea's staying over. She's just in the shower."

"Can I talk to you about one more thing?"

"We're done talking."

"Are we now?"

William stepped forward and took her face in his hands. He held her gaze and smiled. She inhaled sharply, but before she could step away, he pinned her up against her front door and kissed her. Not a gentle kiss, but rather a long, hard, lust-dripping-off-his-tongue-onto-hers type of kiss. He couldn't hold back as everything he once felt for her returned in an instant—the blue of a burning flame.

"So beautiful," he whispered as he pulled away, his breath hard and sharp. He went to leave but changed his mind and pinned her against the door for a second time. He pushed his thigh between her legs, revealing his arousal, and kissed her again—fierce, urgent, and filled with yearning—then stepped back, still holding her face. "So very beautiful."

William turned, strode down the path to his car, and drove away.

Jessa stood on the veranda, the message of William's kiss loud and clear, longing to make love to him and wondering what had just happened. Cocky bastard!

"Who was that?" Lea asked as she came to stand beside Jessa, drying her hair with a towel.

"Just someone who's lost their way."

"Come inside. I want to talk to you about something."

"Isn't it a little late for girl talk?"

"No. And besides, this is boy talk."

"What? You've finally met the man of your daydreams?"

"Maybe, but that's not what I want to talk about. It's about Uncle William. I've solved the puzzle."

Jessa nodded. "I know the story. Dad told me about the accident. You were right all along. William did know Rose. That's why he stopped seeing me, because of who I am."

"Yeah, pretty sad, eh?"

"It is. He confused me with Rose."

"Do you think? Uncle William's not the type to get anything confused. If he said he had feelings for you, he did."

Jessa remained unconvinced. She realized that kiss was his last goodbye. "Enough about William and me. What's this about your love life? Spill."

"Well, I've met this guy at work. He's a registrar, so a few years older."

"Hot?"

"Hot *and* horny." Lea laughed her throaty laugh. "Tall, brown hair, intense silver-blue eyes, and cut like a rugby player. What more could I want? I took convincing initially, thought he was a man whore, but the honeymoon stage is heating up."

"You sly fox, you! Tell me everything. How long, what's the sex like, when's the wedding, and what's his name?"

"Well, it's been a few weeks, but we didn't want to say anything. You know, screwing the crew and all that." She giggled. "He loves my red hair, wants auburn-haired kids, not sure about the wedding, and the pash rash was pretty bad when we first met."

"So, good sex?"

"Fab-u-lous." Lea giggled again, trying to hide her blush. "He's pretty full-on in that department. In more ways than one."

Jessa smiled. "Lucky you."

"His name is Jack, Jack James, and he wants to meet you. I told him I'd score us a dinner invite before you head off."

"I'd love that." Jessa tried to suppress a chuckle, wondering if she should share with Lea the coincidence of her meeting with the doctor.

"What's so funny?"

"You, Miss Lea with an A. You're adorable. Actually, I've met your man before."

"No way. When?"

"At the hospital, the day Mum took me after that panic attack."

"But that was years ago."

"I definitely remember him, though, and you're right, he's hot." She fanned herself with a hand to make her point. "Incredibly hot. But don't you dare tell him I said so!"

"Sharon, do you have a minute?" William stood in her office doorway.

"Sure, come in and have a seat. What can I do for you?"

The two of them had never hit it off. He had no idea why, but he still respected her work ethic. "I need information."

She looked up at her computer screen, fingers hovering above the keyboard. "Okay, what job are you after? Do we have it on CAD?"

"It's not about work. It's about Jessa."

Sharon sat back in her chair and frowned. "You know she's a close friend, and I'm not comfortable discussing her business with you."

"Fair enough. But when we met for a drink over the weekend, she mentioned going to London. Has she told you when she's leaving?"

"You and Jessa met for a drink?"

William chuckled. "Don't sound so surprised."

"So if you're drinking pals, why don't you ask her yourself?"

"Come on, Sharon." He laid on the charm. "I want to surprise her with West End theater tickets, but I need a date."

She narrowed her eyes and exhaled loudly. "The twenty-sixth. I have a friend in travel, and she arranged it for her."

William threw out his line. "Is her boyfriend going?"

Sharon caught the bait. "Jessa doesn't have a boyfriend anymore. He broke up with her. The night he found you guys together."

"How do you know about that?"

"We're girlfriends, and girlfriends tell each other everything, especially over a few drinks. After a couple of wines, Jessa can't shut up."

He smiled, recalling the night at the Watershed when Jessa's car broke down and she couldn't stop talking.

"You still love her?"

"Very much." William paused. "And she still loves me."

"What makes you say that?"

"The other night, I went to her cottage. We kissed, twice."

"Seriously?"

He nodded. "It brought it all back."

Sharon turned off her filter system completely. "You do realize she's never been with anyone but you?"

William stared at her in disbelief.

"You're her one and only," she clarified.

"What are you saying? That Jessa's never had a sexual relationship with any other man? What about Jimmy?"

"They never made it past second base."

"What? But she's such a flirt. I just assumed…" William remembered telling Jessa he wanted to fuck her out of the ballpark and inwardly cringed.

"Me too, but Jimmy told me she wouldn't sleep with him. Look, William, figure this out before it's too late. Personally, I don't get it, but she's carried a torch with your name on it for a long time, so that's good enough for me."

William was still processing the "only lover" information. It gave him hope. He was the only one. Her only one.

"What was it she said?" Sharon glanced up in thought. "You're bound together by a silk thread. I suggested scissors as a solution, but she didn't take me up on the offer."

She laughed, causing William to break into a grin too. He didn't take offense at her ribbing. Her concern for Jessa seemed genuine, and he respected that.

"Thanks for being so candid. I appreciate it." He stood to leave. "The twenty-sixth. That's, what, three weeks away?"

"You have three weeks to turn the tide and splice your silk thread. She's heading to the Valley next Friday for her grandmother's birthday dinner. It's the perfect opportunity for making magic."

He chuckled at her turn of phrase.

"Just saying. And, William, if you need any help, let me know. Maybe that silk thread's still strong after all."

42

THE WATERSHED

As leaving day loomed, Jessa wondered if, or when, she'd see William again. Before that kiss on the veranda, she'd tried to convince herself her feelings for him had waned. But since the kiss…

Her last Thursday at the office was uneventful until the receptionist knocked on Jessa's door. She fanned herself with an envelope as she spoke. "A hot older guy dropped this off." She placed it on Jessa's desk. "Gosh, I'm feeling all lightheaded."

Jessa chuckled as she glanced at her neatly written name on the envelope. William Cook. The hand, the ink, the font—all him. "Thanks."

She waited for the receptionist to leave, then opened the flap and removed a folded sheet of paper and a CD.

Jessa

I hear you're driving to the farm on Friday for Kathy's birthday.

She wondered how he knew. Perhaps Sharon had told him, but why would she do that?

I'd like to see you before you leave for London. I'm going to the Watershed later this evening. I have a commitment on Saturday morning, but I'll expect to see you there at three on Saturday afternoon.

William.

After all this time, why did he expect her to be at his beck and call? With the note still in her hand, Jessa considered his request. Should she visit him one last time?

She needed to go, and that need confused her. Was it love, desire, or purely sexual necessity? Whatever the reason, he still held that silk thread, tugging her in his direction ever so slowly. Jessa set the note on the desk in front of her and dialed Hudson Farrell's number, then Sharon's extension.

"Sweetie, how are you?" Sharon said. "Bet you're getting excited."

"Yeah, I guess. Can we meet for a drink later?"

"You know me, always up for wine o'clock. But it will have to be a quick one. Hubby's cooking dinner."

"Do you want to come over, or shall we go out?"

"I'll come to your place. That way, I don't have to change."

Sharon turned up half an hour late as usual. For her, time constraints were never a consideration. She arrived when she was good and ready and made no apology for it.

"You didn't need to bring wine," Jessa said when she opened the door. "I have wine."

"I'm not drinking Riesling. Too sweet for me, you know that." Sharon laughed as she set a bottle of Chardonnay on the table next to one of Jessa's platters. "I like my wine how I like my men—with a full body and a hint of edge."

Jessa chuckled as they both sat. "I have more than Riesling in my wine cellar of three bottles. Anyhow, I thought I might expand my palate tonight and try a Pinot Gris." Jessa poured two glasses and offered one to Sharon. "Here, see what you think."

Sharon breathed in the bouquet and took a sip. "That's an excellent wine. A hint of apricot, with a touch of pear and passion fruit."

"What? Since when did you become such an expert on the subtle notes of wine?"

"I did a course a while back." Sharon took another sip, her face showing concern. "You look tired. Are you okay?"

Jessa rolled the stem of her wineglass between her fingers, searching for the right words. "I wanted to ask you something. It's about William."

"What about him? Hold on. Hold on. I'm gonna need food for this." Sharon picked up a plate, assembled her snack, and took a bite. "Mmm." She stopped to chew. "You've heard the rumors, then?"

"No, I haven't heard any rumors, and I don't want to." Jessa handed her William's note. "But I wanted to show you this. He dropped it off at the office earlier."

Sharon unfolded the note and read it aloud.

"Well, well, well. Interesting." She spread soft cheese on another chunk of bread. "What's the sneaky bastard up to now?"

"Do you think he wants us to start over?" Jessa asked.

"Look, I hate to be the bearer of bad news, but he's resigned from Hudson Farrell. I'm not supposed to know yet, but I do."

Jessa set her wine glass on the table and moved to the front of her chair. "Resigned? Why would he do that?"

"Apparently, he's heading back overseas." She reached over and patted Jessa's hand. "Are you okay? I know you still have feelings for him."

"I'm fine. A little shocked, though."

"I'm sorry, but I thought you should know."

"Thanks. Maybe it's better this way." So, Jessa thought, the conclusion to the hopeless cause. She stood and grabbed a tissue from the kitchen counter. "It's ironic, isn't it?"

"What is?"

"I left Hudson Farrell because of him, and now he's leaving as well."

"For what it's worth, I think you should go see him this weekend. It may help with closure."

Gratitude for Sharon filled Jessa with warmth. "I'm impressed. You're showing your deep side again. And you're right, but I'm not sure I have the strength anymore."

"Course you do. You have more strength than a sumo wrestler on steroids. I'll come with you if you want, be your support crew. Feed you bananas, water you, adjust your pedal straps."

Jessa laughed. "It's not a triathlon, although I'll probably expend just as much mental energy."

"I never really understood the attraction, but I'm beginning to get with the program. He's not a bad bloke underneath, and he's a good-looking guy, I guess, not that looks are the most important thing, but—"

"A bit of eye candy's always a plus," they said in unison, both laughing.

Jessa raised an eyebrow. "Let's just say when he kisses you, he does so with a loud and clear kiss."

"Meaning?"

"He tells you exactly what he wants without saying a word." She smiled a naughty smile. "Loud and clear."

"Stop. I get the picture. Now I have to work on deleting it." Sharon picked up her plate. "Right, let's make a dent in this platter, and then I should get going."

"Thanks for coming over. I'm going to miss you."

Sharon looked up. "Yeah, me too. You're a good friend."

Later that night, Jessa slipped the CD into her stereo and listened to the tracks, each one representing a moody reflection of her life. William could be so rigid but, all the same, intensely romantic when he felt the need. But why now?

On Saturday morning, Jessa woke with a splitting headache. She'd dreamed of the Watershed, the river, togetherness, and estrangement.

Kathy's party had been fun, and it gave her the chance to say goodbye to her family, but now she wished she'd refused that last glass of wine.

Up and dressed, she kept herself busy with mindless chores. Toenails were filed and painted in a soft nude brown, hair dried and styled, and the headache dealt to with food, painkillers, and lots of water.

But no matter how hard she tried, she failed to shift William and his invitation from her mind. He'd resigned from Hudson Farrell. She didn't know what his plans were. Perhaps he wanted to say one final goodbye and let go of Rose by handing over the cello.

"I'm not sure I'll stay another night," Jessa said to her mother as she entered the kitchen around noon. "I still have a ton of packing to do."

She smiled and stroked Jessa's hair. "Are you okay?"

"Yep, but I'm going to miss you guys."

"We'll talk on the phone. I know I've been reluctant, but maybe this trip will do you good. And I'm going to learn how to use that new e-mail thingy."

Jessa chuckled. "Okay, Mum, you've just officially knocked me over with a feather."

"I am capable of trying new things, you know." She opened the fridge and peered inside. "Right, what should I make for lunch?"

Later, Jessa moped around the house, her thoughts flying to and fro. Should she? Shouldn't she? She wanted to listen to her heart, but her head also had plenty to say, telling her not to be so stupid.

After rereading his note, a hesitant decision was made. She'd return to Clifton Falls later that afternoon, ignoring William's invitation.

Wanting a few moments to herself, Jessa settled on the sofa in the living room and flicked through a magazine as her family moved around her. The next time she glanced at her watch, it was almost three. She wondered if William was standing on the front doorstep of the Watershed, waiting for her.

When her mother walked into the room, Jessa closed the magazine and placed it on the coffee table. She stood and kissed her on the cheek. "Right. I better get going."

"Good idea. If you leave now, the traffic won't be so bad."

After bidding her grandparents a tearful goodbye, Jessa picked up her purse and keys, hugged her father, and headed out the door to her car.

While driving south toward home, her thoughts turned to Rose. How did she feel about William the day she died? Were they happy? Did he kiss her, hold her, and tell her she was pretty? Was it a day like today—warm, sunny, and still—or cold and moody, with drizzle drifting in from the coast?

As she approached the bridge, Jessa recalled making love with William—caring, romantic, Watershed love. Just as quickly, she remembered the hurt and rejection when he left without looking back.

When she reached the Rata River Road T-intersection, Jessa slowed for a moment, then turned left onto the gravel road without considering the consequences. Clouds of dust billowed behind her, marking the dryness of the season—unusual for spring.

She'd traveled it many times, this road of love and loss, and as she passed the small white cross, she whispered a silent prayer. Someone lost their life on this road many years ago. Someone who once loved and was loved in return.

William's SUV was parked in the garage when Jessa pulled into his driveway. Emotions hovered in her gut, and as she left the car, she clutched the strap of her purse.

The front door was open. She called out. Stepped into the hallway.

The house stood proud, exactly the same inside—familiar—but smaller somehow. A vase of sweet-smelling daphne sat on the hall table, the unmistakable scent of spring. Its evergreen leaves were a testament to how some things never change, and its pink buds a definite indication that they do. Next to the vase sat a note with her name on it. She picked it up.

Ink-written words glided over the delicate blue paper he'd always used.

Jessa

Thank you for coming. I'm about to experience a considerable change in my life. Before that happens, I want to spend this afternoon with you, not as lovers from the past, but as friends. I know you said this wasn't possible, but the fact that you're standing in my home means our thread of friendship is still intact.

With your consent, I'd like to take some photos, like we discussed. I understand you weren't keen, but we're both adults—able to sort the true from the false—and I always want to remember you as you are now. I'm down at the boulders. The light is stunning. I've bought you a dress. You'll find it in the guest bedroom.

William.

What?

When Jessa entered the bedroom, ambient shadows filtered through the shutters on the outside of the building, infiltrating the room with muted light. She took a deep breath.

Draped across the end of the bed was a gown fashioned from dark ivory satin and georgette, and on the floor beside the bed, a pair of bronze-colored sandals sat, awaiting their chance to shine. Jessa ran her fingertips over the fabric and held the dress up for size. A pleated georgette overlay softened the corseted bodice, and tiny pearl buttons held the fabric in place on each shoulder seam. Delicate pleats fanned in at the waist, where they gathered neatly before flowing over the tight-fitting hip detail. From this, the skirt floated full length in soft layers of satin and georgette, now free of the pleats that constrained the torso.

It was exquisite.

She sat on the bed for some time, wondering why he'd want to do this. Dress her up like he owned her. Like some living fantasy.

But she couldn't say no.

Not now, not then.

After removing her jeans and top, Jessa slipped the dress over her head. She unhooked her bra and let it fall to the floor. Feeling free and mysteriously beautiful, she did the same with her panties. She'd never worn such a gorgeous creation—one made of satin and dreams.

Jessa stood in front of the mirror, weighing up her options. She could take off the dress and leave. William would never know.

But something stopped her.

As she strolled down the track, the dress floating melodically around her legs, Jessa focused on the boulders and the swift flow of the river, still full after the late-winter rains. William stood upstream at the water's edge, dressed in fawn linen pants rolled up at the ankles and a white shirt open at the neck. With his feet bare, neatly clipped stubble, and hair longer than usual, he looked like a model for an aftershave advert.

"Billy."

William shook his head and smiled at her use of his other-life name. "Jess. Thanks for coming." He took her hand and kissed her on the cheek while his thumbs calmed her knuckles. He smelled as he always did lately, courtesy of Ralph Lauren. "You look incredible."

"Thanks, but this gown's doing all the work." Regret washed over her as she looked at the river, the soft rapids, and the willows bordering the bank before turning to face him. Why was she here, playing her part in his drama? "You look pretty amazing yourself."

His eyes sparkled.

"Do you have your camera?"

"I do, but I want to discuss something first if that's okay." He sounded tense, his voice uneven as he shuffled his feet in the sand.

"We've said everything we need to say, haven't we? Why did you ask me here?"

"I know you're leaving soon, so I couldn't let this opportunity slip through my fingers."

"I'm feeling all kinds of crazy emotions standing here in this dress." She gazed out across the river. Shook her head. "Coming here was a mistake. And please, don't call me Jess. I'm not that girl anymore."

"Why not? You call me Billy when it suits you."

"No, I don't."

"Please, calm down and let me explain. I'm—"

"There's nothing to explain," she said. "I loved you once. I thought I'd love you always and you'd grow to love me. But now I know the full story. You never wanted me, did you? It was Rose you loved and Rose you desired."

"Cut it out, Jess. That's not true."

"Isn't it? In a dark corner of that pedantic mind of yours, you confused me with Rose."

"How can you say that? I admit, when I first saw you, I was shocked. You looked so much like her. Even though she'd been dead for years, she was there, in the very place where we shared our first kiss, staring back at me through your expressive eyes. Can you imagine how I felt?" The words tumbled from him like an urgent tide. "But we have so much more than Rose and I ever had. She was shy and awkward, barely fifteen. Sure, you look similar, but your personalities are entirely different."

"That may be so, but no one told me the real truth. You all kept it from me. And because of my mother's grief, I never had the chance to know anything about my aunt, but..." She turned to leave. "Anyway, I should go."

He took her hand and held it firmly. "Jess, wait. I want to make it right between us."

Jessa tugged her hand free and sighed. "Don't do this, William. We're over." Her voice softened. "We've been over for a long time. But for months, you've gradually taken up residence in my space, turning my head and daring me to feel what I no longer want to feel. That stunt you pulled last week…" She shook her head. "You can't appear on my doorstep and kiss me like I belong to you. Or look at me the way you do, claiming my soul. You have no right to invite me here under false pretenses."

Jessa sucked in her bottom lip to halt the quiver.

"That's where you're wrong. I have every right. Because you do belong to me, and I belong to you. I love you, Jess. I've loved you since you were eighteen, since our Watershed summer, and I always will."

William stepped closer and offered his hands, but Jessa's thoughts held her back.

"You are the most beautiful woman I know, both physically and in here." He placed his hand over her heart. "I don't want us to be a lost promise."

"William—"

"Jess, please. Hear me out." He smiled that knowing smile of his. "Look at you, so exquisite in that dress."

"Please don't say that." But she couldn't help offering a slight smile back. He still held her soul, and they both knew it.

"There's something I want to ask you. I should have asked months ago, but I let my sense of loyalty to people I don't even know cloud my judgment. I now realize the only person I need to be loyal to is you."

Uncertainty swept over her as he reached into his pocket, pulled out a small blue box, and popped it open. Inside, on a pillow of black velvet, sat a cushion-cut lavender sapphire floating in a halo of diamonds and joined by a rose gold band. William knelt in the soft sand and took her left hand in his.

"Jessa Rose, this ring symbolizes the lavender you love and the diamonds you've cut from your coal. I'm here to claim your soul, to deliver that promise, and ask you to be with me, always. Will you do me the honor of becoming my wife?"

She raised her right hand to her face, shaking in disbelief. "William! Are you serious?"

"I've never been more serious in my life. Please, say yes."

"But we hardly know each other. You barely even speak to me. We haven't even been on a date. And what about London? I'm leaving soon."

He got to his feet, shaking his head in amusement. "Jess, just answer the question. Of course we know each other. We'll worry about London and going on dates later. As soon as I kissed you that night, I knew you were still in love with me. Deny it all you want, but that kiss told me everything without a single word spoken. Let's not waste any more time playing games. We've wasted too much time already."

"But I didn't think we had any chances left. I thought our thread had broken forever." Emotion welled in her throat, and she tried to swallow it down.

William kissed her gently and held her for a long time.

"Marry me, Jess," he murmured. "I love you. I've always loved you and don't want tension between us anymore. I can't stand the person I've become around you lately. That arrogant bastard's not who I am. I want us to live together. I want you to say yes."

"Yes," she whispered. "Of course I'll marry you."

He slipped the ring onto her finger, uniting their agreement with lavender and diamonds, and kissed her deeply.

"I can't tell you how relieved I am right now." William laughed as he pulled her into a hug and lifted her off the ground. "I've been a nervous wreck all day. But you didn't put up much of a fight."

"I'd never have taken you for the nervous-wreck type."

"You have a lot to learn." He led her up the track to the deck. "Come, sit." They sat and held hands. "Before we take the next step, I want to give you a chance to tell me how much I hurt you, to get it off your chest, so we can start afresh with a clean slate. Also, I'm sorry for how I acted when I started at Hudson Farrell and for leaving you like I did."

"I understand. We don't need to discuss it any further."

"You forgive me, just like that?"

Jessa held up her left hand. "Maybe this gorgeous ring played a part."

"I'm so sorry I hurt you. Let's promise each other our relationship will always be about open communication from now on."

"I agree and promise."

"I promise as well, and I forgive you for calling me a 'fucking egotistical, arrogant bastard of a man.'" William grinned when she shot him a look of concern.

Jessa's expression shifted to one of amusement. "I try not to use the F-word, but that day, I couldn't think of a better fit."

He kissed her. "I'm so happy right now."

"Me too."

William glanced at his watch. "Right, we don't have much time. You need to fix your makeup, and I should change my pants. Come on." He entwined his fingers with hers and steered her inside, where he kissed her with passion and intent.

She wanted to make love right then and there; the anticipation tingled between her thighs, leaving no room for doubt. But it appeared he had other ideas.

"You have about fifteen minutes," he said. "I'll change and meet you out on the deck."

"Fifteen minutes until what?"

"The ceremony." He kissed her again and turned to walk away.

"William?" Jessa called him back. "Are you saying we're getting married today?"

"Well, you are dressed for the occasion." He chuckled when she stared at him in stunned disbelief. "I assumed you'd be okay with it."

"You ask me to marry you, then give me fifteen minutes' notice before I can even think about it? What about the license and a prenup?"

"I organized the license last week, and we don't need a prenup. I'm not after your Honda or any of your other worldly possessions." His brow furrowed in concern. "You're not having second thoughts, are you? I want to do it now—while we're in the moment. And I'm guessing your family won't approve, so perhaps it's better this way, don't you think?"

He was right. They'd be married and deal with the fallout later. After all, it was their business. "Don't look so worried. I don't want to wait either."

"Good. You were stressing me out for a second there."

"It's just a thought, but do you have a suit here? You look so sexy in a suit."

"When have you seen me in a suit?"

"At the architecture awards." She fanned her face with one hand and flashed William a naughty smile. "So hot."

"Jessa Rose." He grinned. "You're trouble with a capital T."

"Is that right?"

Jessa stepped into the bathroom to fix her hair and makeup. She had no idea what he'd planned, but when she went back outside, there he stood, looking beyond handsome in a well-cut charcoal suit, white shirt, and dark red tie. Three people stood beside him, and as she approached, four pairs of eyes followed her every move.

"Hi. I'm Shelly." The older woman stepped forward and offered her hand. "Your marriage celebrant. This is my husband, Joe, and my daughter, Janie, who's kindly offered to do the photo shoot and be your other witness."

William had thought of everything.

"Hi, pleased to meet you all. Have we met before, Shelly? You seem vaguely familiar." Jessa searched for a memory of Shelly but found none. It puzzled her.

"I don't think so. I knew your family when I had the—"

"General store, right?"

"Almost twenty years ago now. A past life, darlin'."

As Shelly stared, Jessa frowned. "Is everything okay?"

"It's just… you're so like your aunt. You have an entirely different air about you, but…"

"Yes, so I've been told."

William held a posy and a garland of spring flowers: gypsophila, sprigs of just budding lavender, and cream rosebuds. He gently set the garland on Jessa's head and smoothed strands of hair from around her face. "You're exquisite," he whispered as he handed her the posy.

Jessa went up on tiptoe and kissed him on the cheek. "Love the suit."

Shelly cleared her throat. "Shall we begin, you two lovebirds? William, you know what to say, so go ahead."

William beamed with pride throughout his vows, his expression loving and steady. The William she fell in love with had returned.

"Now, Jessa, please repeat after me." Shelly faced Jessa and began.

"I, Jessa, take you, William, to be my husband." Jessa spoke softly, her gaze steady on his. "I promise to love you always, through all lifetimes, and for all of the years we have together on this earth. I promise to respect and care for you, to honor our brief, and see the beauty in our union—every hour, of every day, of every year, for as long as we both shall live." Her soft smile grew into a full-blown grin. His vows were charming, but Jessa wanted to add a few words of her own. "May we always be true friends, passionate lovers, and soul mates into eternity."

William gasped at her words, but before she could ask if he was okay, Joe turned on the sound system, and Gloria Estefan's "Here We Are," the English version, floated over the deck.

It was perfect.

43

AN EXTRAORDINARY DAY

It was after six when William carried Jessa into his bedroom and sat her on the bed. Early evening light cast a monochromatic glow over the room as the curtains floated in and out on the breeze wafting through an open window. He unzipped his fly and let his suit pants drop to the floor, then stood before her in white boxers and his already half-unbuttoned dress shirt. Jessa shivered as he undid the corset hooks on her bodice.

He peppered tiny kisses along her neckline, his hands secure at her waist. "You okay?"

"I'm kind of nervous about you seeing me naked after all this time. And I'm not sure I'll remember what to do."

"Don't be nervous. And I promise you, you won't have forgotten." His lips skimmed her shoulders. "And if you have, I'll remind you."

"And I don't have any panties on."

He laughed. "What?"

"I took them off before I came down to the river, so the dress had a smooth line."

"Perfect."

William slid his hands under the corset and caressed her nipples with the tips of his fingers as he gently nipped her earlobe. "Relax,

Jess. I've got you," he whispered. Then he kissed her—not tenderly as she remembered, but with hunger and wanting, his lips almost bruising hers.

Her fingers inched up and down his torso until they landed on cotton-knit boxers. She guided them past his knees and watched with fascination as he kicked them to the floor, then she lay back on the bed, taking everything in.

William sat beside her. With hands above her head in total capitulation, she smiled up at him. He nipped and sucked her breasts, his tongue gentle over their firm peaks, then harder as their passion increased. His hands slipped over her skin, impatient fingers curling through her light mound of hair as the two of them reconnected. Jessa closed her eyes and took his erection in hand, her touch firm.

"Open your eyes and look at me," he commanded, nudging her legs apart. "I've missed you. You're so incredibly beautiful."

"No, it's embarrassing." Her words were barely a whisper.

"It's not. Don't hide from me."

William moved a hand over hers and coached her, driving his desired rhythm while his other hand gradually brought her almost to the edge. As she arched her back in pleasure, he entered her with strength. She couldn't hold back. Orgasms and tears clung to each other, the perfect partners.

"Tell me."

"In one word?"

"Just one."

"Liberated," she cried.

They lay tangled together in lovers' dreams. After the years they'd spent apart, William still couldn't believe Jessa was his wife. Reluctant to let her go, he pulled her closer, planting soft kisses on her hair as he stroked his hands over her back. She was more beautiful than he remembered: strong and toned, with fuller breasts and broader hips complemented perfectly by a petite waist. He couldn't take his eyes off her. "You're perfect."

She snuggled into him, her tears hot on his naked chest.

"Hey, don't cry," he soothed. "It's okay."

"Sorry. It's been an extraordinary day."

"I know." He traced his fingers up and down her spine. "To be honest, I'm relieved it's over. It stretched my organizational skills to the max."

Jessa laughed through her tears. "Only you could dream up a wedding like that. It doesn't seem real. After all those months of angst."

"Angst?"

"Well, what would you call it?"

"Months of intense sexual frustration coupled with torment and—"

"Angst. Exactly. Anyway, after all those weeks of watching you at the office, thinking we'd never make love again, it's kind of surreal being here together."

"I know, and I'm sorry. I wanted to tell you how I felt, so many times. But I was worried about your parents' reaction. Still am. Also, when I returned from Melbourne, Dan laid it on the line, which stopped me in my tracks for a while."

"What do you mean, laid it on the line?"

"Let's see. What were his words? 'Inappropriate affair'—on my part, not yours—'sexual harassment' and something about what a 'sweet kid' you are. He stopped short of saying he'd ask for my resignation if I didn't back off, but the implication was there, so I did. I wasn't worried about the job, but I didn't want to put you in a compromising position."

"But we'd done nothing wrong."

"As I told him. But, to be fair, I constantly imagined you naked, so he had a point."

"Is that right?"

"I bet you were doing the same. Imagining me naked."

"I was not!"

William propped himself up on one elbow and smiled down at her. "Really? What about the day we went to Scenic Hill? And be honest."

"Okay, you want honest? I wanted you to make love to me that day, right there in the field, under the April sun. To kiss me like you meant it, hold my face in your hands, and—"

"Say it."

She laughed. "I just said it. I wanted you to make love to me."

"You wanted me to fuck you. And that's exactly what I wanted too. That's when I knew I had to get you back, but when you turned down my dinner invitation, I wasn't sure if you still had feelings for me. You're a difficult woman to read."

"Maybe that's a good thing. Anyway, do I live up to your naked fantasies?"

"You surpass them in every possible way." He ran his fingertips across her chest, tracing a line under each breast. "May I ask you something?"

"Of course."

"How long has it been for you?"

"I'm not too sure. You're the one keeping a tally with numbered notes attached to bouquets of French vanilla rosebuds. It's such a relief, though. I sometimes wondered if I'd ever have sex again."

"Are you saying you've not had any other sexual partners?"

Jessa smiled bashfully. "Possibly."

"That's what Sharon said, but I found it hard to believe."

"Sharon told you? Seriously? And, anyhow, why's it so hard to believe?"

"Because you're so sensual and such a flirt."

"I am not."

"Yes, you are. I've seen you in action, remember. Made me jealous as hell, all those tradesmen eyeing you up. And about those rosebuds—"

"William, you can't bring up the rosebud-beheading incident on our wedding day!"

"I found it hilarious, seeing those cut-off rosebuds in my wastepaper basket that day."

"Really? Well, you certainly got me back with your 'Music to Make Love To' playlist. And that little stunt with Gloria Estefan. You made your point loud and clear, even if it was in Portuguese."

William raised an amused brow. "You noticed?"

"How could I not? Anyway, if we're spilling secrets, when did you last have sex?"

"What? We've only been married a few hours, and already I'm getting the sexual inquisition?"

"Honesty, remember? Spill."

"About eighteen months ago, I guess."

Jessa's eyes widened. "You hadn't had sex in eighteen months?"

"Couldn't you tell?"

"Now that you mention it, you did seem rather eager."

"For a while there at work, I thought my balls would burst. And that day at Scenic Hill… Let's just say that the cold surf helped rectify the situation for an hour or two."

"I'm sorry, but it's all your fault. You should have made a move sooner."

"Yep. But that's us, a series of missed opportunities."

"But not anymore."

"No, not anymore."

They slept little that night as they explored the deep passion they'd lost that fateful summer from years before. The next morning, it rained like the middle of winter. They stayed in bed, ate sweet mandarins off the tree in the garden and crumpets with butter and honey, then made love and slept again.

Jessa awoke around noon. Rain pelted the iron roof, but she could hear the bathtub filling over the din. It took her back.

William smiled as he walked into the room. "You're awake." He bent to kiss her.

"What are you doing?" she asked.

"Setting the scene." He kissed her again.

"The scene?"

"For our bathtub reenactment. Do you remember your lines?"

"Should I?"

"Well, you didn't say much last time, just a whole lot of sexy sighs." His eyes glinted, melting her with anticipation. "We're doing it a little differently this time. It's the director's cut."

"What does that mean?"

"I'm the director." He cocked a brow. "I'm in control, so there may be added intensity. We'll see how well you play your part." He smiled again. "Get up and get dressed."

His authoritative tone reminded her of "office" William. "But if we're having a bath, why do I need to get dressed?"

"Because I said so."

He watched her enter the living room, fully dressed as he'd instructed. They stared at one another, anticipation creating the mood while "Rainy Night in Georgia" played on the stereo. William swept her into his arms, carried her to the bathroom, and set her down at the end of the tub. Candles cast ambient light across the room as raindrops hugged the outside of the windowpane. They stood face-to-face, his stubble neatly clipped and shoulders muscular and defined.

"Undress me." William's visual assault intensified as Jessa set his shirt buttons free and tugged his jeans to the floor. The white cotton of his boxers accentuated his tan, and when she pulled them down, his erection sprang to attention.

William slid into the tub and sat back on his haunches as "Runaway" floated in from the living room. He turned her to face him and, without so much as a kiss, unbuttoned her top and undid the drawstring of her yoga pants.

She stood in her bra and panties—delicate black and white lace adorned with tiny pink bows—the scent of essential oils and the soft flicker of candlelight adding ambiance to the room.

"Take them off," he ordered.

As she undressed, he sat back and watched her. Jessa recalled her exhilarating discomfort when he'd insisted on seeing her naked all those years ago, and her nipples peaked harder at the intensity of the memory.

William guided her into the tub and sat her low on his torso, his erection rigid before her. He entwined his legs possessively around hers. Neither of them spoke as her embarrassment matched her intense desire.

He picked up the faucet, edged the ice-cold water into life, and let it drip slowly over her breasts and into the warm water surrounding them. Jessa arched her back with the assault, seeking freedom against his intention.

"What are you doing?" Her breath was hot and thick.

"I love it when you talk husky. Hold still."

"No… don't."

"Yes," he whispered into her ear, then ran his tongue around its shell, sending a clear message directly to her genitalia.

"William." She fought again to free herself. "Don't you dare!"

"Shh, keep still." He tightened his legs around hers, holding the faucet high in one hand while using his other to gently caress her as the icy water trickled down her lower torso.

"Ah—William."

"Horny, Jess?"

"Yes… Stop it, William!" Jessa giggled. "It's freezing."

"Are you going to come for me?"

"William…"

"Yes, you are. By the time I've finished with you, anyway." He halted the trickle and rubbed the pad of his thumb back and forth, bringing her almost to the brink before resuming his cold-water assault. Jessa teetered on the edge as two fingers found their intended target. He increased his pressure and rhythm.

"Which is it, Jess? Are you going to come?" he whispered. "Yes? Or no?"

As a female's voice, singing in French, floated in from the living room, Jessa felt his breath on her neck. "Yes."

"Yes, what?"

"I'm… close. William," she murmured, "I'm… I'm so close."

He replaced the faucet and quickly turned her to face him. Her head fell back as he slowly slid inside her.

As she relaxed into their rhythm, he pushed harder, faster. "Sorry, but this won't take long, believe me. Fuck… Jess!"

Climactic union engulfed them, her pleasure and pain molding into one as he pumped into her repeatedly, holding her tightly around the hips, aiding her movement as his orgasm took hold. "Shit, Jess. Fucking incredible."

She collapsed onto his chest, Spent.

His lips brushed her forehead. "You okay?"

"I'm not sure about this 'added intensity' business."

"You're a woman now. You can't expect to have teenage sex when you're married." He kissed her with a small peck.

"But how will I know how to play my part effectively?" She gazed up at him, her arms entwined around his neck and a slow smile edging her lips upwards. "After all, I've not had any dramatic training."

He laughed. "You're trouble. I always knew it. Practicing our lines is going to be a whole lot of fun. I love you."

"I love you too, so very much."

"Let's eat. I'm starving."

Jessa watched William rummage through the fridge. "What do you fancy for breakfast?"

"Poached eggs on toast with cracked pepper and a side of bacon."

He chuckled. "Perfect. I make a mean poached egg."

"I've been thinking."

He took two pans out of the cabinet and filled one with water. "What about?"

"London. I already have my ticket booked."

"I'm coming with you. If that's okay."

"What? You've already arranged this?"

"Sharon kindly helped book me onto the same flight, and I have some special dates planned."

"Sharon helped you?"

"Why do you say it like that? Sharon and I go way back," he said with a grin. "I couldn't have pulled it off without her. Sounds like she played her part perfectly." William put several slices of bacon in a hot pan and broke four eggs into the simmering water in the other before popping down the bread to toast.

Jessa shook her head. "She's a dark horse that Sharon. Wait till I get my hands on her."

"So, can I come?"

"Well, I can hardly get married on the weekend and take off to London without my husband, can I?" She stood to kiss him and snaked her arms around his waist. "You can come."

"Thank you, Mrs. Cook." He turned back to the pans. "Looks like our eggs are almost done."

She sat at the breakfast bar, sadness weighing heavily on her heart. "The only downside's telling Mum and Dad."

"Your father knows."

"Knows what? That we're married?"

"No, not exactly, but I asked him for his blessing to start seeing you again, and he gave it."

"No way! You're having me on."

"I don't have people on, you know that."

"You have no idea how happy that makes me," she said.

William started plating up their breakfast. "I do, but it still won't be plain sailing."

Jessa lay in bed the next morning and watched as a naked William strolled into the en suite. Still muscular and taut, he looked younger than his years. She'd never imagined him being so comfortable with his body on full display. It made her smile. She'd often mentally undressed him when they worked together. Despite being inappropriate, she couldn't help herself. Just the smell of him took her back five years to that day at the Watershed, when they made love for the first time.

Now, the room was the same, as was the bed, but the sex was altogether different. Like he belonged to her and she belonged to him.

"Jess, can you grab the phone?" His voice from the bathroom broke into her thoughts.

She answered the call. "Hello?"

"Okay, honeymoon's over," Lea said. "Mum and I are bringing a casserole around, so you better stop whatever you're up too and make yourselves presentable."

"You know?"

"Who do you think did your flowers?" Lea giggled as usual. "But we understand why we weren't invited. Big secret and all that."

"What about the dress? Did you choose that too?"

"No. Uncle William did. I can't wait to see it. We'll be over in an hour."

Minutes later, Jessa stood in the shower, cuddling into William's back.

"How are you feeling?" he asked. "I was worried you'd freak out."

"Loved."

"Me too." He turned and kissed her, cradling her face in his hands as he always used to. "I feel much better about us now that you're older."

"Why's that?"

"Because we're equals. I'm no longer seducing a teenager. I felt so guilty about that at the time. And about Rose."

"I'm sorry for throwing myself at you. You didn't stand a chance."

"If I'm honest, I wanted you the first day we met."

"No! But you were so mean. I was just doing my job."

"I know. Guess my defense mechanism kicked in. But that didn't stop me from wanting to have sex with you. I gave myself a stern talking-to after you left that day." William washed his upper torso, then ran the sponge over hers. "But I still couldn't stop thinking about you. You tormented me."

"So it's my fault, is it? I can honestly say you didn't have that effect on me that first day. I never wanted to see you again."

"Yeah, I know. I was a bastard and made you cry. But if it's any consolation, you made me feel most uncomfortable, disturbed."

"Poor you."

He grinned. "When did I start to have an effect?"

"When you walked out of your bedroom with that tiny white towel slung low around your hips. Your eyes danced."

"Is that right?"

"After we first met, Lea showed me photos of you from before the accident. You looked so familiar and cute with longer hair. You reminded me of someone, but I couldn't think who. Lea laughed when I said you were hot."

"You didn't!"

"That's what girls do when we get together—we talk about hot guys," Jessa teased. "But she didn't like me saying that about her favorite uncle."

"We have a strong bond, Lea and I. The two of you are similar in many ways, with your sense of loyalty and strength of purpose."

"Yes, she's a great friend." Jessa pumped body wash onto her palm, then smoothed both hands over his pecs. "Getting back to you wanting to have sex, you know, when you first met me. I thought sex was purely the physical act?"

"It is. But that's what I felt, to be honest. I wanted to have sex with you. I didn't think for one minute that you'd still be a virgin, though."

"Why not? I was only eighteen."

"Because you're a sexy little minx. You were even back then. You're very comfortable with your sexuality. That's arousing to a man. I wanted to pick you up, dump you on my bed, and fuck you until you screamed my name."

"William!"

"What? Don't play the coy card with me. I know now how hot you are for it," he said with a grin. "You took advantage of me."

"I did not."

"Is that so? Anyway, do you know what's wonderful about being married?"

"What?"

"Sometimes, when pushed for time, you can have frantic and steamy sex, even against the wall of the shower, and it's okay."

"And what about fucking me out of the ballpark?" Jessa crouched, rubbing a soapy sponge over his buttocks and down his thighs.

"Please don't remind me I said that. I'd had a bad day. I'm sorry."

"But I've always wondered what it would be like," she murmured, "you know, to be fucked out of the ballpark."

He gazed down at her, their bodies sharing that unique energy two people in love share. "Where are your red shoes?" he asked, a smile lighting up his face.

"At home, packed away in their cardboard box."

"Well, you'll have to wait, won't you? But perhaps I could give you a little taste."

"Sounds delicious. Sometimes, a little taste is as satisfying as a whole plateful if you savor it."

Jessa squealed as William lifted her and pressed her back against the cold tiles. She wrapped her legs around his waist as he entered her.

"Ballpark sex is much more intense than making love, so there'll be no savoring," he said, firmly increasing his rhythm.

"Oh, really?"

"Yes, really."

Once Anna and Lea had gone, William relaxed as the weight lifted from his shoulders and his world turned in harmony for the first time in many years.

"Hey, I have a wedding gift for you. It's upstairs." He took Jessa's hand and led her up the staircase. She stepped into the room off the landing, her eyes widening with surprise.

"Wow." Sheer curtains floated from iron rods, and two large sisal rugs covered the hardwood floor. A small sofa sat at one end, but otherwise, the room was bare. "What a gorgeous space."

"I come up here occasionally to meditate and read, and I sometimes use the room next door as an office." He motioned her forward. "Check out the bathroom and walk-in closet. Plenty of room for shoes."

Jessa took it all in. "You have excellent taste."

"Thank you. That's why I married you. It's the perfect space for our bedroom, don't you think? Once we have the brats."

"Brats?"

"Our kids."

"And when's this happening?"

William slipped an arm around her waist. "Well, I'm not getting any younger, and I do want children. I realize marrying an older man fast-tracks your life, but we should start trying soon—if you agree."

Jessa pecked him on the lips. "Okay."

"You don't sound too convinced." He returned the kiss.

She smiled and shook her head. "We've been married less than thirty-six hours. I need to take a breather before I start pushing out babies."

"I can live with that. Close your eyes."

"Why? What are you up to now?"

"I told you. I have a wedding gift for you." She did as she was told, and he guided her through to the adjoining room. "Okay, open them."

In front of her, on the same low pedestal as the one in his apartment office, stood his gift.

"Aunt Rose's cello." Jessa ran her hand over the fingerboard and strings, connecting to the energy of Rose. "Thank you. You don't know how much this means to me. May I play it?"

"Please do. I've waited a long time for this." William grabbed the cello stool from the closet. "Play me something modern."

"I have just the thing." Jessa sat and positioned the cello between her legs. "You have to guess."

He watched with pride as she plucked the first few chords and allowed the music to carry her away. A lump lodged in his throat as the song's meaning washed over him, and when she'd finished, he couldn't tear his eyes away.

"Lou Reed's 'Perfect Day.' That's the best version I've ever heard."

44

LONDON'S CALLING

Back in Clifton Falls, Jessa stood at the gate of her family home, feeling like a young child about to be reprimanded. She inhaled sharply before walking up the path and knocking on the door.

"Why didn't you just let yourself in?" her father asked as he opened it.

"Hi, Dad. Is Mum home too?"

"She's in the living room. How's the packing coming along?" He frowned at her hesitation. "Don't just stand there. Come in."

"Good. Almost finished." Jessa stepped inside and walked down the hall and into the living room.

Her mother looked up from her knitting and smiled. "I'm beginning to think this trip's a great idea. Look at you. You're positively glowing. I thought you were busy tonight. Are you staying for dinner?"

"No, but I wanted to talk to you both if you don't mind."

"Of course. Is it about money? Because we can help, can't we, David? Whatever you need, be sure to call us. In fact, call us as soon as you get there to let us know you're safe, and—"

"Mum. Stop. I need to say something, and it's hard enough as it is." Jessa sat opposite her, her hands clenched in her lap. "It's about William Cook."

She stared at Jessa in disbelief. "Oh? What about him?" Her voice could have frozen the Tasman Sea.

"You know we met through work?"

"Of course. Though why you ever went to work for Hudson Farrell, I'll never know."

"Well, to be fair, I had no idea why you disliked him until recently, did I? No one let me in on the secret of Billy and Rose. I knew she died in an accident, but that's all."

"Dislike him? That's an understatement. And it was no accident. She never should've been on the back of that farm bike."

"Louisa, please," her father said. "Let Jessa have her say."

Jessa hesitated, wringing her hands together. "Anyway, William and I, we have a special bond."

Her mother frowned at her. "What do you mean? That you and William Cook are friends? That man will chew you up and spit you out, mark my words. Nothing good will ever come of this. It's beyond belief."

"Mum, please, there's more."

"Don't tell me that you're lovers. I couldn't bear it." Her mother's voice grew louder, and Jessa was momentarily lost for words. "Wait, you're not pregnant with that bastard's child?"

"I'm not pregnant. It's…" Jessa locked eyes with her mum, frown matching frown, pain matching pain. "William and I eloped on Saturday."

"Eloped? No! You're married? To Billy Cook?"

Her tears and the primal sob in her voice struck Jessa head-on. She wanted to reach out but realized her mother wouldn't receive or return the gesture. Nor would she want her daughter to see her cry.

"I'm sorry. I know it's a shock, but it's true. We didn't want to wait, so we eloped. We love each other. And we want you and Dad to accept that we're adults and have made this decision for the right reasons."

Her mother stood and paced across the room, then stopped. Turned. "There will never be any possible reason for you to marry that sick bastard. I can't stand the thought of him near you. How could you ever think any of us would accept this?"

"I love him."

"Love? Don't talk to me about love. How would you even know what love is at your age? How could you do this to us? You, our only child!"

"I know what I want. It doesn't mean I don't love my family, but William is part of that family now."

"That man will never be part of our family," her mum shouted. "Do you understand? You've made your choice. You've married him. Married him in secret. It's a betrayal of the worst possible kind. You need to leave. I can't bear to look at you right now." She turned her back on Jessa.

"Louisa. Calm down." David patted Jessa's hand. "Jessa is always welcome here. William talked to me about seeing her again. He asked me for the amber light, and I agreed. I just didn't expect it to turn green so quickly."

"You did what?" she yelled. "That man killed my sister, and now he's taken my only child from me! How could you agree, David? I want nothing more to do with it." She fisted her hands. "Please leave."

"It was an accident. How much longer does he have to pay?" The lump in Jessa's throat grew as she pleaded her case.

"That man won't pay until he meets his maker."

"I'm sorry. I don't want to hurt either of you or Poppa and Kathy G., but I love William. He means everything to me."

"And what do you mean to him, eh? He only wants you because you remind him of Rose. He wants to get back at us. That's all he wants."

"How can you say that?" she sobbed. "He loves me."

Her mother scoffed. "We'll see."

"Louisa, that's enough," her father said as Jessa burst into tears. "It was an accident, and William has nothing to get back at us for."

On the drive back to William's apartment, Jessa questioned whether she'd made the right decision. Had they been too hasty? Would her relationship with her mother ever heal to the point where they were comfortable in each other's presence again? Her family meant everything to her, and now, their bond hung by a frayed thread of her making.

She sat in the car for a while before taking the stairs to his apartment. When she reached the door, the orange had been replaced in favor of navy blue.

"How did it go?" William wrapped her in a hug and kissed her gently on the forehead.

"It didn't. I'm out of the will and on the street." Jessa tried to make light of it, but a single tear escaped down her cheek.

"I should've gone with you." He took her hand and rubbed a thumb over her knuckles. "She'll come around."

"There's no coming around with my mother. You know that. She's cast me out."

"She still loves you. A mother always loves her child."

"I wish that were true, but you know as well as I do that it's not always the case. I hope we made the right decision, getting married when we did."

"Course we did. I'm a selfish bastard and couldn't wait any longer. I love you so very much."

"Thank you." She kissed him. "What happened to the front door?"

"I thought it was time for a change."

45

CONCLUSIONS

MONTHS LATER

David hung his jacket on the coat rack in the hall and stepped into the kitchen. He kissed Louisa on the cheek, filled a glass with water, and sat at the dining table to watch her make dinner. After all these years, he still found her beautiful and wanted to make love to her every day of their lives, no matter how difficult she could be. "Come and sit down for a minute."

Louisa glanced at him and smiled. David hadn't seen her smile much lately, and he wondered what her reaction would be to his news.

"Hold on." She lifted a casserole dish from the fridge. "I'll just pop this in the oven."

David watched and waited. "Jessa called today while you were at bridge."

"From the UK?" Louisa sat in the chair opposite, her smile evaporating. "What did she have to say? I suppose it's all turned to custard in London, has it? I told you it wouldn't last. A leopard doesn't change its spots."

David closed his eyes briefly. Sighed. "Why do you have to be like this?"

"Like what? I'm just telling it as it is."

"No, you're not. You're being your typical negative self, jumping to conclusions about other people's lives when you know nothing about them. And you don't know how it is because you choose not to have a relationship with your daughter. People can change if you give them a chance. And that's what I'm doing here, Lou."

"That man will never change."

"It's not William I'm talking about. I'm giving *you* the chance to change, not him."

Louisa fiddled with the hem of her apron, her face displaying a controlled pout. She heaved a loud sigh. "Well, are you going to tell me what she said?"

"She's coming home."

"What, on her own? Thank goodness for that."

"No, not on her own. They're coming home."

"But they've only been gone eight months. I suppose they want money, do they?"

"Don't be ridiculous. Why would they want money? William's a wealthy man. He owns commercial property all over town and a block up on Edgewood Place, where they plan to build as soon as they get home."

David stood, grabbed a can of beer from the fridge, and took a long swig. "Anyway, she's pregnant. With twins. They're coming home while Jessa can still fly."

"Pregnant? Well, I'm sorry, but I won't be having anything to do with William Cook's babies."

David prickled at the contempt in his wife's voice. "That's enough, Lou. You haven't listened to a word I've said, have you? These babies are our grandchildren. And if I have anything to do with it, we'll welcome the twins into our lives *and* our home. Understand?"

"There is no need to talk to me like that," she said, sulking.

"There's every need. And you'd better think long and hard about how you're going to handle this because I'm almost at the end of my extremely long tether."

PART V

THE RETURN

46

2190 DAYS LATER

"Vanessa called me today." William snuggled into Jessa's back, his hands automatically cupping her breasts under her T-shirt. "She's back and wants to catch up for dinner."

"Sounds good. Perhaps Mum and Dad would have the girls for the night. I'll ask Dad."

"Good plan. As long as you drop them off. Your mother's one scary piece of work."

"Man up, Billy Cook. She doesn't bite."

He pressed a soft kiss to her shoulder and snuggled closer. "I'm not so sure about that."

She rolled onto her back and looked at him. "Didn't Vanessa go out with Nikau back in the day?"

"Yeah, a long time ago." William frowned. "How do you know that?"

"I'm not sure. You must have told me."

"Did I? I'd almost forgotten about it."

Jessa hesitated. "Did you ever think you guys might get together, you know, after that night?"

"You make me so horny when you're naked and that little jealous streak comes out."

"I'm not jealous. Or naked." She skimmed over the same page of her book for the third time.

"But you could be naked soon," he whispered against her neck, his lips leaving tiny kisses in their wake. "And the answer is no. We didn't have any chemistry."

"But you have it with me? The chemistry?"

"Absolutely. Shall I make passionate love to you? I'm aware women reach their sexual peak around thirty, so I have a particular duty to meet your needs. Don't you agree?"

"Not tonight. I'm tired, pregnant, and getting to an interesting part in my book." Jessa giggled as he slipped her T-shirt over her head and flung it across the room.

"Okay, keep reading." William caressed her neck and shoulders, working his way around to her breasts, his touch increasing in pressure.

"William…" She lay her open book face down on the bed.

"Jess?" He turned her face toward him and kissed her again. "Lie on your tummy," he commanded.

The book fell to the floor.

William's lips caressed her neck. "Please open your legs."

"You're so polite when I'm pregnant."

"I'm always polite when I make love to you."

"But not when we're in the ballpark."

"Jessa Rose, how can you say that?" William ran a hand over the junction of her buttocks and between her legs. He eased two fingers inside her, holding her waist with his other hand.

"Oh… that feels so good."

"Does it now?" he whispered. "Do you want more?"

"Yes. Please."

"I thought you'd rather read."

Jessa arched her back, a soft moan escaping as he increased his momentum. "That was before you tugged at my nipple strings. You know what that does to me."

"I do. That's why I do it. They're a direct dial to your sex department."

"And what's yours?" She moved his free hand to her mouth and gently sucked his thumb, gradually adding pressure.

"I wouldn't do that if I were you," he said as he inched inside her and increased his rhythm quickly.

"Why not? You like it, don't you?"

"Jess! *Shit*, Jess."

"Tell me," she challenged.

"Just one word?"

"Just one."

"One word's never enough."

After their dinner date with Vanessa the following weekend, William joined Jessa in the shower as usual. With the twins at her parents', their house was unusually quiet.

"I like Vanessa," Jessa said. "She's so honest and down to earth. And, boy, she looks amazing for her age. I wonder what her secret is."

"I'm pleased you agreed to meet up with her for coffee. She'll be a good person to talk to about Rose."

"Rose?"

The sight of William wrestling with his thoughts concerned Jessa, as he seldom had a problem expressing himself. "I'm not sure how to say this, but it seems to me your connection with Rose goes beyond that of the physical, beyond that of aunt and niece."

"What do you mean?"

He ran a soap-filled sponge over his torso. "You have a special bond with her spirit. Don't you sense it?"

"Sometimes, but I try not to give it much thought. It's all a bit freaky." Jessa leaned her head against his shoulder. "Where exactly did she die?"

"Where that white cross is, down by the river. I erected it six months after the accident."

"Where? On Rata River Road? Why didn't you ever tell me?"

"Guess I assumed you knew."

"I always imagined she died somewhere on the highway. It's strange. I'm drawn to it whenever I drive past it."

"Yeah, me too. Each year, on the anniversary of the accident, I placed eight bunches of lavender around the cross. I did it for many years… until I moved to Sydney. She loved lavender, just like you do."

"Why eight bunches?"

"Eight was Rose's favorite number. She once told me she was born at 8 a.m. The accident happened at 4:31. Do you get the significance?"

Jessa thought for a moment. "Four plus three plus one equals eight."

"Strange, isn't it?"

"Yes. And I was born at 8 a.m. as well."

Once she realized those who truly loved her didn't keep score, Jessa's life fell into place more graciously. Even so, self-doubt still surfaced occasionally when memories of her past collided with unprocessed thoughts, and for some reason, the thought of meeting with Vanessa again made her nervous.

They met at a popular waterfront café. It was warm and sunny at dawn, but by midmorning, humid rain clouds hugged the north coast, and the air had cooled a little. Jessa shivered as a light rash of goose bumps kissed her skin. Kathy G. would say someone had just walked over her grave, but Jessa had never fully understood her grandmother's meaning.

After placing their order, they sat chatting at a wooden table in a quiet corner while they waited.

"Congratulations, by the way," Vanessa said once they had their food and drinks.

"Um, what for?"

"You're pregnant, aren't you?"

"Did William tell you? He can't keep secrets these days." Jessa sipped her cappuccino and broke a slice of biscotti into thirds before taking a bite.

Vanessa inhaled the aroma of her coffee with an enthusiastic hum. "No, it wasn't William." She took a sip. "I'm an intuitive. Do you know what that is?"

"Kind of. You sense things. See flashes of information."

"That's the one." Vanessa smiled before adding, "Sometimes, things I'd rather not sense."

Jessa nodded. She knew the feeling.

"Actually, that's what I wanted to talk to you about." Vanessa hesitated. "Please tell me if I'm overstepping the mark, but have you considered seeing someone?"

Someone? "About what?"

"Your intuitiveness."

Jessa entwined her fingers and rested them under her chin while she pondered Vanessa's words. "I have ways of dealing with it."

"So, you understand what's going on?"

"What do you mean?" Jessa murmured as an unfamiliar awareness surfaced. "Do you know something I don't?"

"Well, I knew Rose." Vanessa held her gaze. "We weren't friends, but we went to the same high school."

"Okay."

"She was a lovely person… kind and respectful."

Jessa picked up her cup, then placed it back on the saucer as William's suggestion about confiding in Vanessa came to mind. "This might sound crazy," she started, "but it's like Rose is guiding me. She's in my thoughts, and… Anyway, it's hard to explain."

"It doesn't sound crazy, at least not to me. But I'm not sure that's what's happening here. With you and Rose, I mean." Vanessa shifted in her chair. "I have a friend who's a hypnotherapist. From my observation and what William's told me, I'm thinking it's something you could explore."

"What's he said?"

Vanessa chewed her bottom lip as if second-guessing herself. "Look, I'm not sure if I should even be talking to you about this, so feel free to tell me to butt out, but do you believe in past lives?"

"Like reincarnation? What makes you ask?"

"Just a thought. It's been niggling away at me since dinner the other night. Actually, long before that." She hesitated. "William told me about your panic attacks."

"Really?"

"Please don't be mad at him. He trusts me, and I would never betray that trust."

"I'm not mad. I'm open to change. In fact, I embrace it." Jessa paused, then smiled. "I guess I know a secret about you too."

"What sort of secret?"

"He told me you were his first."

"Oh, that. He was a sad boy, you know, after Rose died. We spent one crazy night together, fueled by sorrow, loneliness, and way too much alcohol. We both found it awkward afterward, for ages, actually. But that boy sure can kiss."

"Hey!"

Vanessa had a delightful, open laugh, and she used it freely. "Sorry. I'm joking."

Jessa smiled. "Tell me about Rose."

"Everything you need to know about her is inside you. It's setting that knowledge free that's the hard part." Vanessa pulled a flyer from her purse and passed it across the table. "There's a Mind, Body, and Spirit Festival here in a few weeks. You could come with me if you want."

"Do you think?"

"The answers are out there. It's up to you to find them."

"That three-way connection does fascinate me."

"Yes, me too. Right, I'd better get going soon." Vanessa downed the rest of her coffee. "It's good to see William looking so happy and well. I've always had a soft spot for him, and I'm glad you two are finally together and have a family. It's taken a long time."

"Thanks. He's a great dad, and I love him to bits. I'm a lucky girl. I have two wonderful daughters, a stunning home, and a man who loves me unconditionally. If only Mum would offer William an olive branch."

"Ask your spirit guides to show you what steps to take. I have a feeling she'll come round."

"I hope so. And thank you. It's been nice catching up with you this morning."

"Call me anytime." Vanessa offered Jessa her business card as they both stood. "And, Jessa, if you keep an open mind, who knows what you'll discover?"

Jessa's thoughts flew in several directions as they crossed the road to their cars. Over the past few years, she'd accepted the energy surrounding her. But now, she wondered if she had the strength to stir the mud, especially when it had settled and the water was somewhat clearer.

Vanessa's card sat in Jessa's purse for several days while she mulled over their conversation. By the end of the week, she'd decided to explore all opportunities.

The Mind, Body, and Spirit Festival would be her first step.

47

BRAZEN MOVES

William walked into the kitchen, took Jessa in his arms, and kissed her like he meant it. "I've been waiting all day to do that." His hands snaked around her waist as his hungry lips found the soft spot under her earlobe that he knew drove her crazy. "I've missed you."

"Stop it. You're sending naughty signals. Have you finished work already?"

His flirty smile was never far away these days. "I figured I'd knock off early for a change." He picked up a peach from the fruit platter on the island and took a bite. "Where are the girls?"

"In the media room with *Mary Poppins,* since it's raining."

"You okay?" he asked with concern.

"Kind of. I've had an interesting few weeks."

"That's an understatement. Do you need to talk to someone about it?"

"Maybe, but I want to record a video for Mum and Dad first."

"A video?"

"Yes, I've been trying to figure out how to tell them. I don't want to do it in person."

"Why's that?"

"Because I'm not sure I have the strength to carry it through. With a video, I can bare my soul without interruption, and then they can make up their own minds."

He nodded and bit into the peach again.

"Can you help me set it up?" she asked.

"Sure, just say the word. How about tonight? I'll take the twins out for burgers if you want some space."

"Would you? That would be great. I can't decide what to make for dinner."

Despite Rose and Jessa's connection fascinating William, he still struggled to make sense of it. But later that evening, as he watched the video of Jessa telling the story of a life she had no knowledge of —the life of Rose Faith Churchill—he felt as if his heart would break.

Afterward, he walked into their room and sat on the end of the bed.

Jessa looked up from her book, her eyes expressing the question she'd waited her entire adult life to ask: "Well?"

"That's some story, Jessa Rose. How do you feel?"

Tears mingled with her smile. "Free. And at peace. It's a relief to get it off my chest. But it's not a story to me."

William slid under the covers, pulled her close, and smoothed the hair from her face. "I know. Everything's exactly how it happened."

"Is it?"

"You even remembered about me touching her leg on the bus. I wasn't sure if she'd noticed." He smiled. "It was a brazen move on my part."

"Brazen? Great word. Come to think of it, you haven't changed much. You still have plenty of brazen moves."

"Does it surprise you, what you've remembered?" he asked. "It must be quite a shock."

"I'm not sure shock covers it, to be honest." Jessa sighed deeply. "I'm sorry, but I'm pretty emotional right now. I don't know what to think. But you don't seem at all fazed by it."

"I'm not. It's the only possible explanation from where I'm standing. Remember when you asked me about the spot where Rose died?"

"Where you erected the small white cross?"

"Yeah. After the accident, I went there a lot—to talk to her, to feel her spirit. But apart from the first few times, I couldn't sense her around me. It was like she'd moved on."

"Don't you find it strange, what I've recalled?"

"Sure, but the fact we exist on this spinning ball in space called Earth and reproduce other beings with a tiny sperm and an egg is also strange, don't you agree?"

"I guess."

"Now that you know, do you regret coming back?"

"Never. I needed to finish what we started. There was no other option. I couldn't leave you alone to live a life of sorrow and regret."

A lump caught in William's throat as he contemplated how Jessa treated those she loved. "I pushed you away, but you came back for me, Jess. You came back."

"I did." She hugged him closer. "What are you thinking about?"

He pulled back, laughing. "Hmm, the usual. How much I want us to get naked right now. But I'd like you to play the cello for me first."

"What shall I play?"

"Bach, 'Cello Suite No.1 Prelude.'"

"So, we're feeling a little classical tonight, are we?"

"You could say that."

"Did Rose ever play it?"

"Not that I recall."

48

DISTANT CORRIDORS

Dear Mum,

I like to think I have a handle on my emotions, but when it comes to us—our relationship—I clearly don't. The adage you taught me as a child that one should never worry about something until it becomes a problem is now redundant, and often, I struggle to process my fundamental beliefs.

I've mulled over this letter for a while now. In my head, the words flow effortlessly with profound insight, but whenever I try to physically document my thoughts, they awkwardly jostle for position on the page. The words that surface when I lie awake in the darkest hours stay in the far corners of my mind, refusing to reappear when I need them the most. And my efforts to record them remain on my to-do list, along with all the mundane expressions of my everyday life.

While I tell myself I have a near-perfect recollection of my internal monologue, it's an illusion. This letter is one of many attempts and the one I trust you'll take the time to read with an open mind, giving me the quiet and uninterrupted audience I've wanted from you lately.

I understand the reasons for our estrangement, and until recently, I assumed it would always be this way. However, over the past few weeks, I've gained insight and, therefore, the necessity to finally put my innermost feelings into words.

I can't ignore this opportunity to explain my choices—those choices of which you so strongly disapprove. Those same choices I've had the burden of carrying with me—at significant personal cost—without ever being sure of why I had to make them.

Being a mother myself, I understand how the mother/child bond can be damaged by decisions made by either or both parties. My greatest wish is for the bonds we once shared to be restored with acceptance and compassion. I understand why you let your love for Rose drift into the distant corridors of your soul. But in doing so, you denied me the chance to have a relationship with her.

My children are our link. You've no idea how happy we are that you've agreed to see the girls over the past few years and, indeed, how happy they are to spend time with you and Dad. For that, I thank you from the bottom of my heart. You're a good person, and now I'm older and, hopefully, wiser, I accept you did what you felt you had to do, given what you saw as the ultimate betrayal.

What I have to say might sound strange—be hard to get your head around—so I'm asking you to keep an open mind. If you're not certain you can do that, stop now, put this letter and the video back in the envelope, and return it to me. That way, I'll know you're not yet ready to move forward...

Louisa put down the letter, struggling to make sense of its contents. What on earth was going on? She inserted the video, but something stopped her. Instead of pushing *play,* she phoned her mother.

"I've had a letter from Jessa."

"Oh? What does it say?"

Louisa took a deep breath. "Honestly, Mum, I worry about her, and those kids. I really do."

"Look, no matter what you might think of Jessa and William's relationship, she's a great mother, and he's a wonderful dad. They love the twins, so you don't have to worry about that. What does the letter say?" her mum repeated.

"It's cryptic. Rambling, for want of a better word."

"Do you want me to talk to her?"

Louisa hesitated. "She's sent us a video. At least, that husband of hers gave it to David. He said we should watch it together. I guess it's of her and Billy Cook playing happy families."

"Louisa, give it a rest. It's been long enough."

"I'll never let it rest, not as long as I draw breath, and I can't believe you're telling me I should. A leopard doesn't change its spots." Her tone conveyed her irritation.

"Fine, but at least respect Jessa's choice. It's not like she's some lovesick teenager. She's an intelligent young woman."

Louisa didn't want to keep going over the same old ground. She'd forked away at it for years, and still, the same weeds grew. "What do you think?" She sighed into the phone. "Should we watch it?"

"Definitely," her mother said. "I love her with all my heart and know you do too. Sometimes, tough love can be a little too tough."

"Do you have the letter?" Tom asked as he and Kathy relaxed in the Reynolds' living room after dinner several days later.

"I do, but most of it's personal. I'll read you the last part." Louisa took the letter out of her purse and flicked through it until she reached the final page. She cleared her throat.

"I'm not sure if you're familiar with past-life regression. It's held my interest for a while now, and I'd like to share something with you, Dad, Kathy G., and Poppa, but not in person. I need to speak without interruption, hence the video.

"William had no knowledge of this video's contents until I'd finished it. I didn't want his influence to cloud my recollection. He, like everyone else, has struggled to make sense of the 'other me,' and this process has been healing for us both.

"Please, if you're together, watch this video until the end. Whether you make contact after hearing what I have to say is entirely up to you. The ball's in your court.

"Yours in love and light,
"Jessa xx."

David inserted the video into the machine and pressed *play*. Jessa appeared, sitting in the office at their home, papers and books surrounding her. She thanked them for their time and then began.

> "I believe that to move forward into our future, we must negotiate our past. Often, this involves a retrospective journey beyond the physical. You may find what I have to say controversial, but I've decided not to let other people's prejudice affect my thinking or my life.
>
> "As you're all aware, I began having panic attacks in my teens, and from that point on, my life changed forever. William has a friend, Vanessa, who went to school with Rose. You may know her from living in the Valley. Vanessa's an interesting character. She calls herself an intuitive, but others have called her many things over the years, including a white witch."

"What on earth? This is ridiculous!" Louisa jumped to her feet, ready to dart from the room. "I refuse to put myself through this."

David paused the video. "Sit down, Lou. She's our daughter, the daughter we fought so hard to have, and now I'm fighting for her to be heard."

Louisa stared at him in disbelief. "No, David, I can't watch this rubbish."

He inhaled sharply, holding her gaze. "You can and you will. Sit down."

Louisa bristled at his tone but sat beside her mother on the sofa without another word.

David restarted the video.

"A while back, Vanessa suggested I attend the local Mind, Body, and Spirit Festival. Initially, I was hesitant. Even though I realized something was going on, my fears held me back. However, in the end, my quest for the truth was stronger than my fear of the unknown, and it's proving to be one of the best decisions of my life.

"Following the festival, I joined a group of like-minded women who meet once a month to discuss all things spiritual. Through this group, I've learned to meditate and be open to the lessons of my past.

"Lately, I've read several books on the subject of past lives and reincarnation, which led me to a deeper search. At first, I was nervous. After all, reincarnation isn't part of our structured faith, but to me, it makes perfect sense.

"Of course, not everyone believes in it, and I respect that. Opponents claim recollections such as I've experienced are simply genetic memories, stories from our childhood recounted by our subconscious mind. I prefer to view these memories as a search of the soul's database.

"A woman in my group is a past-life regression therapist, and she's guided me through several sessions of hypnosis. Through these sessions, I've recalled significant segments of a previous life.

"I now believe, without a shadow of a doubt… that I was Aunt Rose in my most recent past life."

"Stop the tape! I can't listen to any more of this nonsense," Louisa said, her voice thick with shock and disbelief. "Please, David, this is madness."

David pressed pause on the remote for the second time.

"Well, I, for one, want to hear what she has to say," Kathy said. "If you don't want to watch, we'll understand, but I need to see this. Do it for us, please?"

Louisa stared at her family without comprehension. In her opinion, they'd all gone stark raving mad. "Fine."

"So, we all agree?" David glanced around the room. "Should we continue?"

"As you said before, we owe it to her," Tom said.

> "One thing I remembered after my panic attacks was the scent of lavender. The pump house—the Watershed—was surrounded by fields of lavender when William took Rose there, and I've always loved that smell. William and I have rarely spoken of Rose, apart from before we were married, when he told me of their connection. This is important as I work through the process, as I don't want him prompting my recollection. I guess he's the only person who can truly know what happened the day Rose died, but I want to share my memories of that day. I'll do this partly as Rose for clarity.
>
> "I recalled William, or Billy, as his friends called him, in my first therapy session. He was much younger, with long hair and a fresh face. Before continuing, I want to clarify that when I was eighteen, Lea showed me photos of him from his high school days, and even then, the sense of recognition was strong. So, I admit, I had an image of the younger William in my mind but was certain it came from more than the photographs in Lea's album.
>
> "I liked Billy a lot, secretly wanted to be his girlfriend. He watched me play the cello at school concerts, and sometimes, I went to his rugby matches. He was so cute, and I never imagined he'd be interested in me. But one day, he sat beside me on the bus when I visited Nana, and his leg touched mine. After that, I saw him most days when I worked at the general store.

"Billy kept asking me to go swimming with him and mistook my shyness for indifference. I finally agreed, and after work one day, we rode to the river and swam in the deep hole down by the old bridge. I wore an orange bikini with a wooden center ring. Do you remember it, Mum?"

Louisa stiffened, shaking her head. She'd loved that bikini and wanted one the same. She'd often wondered what had happened to it.

"We walked along the track to the old pump house, now the Watershed. What an amazing space—but solitary. It had once served a purpose but now stood rigid and alone, as if waiting for a time when it could be of use once again.

"I consider buildings, colors, and numbers as having either masculine or feminine energy. This space was definitely masculine, like when you step into an empty church, and the ambiance and solitude calm you."

Kathy spoke. "That sounds like Rose. She talked about that."
"Mum, be quiet," Louisa scolded.

"The light was surreal, streaming through the cracks in the rough-sawn timber, the motes like diamond dust. I remember the tongue-and-groove flooring—covered in dirt and full of borer holes. We made out—innocently. He told me I was beautiful, and for the first time in my life, I felt it. I'd never kissed a boy before. Wow, what an incredible feeling."

Jessa smiled at the recollection, briefly closing her eyes before continuing.

"I needed to be home by five and asked if I could ride the bike to the hay barn. Billy wouldn't let me at first, but I managed to talk him around. He held on tight as we traveled along Rata River Road. It was a hot, dry day, the hills parched to a wheaten yellow. I felt alive and free with the heat of Billy's body at my back and his arms around my waist.

"We were in an accident. But are there truly any accidents in life? I'm not so sure. We hit a sheep. I couldn't stop in time."

She paused, visibly upset.

"Sorry. This part's distressing for me. I slid across the gravel, feeling like I was sliding off the earth. I ended up lying on the edge of the river, close to the track, being pulled from my body by a force so strong that I couldn't fight it, no matter how much I wanted to stay with Billy. He was crying, and there was so much blood. A bone had pierced his leg. He called for me, over and over, until he couldn't call anymore.

"I hovered for what seemed like such a long time, trying my hardest to float back to my body. But I couldn't. I swam in a swift current of mist, drifting away and helpless to do anything about it. I saw myself far below. Blood stopped pumping through my veins as my heart stilled and life drained from me. Although I couldn't see my face, I sensed it was me."

Jessa paused again and plucked a tissue from a box on the desk. Anyone could see she was telling the absolute truth, or at least, what she believed to be the truth.

"I floated through the darkness toward that mystical light we hear about. Even though I knew instinctively that I couldn't return to the body of Rose, I tried to with all my strength."

Jessa frowned and moved her hands prayer-like to her lips as if thinking through a distraction.

"I saw a life that once was—in a similar place, but a different time. You were all there. Mum as my sister, a sister I loved with all my heart, Poppa as my dad, and Kathy G., what a wonderful mother you were to Rose. I have no idea why I got the chance to come back, but I'm so grateful that I did. I never wanted to leave Billy alone… broken and sad.

She took a deep breath and pressed her lips together before dabbing her eyes with the tissue.

"As time passes, I recall other events, some major, some minor. There's still a lot I don't know and much that unnerves me, but finally, I'm reassured that I'm not crazy after all. Aunt Rose and I share the same soul. I'm convinced of that now."

The room was full… of stunned silence.

49

THE POINT

"Daddy." Sophie tugged at his sleeve. "Daddy. There's someone at the door."

William removed his headphones, letting the music flow into space. "Thanks, baby girl. Let's go see who it is."

Sophie jumped up and down with excitement at the sight of her grandparents standing at the front door. "Grandma, Granddad! What are you doing here?"

"Louisa, David." William couldn't believe his eyes. "Please, come in."

"We're here to see Jessa. Is she home?" Louisa asked coolly.

"She's not. Come inside." William stepped back in a gesture of invitation. "It's cold out there."

"Thank you." David ushered his wife inside.

"Mummy's away this weekend," Sophie said. "Sit down, and Daddy will make you a cup of tea, won't you, Daddy?"

"Gwandma, it's you!" Lizzy ran from the bedroom and into Louisa's arms. "What are you doing here? You never come here."

"We came to see your mummy." Louisa lovingly hugged Lizzy's small frame.

"She's at a weetweet," Lizzy said.

"What kind of weetweet?" David smiled.

"In the country. They're getting down on the gwound."

"Grounded," corrected her twin sister.

Louisa and David both looked to William for an explanation.

"It's a health retreat. Jess has been under a lot of pressure lately."

"So we gather," Louisa said curtly.

"Okay, girls, back to bed with the both of you. Come on."

"Daaaddd, can't we stay up a bit longer? It's Friday night," Sophie said, "and we're almost seven."

"Yeah, she's nearly seven, and I'm nearly seven too," Lizzy echoed.

"I want to talk to your grandparents. Come on, back to bed."

"Okay. But you need to tuck us in," Sophie demanded.

"Excuse me?"

She giggled. "Sorry. Please, Daddy."

William was still smiling when he returned from their bedroom to his unexpected guests. "Can I get you anything… a drink, coffee?"

"This isn't a social call," Louisa said. "It's about this… this nonsense on the video."

"What's your take on it?" David asked.

He eased onto the sofa opposite his in-laws, considering his words carefully. "Well, first of all, it isn't nonsense to me."

Louisa went to cut in, but David stopped her. "Let him have his say, Lou. That's what we've come for, to let everyone have their say. Carry on, William."

William was hesitant. "I've tried to figure out this puzzle for years. At first, little niggles bothered me. Jessa called me Billy sometimes when she was stressed and referred to events from my teenage years that she knew nothing about. Some days, the words just tumbled out of her."

Louisa shook her head. "I knew coming here was a mistake. You're all talking nonsense, the whole lot of you. Why can't any of you see it?" She looked away. "There's no point carrying on."

"Louisa," David said, "for once in your life, open your mind and listen. Look, we're all here for the same reason. We all love Jessa in our own way. No matter how much you blame William for Rose's death, it's clear he and Jessa belong together and have two of the cutest kids I've ever seen and another on the way to prove it. It's time to heal old wounds before it's too late." He looked at William. "About that drink—I could do with a whiskey on the rocks if you don't mind."

In the kitchen, William filled two old-fashioned glasses with ice and poured the golden malt over it. He filled another glass with wine, which he offered to Louisa when he returned to the room. She didn't refuse.

He picked up from where he left off: "Look, I've struggled with this too. Please don't think I haven't. I didn't want to fall in love with Jessa. When I found out who she was, I was shocked. I knew it was wrong on so many levels."

William sipped his drink. Whiskey wasn't his tipple of choice, but he welcomed its warmth. "She enchanted me in every way, and I couldn't get her out of my head. The first day I saw her, she was standing in my home, fresh-faced and all of eighteen. She looked so much like Rose—it disturbed and amazed me at the same time. But that wasn't why I fell in love with her."

"There's no denying Jessa and Rose share similar features and mannerisms," David said. "I struggle with it myself sometimes."

"Anyway, we couldn't stay apart. And I tried. I tried so damn hard it hurt. When Tom asked me to give her up, I was a mess. But it took me five years to realize I couldn't live without her."

"That's all well and good, but this past-life nonsense… I cannot, for the life of me, even begin to entertain the idea." Louisa sat tight as a knot, staring at William. "It's all in her mind. She's a sick girl, and that's why we're here."

"I disagree," William said. "I admit, it seems far-fetched, but Jessa has recalled events that she couldn't possibly have known about. So many that I've lost count."

"I've watched that video more than once, and to my mind, it's just a whole lot of romantic fantasy."

"To be fair, Lou," David said, "William will know if what Jessa said about him and Rose is a romantic fantasy, as you call it."

"Well?" Louisa asked. "Tell us. Is what Jessa says about the pump house an accurate account of what happened between you and Rose that day?"

"An exact account."

"And was Rose on the front of that bike?"

"Yes." William sighed. "I'll never forgive myself for that one huge error of judgment. She said she wanted to be free and begged me to let her ride to the first hay barn."

Louisa's face paled.

"Well, tell me this," she continued. "If that's the case, why didn't you inform the police at the time?"

"I did. They said I was lying and warned me to keep my mouth shut out of respect for your family."

"So you did. You kept quiet about it," David said. "But Tom had his suspicions. He told me."

"What?" Louisa glared at her husband. "When was this?"

"Years ago. He asked me to keep it between ourselves."

"But I'm your wife, and you kept that from me?"

"What good would telling you have done? Look, let's get back to the point, shall we?"

"I've heard quite enough," Louisa snapped. "I can't believe you both think this nonsense has any basis in truth." She glanced around the room, not looking at either William or David.

"There's something else," William said.

"Of course there is," Louisa replied. "And there always will be." She got to her feet.

"Jessa wanted to protect you from a pact Rose made with you both."

"Is that so?" Louisa said, sitting back down. "And what is this mysterious pact we need protecting from?"

William gathered his thoughts. "Jessa said you lost a baby through an ectopic pregnancy." He studied them for a reaction. Louisa's lips tightened into a thin line as David reached for her hand.

"How could Jessa know that?" David murmured. "We didn't tell anyone except Rose and Maggie."

"Someone else must have told her." Louisa sat ramrod straight, her face still pallid. "Someone from the hospital."

"So why didn't she mention this in the video?" David asked.

"Jessa didn't want Kathy and Tom finding out. She said, to her knowledge, your parents never knew, and she didn't want them hearing it from her."

"How dare you talk about my lost baby like that! Rose told you, didn't she?"

He shook his head. "Rose never told me. Ask Jessa if you don't believe me."

"That won't be necessary," Louisa said. "I can't forgive you, William. I've tried, but I can't. Not for Rose and not for marrying Jessa behind our back. Come on, David. I won't stay here any longer." Louisa snatched up her purse and stormed toward the door.

"Thanks, William," David said as they both followed her. "We have a lot to take in."

"What do you think?" William asked. "Can you get your head around it?"

"I'm not sure, but I want a closer relationship with my daughter before I'm too old to enjoy it. That's all I want."

50

THE EPIPHANY

"How was your weekend?" William helped Jessa carry her bags in from the car. "And how's our little fella in there?" He rubbed her baby bump.

"Great and great. Very worthwhile—lovely people." She smiled at him. "I've missed you, Billy Cook."

"Not as much as I've missed you. Five days with just the twins for company and no wife to help ease the tension. Challenging doesn't even begin to cover it. Come here." He pulled her close and kissed her with longing and tenderness.

"Mmm, nice. Where are they, by the way? I've missed them so much."

"With Anna. She'll drop them off around seven," he said with a grin.

She glanced at her watch. "So that's, what, three hours max?"

He ushered her into their bedroom, hopping on one foot as he hurried out of his jeans. "Have you thought of any amazing words? For our one-word rule?"

"You'll have to wait and see."

"Hold on a minute." William keyed the sound system into life, and

"Rainy Night in Georgia" floated through the room. "Guess who this is."

Jessa smiled as she listened to the song. "Aaron Neville. His voice is unique." She closed her eyes and stood at the end of the bed, swaying to the music. "He sings it well. It may become my favorite version."

"And am I your favorite version of a husband?" His lips caressed her neck as his hands made a beeline for her breasts.

"Always."

Afterward, they ate grilled cheese sandwiches in bed with their legs entangled, not wanting to let one another go.

"What did you learn about yourself?" William asked. "Any epiphanies?"

"That's a tough one. I have to trust myself to be me. And I realize that's a cliché, but for me, it has an entirely different meaning. I've been rather unsettled lately."

"You have." William took her hand and placed a soft kiss on the center of her palm. "But still, you're on a forward path now."

"I am… but it's hard for me to let go of Rose."

"Do you want to?"

"I need to. I'm not Rose. Sure, she's part of my soul, but I don't want her to define me."

William pushed off the bed and headed into the study. He returned with an old brown envelope.

"What's that?"

"Notes I wrote to Rose. Kathy returned them to me after the accident. Ring any bells?"

"Not sure. Are they love letters?"

"No, not at all." He positioned himself cross-legged on the bed. "Okay, I'm going to ask you five questions."

Jessa grinned. "Five questions? How original."

He grinned back. "I was fifteen, so give me a break. Shall I continue?"

She giggled. "Sorry, carry on."

"Number one. What's your favorite color? Or you can choose a palette."

"Hot pink, green, orange, yellow. A spring-garden palette. Plus, I do love a good navy blue."

He opened the first note and read it aloud.

"A moody sky. I can see why Rose liked that," she said when he'd finished. "And the art at the Watershed—moody-sky palettes, all of them."

"How extremely observant of you, Mrs. Cook. When I came across them in a small gallery in Auckland, they reminded me of Rose. They were hideously expensive, but even to this day, they still inspire me, and that's what art is all about. Question two. What's your favorite song?"

Jessa thought for a moment. "'Landslide.'"

"Dixie Chicks' or Stevie's version?"

"They're both worthy, but I have to pick Stevie's. What did Rose choose?"

"'Taxi,' by Harry Chapin."

"Oh yes, I love that song too. Especially the cello bridge. I think Mum had that album when I was a kid."

"Actually, she didn't. Kathy told me they put it in the coffin with Rose, along with her favorite book."

"Really? And Rose had a locket. What happened to that?"

"She did. She wore it on the day of the accident, but you'll have to ask Kathy or your mum if they still have it. Question three. What's your favorite book?"

She laughed. "*Where's the Green Sheep?*"

"Children's books don't count in this instance." William leaned forward and kissed her softly.

"Okay, *The Alchemist*. What about Rose?"

He read out her answer to question three, but Jessa hadn't heard of Charles, Walter, and Kitty. When he told her the title of the book, *The Painted Veil,* she wasn't familiar with it, even though she'd read some of Maugham's work, mainly short stories.

"Next question. What movie has most inspired you of late?"

"*The Holiday*."

"What? Out of all the great movies ever made, you choose *The Holiday?*"

"Why not? I love that film. Romance sans violence and with a happy ever after. It's the perfect chill-out movie. I never tire of it. What did Rose put?"

"*Brother Son, Sister Moon*. The story of Saint Francis of Assisi and Saint Clare. Do you know it?"

Jessa shook her head.

"You can watch it on YouTube."

"Is it worth watching?"

"What can I say? There's no accounting for taste when it comes to the arts," William said with a laugh. "Now, my beautiful wife, we've come to the final question."

"Okay."

"What do you want most out of life? Think before you answer."

"That's easy. To know my soul's purpose."

"Snap."

"Really? We were the same on the last one?"

"Exactly the same. So you see, you and Rose may be the same soul, but you're the progression of Rose. You like bright colors, aren't afraid to tackle life head-on, and flirt without consequence. Sure, you love romantic movies, books that inspire, and stories of the human heart expressed through song, just like Rose, but you are uniquely you."

"Thank you." Jessa leaned forward and kissed him. "That means a lot. You're a sweet, sweet man. And I do not flirt without consequence."

"Yes, you do. Most of the time, you're not even aware that you're doing it." He gave her a knowing wink. "I'd like you to read the last note. It's kind of significant."

William handed her the thin sheet of writing paper. She studied the page, smiling at the flair of his younger written hand, and began to read:

"An Interview with Cello Girl
"Question Five
"What do you want most out of life?

"Your response to question five is the most insightful yet. Once again, your reply intrigued me. To, and I quote, 'know your soul's purpose' comes from a philosophy many of us don't understand. The point of this questionnaire was to find out more about you. Not the shy, self-conscious girl on the bus, not the girl who hides behind the cello at school functions, not the girl who has a summer job at the general store, but the real you. Your answer is honest and true.

"You trusted me enough to share what you want out of life, and for that, I thank you."

She stopped, then continued slowly, *"May we always be true friends, passionate lovers, and soulmates into eternity."*

"What! My wedding vows?" she said in disbelief. "That's a little too creepy."

"I know. Spooked me out at the time, believe me. Do you remember anything about them now? The blue notes, I mean?"

"I'm not sure, but thank you for sharing them. Is it just me, or were you more of a romantic back in the day?"

"I was a horny teenager. And horny teenagers dream up silly romantic notions."

Later, with the twins asleep in bed, they sat and talked some more. Jessa animated in her enthusiasm about the retreat and William sincere in his interest. He loved seeing her happy and how her face shone when she hugged their daughters. He felt so blessed.

"I've something to tell you," he said as he reached for her hand. "Your folks came around on Friday evening."

"What, here?"

"Yes, here. I couldn't believe it. The last time your mother spoke more than two words to me was at Rose's graveside the day they discharged me from the hospital. I wanted to visit her grave before I returned to the farm." He thought back. "Although, to call it speaking isn't entirely accurate."

"Why? What did she say?"

"She screamed her head off and called me a sick bastard. Your father had to hold her back."

"Oh no." Jessa chuckled. "I'm sorry. Mum has a real potty mouth when she's angry. But what did they want?"

"I gave your dad the video last week."

"What? Billy, I asked you not to until I'd made up my mind."

"I made up your mind for you. That's what loving husbands sometimes do."

"Billy!" she protested again.

"Okay, Jess, I can tell you're not mad at me because you're calling me Billy."

"I am mad at you. So what did they say, William Cook?"

"According to David, your grandparents are surprisingly okay with it. But they've always loved you unconditionally. Your mother's a different story. I wonder if she'll contact you."

"And what about Dad?"

"He's like me. Loves you, no matter what."

Her mood turned serious. "Can I ask you something, and will you answer me truthfully?"

"Sure."

"When did you have your first inkling about Rose and me?"

William recalled how the haunting song he loved so much triggered her panic attack after the awards dinner. "It wasn't until the triple-As that I seriously considered the possibility. 'In My Life' was one of Rose's favorite songs. Her string quartet played it at a recital at my school. But even after that night, I dismissed it."

"I know that song," she said. "I bet I could play it if I tried."

"And there's more. You also knew some of my best lines. Things I said to Rose."

"Really?"

"The day of the accident, I told her, 'Life's too short for regrets and compromise.' Do you remember saying that to me at the Watershed the night your car broke down and adding 'diets' to the mix?"

"Of course. Life's too short for regrets, compromise, and diets."

"Also, when we went swimming, I suggested that Rose take off her bikini top. I said, and I quote, 'It gives you such a sense of freedom, swimming without restrictions.'"

"But she wouldn't take it off. And it was orange." Jessa finally realized the color's significance. "Wait a minute, the same orange as your apartment door used to be."

He smiled. "Correct."

"And the night you gave me the shoes, I talked about swimming without restrictions, didn't I?"

"You did. And then, the last part of your vows."

"That's crazy."

"It wasn't until I confided in Vanessa that all the pieces fell into place."

"Do you have any doubts?"

"None whatsoever. You know details about me that no one other than Rose could know."

"It's scary"—Jessa snuggled into his shoulder—"this thing called life."

William kissed the top of her head. "It can be, but we'll get through it. We're incredibly fortunate to have found each other."

She looked up at him. "More than once."

"Yes. More than once."

51

ESTRANGEMENT

Jessa peered out the window at her mother's car parked on the side of Edgewood Place. She walked the long driveway flanked by lime trees and lavender—her smile bittersweet and mood quietly hopeful—and opened the passenger door.

"Mum, is everything all right? Are you coming in?"

Her mother stared straight ahead. "I can't do this."

"Do what?" Jessa soothed her. "Come on, Mum, come inside."

She stepped out of the car and followed Jessa up the path, then sat at the kitchen table and watched while Jessa made coffee.

"Why do you have this old table in your beautiful home? It looks like you pulled it out of a farm shed."

"It's rustic chic." Jessa smiled. Her mum had never been one to mince her words. "Are you hungry? I made a carrot cake yesterday with cream cheese frosting."

"No, thank you. I can't stay long. How's the pregnancy going?"

"Good. Only six weeks to go now."

Jessa waited for her mother to make the next move. She'd imagined this moment for a long time, but the ball was in her mother's court.

"About this video nonsense."

Jessa's heart sank.

"I'm not sure I can entertain the idea, to be honest," she continued.

"So why are you here?"

"Because I'm unhappy, and I want the truth. I worry about you."

"I'm fine, so please don't worry. And you're unhappy because you refuse to let go of events that make you sad. You wrap your suffering around you like a cloak."

"That's rubbish," she snapped. "Anyway, that's beside the point. This Rose business… You need to see a doctor. Go back on your medication."

"I'm not ill. I don't need medication."

"But you've been so depressed."

"Years ago, not lately." Jessa filled two mugs from the coffee pot and set them on the table. "Look, I admit, it's been a struggle figuring out the Rose mystery, not only for me but for William too. I finally feel at peace with it. I'm more than happy for you and Dad to see the kids, but we can't have a closer relationship if you insist on continuing your campaign of hatred against William. He doesn't deserve it. He's the most loving husband and father. In all the years we've spent together, even though he's a very forthright man, we've scarcely exchanged a cross word. He's my everything."

Her mother pulled a handkerchief from her purse and dabbed her nose. "At least you're making yourself perfectly clear."

"Do you think I want this?" Jessa sat and took her mother's hand. "I don't want it to be this way. I'm a mother, too, and I can't even begin to imagine how it must feel to be estranged from your child. But I'm all too familiar with what it's like when the shoe's on the other foot."

"What do you mean by that?"

"To be estranged from you. It's not a choice I made."

"Isn't it?" She pulled her hand back. "You made the choice, young lady, when you ran off and married that man in secret."

"Yes, well, I'd love to tell you about our wedding day and show you the album. It was the most stunning, romantic day of my life, and no one will ever take that away from me."

"I'm not trying to take anything away from you. *You* made your choice." She heaved a weary sigh. "Anyway, I've decided to study," she added, almost as if thinking aloud. "Do a degree, you know, by distance learning."

Jessa experienced an overwhelming desire to reconnect. To put aside their differences and let go of pointless resentment. "Mum, that's fantastic."

"It's time I did something for myself." She sipped her coffee. "I've lived with the despair of Rose and Billy for a long time, and I want to let it go."

"You can. You can let it go." Jessa took a mental step of courage toward her mother. "Look, you don't have to believe me, but William and I, we're happy together. Sure, we have our moments like any other couple, but he loves me for who I am, and I've always loved him. Ever since I was eighteen. Our love—it can't be undone. It's forever and always, but that doesn't mean I don't love you and Dad."

Her mother sighed again. "So, where do we go from here?"

"Let's take baby steps, shall we?"

"I'm not sure if I can. Not without proof."

"I've given you plenty of proof. But I'm not asking you to believe me or change your views for mine. I want us to be a family again, that's all." Jessa smiled at her. "For me, that's the purpose of our life's journey—learning to live in harmony with those we choose to spend our lives with, finding our truth and letting others find theirs without interfering or passing harsh judgment. It's not an easy task."

Jessa took a deep breath. She needed to say more. "I always assumed I'd mold my children into perfect little beings using lots of love and fair discipline. But now that I'm a mother"—she paused as she thought of her girls and the mischief they made—"I've begun to understand that how they feel, what they have to say, and their reaction to outside stimuli is their way of finding their life's purpose."

Her mother nodded slowly as if she was really listening. "I never knew you and William were lovers when you were younger. Not until recently, anyway." Her tone was laced with acceptance, but she looked sad and weary. "I understand what it's like to love deeply. I've always loved your father in my own way, but when he said he'd talked to William, given his blessing, I felt betrayed. It was like he suddenly had a life of his own that I wasn't a part of."

"I get that. And I'm sorry it had to be that way." Jessa paused. "Dad's a first-best man."

"He is." Her mother rummaged in her purse. "I have something for you."

"What is it?"

She held out a small velvet pouch. Jessa loosened the drawstring and tipped its contents into her palm. "Where did you get this?"

"It belonged to Rose. Mum and Dad gave it to her for her fifteenth birthday. Mum wanted it to go in the coffin with her, but in the end, I couldn't bear to part with it. I took it to the jeweler last week for cleaning. He fixed the clasp."

Jessa ran her fingers over the filigree design of the locket and gently opened the clasp. There, looking up at her, was a faded version of William's younger self, complete with shoulder-length hair and a cheeky grin. She hugged her mother tightly. "Thank you so much. I asked William about this very locket only a few weeks ago. She wore it in the photos he took of her. I feel such a connection to it."

"Well, now you have it."

Jessa remained silent for some time as she contemplated the locket and its contents. She frowned, unsure whether to say more.

"Anyway, I'd better go." Her mother stood, moved to the window, and looked up at the lazy sun peeking through the gray clouds of an overcast sky. "Your father will be home for lunch soon, and you know how he hates eating alone."

"Mum… there's something else I've remembered, but I didn't feel right telling anyone, not even William."

She turned to face Jessa. "Go on."

"Your first boyfriend. He had cancer, didn't he?"

Her mother steadied herself on the chair in front of her. "But, apart from mum and dad, no one knows about that. Not even your father. And Roger's dead. He died before you were born."

"I know," Jessa said softly. "But I remember certain fragments of that time—"

"What kind of fragments?" She sat back at the table.

"Hundreds of boys doing the *haka.* And a white coffin covered in autographs."

"But—"

"Look, Mum, I don't have all the answers. Don't think this is easy for me. Sometimes, it scares me half to death, but I can no longer deny it. I have to be true to myself—and to Rose."

She nodded. "He talked about reincarnation once."

"Who did?"

"Roger, my boyfriend. He loved life and wanted to come back. Have another shot. He told me to keep an open mind and not let religion destroy my inquisitive spirit."

"And did you? Keep an open mind?"

"At the time, I didn't really understand what he meant. I let circumstances shape me, because of loss. I've lost so many loves. Roger, my baby, Rose, Maggie. The bitterness has stayed with me for a long time, but I'm tired of being bitter. What's the point?"

"And William?"

"He loves you, doesn't he?"

"Very much."

Her mother sighed. "I've treated him unfairly in the past. I see that now."

Jessa tried to conceal her shock. "He's a big boy. He let it go a long time ago."

"I wish I'd learned to do the same."

52

THE TIN BOX

"We'd like to thank you all for coming to the Watershed this weekend to celebrate our tenth wedding anniversary. As most of you are aware, Jessa and I eloped in the spring of 2002. It was a typical William Cook affair. In fact, Jessa had no idea until twenty minutes before the ceremony. I even picked out her dress and shoes and wrote our vows. My wife would call me a pedantic control freak and, occasionally, an arrogant bastard…"

As laughter filled the tent, he paused. Jessa chuckled and shook her head fondly, remembering the times she'd called her husband exactly that.

"But I simply saw myself as a man in love." William grinned at her. "We met the summer Jessa left for university. The fact that I was several years her senior and she'd only just graduated from high school was the least of our problems. But, thankfully, a second chance presented itself five years later, and that's why we're here today.

"Jessa doesn't know everything about that day." William glanced lovingly at his wife. "She doesn't know I ordered her dress from New York, and it arrived a week late, or that her ring was the wrong size and had to go back to the jeweler. She doesn't know that the night before the wedding, I hardly slept, wondering if she'd turn up for our three o'clock meeting. By five past three, I'd already convinced myself she wasn't coming. She doesn't know I was so nervous she wouldn't accept my proposal that I couldn't stop going to the bathroom all morning."

He paused and smiled as their guests laughed again. "And she doesn't know that her flowers didn't arrive, so at the last minute, I asked Anna and Lea to make her posy and garland from whatever they could find in the garden. So, our spring wedding was not the most relaxing day of my life, but because Jessa said yes, it was one of the happiest."

William put aside his notes.

"This week marks ten years of marriage for us, which calls for a celebration. We welcomed the chance to repeat our vows in front of you all, our wonderful friends, and, most importantly, our family. That we couldn't keep the guest list below two hundred is a testament to how many amazing people bless our lives.

"Jessa's beautiful dress is the same gown she wore on our wedding day. It still fits perfectly despite her being three months pregnant with our fourth child." Their guests clapped and cheered as William laughed at Jessa's reaction to him spilling their secret. "She wanted me in a suit on the day, so here I am, once again in a suit." He did a twirl, and the tent filled with cheers and laughter. "We're honored to have our daughters, Sophie and Lizzy, as flower girls and our son, Ollie, as my best man, which he always will be, even though he's only just started walking." The guests applauded again while the girls smiled shyly.

"I wanted to have the chance to dance with my wife on the anniversary of our wedding day, something we never did the first time around. So, Mrs. Cook, would you do me the honor?" He offered his hand to her as the band played the intro to "Harvest Moon."

Their guests watched William and Jessa move around the dance floor, lost in a world of silk threads and second chances. Next, Louisa and David joined them, followed by Grant and Doreen, while Kathy and Tom helped the twins join in. Before long, everyone was up dancing, and laughter filled the spring evening until the early hours of the morning.

"That was some speech," Jessa said to William when they were finally alone.

"You didn't think I had it in me, did you?"

"I did, but you said it so eloquently."

"I can be extremely eloquent when I want to be."

"Yes, I know you can, my beautiful man. But wasn't it daunting, spilling our secrets in front of so many people?"

"Not really. I've relaxed a lot over the past ten years, don't you think?"

"Depends on the context." Jessa chuckled. "Thanks for telling two hundred people that I'm pregnant again, by the way."

"I figured it was time."

"I guess."

"Oh, I also have an anniversary gift for you."

"A gift? For me?"

He opened the bottom dresser drawer and removed a tin box.

She lifted the lid and pulled aside the lavender-colored tissue paper. "Shoes! You bought me heels," Jessa said with a suggestive smile. She touched the rich cobalt-colored suede. "They're stunning."

"Well, the blue is a little less intense." His eyes held a familiar glint. "I thought you might enjoy that occasionally, now that you're in your early thirties. What do you think?"

"I'm thinking all kinds of naughty thoughts at the moment. So, why the tin box?"

"It's tradition. The gift for a tenth anniversary is tin."

Jessa laughed, knowing he would have searched on the internet for a list of anniversary gifts. "You are one amazing man. Shall I model them for you?"

William loosened the hooks on the bodice of her dress. "Let's get you out of this gown so we can try them on for size. And then"—his eyes danced—"you decide, red or blue."

"Red or blue. What a decision."

"Wait. I have a new song." He touched his iPod, and "Rainy Night in Georgia" filled the surrounding space.

"There's no mistaking who this is," he said, reaching for her.

"Rod Stewart."

"It's an excellent rendition, don't you think?"

"It is. But don't ask me to choose between him, Randy Crawford, and Aaron Neville."

"Just as well you have only one husband to choose from."

"But who do we have tonight?" She flashed him a broad grin. "William the gentle love-maker or William the ballpark player?"

"I told you—it depends on your choice of shoes. Come here." He pulled her in close. "You're absolutely adorable."

A few days later, William sat at his desk at CookHouse Projects, the firm he and Jessa now owned and worked in side by side. His receptionist appeared at his office door with a small package wrapped in rough brown paper and tied with a yellow ribbon. He smiled as he remembered another package wrapped the same way: the books he'd left for Jessa at Hudson Farrell before he went to Sydney.

"A courier dropped this off for you."

"Thanks, Abby."

William undid the ribbon to reveal the gift. Inside was a French vanilla box and a lavender card. Written in architectural font—neat, black ink, uniform—was her message:

In celebration of the beautiful music
we make together.
May this gift always remind you
to make your way home...
no matter what.
J x

He lifted the lid. On a bed of soft yellow tissue paper lay a tin cello, held together with tiny rivets and strung with fine wire over the bridge. Standing no more than ten inches tall, including the endpin, it was a replica of the cello at home. Jessa's cello. The cello she played for him when they were alone, the cello she confided in when troubled, the cello that was her lifeblood, and now his.

He pushed the button on the intercom. "Abby, cancel my meetings for this afternoon. I need to go home."

The End

Many thanks for taking the time to read *The Watershed.* If you're not ready to leave Clifton Falls and the Rata River Valley just yet, you can read more about William's friend Vanessa Blinkly in *The Watershed's* companion novel, *Field of the White Snow*.

THE PLAYLIST

I wish to acknowledge the following artists whose songs I've mentioned throughout the book. I listened to these songs on repeat while revising, and they helped set the mood.

Bach - Cello Suite No. 1 Prelude
Eleanor Rigby - The Beatles
Fire and Rain - James Taylor
Gold - Ryan Adams
Harvest Moon - Neil Young
Here Comes the Sun - The Beatles
Here We Are - Gloria Estefan
I Need You - America
In My Life - Judy Collins
In My Life - The Beatles
Landslide - Dixie Chicks (renamed The Chicks, 2020)
Landslide - Stevie Nicks
Lucy in the Sky with Diamonds - The Beatles
Needle and the Damage Done - Neil Young
Nobody Does it Better - Carly Simon
Perfect Day - Lou Reed

Rainy Night in Georgia - Aaron Neville
Rainy Night in Georgia - Randy Crawford
Rainy Night in Georgia - Rod Stewart
Runaway - The Corrs
So Far Away - Carole King
Taxi - Harry Chapin

ALSO BY FRANCES COWIE

Field of the White Snow

A perfect companion to *The Watershed.*

All they needed were forty-eight sunsets.

Buy Now @ Amazon.com

The Train Station

Prequel novella to The Watershed.

Some would say they met by chance, others by fate.

Buy Now @ Amazon.com

The List Maker

An Artist — A Dreamer — An Imagined Kiss.

Book One in the standalone Imagined Kiss series.

Buy Now @ Amazon.com

How About Thursday

A CEO — A Temp — An Imagined Kiss.

Book Two in the standalone Imagined Kiss series.

Buy Now @ Amazon.com

Hampton Lane

An Heiress — A Bad Boy — An Imagined Kiss.

Book Three in the standalone Imagined Kiss series.

Lime Tree Hill

He needs a wife. She needs a safe haven.

What could possibly go right?

Book One in the standalone Reluctant Kiss series.

Reluctant Chemistry

"I wish we could live like there's no tomorrow, and love like there is."

Book Two in the standalone Reluctant Kiss series.

The Last Autograph

"Sometimes curiosity takes us places we seldom dream of going."

Book Three in the standalone Reluctant Kiss series.

ACKNOWLEDGMENTS

One chilly morning, I woke with the story of *The Watershed* floating around in my head and the sudden urge to write a novel. Since then, my writing has been met with much enthusiasm, and those enthusiastic people deserve my thanks.

Firstly, I wish to thank Kate and Marjorie from my writing group. Our sessions inspire me and keep me forward-focused. You both have a wonderful way with words.

To Jane and Hilly. It's a blessing to have beta readers who are honest with constructive feedback. To Laura and her book-loving friends, thanks for spreading the word. To Juls, in a roundabout way, you started me on this new path and have taught me so much. Ben, I know romantic fiction isn't your genre, but I still value your support.

To Abby, thank you for lending your voice and red-headed curls to Lea's character, for insisting Lea have a love interest, and for suggesting what Jack James should look like. Louise, thanks for being a sounding board and one of my first beta readers.

Many thanks also to my friends and family who put up with my vivid imagination and crazy ways. Sharlene, your pear-baked chicken is the best.

Kevin, your unwavering support means everything to me, even if I don't want you to read the end result.

Finally, a book is nothing without readers, so many thanks to all of you who have taken the time to read *The Watershed*. Your support is invaluable. If you have a few more minutes, your reviews are greatly appreciated.

May your days be filled with wonderful stories and happiness.

Frances

PS: Some of you may be wondering what a haka is. It is a Māori ceremonial war dance or challenge, often performed at gatherings of importance and also by the All Blacks, New Zealand's national rugby team, before a match.

ABOUT THE AUTHOR

Frances Cowie started writing romantic fiction after waking one morning with the story of an old pump house and three characters—Rose, William, and Jessa—floating around in her head. *The Watershed* is her first novel.

She lives with her husband in New Zealand's beautiful Southern Lakes district and is known to have a passion for cupcakes and Whittaker's coconut chocolate.

For more information, including sneak peeks of upcoming projects, visit Frances online:

www.francescowie.com

www.ingramcontent.com/pod-product-compliance
Lightning Source LLC
Chambersburg PA
CBHW051934240626
47153CB00005B/1489

* 9 7 8 0 4 7 3 3 9 9 7 2 6 *